DISASTER

"We're sinking!" the cry came.

Slowly at first, then rapidly, the deck slid from under them and became a wall in back of them. The Eastland had turned over on her side.

"JUMP FOR YOUR LIFE!" came the screaming words.

Dazed, Sigrid could not be sure whether her own eyes were open or closed, if she was awake, or if she was dreaming. She had two children now, Michael and the little girl.

"Grab my skirt tight," she cautioned the little girl. "I'll need my hands to help us get over the rail. Tight! Don't let go! Hear? Don't let go!"

❧   ❧   ❧

APRIL HARVEST is the final volume of Lillian Budd's celebrated trilogy of family life in Sweden and America. If you missed APRIL SNOW or LAND OF STRANGERS, both are available from Avon.

LILLIAN BUDD

APRIL HARVEST

AVON
PUBLISHERS OF BARD, CAMELOT AND DISCUS BOOKS

AVON BOOKS
A division of
The Hearst Corporation
959 Eighth Avenue
New York, New York 10019

First Avon Printing, April, 1980

AVON TRADEMARK REG. U.S. PAT. OFF. AND IN
OTHER COUNTRIES, MARCA REGISTRADA,
HECHO EN U.S.A.

Printed in the U.S.A.

TO
MARIESTA

"Fair weather cometh out of the North."

Job, 37:22

1

Beyond the lace-curtained window was a new world. The shapes of the cottages across the street had changed, their roof lines softened with overhangs of snow; so had their paints, with white clinging to clapboards that had been of many colors.

The pastor's wife drew the curtain to one side and looked up the street and down. An eerie glimmer appeared in the street lamp, shedding a blurred triangle of light. The triangle was alive with dancing flakes eddying about, drifting downward toward the pavement; then, with the wind reviving them, swirling upward again until at last they had to come to rest upon the ground to make dancing room for the many more falling from above.

A loving smile lingered on the thin face of Kristin Bedell as she sat waiting for her husband. Soon he would come; his short, black-broadcloth-covered legs would move swiftly, like a robin's little matchstick legs scurrying across a summer lawn, to carry him up the steps to her side.

Here he came! He alighted from the carriage at the curb.

As surely as the ancient barometer on the wall told of the weather, those short, black-trousered legs told his mood, and now they moved slowly, haltingly; heavily one followed the other up the steps to the front door.

"Did you see Sigrid home?" she called.

"No, Kristin."

The little gnomelike pastor removed his black fur turban and bent almost double to shake the snow off close to the hooked "Welcome" rug. Precisely he folded the ear muffs in, stood on tiptoe, and stretched both body and arm to hang the hat on a long brass hook at the top of the stately mahogany hall rack. It was a handy thing: he was glad Kristin had salvaged it from discards sent to the

1

church for rummage, when no one else thought it worth giving house room.

Now he shook snow from his ulster and hung it, one sleeve to the right of the long mirror, one sleeve to the left, so that the melting snow could drip from the body of the overcoat into the white marble basin that formed the hall rack's base. Short, chubby fingers undid the clasps on his heavy overshoes; he slipped his feet out of them and strode, not to his wife's chair, but to the big parlor stove.

"Did the Schmotzers take Sigrid home with them?"

"No, Kristin."

He rubbed his hands over the front of his suit. Satisfied that it was warming up, he turned his back to the stove and brushed his hands slowly back and forth over the cloth.

"Did the Allspaughs take her home with *them?*"

"No . . ."

No, he would not distress Kristin by telling her of Mrs. Allspaugh's loud talking after the burial service, embarrassing them all out there at the cemetery. Nor of her pulling at the sorrowing girl's arm, with, "Come on now, up in the coach! No use bawling, 'Twon't do no good. Come on. I'll go right straight on home with you and *stay* until—" He could not blame Sigrid for deciding in that instant that she would walk home. He, himself, had not relished the ride with Mrs. Allspaugh sharing the coach, but had settled himself glumly against the tufted and buttoned upholstery and sat silent, except for the politeness of replying "Yes," or "No," when Mrs. Allspaugh stopped for answer; and even now he was not sure he should not have said, "Yes," when he said, "No."

He shook his head violently to clear it of his thoughts. Kristin was speaking.

"Why, what happened to her?"

"Sigrid's walking home."

"Oh, Felix! In this snowstorm? And you let her walk?"

"I knew she had to be alone in her grief."

"Alone." Kristin shivered. "Motherless. And now fatherless."

Only when he was satisfied that his hands and clothing were free of chill did the pastor go to his wife and bend to kiss her. Swiftly she drew a handkerchief over her mouth, and his lips pressed her forehead, lingered on her hair.

He drew a little rose-carved slipper rocker close to her chair and sat quietly, holding his hand over hers.

"Oh, how I wish"—she spoke at last, so softly he had to lean closer to hear—"that Sigrid could come here—and live with us. . . ."

"Kristin!" His jowls, which hung like scallops at the sides of his face, quivered. "How often I have said that you could read my thoughts before ever I spoke them! But now—now, Kristin, you read my *heart!"*

"We could— Ah, Felix—it would be as if—at last—I had given you the daughter—"

Her reverie was broken by a sudden rush of tears. "But it is impossible." Quickly she placed the square of white linen over her mouth to smother her cough.

"Say not so, Kristin. Sigrid is young. And strong. And you, my dear"—to bring her smile—"feel better with each day! Surely we know that all that is right is possible. Let us pray for guidance to know the right in this."

"I know the right, Felix. It was only—only that I was wishing. I know I could never ask her. . . ."

The mantel clock struck the hours, the half-hours; still sleep hovered just out of Sigrid's reach.

The clock struck five. The night was done. From it she had learned that a night can pass although one is left alone, with the last of a family gone.

With the coming of light she went to the kitchen and put on a gingham apron. The neighbors would be dropping in; she must have lots of coffee ready, egg coffee, and the makings of tea for the few who preferred it, and milk for the children. How many apple cakes would she need? Better make plenty.

Even within the confines of the kitchen she took long, rhythmic strides. She looked taller than she was, for she stood straighter than she might have if, in childhood, she had not been compelled to choose between wearing shoulder braces or feeling the sting of the razor strop; and the curing of round shoulders had seemed the lesser evil.

The neighbors came, as she knew they would; the day passed, teaching of new friendliness, of heartsease that comes through the sharing of sorrow. Toward evening the pastor came, and no sooner had she greeted him than the doorbell rang again.

"Mr. and Mrs. Schmotzer! And Bobby! Come in—come in. Oh, you shouldn't have come all the way from the North Side in this cold!"

"It's not so cold," the husband said, shivering.

"Come, sit down and get your breaths!" Sigrid took off Bobby's overcoat and cap and set his rubbers near the stove.

"We might just as well get right down to business," Mr. Schmotzer began, seating himself beside his wife. "We got to start back right away."

"You'll have a cup of coffee?"

"No. No. No time for coffee. You see, Miss Sigrid, we talked to some of your friends. Close friends." He grasped the sofa's arm, pulled his hand away, and wiped the sweaty place it left with his coat sleeve, then grasped the arm again. "At the—the"—the word came lamely and low, and when it came was an apology—"funeral." His underslung jaw closed tight, fell open, and closed tight again. The lips separated and he drew in air, audibly, through the teeth. Sigrid saw that his lower teeth closed in front of the upper ones, and without conscious knowledge of the doing she reached her lower jaw forward to see how it would feel to close a mouth that way.

That corner of her parlor where Mr. and Mrs. Schmotzer were sitting so straight and formal and uncomfortable looking on the golden-oak sofa resembled the old-time, Old-Country photographs she had seen in Old Lady Muller's red-velvet-brocade-covered album with the big gold clasps, like Bible clasps. The Schmotzers did not look like the Americans they were; they looked like Germans, which they had been. But in all except looks Bazile Schmotzer had come far from being a lower-class European peasant, in the little time he had been in the United States.

Between them the sofa's emerald-green velvet upholstery clashed with the aqua blue of the wife's Sunday-best dress; but Sigrid could see, even from across the room, how beautifully the silk was seamed. The shoulders sat just right; the collar extending into a tied bow was tailored perfectly; there was no "made-by-loving-hands-at-home" look about the dress Mrs. Schmotzer had sewn.

The collar came high on her neck, but it did not entirely

hide the thick, heavy neck of the European peasant woman. She ran her finger between the collar and her neck, pulled gently at the bow to loosen it, although the fit was not too snug. She swallowed heavily, ran her finger inside the collar again. "The American words, to tell you how we feel—they—they come in German!" A string of foreign words came tumbling from the lips she stopped to wet; then she turned helplessly to Pastor Bedell, sitting silent.

He smiled. "Sigrid knows. She knows."

"But we want to do something—"

"Ya. Like I said, we talked to your friends yet. We wanted to find out"—Mr. Schmotzer slipped from his careful efforts at proper pronunciation of American words—"*chust* what it was you wanted most to have, and that was what we decided we would give to you."

Sigrid drew in her breath, getting ready to speak, glancing at Pastor Bedell as if for confirmation of her thought; these people had already done more than anyone could have expected of them, arranging to pay the funeral expenses; but before she could utter any words, the wife helped the husband. "Your father saved our Bobby's life. Ach, Bobby, you would not be sitting there rocking so if it had not been for Mr. C-C-Christianson."

The high-backed cherry rocker which Sigrid's mother, Ellen, had bought from Mr. Ginsberg's rags-and-old-iron wagon, and cleaned and varnished so that it had looked like new, and given to her husband as a birthday present, tipped forward and Bobby slid from its seat. "Don't cry, Mama! Please don't cry some more!"

The empty chair rocked backward, violently, to strike against the wall in its corner of the parlor, then forward and back again before it slowed and stood still.

"The chair! Be more careful!" Mrs. Schmotzer cried. "Ach, Bobby, Bobby!" She wiped her eyes and blew her nose, and settled the boy on her lap. "He is so big to lap-sit." Her apologetic look to Sigrid changed to one of motherly felicity when the boy put his arms about her neck.

Sigrid sent an understanding glance toward the third corner of the square parlor where Pastor Bedell kept the little armless sewing rocker going in steady rhythm; his short legs touched the carpet as he came forward; lifted as he leaned back, and then the toes of his shoes pointed downward toward the floor as children's do when they reach to give added impetus while swinging high on a rope garden swing.

Her mother used to sit in that little chair, rocking Tony. Ellen had called it the nursing rocker at first, when Tony was a baby. Sigrid could see them now, but seeing, the little brother grew until he was almost five years old. He had looked forward with such longing; he wanted so to be old enough to go to school.

She looked at Bobby Schmotzer. Through tear-filled eyes his outline was not clear; and her voice was choked as she asked, "How old are you, Bobby?"

"I'm almost five. When I'm five, then I'll go to kindergarten! Won't I, Mama?" One small hand covering each of his mother's cheeks, he turned her face to his.

"Yes, yes, Bobby."

The room was the same but the day changed for Sigrid. "One, two, three, four," her little brother had counted his fingers, starting with the thumb. "When I get to be this," pointing to his little finger, "I go to school. Don't I, Papa?"

"Yes, when you are five," tenderly her father had assured the boy.

Now the scene changed to the street corner in downtown Chicago. A little boy of almost five had been nearly under the horses' hoofs; no wonder Pa had thrown himself at the runaway team!

"What you want most," Mr. Schmotzer was persisting. "That is what Emilie and I are going to see that you get it. Yes, Emilie, ain't it?"

"Yes, Bazile. Now you go ahead and tell her what it is."

"We asked the friends who know you best," he said again. "And every one—every single one of them—told us the same thing. And so—" The nervous clasping of the golden-oak arm, the wiping of perspiration from its surface with the sleeve repeated themselves until he burst out, "Ach, you tell her, Emilie, you talk so much nicer."

"Nobody, no one could understand, more or better, your desire than I can. It could be mine own wish. Yes, also, it could be mine!"

"Bazile." His wife reached across and laid her hand on his, quieting it. "Please—"

"Yes, Emilie." He moved his large hands to his knees, pulling the trouser legs into wrinkles; and Sigrid found herself pulling at her skirt, wrinkling it; his nervousness was contagious.

"Tell what it is!" Now Emilie's voice raised. "For God's sake, Bazile, tell her what it is before I *bust!*"

"Yes, yes, Emilie. But Miss Sigrid, for it I am too old."

He could be thirty, Sigrid figured. Hard work in the face of poverty in their youth made people from European countries seem older than they were, perhaps, but the eyes under Bazile's heavy, bushy brows were young.

"Too old to go, am I. But not so you." He spoke to her, but turned again to his wife. "Don't you want to be the one to tell her, Emilie?"

"No. No! My Bazile, no! You! *You*—but tell—*tell!*"

A lightning look flashed between Sigrid and her pastor, an understanding look that made lines of amusement come to the corners of their mouths and eyes: the visitor and his wife were like Alphonse and Gaston in the funny papers, always bowing and yielding one to the other. From that significant expression of comprehension Sigrid knew that the pastor half-listened, as she did, for the "You first, my dear Alphonse. No, you first, my dear Gaston!"

Resolutely Mr. Schmotzer gave his hand to his wife's two, to hold, and spoke again, facing Sigrid. "We shall pay for the tuition, for the expense, and you shall go to the university and obtain your degree."

It was as if all of the blood had gone from her brain and left her lightheaded to the point of swimming in thin air. It seemed that she grew small, and drifted, trying to see with some little bit of clarity the people and objects in this familiar room. Her hands clasped the sides of her head and steadied her; now looking through sudden tears at the couple on the sofa, there were a half a dozen of each one, offset from each other, appearing as colored pictures do when the paper has been run unevenly through the presses and each color is a bit askew.

"What—do—you—mean?"

She saw that the pastor's chair came forward and stopped; the back of the little rocker lay almost horizontal, parallel to his back as he leaned forward.

"It is our wish," she heard Mr. Schmotzer continue, "Emilie's and mine, to make it up to you for—for—" The big handkerchief came out of his pocket, and into it he blew his nose furiously, then drew his son to his breast and hugged him until the child cried out, "You're hurting me, Papa!"

Sigrid spread her hands. "Why, I could never accept such a—"

"It is our wish." The father glanced at his wife, and she nodded in assent.

Sigrid laughed. It was a nervous laugh. "Y-you can't have any idea of what you suggest, Mr. Schmotzer! And you can't have any idea how much I appreciate it, but that would take years, the cost would be—oh, it would be—"

"We know what the cost will be. We had professional help; Mr. Emil Bergquist, he is a banker, he came last night and figured it all out. On paper." He settled himself now against the sofa's back; his hand rested quietly on the arm. "I have a good job; since I am in this country I, oh, I have not gone to university school, no, but I have learned much about electricity. I have a good job, a *good* job, and we don't need such a big flat as we've got—four big rooms—no—"

A quick look, heavy with warning, from his wife reminded him that he was not to explain how they planned to manage. "Bazile, ya," she interrupted him. "He is a electrician. And he is a Mason, too! Did you know he was a Mason?"

Yes, Sigrid had known; six pallbearers for her father, members of Mr. Schmotzer's lodge, had come, wearing white gloves. "Yes, I know. And I thank you—oh, how I thank you! But I could not accept this. You have your own son to educate—"

The mother left the sofa and knelt before the chair and folded her hands on Sigrid's lap. "We would have no Bobby to educate if it had not been for your father. And Bobby's education will come. You see"—she leaned close —"my Bazile, he has made up a invention."

"Oh!" Sigrid gasped. She could only hope that her face did not reveal her despair at calling to mind her father's inventions, the perpetual-motion machine, the ventilator, the metal polish, and all the others. No, if an invention was going to be expected to pay for Bobby's education they had certainly better save whatever they had thought of spending on her.

"So, then, it is settled." The boy's father was relieved.

"Wait." She rose and started toward the kitchen. "Let's talk this over with a cup of coffee. I baked *apfel kuchen*—"

"Ach, *apfel kuchen*, ya! Emilie, you go and help her with the coffee."

"No, please, sit and visit, Mrs. Schmotzer. I'll have it ready in a jiffy."

Dear Pastor Bedell, he could see that she wanted to be alone. "What part of Germany did you come from?" he asked Mrs. Schmotzer, detaining her.

Sigrid did not wait to hear. She measured water into the pot, set it over the gas flame, and the turning of the handle of the coffee grinder on the wall drowned out the sounds of voices in the parlor. Grinding with her left hand, she held the right one up level with her eyes: here, in the hollow of this hand, she could hold the thing for which she had longed, the chance to get a university education. It had come close once before; oh, only remembering her teacher's announcement brought back the thrill she had known, "You are to be the valedictorian. You may have first choice of the scholarships." She remembered, too, Miss Lowe's sadness at learning that her "prize pupil" would not be going on to college. "There is always a way," her teacher had said; but she knew better; in her case there had been no way. With her mother ill, and debts to pay, the money she could earn was needed at home. No, there had been no way for her to go to the university; but the reasons were not the kind a person told. Outwardly she had pretended she was overjoyed at the prospect of getting a job; inwardly she had felt the doors of life closing. For life was learning, learning all that had been thought and said and done and accomplished down through the ages. What other way was there to enter the mystical body of knowledge—to move with that body of knowledge—than through a university education?

In losing Pa she felt alone; but this was more than aloneness, not to be able to go to school and learn and know and understand as much as her capacity should prove to be. This was hunger, and thirst! This was a parching of the soul!

But now the everything she wished for could be hers. She had only to take it . . .

"Can't I help, please?" Mrs. Schmotzer came bustling into the kitchen. "That pastor of yours, he is an interesting man; now he is talking electric switches with my man; he's not like a pastor at all."

Sigrid smiled. "I know exactly what you mean. Of course you can help. Let's spread this cloth on the dining-room table. It's so hard to balance a cup and saucer in the hands while trying to eat coffeecake."

"Especially for men," her guest responded with a knowing grin.

"Come, everybody! Please come and have a cup of coffee; and, Bobby, here's a glass of milk for you."

"What do you say, Bobby? What do you say?" His mother prompted the boy to speak the "thank you" his big eyes gave.

"You know," Sigrid said spiritedly while passing the cream, "it's so funny how people are. Even your best friends, who, you think, should really know you, don't know you at all!"

Pastor Bedell shot a quick glance at her. Bright red glowed on her cheeks, and her eyes were brighter than tearless eyes should be. Her laugh was high-pitched.

"I am truly surprised," she went on. "I'll bet, Mr. Schmotzer, that you didn't ask my pastor here what it was that I wanted most in this whole world! *He'd* know what to answer!"

"Why, of course, Sigrid, you know I should have said as—as—as you yourself should have said if anyone had asked the same question about me, of you," he finished lamely. He was confused at her pleading look but completed as best he could what he had started to say.

"Of course!" Again she laughed, a fluty laugh.

"And"—Mr. Schmotzer held a piece of *apfel kuchen* on his fork, halfway to his mouth—"that would be—?"

"That," Sigrid cut him off, "you'd have to ask the person herself, or himself, what it was that his heart yearned most to have."

"That's right!" Slowly the pastor repeated, "That is right."

"But—every one of them—your friends, that I asked—" Mr. Schmotzer, bewildered, stuttering, dropping his fork to his plate. "We asked the Mrs. Taina Something-or-other, and a Mr. Allspaugh, and—"

"Of course, I understand—" Sigrid's voice had softened to its normal low, full tone—"that they all meant well. But they were thinking of me—as I was—when they knew me best, when I was a schoolgirl—and when I was graduated from high school. Why, then I thought that the very bottom of the world had dropped out, because my father—"

With that deep respect for culture all Swedes have, her parents had made heavy sacrifices to give her a high-school education . . . no, it was her mother who had sacrificed. A rush of grief stopped her thoughts: her father was dead; it would be disloyal to say why he had not provided the way. And so she finished—"because I could not use the scholarship I won."

"For having the highest grades all through the four years of high school," the pastor supplied.

"Smartness, that is what I hope Bobby will have." His mother patted the boy on the head, but Bobby caught her wrist and lifted the hand away; he was no little boy!

Sigrid winked at the mother, but aloud she said, "Those good friends don't see so much of me any more, with my going to Chicago every day to work; that's why they don't know that in almost a year I have changed. But—"

The pastor worried at the high pitch her voice had resumed as she addressed herself to Bobby's father. "I suppose it is because I am a girl that the longing for a higher education has been replaced—by—other things. If I had been a man, like you, I would still, most likely, I would still—"

Pastor Bedell saw need to calm her. "Sigrid"—he reached over and laid his hand on hers—"tell us what it is you desire most now."

She drew a deep, deep breath, and he saw that her lips and chin quivered. "Oh, how I would love to own a blue velvet dress!"

He drew his hand from hers; his eyes opened wide and their lids blinked busily.

"In that beautiful shade of blue," she was saying, "that comes in the sky soon after the sun has set—just before it darkens—"

"Well, if that isn't just like a woman!" He laughed, addressing Mr. Schmotzer, because he felt this was what Sigrid wanted him to do.

"So," she was begging with her eyes, letting them rest first on the husband, then on the wife, "if you really want to do something for me—really—that I would love, make me a dress of blue velvet—to wear to parties—"

"*Gott!*" Mr. Schmotzer blurted. "That would be nothing, absolutely nothing! A few dollars for a couple of yards of goods, a few hours of Emilie's time, it would be nothing—less than nothing—for all we owe to you!"

She looked helplessly to her pastor, beseechingly.

"I think," he responded, "that if that is what Sigrid wants, that is what you should try to give to her. I am sure it is not as small a thing as you would make it sound."

Violent shakings of the heads of the two Schmotzers almost caused him to give up trying; but then he looked at Sigrid, and tried again. "Certainly, if it will make her heart glad, you would be willing? Wouldn't you, Mr. Schmotzer? And Missus, too?" He stroked his jowls, waiting for an answer, but none came. "At this time, after—what she has gone through—I think we should try to make her woman-heart glad, don't you?"

"But it is so *lit*'tle!" the husband cried.

The wife jumped up. "Borrow me a tape measure! Ach, I am a woman! I can see through—" She shook her finger at Bazile. "Even if you cannot!"

See through what, Sigrid wondered, but opened the sewing-machine drawer.

"Men! So blind you are, you men!" Emilie said positively, and reached to take the tape measure.

She unrolled the tape and Sigrid stood open-mouthed at hearing Emilie's logic: "After all, the university, it is hard work—not for a woman—a good-looking young woman like Sigrid! Maybe, even"—Sigrid felt the tape encircle her bust, waist, and hips, and smiled to hear—"you think of a young man? Maybe?"

Her blush gave Mrs. Schmotzer confidence. "Ya—see? Maybe of marriage you think yet? No? Vell, anyway—"

The tape was measuring the length her skirt should be.

Emilie's fingers were going to make her the "beautifulest dress" she ever saw. . . .

"Why did you do it?" Pastor Bedell plomped himself, hard, into the little rocker.

Sigrid walked past him into the dining room, laid her arms on the table, and dropped her head on them.

He came and stood beside her chair. At last she raised her head. "Please sit down." The smile that came was wan as she extended her hand, palm upward. "I was about to say that the Blue Bird of Happiness flew right into my hand—and—I opened the hand, and let it fly away."

"Why? *Why* did you?"

"But it wasn't—"

"Why did you choose a party dress?" He rested his elbows on the table and gesticulated with his expressive hands. "Why didn't you—if you wanted something blue— tell them about how you walk out of your way every evening to go past Jake's Pawnshop and stand and gaze into the window, looking at that old piece of blue cloth hanging there? They would have given you that just as well. But a dress! What made you choose a *party* dress?"

"I don't know." She looked at him dumbly. "But I realized that I was going to have to let them do something for me. I saw the exquisite sewing that Mrs. Schmotzer had done on her dress, and—I've always loved the color blue—the thought of a dress just popped into my head."

"But why didn't you accept their offer? They were sincere, and your ambition has been to go to the university!"

"Because, oh, Pastor Bedell, I started before to tell you, to say that the Blue Bird of Happiness had flown right into my hand; but that was not true. There would have been no happiness for me in taking—from them. I knew all of the time I couldn't. But, even so, for a minute I was tempted.

"Listen," she leaned toward him. "When the undertaker called me, asking me to come and select a casket, I went. He said, 'The Schmotzers want you to have the finest, the best of everything, for your father's funeral,' and showed me a mahogany casket with silver handles, and said that was the one they had picked out. I asked, 'It is the most expensive, isn't it?' And he said, 'Yes, it is.' But nothing was to be too good. And so I asked, 'Is he, are they, very rich?'

"You know Mr. Kampp, and how nice he is; he put his hands on my shoulders, and with those deep-set black eyes of his looked straight into my eyes. 'No,' he said. 'Not in money; only in the goodness of their hearts.' Then, as if he wanted to be of help, he said. 'This is in confidence; I am not sure he would approve of my telling you, but I think you should know. He has made arrangements to pay your father's funeral expenses in weekly payments; every payday, on Fridays, he says, he will stop in and pay what he can spare.'" She threw her hands wide. "You know as well as I do that there is nothing to make him pay anything! But Mr. Kampp finished by saying to me, 'And I have the feeling he will spare until it hurts.'"

She stared dreamily at nothing in particular until a hopeful look came into her blue eyes, and she asked, "You saw Pa's casket, Pastor Bedell. You would not have guessed it was the cheapest one, would you?"

"No, Sigrid, I would not have guessed."

"No," she echoed him. "I could not take more than a dress from them. But don't look so sad about it, Pastor. I'll get my education. I'll find a way."

2

She stood inside her front door, where the long plate-glass window framed the winter night lying in daytime clearness under the cold white moon, and parting the lace curtains watched the little figure trudge through the snow toward his home.

A cloud drifted by, hiding the moon's face so that the white night lay in half-light, mysterious, and when again the moon shone full Pastor Bedell had turned into the parsonage and was gone. The freshly white-painted house looked gray now against the purer white of moonlit snow. Only the footsteps leading from her front steps broke the smooth, even, and deep white carpet. Moonlight heaped the ice-bound elm with crystal gems, each twig a diamond, the branches shivering, cracking, in the cold. With a catch in her breath she saw the house roofs no longer as roof-tops but as diadems, sparkling, glittering.

Her arms slipped into her winter coat and, pulled by some magic magnetic power, she walked out into that fairy world of frozen magnificence.

The settling cold brought a stinging in her nostrils, and as she followed the path the Schmotzers and the pastor had broken, her breath made clouds of vapor. Soon there were no tracks and she had to lift each leg high as she stepped, plunging one foot after the other into the snow, leaving deep holes behind her.

Snow. It must lie ten inches deep.

It would be ten inches deep, too, on the new grave in Rose Hill, making a white mound over the loosely piled dirt and the blanket of red roses. It would have placed a white lace edge around the huge red heart of close-set carnation blossoms, to make it look more like a Valentine than a "Broken Heart" sent by the friendly neighbors of Calico Row.

15

"A hero," the newspapers called him, and he was her father.

She retraced her steps, but when she came to the parsonage she stopped. If she did not have her own house that she must try to keep wouldn't it be wonderful to live in such a home, where only kind and loving words were spoken, where the display of Kristin's love of the beautiful did something to a person's very heart?

It would not all be taking; there would be some giving, too, if they would ask her to come to live with them; she could be of help to Kristin. And Kristin needed help.

She could never ask them. Forlorn, she walked into that awful emptiness there is in a house after a casket has been carried out. From now on she would be alone, with only the memory of little Tony, without Mother who had died such few months ago, and without Pa.

Without Pa. It was as a mother would feel at losing a helpless child, in a way, the loneliness she would feel for him. Throughout his lifetime perhaps he had lived in trivial ways: she thought it generously, but she had to drive through to the truth about him. But only the good of him would she remember—only the good. And there was much to remember.

With tears welling she went into her bedroom and sat staring at the pussy willows on the wallpaper, gray and white, with brown stems and little reddish markings on the pussies, and light gray leaves against the darker background. She did not have to close her eyes to see the fluffy white pussy willows change to fluffy white snowflakes falling on Pastor Bedell's bared head as he spoke to the hundreds of people who came to Rose Hill to pay respect to "Chicago's hero."

Of a sudden it had grown colder there in the cemetery; the snow no longer fell as flakes, but as hard, globular miniature mimosa flowers, and pitted against the faces of the gathered crowd like tiny hailstones. Many of the men had re-covered their heads, but not the pastor as he went on with the eulogy to "Carl, the loving husband to Ellen, dainty flowerlike soul she had been; the generous neighbor, doing without in order to help another in distress; the good citizen, always the first at the polls on election days; the Union craftsman, lending his skill to the building of many homes of those who stood and listened." And Carl Christianson had not been, to the pastor's mind, an "immigrant," not a hyphenated American, but an "American of the first order."

Sigrid drew on her bedroom slippers, man-sized slippers, fluffy and warm. Both were made for the same foot, but—fun sparkles came, unbidden, to the blue eyes—what did that matter when they had been such a bargain?

Sitting cross-legged on the bed, she swung one foot; one too-large slipper dangled from a big toe and, while the leg swung, the slipper slapped against the sole of a long, narrow foot, tapping as fingers do on arms of chairs as old men sit thinking.

If only Ellen might have shared the pastor's praise of Pa! But little Ellen lay far away in Sweden, beside her own mother, in her hand the dried bunch of wildflowers—buttercups and berry leaves that the years had turned all the same faded color—those flowers she had brought with her to America, and carried "home" again.

Home. Sigrid spoke the word aloud, but she would never be able to give it that minor sound that told of Ellen's yearning, regret, nostalgia, pain, through all the years until that day she knew she could return to Sweden. Then the word "home" had sung from the heart of Ellen, flowed from her lips sounding like the singing strings of the old zither.

Sigrid looked down at her hands. In them she had once held that poor bouquet that now and forever more would be clasped in her mother's little hands. . . .

Again a surge of grief overcame her. Oh, if Ellen could have heard the pastor tell about Pa's sitting on the front porch with the young people of the neighborhood gathered about him, filling the porch railing, lining the steps, learning their history lessons! "There was no time for going with the gangs when Mr. Christianson talked, for then the Pilgrims came; he awakened their eyes to clearer sight, made noses keener to smells, until the boys and girls sniffed at talk of wild turkeys roasting on the spit for that first Thanksgiving Day; or Lincoln came, and they could hear honest Abe's cutting through wood for his hearth not only to keep warm by, but to read by—to learn by."

Sigrid's head bowed. Yes, Pa had had virtues as well as faults, though it had been easier for many people to see only the faults. If only he had not allowed one incident in his youth to warp his life! That was the tragic thing, the way he had taken his father's selling of his pet horse, tearing himself from home, holding a grudge against both mother and father, renouncing God because the father he hated prayed to God.

It would take strength not to be a martyr to a single circumstance, not to try to find forgetfulness in drink, more strength than Pa had had.

But the pastor was one to see the good: "So, let us commemorate today"—his words had gone forth to the farthest fringe of the crowd—"not that Carl Christianson has died, but that he lived; that, living, he knew the triumphant moment which few men know, the moment in which he drank of that draught of life's greatest fulfillment when a man, in giving his life for another's, sees his own spirit reach its godlike aim!

"And who knows"—the pastor had held his book high —"who knows but that Bobby Schmotzer, the boy whose life Carl Christianson saved, may one day become a very great man? Who knows but that one day he may even become the President of our United States?"

As one the two Schmotzers had knelt in the wet snow, arms clutching the bewildered Bobby between them, but clasping their hands and raising them toward the low gray sky. "Dear God in heaven," Mr. Schmotzer said then, so all could hear, "to think that we can live in a land where such a thing is possible!"

That was like something Pa might have said. . . .

His pet, a calico-colored kitten, came from somewhere and jumped into her lap, settling itself comfortably.

"Sarsaparilla," she said softly, "you are lonely for him, too." The orange, black, and yellow fur gave sparks at her stroking. Rumpling the white fur on the underneck, she crooned, "Sarsaparilla, that's much too long a name for Pa to have given a little cat like you. Sassy, that's better; Sassy, for short." Her eyes roved, resting on each object in the room, and wandered toward the parlor, and dining room, the kitchen. "Oh, Sassy!" She hugged the kitten to her. "Isn't it good to have a home!"

The Welsbach mantles gave a homey light, red glowed from behind the squares of isinglass in the doors of the big base burner in the dining room. After some hot coffee and a fried egg with bacon—

With a start she recalled that only a few hours past she had been certain she would never be able to relish food again.

"Come, kitty, come, Sassy, I'll get you some milk. You must be starved."

The meal over, she set her plate on a newspaper under the sink so Sassy's sprightly tongue could clean off the last of the taste and smell of bacon.

Tomorrow she would go back to work, after these days of absence, and so tonight she had better sort her father's belongings. There was not much of any value, but the Salvation Army was always glad to get men's shoes and suits. There was the cardboard shoe box marked, "Private papers." View of what was inside had always been denied her, and so she hesitated now in untying the string wrapped twice around it. So often Pa had bound it around and tied the bowknot; as she wrapped the cord over her fingers, then laid the figure eight it made aside, she saw her father, not as a man, a husband to her mother, a father to be loved—oh, so painfully loved—but as a little boy wrapping his precious belongings up and tying them around with a string.

Opening the box, she saw the man he had been more clearly now than ever before in this neat stack of papers: the deed to the house, the mortgage papers, the paid tax bills; the oil stock certificates and shares in gold mines, all marked "Worthless" in his even script; and also, penned by him, page after page of foolscap paper. Another day she would read them all, word for word, but now she replaced them as they had been in the box, with his mother's address right on top, all except the envelope marked, "My Will."

Once he had described to her the seeing through the mists as one stood under the falls of Niagara; just so did her eyes see his last will and testament: "On you, my daughter Sigrid, I have bestowed the heritage of Sweden, and now I leave to you the promise of America."

It was more like a letter than a will: "I know you bore the ridicule, often, of being an immigrant's child. But who is there in this country who is not the child of immigrants? Only a few full-blooded redskins.

"Hold your heads high, you children of immigrants, for you are Americans!"

As she read she saw her father as the personification of the boy in the Old Country who had threaded the loom for the Old-Country mother, setting the warp, sitting watching the patterns grow as her hands threw the shuttle. Always the peasant folk had found ways to combine beauty and utility, bringing now to the mind's sight a graceful gull, inlaid of brass, flying with the flying shuttle.

The picture of the Indian America that had been hung before Sigrid like a woven piece portraying virgin woods, deep rivers, sparkling rivulets, side by side with iridescent threads that were ruby-throated hummingbirds, and hills, as background for the major pattern—wigwams and war-painted faces, tomahawks, headdresses of feathers plucked from the eagle, and papooses slung on squaws' strong backs. And scalps.

She saw Time lay aside that tapestry which had been America *at the coming of the immigrants*.

Reading on, her father now became the immigrant, a composite of all of them. "Why did we come to America? We all had our reasons for leaving our homelands; but always remember, if it had been good for us there, we would not have come here at all. None of us!"

Now he pictured for her another loom, set with the same warp, but here came new threads, not only from Sweden, from everywhere! One was rebellion against distinction of class, one was a quest for freedom of religion, one a revulsion against compulsory military training. There was the building of a little white church, the singing of a hymn, there was the sparkling thread which was the art of glass blowing brought by the Bohemians—new threads—weaving a tapestry which was to be the new America!

Nor were they all strong and beautiful, those threads. "We came," her father's words said, "from all countries, bringing our cultures, our skills, and our faults. It was not to be expected that we could leave our undesirable qualities behind, our hatreds, our personal limitations, our weaknesses of character; they all came with us. We brought our discontent—or maybe that was good?—and our antagonisms."

But they brought many good qualities, those wanderers from foreign lands, and courage was one.

"Faith was the shuttle, hope was the little inlaid brass gull flying with it to weave in and out—alternating between the threads which were the skills of woodcarvers and painters and sculptors and carpenters and bridge-builders and railroad builders and coal miners and school-teachers and farmers and herdsmen and bakers, between the celebrations of feast days and fast days—the shining thread of courage, blending all together to make the magnificent picture which is America."

Courage. . . .

No, it was more like one of their old-time chats than a letter, this will. "Oh, yes, Sigrid, it takes courage to leave home and relatives and friends, disguise it as a man might try to do by showing anger, or indifference, or bravado, to leave customs and traditions and friends and kin, to sail away toward another land whose language he does not speak, knowing he will never come back.

"Oh, the times I wondered how much longer my heart could beat without sight of my mother's face, her hands, wrinkled and work-worn, which I had hated because, to the boy I was, they were not beautiful!

"We immigrants came. Was it because of religious persecution, of limited security for the individual, or the lack of an acre of ground on which to grow his food, or the absence of opportunity for education, or the hatred of a father who could betray a son; whatever the reason, it was not so good for us there; and when America held out her arms to us, saying, 'Come, I will give you opportunity; come, I will give you land; come, I will give you equality; come, I will give you freedom,' we came.

"Has America given what she promised? Ah, so much more, so much, much more. Some of us have failed America; but she has failed none, not a one of us.

"In what other country on the face of the globe could a man like Jesper Seastrom have come to be what he is, the biggest building contractor in the Middle West? I worked for him; I know his background well, from his own lips. Twelve years old, alone, he came from the far north of Sweden. He was large for his dozen years. He had to squeeze into a little seat in the first grade in public school, in a room full of six-year-olds, because he did not know a word of English.

"Do you see that that took courage?

"Oh, yes, compulsory public-school education had come

to Sweden when Jesper Seastrom was a boy, but he was far from a schoolhouse and he learned his alphabet from an itinerant teacher who came six or seven days in spring and fall and taught the children their letters by smoothing off a square of soil and marking the a's and b's and c's upon it with a stick. But too soon the letters must be rubbed out, in spring to set the flax seed down, or rye, or barley seed; in fall to cover the ground with herring, slit open, drying and stinking in what sunshine should come before the snowfall.

"A week of schooling twice a year! Only so few days could those inches of earth be spared for teaching, for learning; then the letters must be erased, for there was so little land—so little land.

"They did not know what it was to have paper, pencils, slates, or books, in his old home. To be sure the young Jesper practiced his letters on the new-fallen snow in wintertime; but there were fancier lines a boy must draw to keep life in his body and those of younger *syskon*, the lines made by ski as hunting he would go for reindeer meat or hare.

"Jesper Seastrom came to America; by working for his board and keep, delivering newspapers, sweeping out stores or washing plate-glass windows after school, he finished the grammar grades. He was graduated from high school. Some who are born in this country cannot claim as much, but it is not because the opportunity is not here for them. Alas, they are the ones who have come to look with apathy on what America offers in the way of education. Maybe, being too easily in reach, they discount its worth?

"Jesper Seastrom went on studying, attending night school, and look at him now!"

She would like to look at him. Instead, Sigrid looked at the wall ahead, but did not see it. She saw herself in her job at the printing office; nine months she had worked there, ever since she finished high school.

"Mr. Seastrom—by going to night school—"

She knew in this moment that she was going to keep on going to night school even after she completed her typewriting course. Exalted in spirit, she turned again to her father's writing. "The immigrants were the weavers of America, and they filled their wastebaskets with the imperfect threads of government, those that showed taints of monarchy, dynasty, or despotism. Likely heir to them all, did America copy the old countries? No, she set the pace, not only in economy but in the way of life, in the way of government. How far ahead she has gone of every parent country! Just as any child should progress farther than his parents. If he does not, of what avail is life?

"America is so young, yet think of what she has already achieved. Then think of what must lie ahead for her! Think of her destiny—and yours!"

It was long that Sigrid sat, looking and thinking. Her country was the only country in the world that was the child of all nations. Here all strains of blood had mingled, and were mingling, to make American blood. With a deep sense of elation, strong with emotion, she spoke aloud, "And I am an American!"

At last she brought her eyes to rest again on the words her father had written. "I?" she read, and a wave of sadness brought tears. "Well you may ask, what is it I have done? Only this, I opened the way for you. And so, to you, my Sigrid, I bequeath the richest legacy in all the world, the promise of America."

Pensive, she sat looking at the neat, even handwriting until the large hand had circled the clock face; only then did she fold the written pages and slip them back into their envelope. She knew her father better now, in death, than ever she had known him in life.

Too bad that his mother had not known his feeling for the land whose lighted torch had drawn him. "But now she can know." Sigrid reached for an envelope and on it copied the address from the slip of paper lying topmost on the stack. Her father had not written to his old home in Sweden since the day she was born. Why? Because he had not received an answer to his letter telling his mother he had named his child for her. And it was not only that, it was the letter he had tried for years to write, the feeler—sent to his home to learn if knowledge of their errant son was welcome still.

How did he know the letter had ever reached his mother? Ellen had asked him; so often she had begged him to write again; but no, his pride hurt, he had clung to the Old-Country way of only answering a letter received. Stubborn, he would not write again; feeling rejected, he would not. Bitter, he in turn again rejected the mother from whom he had not received the expected letter of forgiveness for running away from home, for hurting her as he knew he had done on leaving.

But now, at last, here was his mother's address for her to use, and Sigrid looked out of the east window where day sent its first lightening from the heavens. She would be eighteen years old in June, so for more than seventeen years his mother had not heard from her son, Carl.

"Dear God, let her still be living, so she will get this letter." Sigrid wrote in English, for that was all she knew, telling of what she had to tell. But surely balm must spread over the wound when her grandmother, Sigrid of Norden, in Bohuslän, Sweden, would read these clippings from the newspapers describing her son's heroic act in stepping from the curb on a crowded Chicago street and in the instant that the runaway team was abreast of him, grabbing the bit of one, twisting it, setting the big horse down on its haunches, stopping both horses, and saving Bobby Schmotzer.

His last words her father had said in Swedish. Now, with the Swedish-English dictionary before her, she could see how his native tongue had been corrupted by disuse and Middle-Western American contact. *"Förlåta,"* he had said it; but she wrote, *" 'Förlåt mig,'* he begged, as I leaned over him and kissed his lips, and he spoke to me as if it were his mother's face he saw before him, 'forgive me.' "

Oh, yes, certainly the grief of the mother of Carl must be assuaged in learning that his last words on earth had been, "Mother, forgive me, in His Holy Name."

The rosy dawn made diamond sparkles on the snow outside, reflecting their colors through the south windows on to the parlor ceiling. Sigrid looked up to see her own reflection in the shiny nickel trim of the base burner, her red cheeks matching the color of the sun rising now on a new day. Already the bitter dread of loneliness had lifted with the hope that she was not to be entirely without kin, that she would have family still; already she felt a closeness to the one whose name she bore.

But even as she signed, "Your loving granddaughter,

Sigrid," the north wind whistled a warning and the icy hand of winter reached inside of her and froze her heart: it was too much to hope for—that the Swedish Sigrid could be living still.

3

It was Mrs. Allspaugh, whom Sigrid had been taught in childhood to call "Aunt Hattie," who had called the attention of the crowd to her at Rose Hill. "There she is, over there! If she ain't feeding the horses! Well, like I always say, 'The acorn doesn't fall far from the tree!' That's ex*ack*ly what her father would have been doing!"

"Oh, you knew him, then?" someone had asked. There were so many there who had never heard of her father before his death.

"Knew him? I'll say I did! Why, I'll never forget—if I live to be a thousand—the first day I ever met him!" Smugly, "You can bet *I* told him off!"

She had seen Mrs. Schmotzer tug at Mrs. Allspaugh's arm in vain to silence her. But, "It was on the train, coming between Hillsdale and Oakhurst. I said it then, and I say it now, if a man has to smoke while he's on a train, let him go forward to the hog car where he belongs."

She had bitten her lips at Mrs. Allspaugh's laugh; it seemed so out of place to laugh, at a funeral. But Aunt Hattie was determined to finish. "The car pervided expressly for pigs. That's what I told him. Yes, sir-*ree!* Smoking! *Ugh!*"

Even getting into the coach had not silenced Aunt Hattie; she leaned out of the door, calling out, "After that, you see, I rented them a flat—and later—"

It was Hattie Allspaugh who held the mortgage on this home.

And now Aunt Hattie sat across from her at the kitchen table, sat with elbows propped up and chin resting in her hands. "You may not know it, but *I* know that a young girl like you can't keep up mortgage payments."

"But I have a job. I—"

26

"Don't you go interrupting your elders! And, anyway, I don't approve of your living here alone."

Sigrid was only half-consciously aware that Mrs. Allspaugh kept on talking; she knew only that Aunt Hattie did not understand her need for keeping "Ellen's house." But she had her mother's challenge: "Sigrid, if Pa doesn't find work, it will take character for a young girl to keep up payments on a house." And her mother had wanted her, most of all, to have character. More than comeliness. More than schooling, and schooling was one of the most important things in life! More than wealth, or material possessions; oh, so much more than wealth. More than health, and without health life was nothing.

Character. Doing the things you have promised yourself to do developed character, Ellen always said, such as sewing at least one calico patch on the quilt you have started before you allow yourself to go to bed at night, no matter how hard or heavy the day has been, no matter how tired your mind and body are; such as brushing your hair a hundred strokes on each side every morning, if that is what you have said to yourself you were going to do; such as refusing the glass of liquor that promised forgetfulness of trouble; such as making payments on a house.

"I said," the old friend's voice sharpened, "you can't be having that *Enoch* calling on you, here, if you live alone."

Sigrid felt her color heighten. Aunt Hattie knew very well that the Yingling lad had changed his name to Jack, he was trying so hard to become an American; but she would insist on using his Swedish name.

Dear Jack, such nice manners, always standing holding his hat over his heart when she met him on the street in that delightful Old-World manner that she had so loved in Pa. Aunt Hattie called Jack her "beau."

He was; at least he was her best friend among the young people. She often wondered at his frail frame coming from the same parents as the elder brother, Jonatan, the Swedish stairbuilder, with whom he lived in the salmon-colored house on the corner. Jonatan and Beda and their five small boys, all under six. Aunt Hattie wondered why he did not leave the home of his brother where life was nothing but heavy words—and diapers; but she never wondered about that. She knew. He had not yet found his place, a job, in the new country; he had not even mastered the language.

Mrs. Allspaugh had been sitting staring at Sigrid's strong-looking hands, at the ring she wore on the third finger of her left hand, a big pewter ring with store string wound around the inside to make it small enough to fit.

Her eyes had risen to follow the line of Sigrid's as yet undeveloped bust; two little brown moles cast shadows on the white skin of her long neck; her right brow arched higher than the left; the left brow, while not straight, was lowered some; and it was not that the left eye was smaller, but somehow it looked smaller. Was it that its lids were contracted to reflect defiance?

"I *forbid* your living here alone."

"Forbid? Why, Aunt Hattie! What do you think I am—a child?"

Yes, Mrs. Allspaugh was thinking, she is more like her father than I thought; so easily turned to anger. Look at her, red as a beet in the face! Well, she has had a good example of what uncontrolled temper can do to a person!

As Sigrid rose, now, pacing the room, something about her reminded Mrs. Allspaugh of the great wheatfields she had seen in North Dakota. The girl walked with a rhythmic motion, her body like a slender wheat stem undulating as if it enjoyed defiance of an angry wind.

"Don't you realize that I am almost eighteen years old?" she asked.

"*Humpf!*"

"And I am not going to—just walk out—and give up the house—like that!" She snapped her fingers. "And lose all that my mother worked so hard for!" At seeing a look of pain flash over Mrs. Allspaugh's face, Sigrid stopped abruptly. She must not forget that when she was thirteen years old, and her father had been so steady on the carpentry job that his contractor boss would waive the hundred-dollar down payment on one of the cottages in Calico Row if her parents could find someone to take up the mortgage, that it had been Hattie Allspaugh who had been willing to take the risk. Let her not forget that all this time it had been because of her she had this roof over her head.

And the calico cat, and all the litters of kittens. Sassy would not have had this home, either, if Hattie Allspaugh had not taken up the mortgage. And there was the time she had helped Ellen, when Tony was born; she had been good to Ellen. . . .

Aunt Hattie was rich; but how poor she was! Did anyone ever think of anything in connection with her, or mention of her, except money? Did anyone ever think of love?

Mrs. Allspaugh was the last person in the world on whom she would have thought she would want to bestow an embrace, but now Sigrid put her arm about the older woman's shoulders. "Aunt Hattie, I know you are only thinking of what's best for me. I know how good you have been to me—to my mother—to little Tony—it is not that I want to make you mad at me, but I *have* to keep my mother's house as long as I can. I simply have to! Let's make a deal: as long as I can work, and don't miss a payment, you'll try to see that I'm wise in—"

Grudgingly the answer came, "Well, as long as you don't miss a payment."

"I love you, Aunt Hattie." She placed a kiss on the wrinkled cheek, and found it hard to keep from laughing at the look of astonishment that greeted it.

"Well." Mrs. Allspaugh cleared her throat self-consciously, before her thin lips tightened. "Anyway, it's a pity that your father couldn't have left you a little something—beside debts." Her head tossed so violently that its white pompadour looked to be in danger of tumbling.

"Oh, but he did."

"What's that you say?" Bespectacled eyes popped in registering Hattie's surprise before one side of her nose screwed up and her lips curled in disbelief. "How much?"

She did not notice the trace of mischief that brought a twinkle to Sigrid's face. "He left me what it takes to keep on sending me to night school." And so he had. He had left the desire, the encouragement. Need she justify herself in not telling the whole truth to Mrs. Allspaugh? "He left a will."

"A will? Seems to me you could of said something about it before now! For Pete's sake! A will? Well, I'll be swanned! I'd never have thunk it possible—*him*—leaving a will! Well, I s'pose you've got to give even the devil his due! S'long!" Mrs. Allspaugh hurried away.

It was easy to guess that the reason for her haste was that she could not wait to burst in at the Heinebachs and

Yinglings and Mullers to be the first to tell the news that
Carl Christianson had left a will, and left enough to—
Sigrid's eyebrows raised—there was no telling what it
would turn out to be, that he left enough for, by the time
it had expanded in the repetition for which it was destined
with Aunt Hattie spreading the news.

Mrs. Allspaugh had not been able to contain herself
long enough to hear the news, that she, Sigrid Christianson, had at last found a way to earn her night-school
tuition at the business college; that the wages she earned
clerking three nights a week in the dry-goods store no
longer would have to be used to pay the tuition, so she
could put that money toward paying on the house!

It would not take very long after the close of each class
to dust the typewriters—there were only twenty machines
—and wipe their platens with alcohol, and brush the type
with benzine, and keep a check on ribbons to make sure
they were replaced when worn. Mr. Wyatt was going to
let her borrow the advanced lesson books, so the only cost
was the paper and the extra five cents' carfare three times
a week. She would manage that easily by cutting down a
little on the groceries. Nothing would stop her now that
she had started; she would do as Pa said Mr. Seastrom
did, keep on studying. After she mastered typewriting she
would study shorthand; after shorthand would come the
study of the Swedish language. After that she would enroll
in classes at the University of Chicago night school and
start accumulating credits toward a degree.

Every time she thought of a university education she
thought of the Schmotzers. How long would it be before
she would see the blue velvet dress? It was only an un-
bleached muslin cutting off of a pattern that Emilie had
fitted to her so far; the dress itself was to be a surprise.

And so would she have a surprise for Emilie. Deftly her
fingers plied a fine needle over and under blue silk threads.
Squinting, bringing her face close, she wove, then held her
work up to the light. Surprising herself in being able to
accomplish what she had set out to do, her eyes lit up with
satisfaction. And for the dress that Emilie was making she
could hardly wait. Yes, in expectation that velvet dress
was the thing she wanted most!

Except to get a letter from her father's mother.

Except to know Swedish.

If she had known the Swedish language she could have written to her father's people in their own tongue. More than a month had gone by now since she dropped her letter into the mailbox on the corner.

Although no reply to it had come, April had; both come and gone. Now it was May, and May was a month to make a person want to breathe deeply of the scent of spring flowers, as she stepped out on the porch in the early morning, and be glad! The blue sky told that the heavy snow clouds of winter were gone. What clouds there were were really not clouds at all, only frail, wispy brush strokes of white. She watched a familiar blue-clad uniformed figure as he came walking from house to house, stopping to sort the papers and envelopes he carried in his hands, walking up steps, dropping a letter into a mailbox slot, or trying to balance a rolled-up magazine on top of a small letterbox.

"Good morning, Mr. O'Mahoney!"

"Good mornin', Miss Sigrid, and how're you today?" Not looking up for answer, twice he sorted the letters in his hand, then with a big grin swung his mail sack forward, dug into it, and swinging it back to rest on a large leather patch, held up a big square blue-gray envelope. "From the Ould Country, it is!"

"Oh, thanks! Thanks!" She held the letter high as she ran. "I've got to hurry or I'll be late for work!"

"All aboard!" The lively call of the conductor reached her.

Still running, she slipped the letter into her pocketbook before she reached for the grab rail and jumped on the car. Clinging to a hanging strap, oblivious of the jostling and pushing of fellow pasengers, she swayed or was thrown, matching the movements of the streetcar, and her thoughts were on the letter. The return address on the back of the envelope would say, *"Fru Sigrid Kristiansson, Norden, Bohuslän, Sweden."*

Twice he repeated his invitation before she heard a gentleman say, "Have my seat, lady?"

"You are very kind." In these changing times, with so many women and girls going to work on the streetcars, it was not often that a man offered his seat, except, of course, to the elderly. And there was that business of "equality with men" that women were after. "So let them stand," the men said. But not all men; and so she sent a warm and thankful smile to this gentleman, and he tipped his hat and bowed.

Now she could have her hands free to open the letter! They quivered so that she fumbled with the pocketbook's clasp; the letter shook in her trembling fingers as she read her address spawled boldly over the entire front of the large envelope. She turned it over.

It was not from Sigrid Kristiansson.

If her grandmother were alive she would have been the one to answer.

This letter was from *Norden, Bohuslän, Sweden,* yes; but the sender was one *Fru Johann Sandell.*

4

Seventeen years was a long time. It had been too long.

Sigrid took a wire hairpin from her braids, slid its one prong into a corner of the blue-gray envelope. Carefully, so as not to cause a ragged tear, she slit the top fold open and removed the letter.

"Thank God!" It *was* from her grandmother! Although the context of the letter was written in English, the salutation was in Swedish: *"Min Älskade Karl's Dotter*—My Beloved Karl's Daughter." The swaying, screeching, grinding of the streetcar no longer was a part of Sigrid's morning, for these pages were not paper any more, but thankful cries from a grandmother's heart. "At last, at last I have found you! At last has come word of Karl!"

There was grief, spelled out as only a mother can know the words at loss of her own flesh and blood, but there was joy at learning of her son's return to the faith of his boyhood, at knowing of his plea for her forgiveness. "If there was aught to forgive, then I forgave it long ago." There was pride at reading that "The Hero" was her son.

She knew puzzlement, she wrote. "How can it be that my granddaughter's name is Sigrid Christianson; how is it hat Karl is written of as Carl Christianson, here in the lippings, when it was as Karl Petersson he left his home?"

Sigrid looked, without seeing, out of the car window; she had been remiss in not having explained. Her father had told her that in the old home in Sweden he had been known as Karl Petersson, for he was Peter's son. Once in America, however, "Your name may be spelled K-a-r-l in the Old Country, but in America we spell it C-a-r-l. And if your father's name is Kristiansson, over here *your* name is Christianson—see?" the official had told him, and so a stroke of a pen at the Immigration Station in New York had changed his name.

And the step her father had taken, out of his home, had changed hers! If she had been born to her father in his homeland she would have been known as Sigrid Karls-dotter!

Tenderly she smiled; even so she bore the name. Not on the courthouse records, no; not on the page of births in the family Bible, but in her grandmother's loving heart, in this letter with its greeting, *"Min Älskade Karl's Dotter."* Again she turned to it. "Whatever the reason for the change in name, now does that circumstance answer my years of questioning. Now do I know why I could not locate Karl. Look you upon the address written on the crumbling envelope I send enclosed with this, see there-upon the handwriting of my younger days, 'Karl Mattias Petersson.' There, within, is my answer to my son, singing my joy at learning of your birth, speaking my pride at hearing that he named you, his child, for me."

Now, when it was too late for him to know, also came the answer to her father's years'-long questioning: after he had put by his pride and written home, why had he not received a reply? He never knew that his mother's letter had been routed on the German steamer *Elbe,* the luckless vessel doomed to founder in the North Sea.

"Note the memorandum, 'Opened by Dead Letter Office, United States Post Office Department. Unable to locate K. M. Petersson. Return to Sender.' Thus did my letter come back to me."

A sob escaped Sigrid. "Such a little thing to—"

Little things, letters? Little? Oh, no! Links in a magic chain, binding when earthly circumstances part, links stretching a chain of silent eye language over the miles from heart to absent heart. No, no little thing: this piece of paper could have prevented the bitterness Pa knew! All of their lives might have been different if he had been able to retie the home bond he had cut in heartbreak and in rage.

"But now I have found you, my Sigrid! Daughter to my eldest son! First granddaughter to be born to me! First, and the only one, to be named for me! Ah, God speed the day when I can hold you in my arms! When I can hear you speak! For you will be coming home?"

Reluctantly turning from joy to sad remembrance, her grandmother went on, "Again I wrote, again, and yet again, but always addressing the envelopes, 'Karl Mattias Petersson.' They all came back unclaimed. And still, though he never wrote again, I seemed to know he was not dead. I could not know—dear God, I could not know—that in America he was known as Carl Christianson, nor that he had moved from the only street number I knew. I wrote to the Lutheran pastor of the *församling* of Chicago, and he knew Karl not; not in his parish was there a Karl Mattias Petersson from Bohuslän. I wrote to the place of records: there showed no daughter born to one of such a name. And so I prayed that once again might come a letter from America. My prayer is answered. Your letter shall rest close to me; it shall be a part of me from now until forever."

Try as she would to hold them back, tears would come. Nearing the office building in which she worked, Sigrid brushed them from her cheeks.

"The past is done. The present is good, for I have found you. Tell me—are your eyes blue, like Karl's? Are your hands big and strong, used to the feel of the earth, as I would hope them to be? Can you, my Sigrid, stand in rain and feel God's goodness as well as in the sunshine? Ah, my Karl's daughter, come to us soon, that we may clasp you by the hand!" Now her grandmother listed the names of the many at Norden, her children and her children's children. "They all send loving greetings to our Sigrid. And no less, says Johann my husband, does he send love, than I."

Her grandmother was remarried, and to the old family friend, Johann Sandell; but Pa had never known of that. His father, whom he had hated so, Peter, was still alive when Pa left home.

The letter was concluded, as begun, in Swedish. *"Från eder kära farmor*—From your loving grandmother, *Mor* Sigrid of Norden."

"Mor," the Swedish word for "Mother." What a lovely-sounding word it was, said as though it were spelled "moor," with the long double "o" sound, the "ōō" that had been so hard for her parents to overcome in pronouncing American words spelled with a single "o."

"Mor"—Mother, "Far"—Father; and so her father's mother was her "Farmor." Or, if one were to describe a mother's father, that person would be spoken of as "Morfar." It was easy to distinguish relationships, using the Swedish way.

There had been a Morfar in her father's home. Almost, it seemed, she might have known him, he was so real to her, come so alive from Pa's descriptions and tales of him. Morfar could have been the hero of a legend, beloved on sea and land for his good deeds and generous heart, but he had been her own great-great-grandfather. From such she had sprung!

Morfar. Farmor. What beautiful words to come singing from the tongue! Folding the letter from her Farmor, she said the name over and over in her mind, and stuffed the envelope back in her pocketbook. Happily she hurried; the sky was blue, the air smelled of the freshness of Lake Michigan, she had a job, she had a home, and she was studying. She was rich! She had kinfolk who loved her! They called her "our Sigrid"! She was not alone, would never be alone. With the coming of the letter her family, which up to now had been only a dream, was made real.

More slowly, when evening came and the low sun sent horizontal rays to change the skyscrapers' windows into rectangles of shining gold, Sigrid walked from the printing office. The spring had gone from her walk; one foot followed the other tiredly. The usual joy at laying her fingers on the unlettered keys of a schoolroom typewriter was gone; she merely went through the necessary motions.

Three hours later she climbed her front steps. Sorrowfully she stroked the handrail. Ellen's home: and this was not only a home, it was a monument to the time her father had stopped drinking. They had been a happy family in those years when Pa was sober. Then Tony died, and Pa had always blamed himself for that. When drink, later, had loosened his tongue, he had let slip enough so that she knew his agony. "Oh, God," she had heard him moan, calling on the One his lips denied. "Why did you not take me instead?" The anguish he knew! And he knew no other escape than losing the unbearable through drink.

Now she was going to have to lose this monument to the good which had been Pa. Her parents had been so right in knowing it would take a long, long time to pay off twenty-five hundred dollars; it would have taken years yet to pay for this home—the home Ellen had loved, the home she loved—her lovely garden—

She went through the house, turned on the porch light, and went into the back yard. Feverishly she dug the trowel into the soil. As spring was heading into deep summer she could see how the plants had developed. The fiddlehead ferns were unfolding in their new height; the wild roses she had transplanted from the prairie had taken hold and were putting forth new leaf buds, tender and light green.

Her trowel jabbed into the ground to loosen a long dandelion root. It was the size of a carrot already! But even it was dear.

All this she would lose now. Because when Mr. Sam, her employer, had learned that due to her daydreaming about the letter from Sweden she had passed, with her red-penciled "Okay" and sent to the *National Household* magazine, an advertising piece with the cut of a toaster paired with the description of a percolator while under the picture of the coffee percolator the type was set to tell of how well it toasted two slices of bread at the same time, instead of saying—as she had hoped he might, but knew he wouldn't —"What marvels electricity can perform!" he had said, *"You're fired!"*

Tomorrow she would start looking for another job. But jobs were not found in a day, or a week. It might be a month; and then she would have to miss the mortgage payment to Hattie Allspaugh.

5

"I didn't fold it and put it in a box, 'specially to keep it nice." Mrs. Schmotzer puffed as she led the way into Sigrid's parlor. Her husband followed, holding his right arm high, trailing a long white sheet from a wooden clothes hanger, letting the screen door bang behind him.

"Here, Bazile, hang it from the chandelier. So!" Her face was flushed. "I—I hope you like—"

Sigrid brought a smile. She had trudged all day, from one employment office to another; but now she danced excitedly around the hanging sheet. Now was not the time to think about how much better she could have used the money the dress material had cost.

"So, now soon comes the unweiling. No, Bobby! Stand back! There, go sit in a chair, that's a good boy. Hear me? Always got to be right out in front! Let Sigrid be the one for onct!" Emilie took common pins from the sheet and stuffed them into her mouth, talking around them. "Sit nice on the chair, Bobby. Ya, ya, Sigrid, I hope you like."

As if she were shooing chickens with an apron, she picked up the sides of her skirt and chased her husband out of the parlor. "You go out into the back yard, now, till I call you. I want to put it on her, see?"

"Yes, Emilie. Come, Bobby."

"I'm gonna stay. Can't I, Mama?" Whining, "Can't I stay?"

"Ach, you don't mind the boy, Sigrid? He's only a baby, really. Yes, Bobby, so long as you sit. Hear me? Sit. Now, Bazile, you get!"

At seeing Emilie's mouth so full of pins Sigrid felt herself half-afraid to swallow; but her fingers already were busy; she did not need Emilie's "Take off your shirtwaist and skirt." They were already off.

"Now shut your eyes."

38

She felt a silky softness slide over her head, down her arms; smelled the newness of cloth, stood with eyes tightly closed and waited until Mrs. Schmotzer had spit out the pins, then felt confident hands smooth the bodice before hooking it up the side.

"So many hooks?" There must be two dozen!

"Ya! There is no gapping, no bulging, when Emilie Schmotzer fits to your figger."

"Isn't it time yet to open my eyes?"

"Just in a minute. Come, Bazile. Bazile! Now where did that man go to? B-a-z-i-l-e—? Bobby, go and get your papa!" The mother swatted the boy's backside in loving gesture and started him toward the back door, only to jump, startled, at her husband's, "Here I am," come from behind her, just inside the front door.

"Now—"

Sigrid yielded to the firm hands that turned her to face the long console mirror, and opened her eyes. Oh! Was it truly herself? Her hands lightly followed the tight line of the bodice in the front to where it reached an inch or so below the natural waistline; moved to the back, to where it dipped low to a point, flowed lightly over the bustle effect; moved down over the skirt as it hung in silky velvet folds below four rows of hand shirring. Any girl's shoulders would move up and down, forward and back, to display their bare tips above the tiny roll of self material finishing the low neckline.

She stepped back from the mirror to view herself at full length: the hemline came slightly above the ankles.

"You like." Mrs. Schmotzer's head bobbed up and down. "I can see you like what I have made."

"Oh, Emilie!"

"Here, take my skirt. It washes. Cry into it. Ya, come, I cry, too." Half-laughing, half-weeping, they embraced.

"But"—Bazile's hands made a questioning move—"what about the—the other? Emilie, did you forget the—other?" He ran one hand, in pantomime, from the tips of his fingers up one arm.

"Ach, *himmel*, yes! Here!"

Sigrid opened the tissue-paper-wrapped parcel Emilie handed her. Of the same blue silk velvet the seamstress had fashioned a pair of gloves, long, almost reaching to meet the little sleeves high on the arms.

"Here." Bobby stalked forward now at an encouraging push from his father. "Here, take it." Poker-faced, he thrust an envelope at her. "From me," he clipped, and stalked back to his father's side.

With a corner of Emilie Schmotzer's sheet held gingerly in blue-gloved fingers close to her face, to catch any vagrant teardrop, she read the note pinned to a ten-dollar bill, "For slippers, to match, and silk stockings."

No words would come, and so she handed Emilie the surprise she had made.

"A label! Like from a salon, it will make your dress!"

"No, Emilie, it is not for my dress. It's for you, to put into your own best dress. It's only a little 'thank you.' "

Now the seamstress looked closely at the little strip of woven silk. "Where—*where* did you—get—such—?"

"I made it."

"Bazile! She made it! She weaved it, a label! *With my name on!* Ach, it must have taken longer than for me to have made her whole dress!" Emilie brought it so close to her husband's eyes he had to draw back in order to see. She bent so Bobby could see it. "How in the world could you make it—such a label?"

"I got a little oblong pillbox from Mr. Bradley's drugstore. Then I stuck real fine needles through each short end, up from the bottom, and on the needles I strung the blue silk thread back and forth, or 'forth and back,' as my father always said, like warp on a little box loom. On those threads I wove, with the gold-colored sewing silk, making the writing in the long satin stitch."

"Ach!" The older woman's head swung in amazement. "Like Paris it is—a label—in script writing—a label—"

"What does it say, Mama?"

"What does it say? It says, *'Emilie—Modiste'*—it says."

Mrs. Schmotzer kept repeating, "Emilie—Modiste," mumbling as if she were talking in her sleep. Then, "Emilie—Modiste—ya! Ya, Sigrid! In this, your America, from Emilie the immigrant, *could come* 'Emilie—Modiste!' " She started toward the door as if she had an appointment with Fate and must not keep Fate waiting. "We must go! Come, come, both of you! Good-by, Sigrid! God bless you, Sigrid!"

At the screen door's closing behind the Schmotzer family Sigrid gazed into the mirror. Standing there, dressed in the exquisite blue velvet, she heard the screen door open again, and in her imagination saw Jack enter—tall, blond Jack—and slowly she turned to face him; but the figure that had entered was Mrs. Allspaugh's.

"Well! Where'd you get that finery?" Her neighbor's sharp voice burst the fairy bubble.

"Oh, Aunt Hattie! Isn't it beautiful?" She spread her hands and followed the fit of the velvet.

"But—blue?"

"Yes. My favorite color."

"Humpf! Should've been black. You know you're still in mourning, or ought to be. A year ain't gone by yet, not by a long sight."

"Come." She took Mrs. Allspaugh's hand. "Please come, I want to show you something."

"What?"

"Something Pastor Bedell showed me after my mother and father died."

Reluctantly the old friend allowed herself to be led.

"I asked him if I should buy a black dress." They were in the back yard now, and close to the fence Sigrid lightly brushed aside the peltate leaves of the crawling nasturtiums and pointed. "See, beyond the 'nose twists' there my little clump of wild blue-eyed grass?"

Growing six or seven inches tall, the flat stems bore purple buds and sapphire blossoms that could be mistaken for tiny dwarf flag lilies. She ran her fingers under one stem that was wilted, shriveled, and lying on the ground. Its brilliant colors were gone. "As Pastor Bedell said, 'This one has died. But do the others shed their bright blue and don somber black? No. The others bloom blue, starry-eyed, and happy.' "

So did her eyes shine as she said softly, "They would want me to have blue, both Mother and Pa," and walked as in a dream back to the console mirror.

Sigrid walked from office to office, from factory to factory, and the only greeting she received was, "No help wanted."

"Maybe, if I could rent the house for a while?" An idle thought, for even in the fine brick twelve-flat building on Chicago Avenue there were twelve "For Rent" signs. The owner had laid off the janitor and turned off the water

and lights so that the three-story building stood dark and
silent, with lawn parched and brown, a reminder of slack
times.

"There must be some way of earning a living." She spoke
of it only to the kitten, and Sassy paid no heed. Sassy's
mind dwelt mainly on ivory-colored milk pouring thickly
from a glass quart bottle.

"My mother always found a way."

And how? By doing something people needed done. By
giving a service for which there was a demand.

"Of course!" She jumped to her feet so quickly she
spilled the kitten from her lap. "Everyone *eats!*"

From yellow house to pink house to gray house to
salmon-colored house. "Mrs. Pike, would you like to buy
some homemade bread?"

"As good as you make it? Yes!"

"Mrs. Muller, would you buy a white layer cake?"

"Your fresh-ground coconut kind? *Indeed* I would!"

"Apple cake, Mrs. Jacobson?" "Taina, would you
like—?" "Mrs. Peterson, how about some limpa rye
bread?" "Beda Yingling—?"

Yes, Yes! And *yes!*

And so Sigrid walked in the pleasantness of the June
day, delivering the orders she had taken, carefully taking
meringue pies or frosted cakes from her own old baby carriage and carrying them to eager customers. *Cash* customers!

As Sigrid walked, Pastor Bedell sat in the parsonage
parlor. Putting off the thing he planned to do, he turned
his thoughts to Sigrid.

Yes, she was strong; her build, her ruddy skin, all of her,
made a person feel her strength, as so often a foreign
peasant woman's does, in some subtle way by the broad
shoulders, the long hands and feet, the certainty, the erect-
ness with which she carried her tall height. Even that ring
she wore, as if it were a part of her, bespoke her strength
—a huge ring, crudely fashioned of pewter, or more rightly *malm*, bell metal, as they called it in the Old Country—
a man's ring come down from Viking ancestors on her
mother's side—sent to her by her mother's sister after
Ellen's death.

And yet—not refuting her ruggedness, nor lessening it,
there was about her a delicacy, as of not entirely outgrown

adolescence—something that made him yield to Kristin's fear for her. . . .

Out of the corner of his eye he watched his wife's fingers idling over the keys of the organ. He was glad she was not looking at him, for his spectacles were much too far down on his nose bridge for seeing through, and the book might as well be upside down for all he read its pages.

Rocking, he looked up at the ceiling; rocking more violently, he raised the volume close to his face so if she glanced his way she would not see that his eyes did not rove from line to line.

Why should he hesitate so to say the words he knew would please her? Oh, he knew how astonished she would be, and wonder what had got into him, a Lutheran minister, to suggest that they go to the theater!

Love, that had been like the throbbing of an ocean in his youth and grown deeper, stronger, through the years, lit up his face at thought of that lifelong wish of Kristin's, to see one time the gayety and grandeur of the inside of the theater, for he was going to grant it now. His lips moved in silent prayer, "Dear Lord, you know we've never been to the theater; I never thought I'd want to go; but I'm going to take her once, Lord, before she goes."

But if she should ask, "Why?" after all these years. "Why, *now?*" What could he say? From the fullness of his eyes, or in his throat, would she guess the real reason for his asking her? This new medico, Dr. van Vlaardingen, was not one to beat around the bush, but, "Why should she have to know her time is almost gone?" he had said. "It might only serve to discourage her; and with this great white plague it is encouragement alone that helps."

Pastor Bedell stopped rocking. He was afraid; more scared than he had ever been in all his life. What if she saw through his plan?

"Kristin"—he slid his half-spectacles to his forehead—"do you suppose you would feel up to attending a performance at the theater?"

Her hands fell full across the keys, sending a discordant chord into the room as if to match the absurdity of his question. "Dear Felix, what's that you say?" She leaned forward, pushing in the organ stops.

He fought to keep back tears. Keep her happy, the doctor

had said, for the little time there is left for her. It took so
little to keep Kristin happy. And all through the years of
their marriage it had been little he could give her. She had
denied herself so many things, stifled the longings she had
known. For him, because he was a Lutheran minister, and
she loved him, she had put her yearning for the theater,
and dancing, and how many other things, aside.

Was she starved for the joy that such would bring? Was
that why her face looked now the way it did, almost as if
heaven itself had opened up before her? Ah, yes, he was
glad he had thought up an excuse to grant that wish of
hers.

"I say, my dear, would you like to go to the theater?"

Her face showed her remorse, now, at ever having mentioned this desire, which, through the years, he knew, had
grown in importance to her. "What would the women say,
in the church, if they learned the pastor's wife had gone to
the theater after being too indisposed to attend church for
the several Sundays?"

"It is God who is our judge, Kristin."

"You mean—you would do this—for me? But—why—
now?"

He could not keep his face from taking on a silly look.
"No, I would be doing it for me. For myself." He got up
and walked back and forth over the carpet, with his hands
clasped behind his back, with the swallow tails of his coat
flapping. "It would be the most 'human' thing I ever did!"

"Human?"

"Oh," boyishly he faced her squarely, and bragged. "I
would make a good social secretary, Kristin."

"A good anything, you would make."

"Thank you, my dear. Now perhaps you might like to
go to McVicker's?"

"Oh, Felix, Felix!"

"There will be presented the Cines photo drama *Quo
Vadis.*" He had picked up the Chicago *Tribune* and opened
and folded it at the theater news. "Or to the Majestic, to
see Lillian Russell do her monologue on health and beauty.
Or to the Garrick—?"

"Oh, either—either—but—why—why, *now?*"

"You see—I—I, well, Sigrid should have some fancy
place to wear that grand new dress of hers. If we do not
figure out a place, where would she ever wear it? The

young man, Jack, he"—the pastor's tongue was in his cheek, thinking of his own purse—"he can't afford to take her to grand places."

His wife came and stood behind his chair and ran her slender fingers through his little fringe of hair. "Ever the thoughtful one, my Felix, ever, ever so. But"—breathlessly—"what is playing at the Garrick?"

"When Dreams Come True." Her warm cheek against the top of his head stopped him. His life with her had been dreams come true; no play, written by man, could equal this story of their lives writ by God.

"That is the name of the production, Kristin. Do not worry, for times are changing, and more and more of our church people are attending the theaters"—he grinned—"even if they do not tell their pastors. And the women of the church should not object too much for here it says that William Pinkerton, the world's greatest detective, and a clean-living man, says, 'It is very seldom that I sit through a performance twice, but this is full of catchy music, fine performing. Absolutely clean, very sweet and pretty.'"

"But, Felix, see—down further, 'Joseph Santley dances his own tango!'" Her mouth drooped.

"But see also, 'Clean as a hound's tooth!' says the New York *Morning Telegraph.*"

"Even if there is dancing in it—you—would go?"

"If you feel up to it, Kristin, we are going."

"Pastor Bedell," his wife tormented him, "could not have arranged a fine enough party anywhere else, could he? Not at his home, nor even in the church? Could he?"

"No, Kristin." Gently he drew his wife to sit on his short lap. No, not at his home, nor in the church, could his Kristin have her dream come true, to see the inside of the theater. Aloud he said. "No, Kristin, not anywhere else could Sigrid wear that new dress of hers in propriety."

On Saturday evening Jack called for Sigrid. He reached to touch her dress, but his arms fell limply at his sides. Then he spoke volumes with his whisper, "An *angel,* you are—a beautiful blue *angel.*" And he sat silent, with the pastor and his wife and Sigrid, packed into Mr. Benson's automobile, as they rode in style to Chicago's Loop. Now they stood in the lobby of the Garrick Theater and watched well-dressed patrons drift in.

"There is no more beautiful dress than mine, is there?" Sigrid asked the pastor's wife.

"See how they all glance in your direction? That should be answer enough."

Happily Sigrid squeezed her friend's hand, although she could be almost certain it was at the pastor they looked, for unapologetically here in the theater he wore the habit of his calling, black suit and white collar with its two starched tabs.

Nervously the pastor tightened his hold on his wife's arm. Now that he was here, working out the thing he had schemed, he felt like the choirboy who, striding to the loft, sees glances cast at his back pocket and knows that his surplice has caught over his slingshot. But he saw that although his wife kept the handkerchief pressed against her lips she was serenely happy.

He allowed his party to be pushed by the crowd, and soon they were following a party of three made up of a middle-aged, fat, red-faced man and a woman dressed in flashy purple with a sparkling tiara on her bleached hair and with shining bracelets and rings worn outside of her purple silk gloves. The third of the party was a young woman dressed in black lace, her décolleté so low in front that the line between her breasts showed deeply. Her full lips were rouged.

Sigrid could tell by their attitudes that the three had disagreed. "Well, why did you *come* then?" she heard the young woman growl at the heavy-set man, and had to pinch herself to make realization come that there could be cruel words in such a place as this, under the stimulus of the electric-lighted crystal chandeliers, the richness of red velours draperies, the brilliant roses in the carpet, and the chitchatting of happy folk. A heavy wave of generous feeling swept over her, and she felt deeply sorry for this unknown man.

"Why, good evening, Mr. Shannon." The pastor extended his hand. "How pleasant meeting you here."

"Ah—eh? I, eh—"

"Bedell is the name, from out on the west side. Calico Row." He shook hands warmly. "Perhaps you don't recall me; we met at a political rally in Turner Hall."

"Ah, a fellow Democrat!" Mr. Shannon pumped the pastor's hand.

"No. No. I am a Republican."

Sigrid shook with inner laughter at seeing the pastor's hand dropped as if it were a red-hot iron.

"We Swedes," he was saying, "you see, came from a kingdom to a republic, and that word means a great deal to us, just the sound of it! It is only natural, I suppose"—he smiled broadly—"that most of us should have chosen to be Republicans. But I'd like to have you know my wife, Mrs. Bedell. And our friends, Miss Sigrid Christianson and Jack Yingling."

"I—ah—er—" Mr. Shannon ran his finger between his stiff collar and heavy neck, and Sigrid saw an angry red line where the collar had chafed the skin. "Pleased ta' meetcha. And this here's my wife, and my daughter, Grayce."

"Why—Gracie Shannon!" Sigrid raised both of her hands. "How *nice* to meet you again, after all these years. How many years is it? Not since we were children!"

"It's Grayce, please," Mrs. Shannon said haughtily, bringing a lorgnette with a long jewel-studded handle to her eyes.

Sigrid winced at the tone, and under Gracie's head-to-toe scrutiny her hands, even in the silk velvet gloves, grew clumsy; her feet, even in the new blue slippers, seemed bigger than the size six they were.

She could see that Gracie gloated at her discomfiture as she walked with hips dipping in sensuous motion close enough to Jack to brush his sleeve before slipping her arm into the crook of her father's, before tossing her head and saying, "Oh, yes. Now I remember you. You're Sigrid, the one the kids used to call 'Cigarette.' Sure, I remember you; you lived in a basement, and your mother was a wash-woman."

6

Even as a child Gracie had known how to pick out the tender spots, cruelly saying the thing she knew would hurt most. But Ellen would have been proud of her daughter if she could have seen her biting her tongue to keep from snapping back at Gracie, "Yes, and your father was a saloon-keeper!" She had felt sorry for that red-faced father.

But the inside of a theater had been a place to make four happy people forget Gracie's gibe. Sigrid lived over the evening: if she had not experienced that thrill at the curtain's rising, if she had not seen the actors, if she had not sat open-mouthed at the play, if she had not felt Jack's hand pressure on hers in the tightly packed automobile on the way home, that night would have been enough to be a heart's most precious memory, for the watching of Kristin's face.

Such *joy* as the pastor brought to Kristin—such pure, pure joy! And to her.

That was on Saturday. Now it was Monday night. She dragged one foot after the other, clung to the railing as if she were old, and pulled herself up the steps, humping the empty baby carriage after her.

"Sassy, you've no idea how hard it is to gather together twenty-five dollars!" The sleepy cat came stretching, too sleepy to meow, rubbing against her legs.

Her front door was no welcoming rectangle of light; inside it was as dark as the outside night; no smell of cooking greeted her, to hasten her step or lighten it. Only Sassy waited for her to come home; and the lentils waited to be sorted and cleaned and put to soak, to be ready for tomorrow's supper.

"Your *first* visit to the theater?" Gracie had said.

Remembering was bitter: as a child Gracie had had everything she had wanted, a rich home, a mother who did

48

not have to work for other people, silk dresses, a bisque doll with real hair and joints, and a doll buggy with a silk parasol that folded and rubber tires on the wheels. And now that they were grown, Gracie was so fortunate as to have her mother and father living!

"Oh, my! What ever have you done to bring any beauty into your drab life without the theatah?" Gracie had gone on.

Her drab life: emptying a package of lentils on to the sink; taking out the shriveled ones and throwing them away, scraping the good ones into little piles—

Her head dropped on her arms. "Dear God, help me. It's only that I'm so tired—so terribly tired—"

She must have napped. In the brief moments of a dream she had seen herself carrying a bowl of steaming lentils to the pastor's home; Kristin was so fond of lentils. My, how pretty they were! Soft grayish beige with overtones of rose—overlapping each other—soft-colored seeds changing to soft-colored shells, overlapping on some imaginary beach, as she sorted them. How could Gracie think that anyone's life could be drab, with the beauty there was all around?

That Gracie! If she could have seen her own expression when Jack answered her, in a long outburst of rapid Swedish! She hadn't understood the words, but no one could have misunderstood the tone. Sigrid laughed outright, to make Sassy look up and miss taking, in fast time, one mouthful of leftover stew.

Her own plate of stew grew cold and fatty in front of Sigrid as she counted the day's receipts, setting aside five cents out of each full dollar's worth of change. Now to figure out the cost of replacement of the staples used in the day's baking and slip the rest into the envelope marked "Mortgage." She drew the nickels toward her, reached for the mechanical bank, and laid one five-cent piece at a time on the quarter-sized tambourine stretched toward her by a cast-metal Salvation Army lassie. She pressed the lever in the back of a shaggy brown dog of iron who wagged his tail up and down and opened his mouth as if he were barking, but no sound came except that of the tinkling bell the lassie held in her other hand. And the coins slipped through the slot.

Two nickels toward the realization of her heart's desire. . . .

She picked up the bank and rattled it. A look of childlike joy spread over her face. Again she was a child, hearing her mother say,

> "Little drops of water,
> Little grains of sand,
> Make the mighty ocean
> And the pleasant land."

Two coins. So little. But it was a *beginning!*

After a gentle knock she walked right in. "Kristin?"

She set the dish of hot lentils on the kitchen stove and sped toward the bedroom. "Kristin, oh, Kristin!" The light in sunken eyes told Sigrid how glad the pastor's wife was that she had come.

The pillowcase—all stained with bright red blood.

The feeble lifting of the handkerchief.

The cough! Oh, what that cough did to Kristin!

"Have you, has this ever happened before?"

"Yes, Sigrid." She would be all right: as soon as this devastating weakness passed. Then she would be all right again.

Sigrid looked around. They needed her here. By now she sensed that they would never ask her to come. But they needed her. With a soothing word of reassurance to her friend, she changed the bed. She put on a kitchen apron; soon the teakettle sang a lively tune on the cookstove, gaslights burned cheerily in all their outlets. Supper of lentils was set on the bedside table for the pastor, and Sigrid fed Kristin warm broth.

In the morning the pastor served as messenger, delivering regrets that for this one day the bakery orders could not be filled, and Sigrid went about setting the parsonage in order.

"I'm so glad you feel better this morning, Kristin!" She peeked into the bedroom.

"I'm so sorry to be of such trouble. It's only that when the hemorrhages come—"

"No trouble at all! You know I love to come here."

"And how much it means to me when you come."

Changing her expression, "One can learn much, even about a well-known friend, watching her dust."

"You could see me in the other rooms?"

"I could see that you love the rare pieces—the old—as I do. It takes you longer to dust those—"

She blushed. "You mean the chair, Kristin. And—"

"The Baltimore Chippendale chair, yes. And I saw how you lingered lovingly over the little Geib piano, stroking the wood—"

"It's just like silk-satin!"

"Yes. The patina, a finish which only age can give. But the organ. You dusted that, but that was all. It is a cheaply made, modern piece—"

"But I didn't *know!*" Sigrid spread her hands, palms upward.

"You knew you thought them beautiful. That is enough. It is something that comes from inside of a person, this love for the beautiful—the old—"

"I've loved them ever since I first came into your home, Kristin, since I was only a child. And the two knife boxes on the sideboard?"

"Sheraton. Mahogany, inlaid with satinwood."

"And the hall tree? Are they heirlooms, Kristin?" Certainly they were much too expensive to have been acquired on a pastor's pay.

His wife smiled. "Somebody's heirlooms, Sigrid, but not my family's. My parents were first-generation Americans, from Europe, as yours were, and came here almost empty-handed."

"Then where did you get them? Oh, no, I've tired you. Don't try to talk more."

"Not too tired to talk of beautiful things." Earnestly, "Let me tell you, Sigrid, cultivate this appreciation that you have—"

"You know I do have a milk-glass plate—and—"

Kristin nodded. "Yes. But study, and then go searching in likely old shops. I found the knife boxes in an old dirty secondhand store, like Jake's. Someday they may be very valuable, but thirty years ago I paid only six dollars for the two."

"Jake's, you said. Have you ever noticed that blue piece of drapery that hangs in the back, to the left, behind the big copper pot? You haven't? Oh, Kristin, it is the rarest blue—it is—"

Softly speaking happy hopes of one day owning the blue material, Sigrid bathed Kristin Bedell in preparation for the morning call of the neighborhood's new doctor.

"What is it? A curtain, or a spread, or what?"

"I really can't tell, the windows are so grimy. But some-day—*some*day I'm going to go in and ask the price of it."

"That is the way I 'courted' my knife boxes before at last I was able to go in and price them, with some money in my hand!"

They laughed; and Sigrid combed Kristin's hair and tied narrow pink ribbons at the ends of the long pigtails.

"Would you like to have your toenails done? That always makes me feel just like I've had a second bath."

"Oh, Sigrid, *would* you?"

The little scissors snipped; the toothpick swab gently pressed back cuticle. Absorbed in what she was doing, Sigrid did not hear a step enter the bedroom. She looked up, startled, at hearing, "Ah, Mrs. Bedell, I see you have a nurse?"

"Sh-h-h, she is sleeping."

"Yes, so I see." Extending his hand. "I am Dr. Van Vlaardingen."

She stood. She looked up into his big, open Dutch-looking face—into his eyes—

His eyes! They seemed to be smoldering with a steely fire. It was as if sparks came from them.

"And this is my son, Nico."

7

Like turning a sudden corner, after traveling a maze of narrow city streets, and seeing before one's eyes a broad expanse of meadow, in that instant of meeting the doctor a plan for the solving of her problems had come to Sigrid. If events worked out, as she now hoped so desperately they would, she could be true to the memory of her mother's wish and keep her home, she could be of help to Kristin, and oh, the happiness she herself would know!

It all depended on the doctor.

The pastor always said you can't only pray for what you want out of life, expecting to receive it; you have to go about doing for yourself, to help God answer prayers. First, she would plan to have a watermelon feast in her back yard, a sort of welcome to Calico Row for Dr. van Vlaardingen and his son. She would ask each of the neighbors, who could afford to, to contribute a melon.

Planning, she followed the many ways demanded by her days, that way beginning with the lighting of the oven at four o'clock in the morning, the many paths she traveled to deliver the baked goods, the final path on three evenings a week leading to night school, on three to the back of the counter at the dry-goods store, the path to home by way of the window of the pawn shop, the way to the icebox for Sassy's milk, the path leading to church, and there was only one face she saw at the way's end. Kristin's.

Poor Kristin, who, living in the happy hope of another visit to the theater, did not know how few were her remaining days. Poor Pastor Bedell, who did. And yet, knowing, he could smile. Sigrid marveled that he could. He was the living example of faith in a glorious hereafter. Death was only a milestone, not the end, to him. Perhaps that was the reason he could lead his flock so well into believing, because he himself knew such implicit faith. So often he

53

would link his sermons to the ways of nature; and so many times as he walked with her he showed her how, in nature, God sent His messages to him.

Seeing her home after her visit to Kristin, they stood looking into the mimic blue sky which was Fuller's Pond, and watched the water striders dent its surface. "People call it the Jesus bug," he said. "Because it walks on the water. Those six long legs have waxy feet that do not break through the surface tension. But see, Sigrid, look at the dragonfly, with his beautiful lacy wings of glossy texture, see how he skims about, coming close to the surface; see how he hovers, his immense eyes peering hard below? What does he see there, living in the water?"

Soon he answered himself, "Grubs. Grubs, such as the dragonfly himself was before he crept out of his muddy skin. And then he found himself crawling, up the stem of a cattail, up into the air and sunshine. It meant agony to him to rid himself of the garment he wore below, before he emerged this lovely green-and-silver thing." He looked from the water to her. "Does he fly low to try to tell those he has left behind of the beauty he has found above?"

She understood his comparison to earthly beings, to death, and to a heavenly place. She understood when he finished, "They crawl below, entirely oblivious of him, not knowing that he once was one of them."

Oh, for such faith as the pastor knew! Then she could know that her prayer would be answered and this plan of hers would work.

The day she chose was a beautiful day for a watermelon feast, and for gathering, out-of-doors, to meet the new doctor. "Dr. van Vlaardingen," she introduced him to the neighbors as they arrived. "And his son, Nico."

The newcomers mingled well with the old-timers of Calico Row, Taina and Louis Heinebach, Beda Yingling and Jonatan and their boys, and Jack, and Mr. and Mrs. Allspaugh, and all.

The Van Vlaardingens. She studied them. Try as she would to describe their faces to herself she could not—neither Nico's nor his father's—except their eyes. She had seen many blue eyes before, of varying shades, light, dark, gray-blue, greenish-blue, but never such eyes as these two had. They were not wide open to attract attention; although the upper lids were not drooped and the lower ones did not reach upward, there was a partially closed expression about them. But when they opened wide, they were such different eyes. Steel-blue, but not a cold steel; near to the color of the zenith of the clear sky, with something added, that steely fire.

The father's voice was deep and ringing; there was only a trace of an accent, a "z" softness to his "s's," which Nico had caught, to give an added interest to his bass man voice.

The doctor was big, and solid, like a large oak tree. Whimsy replaced the seriousness which had settled on Sigrid's face: he was the kind of tree you would choose to carve your initials on, with a heart, and an arrow, and the initials of the one you loved. Sturdy, he was, the kind you'd pick out of all the forest monarchs to brace yourself against if trouble came, to lean an arm against while burying your head in the crook of that arm and crying your heart out.

Lost in her thoughts, she missed whatever had been said to precipitate Jack's stating flatly, and with uncommon force for him, that he, "or anyone else, could be yust as good without going to church."

She wished, for the pastor's sake, he had not said it, but the doctor did more than wish; he spoke, "Perhaps so." And generously, "I grant you so." His big round face then took on a stern look. "But the American way of life is based on Christian concepts. Do you think it is entirely fair to live under the light of them and take no active part in nurturing them?"

"*Our* way of life," Hattie Allspaugh retorted, giving emphasis to the first word as if to exclude the Holland-born doctor, "is based on the Constitution!"

"And the Constitution," the doctor asked patiently. "On what is that based?"

"Well—er—"

"It is based on Mosaic law, is it not?" Then he turned to Jack. "While granting freedom of speech, freedom of religious thought, and the right to petition, while granting trial by jury, and security from unreasonable searches and seizures, while preventing slavery, it vests judicial power to punish piracies, treason, felonies, and other heinous crimes. In that way our"—and now he emphasized the word—"Constitution says, 'Thou shalt not steal, thou shalt not kill.'

"These," he continued, "are no overbearing impositions, set down arbitrarily by Moses or our Constitution; they are natural moral laws come out of man's living with man, proved by time to be the best for the most. Not, in spite of the wording, 'Thou shalt not,' restricting us, but protecting us. Is is not, then, the least we can do to support in some way the institution which has elevated our sphere from that of the savages and heathen?"

Pastor Bedell's face beamed as he listened.

Jack looked at the floor.

"If we accept the privileges of living in a Christian world, we must also accept some of the responsibilities. Any church—just so we contribute something of ourselves to a plan that gives to us so richly—any church, but we should support some church." The doctor's eyes shone. "Certainly, if our ability to help in material ways is small, we can make up for that by lending our presence."

A long silence lay over the neighbors. They had respect for this newcomer; all were thinking deeply on his words, and the deepest thoughts could well have been Sigrid's own. His conversation had a professorial sound, as with others she knew who were of foreign birth, but his use of "bookish" words did not seem to make him any the less one of them.

And they all liked the son, who had been left motherless at birth.

Sigrid turned her attention to the son. She had never heard anyone, before Nico, call a father "Dad." It was usually "Pa," or "Pop," or, of course, "Father." But "Dad" had a connotation of admiration, and closeness, and respect, and more than either or all of these, love. She would have liked to have called her own father "Dad."

Aside from his eyes, Nico looked like any other young fellow his age. The part in his hair was never very straight; and his clothes, while new, were too large for him. Boys of eighteen seemed so immature and clumsy alongside girls of the same age; she was grown up, more on an age level with Jack, who was twenty-one.

She could see how the doctor idolized his son. "My shadow," he called him. "Trying to pick up Dad's professional manner," Nico said, laughing, for he had decided he also was going to be a physician. Nico was not tall for his age; he would have a long way to go to match his father's height, yet the father and son were much alike and in that similarity were different from anyone else she had ever met. She hardly thought of them separately, just as "the van Vlaardingens." Still, they were different; the father was so serious, but Nico put fun into everything he did. It was he who cut the melons and sliced them lengthwise so as to cause the Yingling boys, in eating them, to screech to each other, "Your *ears* are dripping!"

She kept the doctor in her sight, waiting for a chance to speak to him alone.

He stood apart. Now—!

"Doctor? How do you like Calico Row by this time?"

"Very well. Very well."

"You—you wouldn't be thinking about moving—to the Row—now that you're establishing a practice here?" She felt her pulse beat against the heavy ring.

"Well, as a matter of fact, I *should!*"

"Could I—would you let me show you my home, inside, to see if it might do for you to rent?"

He gave her a sharp glance. "Why? Are you thinking of moving away?"

She bit her lip.

"Excuse me. I didn't mean to get personal. Yes." He took her arm. "Please, do show me."

This was the kitchen. A cheerful room of good size, didn't he think? The dining room was dark, yes, the houses were so close together the eaves met, keeping out the light; but the parlor! It faced south so it was sunny. The bedrooms—the attic—the basement—

"Yes. Yes, I see."

She could tell it had not impressed him. "I only thought—"

"And I'll think it over," he said kindly, and led her back to the noise of laughter and fun making.

It hadn't suited him. How could she ever have thought it would?

Sadly, she said to Jack as he was leaving, "I'm not as smart as I thought I was."

He did not spare the words to question, only answered, "Smart enough for me."

As the last of the guests disappeared through the narrow

gangway a fuzziness entwined her ankles. "Sassy! Poor Sassy, where have you been? Why, you're nothing but an old alley cat lately, with my being away so much, and no one here to take care of you." But Sassy purred contentedly, with a new kind of contentedness, not paying any attention when her mistress said in a determined voice, "Well, it looks like I'm going to have to think up another plan."

Sigrid barely touched the doorbell, then turned the knob. "May I come in?"

"The day always seems brighter, we always breathe more easily, when Sigrid comes. Is it not so, Felix?"

"It is so." The pastor beckoned her to a chair, but Sigrid did not sit.

"I've come to ask a favor."

"Speak it, and it shall be granted."

"Would you—give a homeless—young woman—a home?"

A look passed between the pastor and his wife, a worried look, a look of pain, and yet a look of joy. Both opened their lips to speak, but Sigrid's tongue would not be stilled. "The doctor is going to rent my house. For enough to pay the monthly payments. And enough to pay the taxes. Upkeep—he's going to take care of that, too. And the only thing—the *only* thing he asks is that I let him have some remodeling done. As it is, the house doesn't exactly suit his needs!

"Think of it!" She danced around the room, stopping to hug Kristin, and not noticing the ever-present handkerchief, tapping the pastor on the shoulder as she pirouetted around him.

Suddenly she stopped. Trying to look crestfallen, she grimaced. "But I won't have a place to hang my hat—a bedroom to sleep in—if you don't take me in."

"We—we—"

"Where else should a girl go to ask for shelter, if not to her pastor's home?" She shrugged her shoulders and opened her hands as Pawnshop Jake did so expressively.

The pastor looked at his wife. Dear God! The hope that filled her eyes! The gladness! "Bless you, Sigrid," he began. Then, stuttering, "You know how it is with us, and still you want to come?"

"Please, let me come?"

"Let you?" Kristin exclaimed. "*Let* you?"

As if it had been rehearsed, two women spoke as one. "I knew God would take care of me."

Sigrid served Kristin well in the months that followed, until one day the doctor placed his arm on her shoulders and walked her from the room, leaving the pastor at his wife's bedside, closing the door on the last moments of a perfect love.

Now it was the pastor, he who had comforted so many through the years, who needed comforting. Sigrid noticed that his spectacles were besmeared. Gently she lifted them from his face, ran warm hydrant water over them, dried them on a linen towel, and polished them. When did he cry? Not before any of them.

He looked up. He was like a little troll, trying to make smiles out of material in which there are no smiles. "Sigrid, you understand, don't you? My faith, it is still the same. But it's hard to be strong when it's your own heart, your own love. It's different then."

For her staying with Kristin, for making Kristin's last days happy, he would never be able to thank her. And would she stay, for a while, and keep house at the parsonage?

"It is what I want most to do. This is my home now."

As a self-conscious groom often left a five-dollar bill in a plain white envelope, with studied carelessness, on the pastor's hall table—not pay, only a meager thank you for the great service rendered—one day the pastor laid a plain white envelope on Sigrid's dresser.

She looked inside. Now she could afford to put an ad in the Chicago *Tribune!* Now she would get a job! Oh, she would repay the pastor for this!

In all enthusiasm letters to her grandmother told of her new job. She was a full-fledged typist now, earning twelve dollars and a half a week (if the cyclometer on the back of the typewriter showed the required number of strikes each day!). And she and Nico were laying a platform of cement, for the garbage can to stand on, near the alley fence. All of this she wrote to Sigrid of Norden; and that before Nico had offered to help, it had been only a chore; that after Nico had come to help with the shoveling of sand and gravel from one pile to another, and back, the heavy shoveling had turned to music, the dripping of the hose a metronome, the tune a tune of laughter.

"I'll bet we could build a whole garage together, for Dad's car," he had shouted, over the scraping of their shovels, never losing a beat. She had straightened, and looked at him, and laughed. But he had touched her secret wishing place: her hands were workman's hands. So would she bet they could build a garage. . . .

But of the doctor's Sunday-afternoon call she did not write. "Tell me," he asked. "How long had you known Mrs. Bedell?"

"Since I was about ten years old."

He laid the back of his hand lightly against her cheek. "Do your cheeks always get as rosy as this come afternoon?"

"Oh, yes. I've always had a 'high complexion'—just like my mother's."

"Your mother. She was young wasn't she?" Tenderly, "What caused her death?"

"The galloping consumption."

"I see." He reached for his clinical thermometer. "Do you, my dear, ever expectorate anything?"

"You don't have to say any more, Doctor." She gritted her teeth hard and clenched her fists. "I'm afraid I know what you mean."

8

A left arm, swollen, red, feverish, and throbbing, told the awful verdict. Never had she thought before of how precious life is until Dr. van Vlaardingen said, "You'll have to fight."

The test would be followed by small doses of tuberculin, increased every five days so that her body would build up against the disease. Fight? Of course she would fight! But the lassitude; did the doctor know how hard it was to fight that? Could he guess the effort it took to keep on going to work, to school?

Every five days, so many cubic centimeters injected into arms already sore . . .

Every day a prayer to renew the courage to fight . . .

Every hour a prayer for strength to keep on going . . .

A constant prayer for constant faith to believe she would get well.

The hours and the days lengthened into weeks. Now she was studying shorthand at the business-college night school. Nature began to button up and gird the land against the winter. Her zinnias grew to look like cripply old people, sprawling all over their beds or leaning against the fences. "Sun dust," the gold of sunflowers and golden-rod, was splashed over the prairies; the rushes in the marsh were drying, and the cattails gone to seed. Pale blue and white wild asters—wee, multiflowered—enjoyed their season before the inevitable coming of their cousins of purple and deeper blue. Cottonwood trees were changing their dresses from green to ones of yellowish tint. Sigrid waited for the tops of her rhubarb plants to wither, then dug half-a-dozen large clumps from her garden row, leaving a ball of earth around the fleshy roots. For six weeks she would leave them in the areaway so they could freeze now and again, as the temperature rose and fell. After this dormancy she would set them in the darkest corner of the basement, water them well, and in a month—in the middle of winter, at Christmas—she and the pastor would be having rhubarb sauce, fresh, pink, springlike, and delicious.

Christmas. The happiest time of the year, erasing trouble and illness. And when a person has two Christmases, then it makes for a finest Yuletide of all. And she had two, a Swedish one and an American one; for vicariously, as real as if her feet trod Swedish land and snow and room boards, she was a part of the Christmas at Norden. As real as if she sat cross-legged on a homewoven carpet on the floor of the dwelling in which her father had first seen light of day and grown to manhood did she hear her Far-mor's telling of the legend of Santa Lucia, retold on the Day to the newly old enough to listen. For there were always young ones coming on in Bohuslän.

Her grandmother's voice would be low, and sweet, and full of the love of life and the piety of Christmastime: "Though Sweden is a Protestant country," the voice rose from the written letter page, "nevertheless it observes, as the opening event of the midwinter schedule, the celebration of the Santa Lucia festival on this day, December the thirteenth. Now the year's threshing and spinning and weaving all are done, and the house and barns all freshly cleaned.

"Aye, there was a time, long years ago, when this was a church festival only, but with the Reformation it continued as a family rite. Santa Lucia"—the way Mor Sigrid would say the word, with the soft Swedish "s" sound for the "c" made it a song in Sigrid's ears—"a martyred young woman of Syracuse, in Sicily, was the guardian saint of the poor. And a young man fell in love with her, with her beautiful eyes. But he was not a Christian. According to tradition, when she learned of his great passion for her eyes, she took them from their sockets and sent them to him on a platter, as inducement to him to become a Christian.

"Lucia, one day thereafter, knelt in prayer. As she knelt, God gave her eyes—new eyes—more beautiful than the ones she had had before; and again she could see to walk, on the white snows in her long white robe, to carry food to the poor. Santa Lucia, the beautiful—whose arms were so laden with food and medicine for imprisoned and persecuted Christians in the catacombs that she tied candles around her head to light her way through the darkened labyrinths; Lucia, to whom light was returned after darkness—Santa Lucia's Day, at the winter solstice, the day which once again shortens the darkness of night, to speed the return of the sun!

"I wish you could come home, dear Karl's daughter, to spend the whole of Yuletide with us here."

Sigrid closed her eyes; the words on the letter paper burned through their lids: she lay abed, at Norden, between sweet-smelling homespun linen sheets; she listened as the eldest maiden rose, was dressed in white, and stood while a wreath of berry leaves was set atop her tresses, stood breathless as the seven candles—one for each of the principal virtues as set forth in the highest code of morality in medieval Christian ethics: purity, obedience, benevolence, faith, hope, love, and humility—were set into the crown and lighted.

Sigrid heard as Mor Sigrid said seven prayers for the happiness and good health of her family, and seven times prayed for the sun's return; and as the maiden, Hjördis, daughter to Agda, carried a tray from bed to bed, with due lavishness serving coffee and Lussekaka to the family members, singing of Santa Lucia, "who is the embodiment of the Christmas spirit, and the symbol of returning sunlight," Sigrid's eyes opened to read. But then they closed again and once more she was in Sweden, a part of the family, and Aunt Agda's daughter served her pastries from a silver tray. . . .

She was there, too, at the raising of the sheaf.

"Only by saving the last sheaf cut from the field, the one in which the spirit of growth is imprisoned, and placing one-half part of it outside the dwelling, can the spirit restore the strength of the sun and entice it back to bring a new season of growing grain. In all seriousness has the knowledge of these festivities been handed down from father to son; aye, in all earnestness have the customs been perpetuated, for always there have been so many mouths to be fed from the small earth plots, and it is on the sun the farmer is dependent to get that living from the ground.

"Necessity, coupled with legend; so might one speak of the festivities, the customs, of Sweden. And who is so sure that it is all superstition that he would dare so tempt the Fates as not to hang the sheaf, come Yuletide? The learned ones say it is only because they wish to feed the birds; well that may be, my Sigrid, but, as much a part of the Yuletide as Christmas Day itself, as the giving of gifts in the manner of the Wise Men's bestowing them on the Infant Jesus, is the placing of the sheaf high on a pole near to the dwelling house.

"It was always Karl's chore to scrape away the snow from the lawn about the pole, so that on this bare spot the birds might dance."

Sigrid was not in the cottage in Calico Row, a suburb of Chicago in the United States of America. True, her body sat there, but *she* stood on the spot in the house yard at Norden, in Bohuslän in Sweden, and helped to raise the pole of spruce—there, where her father had helped to raise it, and his father, and his, on, back to the time of the Vikings—and the word "home" went through her like an arrow. . . .

"If many finches and sparrows come," her grandmother wrote further, "to share the golden feast, then the coming year promises to bring an abundant crop of grain. And many birds always come at Yuletide!

"From the other half part of the last sheaf now we bake the 'sowing cake.' This shall we save all through the winter, but when spring comes and the tilling of the earth is about to be begun, then shall we divide the sowing cake evenly between men and animals at Norden. So do we honor the spirit of the growing grain. So do we secure a bountiful harvest from the seed of April's sowing."

Yuletide in Sweden! From the time when they at Norden went into the woodlot and clipped straggling low evergreen branches to make the Advent wreath—to the lighting of one of its tall candles on each of the four Sundays of Advent—from Santa Lucia's Day to St. Knut's Day, Sigrid was with them. Christmas is of the spirit, and the spirit of Sigrid shared, through her grandmother's written words, "the month when all of Norden's world knows contentment, when the cows and the horses, and the sheep and the dogs, even the little kittens, almost speak the words, 'Keep ye well, for this is Christmas!'—when the fish in the sea can swim without the fear of nets or lines; when birds may spread their wings, eluding not the swiftly flying shell or shot; when even the wild animals in the forests seem to know that no traps nor hidden snares await them!"

Steeped with the spirit of a Swedish Christmas, Sigrid called *"God Jul"*—"Good Christmas"—to friends, and came trudging home through the snow carrying a goose for roasting, dragging a Christmas tree behind her.

Flakes settled on her eyelashes so that she had to blink when she neared a street corner in order to see clearly the triangle of feeble yellow shed by the globe atop a tenuous tall pole, itself only a shadow in the thickly falling snow.

She stopped below the light to shift the goose to her other arm. Where the parcel had rested, one snowflake came to lie, apart, in its six-pointed perfection, on the dark broadcloth of her coat sleeve. How often Pa had pointed out the beauty of the snowflakes, "in their symmetry witness that some Final Order rules the outward chaos of our worlds." Here lay a crystal made up of thin, delicate, ornamented spokes, with projections sprouting more ornament, lying in sparkling white tracery on the black sleeve. Oh, yes, to see snowflakes was to think of Pa, and of the way, paradoxically in his professed unbelief, he had described them, "Reflecting the perfection of the Universe."

"Yet"—and she caught her breath—"after seeing such perfection there are some people who don't believe in God!"

Panting from the cold and the exertion, still under the spell of the Swedish Christmas, she answered the pastor's welcome with, *"God Jul!"*

It was a happy Christmas Eve for her, this second celebration. How could it be, with the sorrow the year had brought? Kristin's death, and Pa's, and the terrible knowledge of the frailty of her own lungs.

And yet it was.

They dressed the table tree, set on the little Geib piano, and Sigrid stretched, so that her shirtwaist tail pulled out of her skirt belt, to drape the tinsel over the topmost branches, and put Ellen's Christmas star on the very tip. Pastor Bedell was too short to reach, so he stood on a dining-room chair spread with yesterday's Chicago *Daily News.* It was while she made the gravy that he spread the white sheet under the tree, and ruffled it to make it look like drifted snow, and laid the presents around. Yes, they

could—but with difficulty! wait until the goose was devoured, to unwrap them. Devoured, it was; and cranber-
ries, and little onions in cream sauce, and crisp white
celery, and sage dressing; and to finish the meal, warm
mince pie.

Acting as Santa Claus, the pastor brought her the parcel
which had come from Sweden. "I can't undo the knot!" She
looked to him for help, her fingers shaking, her eyes swimming with happy tears.

His fingers helped her. It was a large box, bashed in at
the corners from the many handlings over its long travel;
and when she lifted the cover it was as if she saw Mor
Sigrid of Norden tending her sheep, whispering into their
ears as she wielded the clipping shears; carding the wool;
preparing the dye vats after plucking red and purple
berries and digging yellow roots; as if she saw her grandmother flinging handfuls of flaxseed over the open ground
and hoeing between small plants and matching the blue
of the flax flowers to the blue of the sky; scutching the
long, slender stems with a large wooden swingle; sitting
at her wheel spinning the linen thread, at her loom weaving this coverlet.

This was the "Winter Rose" pattern in red and green
and yellow and black wools on white linen, bringing her
Farmor close. . . .

Long they sat silent as Sigrid fingered the coverlet. So
much was there to be gleaned, from the stitches, about
the stitcher. So much to be learned, "seeing" her grandmother through touching the pattern of wool on linen, in
the same way that Helen Keller, the blind woman who
gave a lecture at Town Hall, could "see" a picture through
her fingers while reading characters in Braille.

Now, on seeing this, she knew what she would make as
a gift for her grandmother, something of America, something of herself, so her grandmother could read from the
picture she would stitch something about her who stitched
it: on white percale she would center a large eagle, with
full-spread wings, appliquéd of calico prints in grays and
browns, with yellow for the feet and bill. In back of the
winged eagle she would run tiny quilting stitches, white
on white, to show the American Flag blowing in the wind.

Quilting stitches would run in rays, in long, straight
lines, from the Stars and Stripes to the quilt's border. That

border she would make of squares, one for each state in the Union; in the center of each square she would place the state flower, appliquéd in true color, and below the flower the name of the state embroidered in outline stitches of black D.M.C. There would be the violet of Illinois, the poppy of California, the dogwood of Virginia, the sunflower of Kansas: all of America would be there, in that bouquet, to send to her Farmor in the Old Country.

A tapping on her shoulder, and "Come, look," brought her back to the evening and she followed her pastor to the kitchen.

Even Sassy was imbued with the spirit of giving. Under the gas stove her basket wriggled with life. Too busy for purring, she licked each kitten, and if a cat can lick proudly, that was the way Sassy licked. Then she uncoiled and lay stretched out on her side.

The slim twisted tallow candles of red and blue and green and yellow and white on the tiny green tree burned to their bottom ends, laid down their wicks, and snuffed out their flames; the only light came from behind the isinglass windows of the big stove. Sigrid sat on the kitchen floor and gazed in wonder, on this night the miracle of birth, as six soft little noses pressed busily into Sassy's warm breast fur.

"Merry Christmas!" her heart sang; but she could hardly bid the pastor be merry on this the loneliest of all his Christmases. And so her voice poured forth, to bring his smile, *"God's in His Heaven. All's right with the world!"*

9

March brought the spring winds, and an ill wind blew toward Sigrid the day her employer, Mr. Wessly, said, "You never told me, Miss Christianson, that you had t.b."

"I have not tried to make a secret of it, sir," she had answered. "And I haven't been absent a single day."

"Well, although I admit you are the best typist we've had here, I'm going to have to let you go; I don't feel that we can afford the health risk," he said, drawing away from her.

Like a loving, protecting father the pastor eased her worry. "This is your home, Sigrid. You have food and shelter here. Take your time to look for another position, a week, a month, or several months, it matters not how long. Only keep faith, Sigrid, and know that God watches over you and will take care of you."

She was surprised to learn how good it was to sleep late in the mornings. Her restless mind slowed down, slowing her restless body. Pleased, the doctor said, "This rest is doing you more good than all of my medicines!"

She had time to visit the new neighbors, Patrick and Molly O'Toole, who moved into the little house next door to her own. They were from Limerick, Ireland; fourteen years married, fourteen years childless, and now, "Even before I had time to hem and hang the lace curtains to the front windows," Molly had scarcely been able to speak, she was so excited that at last she was going to have a baby, "we know this American house has brought us good luck."

The pastor sat reading while across the room Sigrid's long, vigorous hands, as apt with a hammer, a saw, a garden spade, or No. 120 sewing thread, daintily cast on thirty stitches of baby-blue yarn. Then the knitting needles flew, and her thoughts kept up with them. Pat worked at the big plant, and it was he who had spoken for her, so that she was to be given the stenographic job as secretary to gruff Mr. Horgan. And now she was teaching shorthand and typewriting at the business college, in the evening classes where she had studied. She guessed Mr. Wyatt thought he was paying her a compliment, saying she looked old—old enough to be a teacher.

He might have changed his mind if he had seen her with Nico the next day, like children pressing their noses flat against a candy case, peering through the begrimed window of Jake's Pawnshop.

Suddenly Nico had burst out laughing. "I'll bet we'd look funny from the inside!"

"Someday I want to own that blue cloth," she had said seriously.

"What would you do with it?"

"Why—I'd just—just look at it."

Then he grew serious. "Do you know, Sigrid, it's just about the color of your eyes."

She wished Jack would think of such a nice thing to say to her. Jack, the faithful one, waiting at the streetcar to escort her home after night-school sessions. Jack, the silent one; sometimes he never spoke a word all the way home.

It was June.

Wild roses bloomed on the prairie. Would he care, she asked him, to go with her to church and afterward walk with her amid the roses' fragrance? No, not to church: he'd had enough, too much, of church, with the everlasting arguing at home about going three times a day on Sundays, he'd had enough. Let his brother Jonatan go to church—for the both of them!

Instead, then, she walked alone, her body swinging; and when she found an early gentian, bluer than a blue-jay's crest, it was as if she had found a gold mine.

To the amusement of the union carpenters who were doing remodeling inside of the house, the cement floor of the garage was laid; "S.C." and "N.vV." were drawn with a twig into the wet cement, inside the doorsill, to tell posterity who the builders were.

Now, for the walls, she held the level against the two-by-four uprights while Nico hammered. For hours they would work together, almost like two hands of a single artisan; then they would quarrel, and peace would fly. He would leave, hair ruffled, his bass voice flinging back lines from *The Taming of the Shrew*.

But she knew he would come back: not because of her, but because this thing they were building with their own hands had become a part of him, as it had with her.

She had lost the angular, gawky look of adolescence; her body was filling out where it was most becoming to be filled out; her cheeks were rounding out; the ruddy look of health daily grew more pronounced, replacing the fever glow. Life in the parsonage, if not in the world, went on smoothly, serenely. They learned of the world's troubled affairs through the newspapers. And the way they played things up! "To the hilt!" as Hattie Allspaugh said. Sigrid threw a glance at the day's Chicago *Tribune*. The headline screamed, "ARCHDUKE FERDINAND OF AUSTRIA-HUNGARY ASSASSINATED." But nothing could interest Calico Row less.

Summer passed.

Cattails stood fuzzy where the marsh had been. Dry, their leaves rustled in the wind like cornstalks at Halloween. A pheasant darting through the miniature forest on dried, cracked ground made the only other sound. An oak leaf fluttered down from some tall height and as Sigrid watched it, it drifted lazily, horizontally, in indecision as to where it should land to make its winter home.

Heavy late fall rains beat down the cattail stems in the swamp and they lay broken, floating, miniature logs on the water covering the floor of the marsh so lately caked and cracked. Redwinged blackbirds no longer sat atop the seeded cattails and swayed; winter was coming, and the birds were gone.

The rains let up, and the days grew cold. It snowed. The snow melted. One evening in early January the rains came again, colder than before, and Sigrid swung herself, with the aid of the grab rail, off the streetcar.

Had the rain stopped? No. She looked up into the ribs of a big black umbrella. "Why, Nico, where did you come from?"

"Pastor Bedell was called to Austin, so Dad and I thought we'd like you to come over to our house—well, really, your house. Dad's at the O'Tooles', but he'll be right back. We've got something to show you."

Outside of the O'Tooles' stood Leaping Lena, the doctor's Ford automobile, so named because of its propensity to leap on starting. Nico, carrying the umbrella firmly against the wind and rain, led Sigrid to his front door and opened it.

She stepped inside, then passed her hands over her eyes to make sight clearer. Was this the cottage she had called her home?

The little square entry hall was gone. She entered a small formal parlor, with a leather-covered sofa and tall wing chair grouped at one side and two plain mahogany side chairs flanking a low bachelor's chest. Above it hung an eagle-topped mirror. "Chippendale," she said to herself. An oriental rug covered the floor; at the door was a small throw rug to catch the drip of rain or snow from overshoes.

Her rubbers came off, and not waiting for invitation she walked through the wide doorway into the room that had been her parlor.

"Oh!" The wall dividing it from the dining room had been torn down. Here, now, was one long, large room. The mirrored console, the dining-room windows through which no daylight ever had streamed, were gone. All of the walls on three sides were lined, from floor to ceiling, with bookshelves. And the shelves were filled with books!

Where the china closet had been was a fireplace: the adjacent chimney that had always made her dishes feel warm had been enlarged; and now the grate threw cheerful warmth into the large room.

What had been golden-oak woodwork was enameled white. Flanking the fireplace the whole wall was paneled, and against the white of it stood an antique snake-legged reading stand holding an unabridged dictionary. Deep upholstered chairs were spaced around the room in pairs, with a low lamp table between each two.

She went about the room, touching, looking at book titles. When she turned to look for Nico he was gone.

A library—she would wait here, in this room which, without her knowing it before, had been her lifelong hope to see. If she could come here, and read, and study—yes, now again she knew that her greatest desire was to learn— to learn—to *learn!*

Absorbed in a book, she jumped at Nico's, "Dad wants you right away, at the O'Tooles'!"

Dr. van Vlaardingen met her at Molly's bedroom door. "Mrs. O'Toole is in labor too soon. Her nurse is on another case. I can't get hold of anyone else in time." He moved swiftly and with assurance, despite his bigness; spoke swiftly, too. He did not ask her to help, he merely ordered her. "Scrub your hands and arms for five minutes with this soap. Slip this garment on." All the while he was tying a gauze over her mouth and wrapping a towel around her hair. "Put these instruments in water in this basin, over the gas flame. Keep them boiling. Pat, bring an armful of newspapers." As a teacher would, he turned to her. "Newspapers make good padding to protect the mattress. And, Pat, you and Nico stay away from here now. Here, Sigrid, slip on these rubber gloves—here now —help me, here. I'm glad you're not the fainting kind."

"Thank you, Doctor."

"In moments like this—I—feel—so humble." He turned for an instant to her, and his look allayed her queasiness, then back to the infant entering the world. "It's a boy, Molly."

"Ah, Pat will be glad. Fourteen years he's waited for his Michael."

Sigrid stared in wonder, until the doctor held the baby toward her. It was the ball of fire sent from his eyes that scared her utmost being, cauterizing the wounds life had inflicted on her. She was on a new plane, a high plane, as she held this newborn infant in her hands and felt the doctor's hands under hers.

"It's like looking at *God*," she whispered.

Their eyes locked in understanding. "You ought to be a nurse," Dr. van Vlaardingen answered, so close she felt his breath, before he turned to attend the mother.

Michael's eyes opened to Sigrid. Blue and serene, they seemed to be the biggest part of him; they looked into her own, and vibrant undertones of hope sang through her. It was as if she gazed into the naked soul of man—into eternity! Her heart beat against her ribs like thunder in a mountain valley. This was the miracle of life!

Day-by-day routine: mornings and evenings of hanging to a strap in the streetcar, swaying with the motion of it, bumping against men smelling of sweat, or being pushed by men smelling of sweat and beer; working; skimping; fighting *to win* against tuberculosis, this was the fun of living!

And life was good.

The van Vlaardingens' library became the gathering place for the studious of Calico Row. Evenings saw the doctor sitting smoking a Delft pipe, reading. The pastor sat in the rocker, reading, thinking, or napping. Nico, studying, was deep in college work preparing for medical school. Jack studied for examinations for citizenship. Sigrid began with Volume I of the *World's History,* but only too often found herself engrossed in *The Practical Book of American Antiques.*

Tonight, at the doctor's request, she had brought her father's old cardboard shoe box. "Please share with us his reminiscences. It may be just possible that there will be material there that Nico needs for his Humanities paper."

"Speaking of Sweden," she said, "and immigrants." Neatly she stacked the papers while talking, replacing them as she had found them in the box, and picked up a booklet telling the *Story of Castle Garden.* "In so many ways Sweden is linked to America. Did you know that our custom of rising on hearing 'The Star-Spangled Banner' was originated by Daniel Webster when it was sung in Castle Garden by Jenny Lind?"

No, they had not known.

"The Swedish Nightingale, as my parents always spoke of her."

"Not only your parents," the pastor interrupted. "Jenny Lind truly lives on as the unrivaled master of coloratura."

She placed the story her father had written about his adopted city over the booklet. Still another piece of his writing, like the others pieced together where they had once been torn across, she held toward Nico. "This one may be of interest to you, for your paper."

"Read it aloud to us, Sigrid," the doctor asked.

"If you want me to. *Harps on the Willows,* he entitled this, and opens it with a question from the Bible, 'We hanged our harps upon the willows. . . . For how can we sing in a strange land?' "

She read then of the pain, the inner turmoil, her father

had known on tearing himself from his homeland, on coming to a land of strangers. It was written in the third person, but Sigrid knew it was her father's heartache. As she read, the others also knew. Ridicule was the thing that had hurt him most. "A green Swede," he had been; that name calling had hurt him more than the chicanery which had cost him his job and friends in Geneva, more than the cunning which had cheated him of rightful earnings, not once, but time and time again. Ridicule was the knife to stab into an immigrant's heart and make it bleed.

Her voice trembled, following the story. The one of whom her father wrote he had named "Karl," but she knew it was himself, Carl Christianson; she knew that, in following Karl's footsteps, she was following her father's steps. She felt the hunger that gnawed at his middle as he walked the long and lonely road, lost sight of the fact that she was reading, to hear a farmer say, "Work? Yes, I can always use a Swede. Strong backs you Swedes got."

He was a "green Swede," so he was hired to husk corn. But that was something new to learn. He had never known of corn growing in Sweden. He would stay on here, bearing the raillery, for he saw an opportunity to make big money beyond what he would earn as a husker. Why had not others done it before him? It was that way with everything, inventions or discoveries, anything; it was all so simple after someone had shown the way.

The corn silk was of such fine texture, was it of it that silk was made? "Oh, yes," according to the boss, who smirked in that silly way he had, while outlining the process. Why did they not gather it and sell it, then? They did not have time enough; this was a day of specialization; their main product was the corn itself; however, if the young Swede could keep up with the husking, he was free to gather the silk as they went and tuck it under the shoveling board in the back end of the wagon, and he might keep all the money it brought.

Faster than ever he worked husking, and gathering the silk. It seemed a shame to waste even the few strands of it that stuck to his pants legs when he wiped his hands against them.

One barrel was full; and he had kept up with the huskers. A second barrel was filling. Saturday night. He would spare time to ride to town in the wagon filled with work-hands from the farm, listening to the singing of

> "Down went McGinty
>   To the bottom of the sea,
>   And he must be very wet
>   For they haven't found him yet,"

and "The Band Played On," a brand-new song. Oh, it was too hard to concentrate on learning the words for thinking of the fortune he stood to make on the corn silk.

"There he goes." The words reached him as he walked toward the village hall, counting his change as he walked so as to have it ready for the entrance ticket to the magic-lantern sociable. Straightening to his full height, walking spryly, jauntily, cocking his ear to hear again and again, he listened to, "Yes, that's him."

They must be talking of his barrels of corn silk. He opened his vest buttons so his chest could swell.

Fame!

And this was only the beginning. What would it be after he had sold the silk, if all this interest could be shown in him in the mere knowledge of what the future held? Ah, he would smoke big black cigars as all successful rich Americans did. He would—

"Oh, why didn't somebody warn him?" Sigrid asked of the pity on Jack's face.

"How could anyone *be* that dumb?" broke from Nico's lips.

"Do you think"—she eyed him frigidly—"you would be any smarter if you went to a different country where everything was strange and new, and even the language didn't always say the thing you tried to make it say? What makes you think you would be any less ignorant about unfamiliar things?"

He flushed; and she resumed the reading.

A folding chair, near the front edge of the crowd, that was the seat to choose, to sit on and hear the five pieces of the village band begin to play.

"Let's sit here," a coarse whisper came from the seats behind Karl's. "We'll have some fun." And, "Jiminy, how dumb do they come?"

Over the notes of "Ta-ra-ra Boom-der-ay" he heard them,

and they spoke of him, of the fool who believed corn silk had any value, that silk cloth could be made of it. Corn silk! Everybody knew that it was worthless! He heard now that this was a joke that was pulled on greenhorns, but only one in a thousand was green enough to believe it.

So the boss had fooled him, and the whole town knew of it and was laughing at him. His fists clenched. He started to his feet; he would thrash the daylights out of all of them! He would start with those two *bourgeois* behind him and knock their heads together until they cracked!

The music stopped. Before the lights went out the roomful of people saw him standing there with beet-colored face, tall, shaking with rage, with humiliation. And they laughed.

The light from the magic lantern danced around on a white sheet drawn tight against it. Tears blurred the lights from the lamps hung atop exits. The chill of October blew in from the side door, opening to admit an elderly residenter, and froze Karl's heart. Yes, he found his way to the door, but not too soon to hear, "There he goes. Can you imagine it? A use for corn silk! Ha!"

And amid laughter, "Aw, what more could you expect of a green Swede?"

Sigrid's hands shook as she laid the last page of foolscap face down over the others and finished her father's message, "I hanged my harp on the willow."

Jack's eyes were moist as her gaze met them.

"Later he writes differently," she began.

But Nico interrupted. "I never fully realized before how hard it was for them—to pave the way for us."

"We don't, do we?"

"Your father"—he leaned forward eagerly—"his writing makes it all so clear, the transplanting, the suffering. Did he ever try to be a writer? Professionally, I mean."

"I believe he always may have had a secret longing to be—but—"

No, she would not say that her father had not been what people call a successful man in anything he did. Because, of course, that was not true. Whatever he was, or was not, let her always remember what he had given her: faith in her country, and he had given her her country! Faith in herself. Faith in her God. Through Pa she had first learned the love of God through the love of nature, become sensitive to the message of the meadowlark; because of him—or them, because Mother and he surely were as one—she knew to kneel in thanks before a hayrack piled high with the first harvest.

Because of Pa she knew how to appreciate all that America gave her; because of him her country's history had come to her as an interesting, living story.

Absently she folded the foolscap sheets, pressed them into a small tight packet, of size to fit a letter envelope, hefted it, wondered how much postage it might cost to send it to Sweden, when suddenly, forcefully, a vague fear gripped her: why had it been so long since she had had a letter from her grandmother?

Swedish Interlude

Except for the deep furrows on her brow, the sixty-seven years of her age sat lightly on Mor Sigrid of Norden. Big Johann watched the dancing firelight from the grate make shadows on her forehead, and he thought of the many deep furrows—deep and even—she had plowed on Norden's land. Just so had cloud-shattered sunlight played over the ground her homemade plow had turned those many springs until she had become his wife.

Softly the rain fell; through the open window and into the big room came the fresh, sweet smell of it.

Spring was early, and now the heavens sent the gentle rains to wash away the last of winter's snows, to swell the bulbs and roots low in the ground until no force could keep their stems and flowers from bursting through into the air to stand with upturned faces, drinking in the wetness.

Spray came through the open window; he watched his Sigrid turn her face to feel the rain. So beautiful, that face, on which the lines of age and pain and labor only set off the major work, a flawless portrait of motherhood and love. Faith, too, was there reflected to make the picture true.

If there were strands of gray in her hair, he could not

see them; the golden sheen of it outshone them. No hump distorted the back of her neck and shoulders; she was as tall and straight as when she was a girl, unmarried still to Peter who had been the first to claim her. And when she walked, how he loved to watch the rhythmic grace of her!

He saw that her son, Johann, his crippled namesake, watched, too, as the spray from spring rain dampened her face, upturned to meet it; and with the closing of her eyes, he knew she prayed. . . .

She picked up her pencil. "My beloved Karl's daughter," she wrote, and then as she had done in letters ofttimes before she put down the words her heart bade her say, "I wish you could come home." Her chin braced itself in her hand, elbow resting on the table: it was a sad thing to think of a young girl living alone in a strange, far country, without mother or father. Yet, it was true that the birth-land would not be strange to that girl child who bore her name. Ah, was it because of that she was so infinitely dear? Or was it because this was the child of her first-born son? The young Sigrid: true, it was her native land in which she lived. But home was where one was surrounded by kindred and the close ties of blood.

Norden's grounds were spacious, even the small house seemed big now, and somewhat bare, since so many of her children had gone from its rooftree; it would be jolly to have young Sigrid in the home. Aye, there was such a plentiness of room here.

Again, as so many times she had done before, she went to the fireplace, removed two loose bricks, and from the niche brought out the letter Karl's daughter had written telling of his death; again she unfolded and reread that letter, yellowed now with two years of age. It had brought grief, yes; did still; but oh, such glory as was mixed with the sorrow of his death! For her son had died a brave man. The clippings from the newspapers named him "a hero."

That was her Karl.

What his daily life had been in the new land she could only guess, the life of an ordinary workingman wed to a young woman also from Sweden. Sigrid's letters, while telling much, told so little, after all. America had beck-oned; America had promised. Could it be possible that that new land had been able to give happy answers to the hundreds of thousands who had gone from their European homes?

Karl had turned out to be a carpenter. Least of all could she have foreseen such! His fingers had never seemed to her to be as apt or clever as his head. A worker with his head; that was the gift she had hoped to mark him with, before he was born, even as she had marked Elisabet's cheek with the hairy birthmark.

"God's will be done," she breathed; her "ugly duckling" might never have known the joy of becoming as the "beautiful swan" if things had been different in her life. Dear Elisabet, her first-born; but Karl was her first-born son. She named the rest off, as they had come to her: of the life of each of her children could a book be written.

So much of pleasure would be written in the book of "Karl," if she could write a book; even the pain of giving birth, breech that it was, had given way to joy, for at last a son had been born and the long line of female succession in Norden's family was broken. Shoveling a tunnel from the house to barn, there she had been, cold, hungry, and alone, while Peter lay abed still snuggled close to Elisabet. Her shovel, "Far," was her interpretation of the Snow God; she had carved him from a piece of oak, cut the utility end into a small, well-shaped shoveling area. But the face on the handle was merry; it smiled back at her now as she looked at it standing beside the fireplace. It was silly to name a shovel "Far," Peter had said; but it had been fun to be silly so, for she was young then. Only nineteen years of age. The exact age young Sigrid was now. He had been company for her, Far had, on that day until Karl was born.

At that moment she had thought that never would she doubt the wisdom of her marriage to Peter, for he had fathered her a son. Male issue had come in her union with Peter, and she had named him Karl, for her Morfar. Closing her eyes, she could see herself as a little girl, sitting at Morfar's feet, listening while he told her of her forebears and of himself—how he had poured all of his love into the raising of his daughter, Sigrid Karlsdotter, who had become her mother after her marriage to Elias Johansson.

She, Elias' daughter, had borne the name Sigrid Eliasdotter, and she had married Peter Kristiansson. Why had she married him? Was it the way of nature that in the spring young blood answers young blood? Ah, if the young could only know that God had raised men and women from animals' estate, giving them intelligence to use to choose a mate with thought and brain, to bear in mind the future time when reproduction was not the main of bodies' works. If only the young could brave that first wild urge to mate!

But who ever found an old head on young shoulders? She had married Peter. And she had borne a son, Karl Petersson.

Karl. She had taught him to ride the colt, Hjärta, dedicated to him before he was born. She had taught him to ski, to read, to write, to swim; to bring in the herring, the cod, and the mackerel; taught him to sow and to reap, to sing, to play, to pray.

He had loved the horse, Hjärta. Too much, perhaps. It was the thing that meant most in his whole life. In it he found his dreams for all his future. But then, Peter sold the horse—

Mor Sigrid shivered at remembering, and felt that a shawl was being drawn over her shoulders. Only a quick, loving glance, a little curving upward of her lips to Big Johann as he placed it there, no more, knowing so well that he would understand.

Karl had blamed her. How could he? How *could* he have felt so?

He then declared he would go to America; he could not stay in Sweden, he said, feeling that the whole of Sweden mocked him, laughed at him because he did not know where it hid his Hjärta! Yes, that was his heart's reason for his going. Perhaps his mind knew ambition for what opportunity the new land offered; perhaps; but it was his heart tore him from home.

If it was his soul's wish to go to a land of strangers, then she would help him; and so she had sat, night after night, lovingly carving a set of chessmen, sixteen, out of pieces of clear, light birch and sixteen out of bits of rosewood. There were portrayed, when she had finished them, King Oskar II and his Queen, Sophia, and heads of state; and pawns portraying common men of her acquaintance. Arrayed against a Russian foe, they had been real enough so that the children could name them one by one. And so had the King been able to also!

Aye, she had seen her king, shaken hands with him, laughed with him, talked with him. He had given her gold pieces in token for the chessmen, and she had brought the money home. She had brought it home. Here, in this room, she had held them out, the gold pieces, to her son—her beloved son—only to have him greet her return in sightless anger, in senseless rage—blaming her for what his father had done to him. He had turned from her without even seeing the gold held out to him.

Then she had heard the water giving to the oars, and he was gone. . . .

That book of "Karl," if she could write a book, it would have pain upon its pages, too.

So had she left the dwelling house on that day. Not seeing, not knowing where she went, she had walked through the dark fens of the swamp, walked stumbling around the island, down to the sea. There she had stood on the shore, with waves breaking around her feet, for hours, alone. Aye, she had wept.

She started now. A little tinkle, the sound of metal striking wood, woke her from her daydreaming. Through misty eyes she saw that Young Johann's crochet needle had dropped to the floor, and she half-rose from her chair, wanting to fetch it for him, and yet—she hesitated, half-standing, half-sitting—

"Nay, mor," he chided her. "Get it not. Remember, we agreed between us long ago that I must always help myself."

"So we agreed," she said to her son, trying hard to put a lilt into her voice, and went back to her letter writing. The English words she sought came easily enough, her fingers were willing enough to write them, but not yet did they cover the paper. She chewed on her pencil: the man's work she had done, farming on this island off the mainland coast of Sweden, and fishing, and finding a living for her many children, the giving birth to the thirteen *afkomma*—the offspring to whom Peter had given his seed—the years she had lived as wife to Peter, the nights spent lying in their bed submitting to his lust, they were as nothing. As nothing, now, to this. Out of the corner of her eye seeing crippled Johann, with sweat pour-

ing from him, retrieving the needle with almost super-
human effort, all but tumbling head foremost from his
wheel chair in the doing—

"See, I have it!"

"Of course you have it. It is only that I—"

"We know." He winked at Big Johann. "It is only that
so many years of waiting on everyone forms a habit it
is hard to break."

The needle dropped again to the floor. His mother saw
that he smiled as he explained, "This is an unusually
intricate pattern I am following."

He smiled. Yes, if it would be the death of him to use
his strength to bring a smile to that face for her, she knew
that he would smile.

"My fingers," he went on, "do not keep up with my
thinking, with my eyes, on this; that is the reason for this
absurd clumsiness."

And why did the fingers not? Her own fingers dug deep
into her palms. They had not mentioned it between them;
carefully Johann avoided mention of the demon that
worked so ruthlessly, so silently, to take the life from willing fingers.

"It is to the American Sigrid that you write?" he asked,
to draw his mother's thought from seeing him strain to
pick up the capricious needle.

"Aye." Perhaps he would like to add a line?

"Have you told her, yet, of how the earthen jug is filling
with coins to pay for the ticket so she may come to
Norden?"

"Not yet. But I shall."

"Do not say that most of the coins are of öre value!"
He smiled a different kind of smile than that other. "If she
knew it was at a penny a time we save, it would not serve
to build up much hope."

"Nor say that it fills slowly." Big Johann drew out the
last word, dramatizing it.

Young Johann laughed. "Slowly filling, perhaps, but
filling."

"Two years now," Mor Sigrid ruminated. "And not
sufficient money gathered for passage to bring her to us.
Two years she has been alone."

But now, as she had bade Big Johann do, to try to

uncover some interest of her son's so they might steer the work of the crippled one into channels where his hands need not play so big a part, he made effort. "You say your fingers, in this case, do not keep up with your thinking. Is it not time, then, to give the fingers a well-earned holiday, and let that mind of yours—"

Foreign to the face of Young Johann was the serious look that spread over it as he spoke low to his stepfather. "Think not that I have not tried to figure out a work that I can do." He sent a furtive glance to assure himself that his mother had not heard. She must never think him disheartened with his life as it was coming to be.

Her ears were keener than he knew. Her pencil was ready, but it merely touched the paper and did not make words. She did not evade the truth that young Sigrid could not claim the necessary portion of her thoughts for the thinking of her son. Even the war, raging on the continent, could not; nor pity for the mothers of sons fighting on the battlefield. She had to find a way to help Johann.

She laid the pencil down. It was of Johann she must think now, a way to help Johann. . . .

The movement of his arm caught her attention as he wiped the sweat from his face and neck. There he sat, trying to hold his crochet needle, dropping it to his lap, picking it up with stiff and gnarled fingers, biting his lips until the blood came, trying so hard to make the needle do his bidding as it had used to do; and then, when he caught her eye, smiling. *Smiling!*

She pushed the letter paper from her. He could smile when his whole life's meaning was passing from him. If he would rant and rave against his fate, as Karl might have done—as Karl would have done—then maybe she could feel less heartache for him.

Was it not enough that his legs were crippled? Dear God! Why did he have to bear the crippling of his fingers and his hands, too? For thirty-seven years he had sat in the wheel chair. Was that not enough?

Dear Johann Gustave, her fourth child, her second son, named for the good friend, Big Johann, who, after Peter's death, had become her husband. She sent a fond smile in his direction now, and he was quick to answer it. A good and loving husband, Big Johann, sitting there grasping the

chair arms to keep himself from rushing to give the help
the crippled one did not want; a better father to her
children than ever their own had been.

When Elisabet and Karl and Maria had gone to the
mainland to attend the elementary school, how joyfully
little Johann had looked forward to the time when he, too,
could go! Then to fill his lonely days, with *syskon* gone
away to school, she had taught him to crochet, and he had
made a stocking cap for Lucifer, the sea gull, who had
come with bleeding broken wing seeking shelter from a
storm—Lucifer, never again to leave them, but to stay
and stay—

They had guessed the name would suit; at least Lucifer,
in all the years, had never laid an egg!

With his stocking cap on he had strutted in front of
them, proud, as if he were a mannequin in a Parisian
salon. She could laugh, now, in remembering—*if Johann's
needle had not again fallen to the floor.*

Johann had "danced the tree out" on that last St. Knut's
Day that he could use his legs. Yuletide was done, and
the tree would leave the corner of honor in the big room.
No different than the ceremony of all other Christmases?
Aye, different. For that was before—

Johann had danced! For lack of breath, he had stopped
dancing, not for lack of legs. Not then.

Then came that day in spring. That day. . . .

Dear little Johann, barely five years old, trying in his
childlike way to be a man and do a man's work. Only
one more load of manure, scraped from the barn bins, to
spread over the ground. Johann had stood on the wagon
floor digging in the fork, tossing a forkful over the side—
then the horses bolted!

Oh, that a mother's eyes should have to see what then
she saw—Johann clutching tightly the handle of the dung
fork; Johann falling over the low side of the wagon, his
hold on the fork handle loosening; Johann twisting, and
the fore part of his body and the handle hitting the ground;
Johann's legs becoming impaled on the tines of the dung
fork.

Remembering, her teeth bit through the pencil and
ground against the splinters.

Big Johann looked up sharply at the sound. Helpless,

respecting her need for solitude, yet yearning to put his arms about her hoping in some small way to share her burden and thereby lighten it, helpless he sat.

And rigidly she sat, her face turned to the rain.

Only her prayers to God had given her strength to overcome the blackness that had threatened to engulf her on that day. Through prayer God had given her strength to walk toward the dwelling carrying her child. God had been kind to give her fortitude enough to pull the weapon from the wounds, to thrust the white-hot knife-sharpening steel into the four holes in little legs, cleansing them of that most dreaded of all foreign matter, animal excrement from the barn.

Remembering, she drew her nostrils together until they whitened; that smell of burning flesh!

Then came the lockjaw.

Some miracle had saved him. Saved him to sit for all the days of his life with shrunken legs, never to go to school, never to know the outer world and the folk who lived in it, to know nothing but the four walls of his home.

She had read to him before he learned to read. Then they read together. One day they came on the words of the great Augustine, and seeing them too late to skim around them, she read, "The world is a great book, of which they that never stir from home read only a page." Sadly she had seen that he realized, young as he was, that the great book of the world, for him, would have to remain tightly closed.

But no. Though the miracle of her Morfar's books they had traveled together all over the great wide earth, from Egypt to America, from Africa to Greenland. His learning had not suffered; he had gained knowledge through the years.

Another miracle had happened, and through the crocheting that he loved so to do. "I could sit and crochet all the day long," one time he had said; and through the doing he had traveled as far as the great cathedral! He had made an altar cloth, which Big Johann had said was "fine enough for a cathedral," and their pastor had sent the exquisite lace and written the story of its making to the bishop; and he sent for Johann and her and Peter, and they walked down the aisle of the cathedral. They had listened as the cloth was blessed.

From the time when his fingers first fumbled as he tried to pick up a vagrant stitch, when his teeth chewed against his tongue in concentration on the patterns she had drawn for him to copy, he had been happy in creating the beautiful handiwork. He knew fame: worthy companions to the works of great painters whose pictures graced churches and chapels all over Swedenland were the laces Johann had made.

But now did idleness confront him?

He must not see her looking at him with pity in her eyes. Yet now she looked. The insidious maimer had crawled slowly at first, crippling the hands only slightly; but of late weeks it had raced. Now his fingers, distorted with large bumps and swollen joints, lay in his lap. The needle lay on the floor. His head had dropped forward, chin resting on his chest. As she watched a tear fell to his shirt front. Johann had found happiness in work. Was this, then, to be the end of happiness for him?

What other could he do? What was there that she could help him do? Even Elisabet, ever the resourceful one, had not been able to figure out something to suggest to Johann that would fill his mind with challenge, that would be work to fill his days without the assistance of his fingers. No, not Big Johann, either, had been able to. But she was his mother. She had to find a way to help Johann. She had to! Yet, what could she *do*?

She pulled the letter paper toward her. At hand, at this moment, was something she must finish; a letter received was a letter to answer, and she had put it off now for a month of time. Nay, it was more like two—or it could be three—it would be no easier to write joyously tomorrow. She must set thoughts of Johann aside and write this letter now—*now*—and send it on its way before another nightfall. The granddaughter, too, was dear. But another time she would tell young Sigrid of that glad day in the future when the earthen jug most certainly must give coins enough to buy her a passage over the Atlantic.

It must be the shortness of the pencil that made the writing so difficult to do. Let it last only to write a conclusion, then she would throw it away.

She finished, "From your loving grandmother, Sigrid of

Norden." As with the salutation she put the words down
in Swedish, folded the page, stuffed it into the envelope,
and affixed the stamp. Then slowly, looking straight ahead,
she walked out into the gentle rain.

10

Where was the dividing line between spring and summer? It was not spring one day and summer the next, as one might be led to believe by looking at the almanac. The seasons had joined, melting one into the other, and already it was July. Jack had saved enough to take Sigrid to the Great Northern Theatre in April. She had worn her blue velvet dress and, sitting close, they had seen Charlotte, the figure skater, write her name on ice. Afterward they had gone to Henrici's for apple omelet and coffee.

For more than a year she had been Mr. Horgan's secretary. He was still gruff and demanding but she was finally getting accustomed to his ways. She and Nico had completed the first semester of elementary Swedish in the evening classes at the downtown branch of the University of Chicago.

Did Nico really feel the need of knowing Swedish, "in case he practiced in a Swedish neighborhood," or had his enrollment with her been a yielding to his father's over-solicitious concern at her being in the Loop alone after dark?

She was enjoying the friendships made during noon hours, with the girls of her own age. And the mechanical bank was getting heavier. And the tuberculosis test no longer showed "positive." The living was good—so good it almost made her feel afraid.

Her hollyhocks hid the fences at either side of the narrow city lot on which the parsonage stood. Blue larkspur nestled against them. Here was a clump of columbine, her mother's favorite flower, there lady-slippers, and stocks whose spicy fragrance had almost overcome the smell of gunpowder of exploded firecrackers on the Fourth.

White petunias now took the place of tulips that had encircled the border, and sweet alyssum sprouted here and yon, even in the grass. They looked so pretty there, she did not have the heart to cut them down with the lawn mower, so she clipped the grass close around them with a pair of scissors, and let them grow wherever they would. Full summer ripened the brown heads on the cattails in the marsh.

July. Another word for heat, and sweat, and dry, parched lawns; but a word too for red clover blossoms, phlox, flaming menarda, and tiger lilies; a word for vacations, and excursions, and picnics.

Saturday. A hot and sticky July the twenty-fourth.

Jack worked at the plant now so he, too, would be going today on the excursion planned by the management for the pleasure of its employees, on boats across the tip of Lake Michigan to the beaches of the dune-land coast of Indiana.

The day was so silent just before dawn. The big old elm stood hushed. No sound of morning came to her as she stood at the top of the nine steps that led steeply from the front porch of the parsonage to the cement sidewalk below; not even the sound of iron shoes on a milkman's horse disturbed the early quiet of this dark and muggy morning.

The milkman's horse was one that never would be replaced by an automobile engine. Certainty settled over Sigrid's face. A mechanical horse could never follow along on a street knowing the route so well as to stop in front of the next customer's house as the driver followed, all the while setting off bottles on a porch or step.

Were horses truly "on the way out"? If she could dream of a world without horses, would she be able to visualize what her father's life might have been if he had lived in such a time? A shudder shook her. How could that grandfather, Peter, have sold the stallion that had meant so much to his son? She could be glad her own father had not "taken after" his.

Despite his great love for them, it was a horse that had caused her father's death. Even now she could see him being trampled under those hoofs; but constant in her mind's sight was the look on his face as, before he died, he prayed to his mother and his God. She shook her head. No, it was much too hard to try to think of a world without horses.

Now from around the corner came the milkman; the cheery clip-clop of hoofs against asphalt brought her back to the morning. What a one to herald a picnic day! Dark. Damp.

She extended her hand beyond the protection of the porch roof. It was not actually raining, but the very air was wet; only a drizzle, but perhaps the old saying still might hold true, "Rain before seven, clear before eleven." Where the light of the gas mantle threw its beams from inside the parlor, across the porch floor and through the spaces between inch-by-inch spokes of the railing, it showed droplets clinging evenly along the arched green branches of bridal wreath and mock orange, hanging quivering, sparkling.

"Like a diamond necklace," she said to herself.

Her hand raised, and the fingers touched the strand she wore, a homemade necklace of orange-red berries from the mountain ash, strung by her grandmother's fingers; a shriveled necklace, now, having come as a gift for remembering last year's Santa Lucia's Day. "As like two peas to the one your cousin Hjördis shall wear as again she is our Santa Lucia's handmaiden." And, "after she has gone from bed to bed, singing the song of Lucia, then," wrote Mor Sigrid, as they had done with Elisabet in bygone years, and with Marta after her elder sister was married, and with Agda in her turn, they would seat Hjördis on her throne, "a little three-legged stool that has known the home longer, even, than I," far away enough from the walls in the festive corner of the big room so that they all might dance around her. "In your absence," Mor Sigrid's letter had concluded, "so shall I clasp my hands in prayer for you."

Those hands would be wrinkled, too, as the berries were. "Longer, even, than I," those hands had written. The melancholy of the morning penetrated deeply into Sigrid. Such a long time her grandmother had lived, almost her allotted threescore and ten. She was old, sixty-seven years old. . . .

The clip-clop passed. Horses. Because of a horse her father had left his home in Sweden. So it was because of a horse that she was an American. No wonder she loved them.

Saturday. July the twenty-fourth, nineteen hundred and fifteen.

She watched, waiting for the front door of the O'Tooles' house to open. Standing in their back yard last evening, "It'll be the first time I have ever been out of Illinois!" she had said, enthusiastically, to Pat. But making little woodpecker sounds against the fence post with the toe of his shoe, he had stood crestfallen. "Molly ain't so keen on goin'."

"Oh," she had assured him. "She'll be happy about it tomorrow."

Suddenly, as if a dozen well-timed cuckoo clocks had sprung their doors, as many front doors opened in the block of the subdivision; and from one came Pat with Michael, already six months old, on his arm.

"I'm so glad you decided to go, Molly. See, Pat, I told you—"

Yes, and they would be coming home early, of course, because of taking Michael along. It was in low tones Molly spoke, not in excited ones such as all the rest were shrilling.

Pat greeted Sigrid. "What an 'ell of a mornin' for a picnic! But what do we care? We've got our 'parashoots'!"

Yes, she saw that he had his parasol, a red-and-white striped one about twelve inches across, with silvery bells at each spoke end. So did she have one. So did almost everyone who gathered for the march to the Chicago Avenue streetcar.

They had to hurry, Pat reminded them. In order to come home on the first boat they would have to sail on the first boat, if they were to have any time at all at the picnic; seven thirty the *Eastland* would leave her dock. That meant they had to be downtown and at hand not later than six thirty when the ship opened her gangway, to be sure to get aboard; it seemed every one of the seven thousand ticket holders wanted to leave on the first sailing.

"Sigrid," Molly whispered, "don't you feel—something?"

"Only a little drizzle." And Sigrid lifted her face to feel the full effect of its cooling wetness.

Pat led the parade toward the streetcar. The Mac-Kenzies, the Schmidts, the Petersons, the Jacobsons, the Pikes, full families they came, with bells on striped parasols tinkling, with babies snatched too early from their beds wailing, with men and women wearing doll-sized paper hats singing, "For He's a Jolly Good Fellow!" Let it drizzle, let it rain if the skies wished, nothing would dampen the spirits of the picnickers now that they were on their way, least of all Sigrid's. Nothing!

"O-kay! Up on the streetcar!"

"Everybody Works but Father!" The words of ragtime songs spilled out of the car, and people standing on the streets or leaning out of open windows heard, waved, and called, "Have a good picnic day!" Then they'd look up at the murky sky and laugh.

"We Won't Go Home Until Morning!" The air rang with harmonizing. "Jazz" was what they were beginning to call it now.

The streetcars unloaded their noisy cargoes.

Only a short walk, and "There she *is!*" Big, as an ocean liner must be. Sigrid drew in her breath at seeing the *Eastland*. She didn't blame them at all for running; she was as impatient as the rest, could not wait to get aboard, to be sure of getting a good location on the deck. Only Molly hesitated.

Sigrid looked around. "For heaven's sake, you behind me, don't push us so!"

"Please," the crewmen urged. "P-lease, go above. Plenty of room above! Use the companionways—to the upper decks—pulease!"

"Glad to." Sigrid led the way, shoving Pat and Molly before her.

"Come, Molly." Pat pulled her arm. "I want you to meet my boss."

"No!" Molly screamed, as she lurched to keep from losing her footing.

"Mind your manners, Molly girl." Pat's voice was stern. "A-wailin' like a banshee. There's me boss. What'll he be thinkin'?"

"Here"—Molly fairly thrust Michael into Sigrid's arms—"take care of him till we get back."

Out of breath, feeling battered from the jostling and pushing, Sigrid would sit right here with Michael. "No, thank you," she answered one of the foremen from the plant, she did not care to sit where she could see the river; this was good enough. If all she could see here was the loading dock, then that was what she would see. She had been pushed around enough.

The foreman tried to explain. The confusion would soon be over; it would only be a few short minutes that they would be tied up at the dock here on the south bank of the Chicago River, a bit west of the Clark Street Bridge, so they might all just as well watch those poor hard-working devils hurrying to their jobs in the Loop! As soon as the boat steamed out everyone would be more comfortable, be able to sit and revel in this grand trip on the lake.

"Why is the boat rocking so?" She clutched the side of the deck chair and tightened her hold on Michael.

"Rocking, miss? What kind of sailor are you? Not getting seasick while we're still tied to the dock, I hope?"

She knew what she felt, and she felt the boat swaying. "Listing," was the way Pa would have described it; the crowd was surging to the port side, almost everyone was going that way to get a better view of the river; but she felt sick. Maybe it was her eyes. The buildings on Clark Street went up, and then they went down—fast. Too fast! The fingers of her free hand reached to grip her throat. Holding it tight might help to keep her from vomiting; and she closed her eyes to the crowd.

"*Herre Gud!*" Only those Swedish words, reaching out from early memories to help her, could give utterance to her plea to Almighty God for help as her deck chair slid from the railing to bump, crashing, against the bulkhead. Furiously clutching the screaming Michael, she opened her eyes, to see a baby tossed from its mother's arms as they were thrown at the violent impact.

"*All passengers to starboard!*" The engineer's warning sounded in a frightening roar over the boat.

"There, baby, there; you'll be all right." Sigrid crawled one-handedly over the slanting deck.

It was dead.

There was a hole in its head where it had struck against a hawser clamp. . . .

And the poor mother. Her face was frozen in nameless horror, until in a fleeting instant the face changed. Sigrid tried to close her eyes to it, but the lids refused to drop. How, at a time like this, could anyone think of the old clock face, up in the attic, from which the hands had been removed? Here it was, in front of her, such a face, with no meaning, without thought or emotion—a face topping a swaying body sitting cross-legged on an inclined deck, a face out of which, in ventriloquist fashion, came a thin, beautiful voice singing "Brahms' Lullaby."

She wanted to bury her face in her hand. But she sat looking, and could not stop looking.

It was an icebox that came crashing, and as it hit the bulkhead a hundred-pound block of ice hurtled through the doorway. She stretched out her arm in a futile effort to deflect it, and she could only moan as it stilled the mother's lullaby.

Ripping off her wide sash, she tied Michael to her. Then, staggering, trying desperately to grab some stable object for support, she fell and rolled on the horrible incline that had been the deck. A little girl—she couldn't be more than two—was close enough to grab.

Oh, no! Only by an inch she had missed. And she had almost *felt* the little dress. "Dear God, make my arm longer, so I can reach—"

Another little girl—with curls—

Another grabbing—straining—reaching—

"I've got you! You'll be all right!"

"Will you hold my hand—tight?"

"Yes, dear."

"My name's—"

Paralyzed with fear, Sigrid did not hear, but cried to God for help. Was there no air to breathe? Only a weird moaning, screaming hum of terror. It was choking her! She reached the arm that wound around Michael and the hand again grabbed at her throat.

"We're sinking!" the cry came.

The touch of the necklace of orange-red berries steadied her, and as if strength came from the one who had strung them, she raised her head. "Of course not! How could we sink? We're right in the middle of the city of Chicago! Look—we can almost reach out and touch the buildings!"

"God bless you," a man said at the comfort her words gave; but at once, terror-stricken, they saw—slowly at first, then rapidly—the deck slide from under them and become a wall in back of them. The *Eastland* had turned over on her side.

"Jump!" someone shrieked.

"JUMP!"

"J-U-M-P!"

"JUMP FOR YOUR LIFE!" came the screaming words.

Dazed, Sigrid could not be sure whether her own eyes were open or closed, if she was awake, or if she was dreaming; there, in front of her, were many eyes—eyes filled with terror; eyes filled with fear, with despair; questioning eyes, pleading eyes, coming toward her, passing by; eyes, now above, now falling like shooting stars; eyes bulging from their sockets! Dead eyes—staring—

"If they were on the port side, they're under!" she heard.

Where were Molly and Pat? Had they reached the port side? Where was Jack? She had forgotten all about Jack! *"Molly! Pat!"*

It was blood, streaming from her head, that was changing the color of things, painting the swishing waves with sunset hues while it was morning.

She had the two children now, Michael and the little girl. It would be kind to say more soothing words to them; but her tongue stuck to the roof of her mouth. Floundering human beings surrounded her, grasping for anything, anything to hold on to; men and women, and she herself, clinging to the two little ones, saw the upturned hull beyond the starboard rail. There might be safety there.

Her voice returned. "Grab my skirt tight," she cautioned the little girl. "I'll need my hands to help us get over the rail. Tight! Don't let go! Hear? Don't let go!"

The child put one hand up and caught a ringlet.

"Hold on to my skirt with *both* hands—we're almost over! Don't let go!"

"They're natural," the child said.

They were over the rail. Now she could grab the child's hand again.

"See?" The child let go her hold to slip a finger into the ringlet and started sliding on the slimy hull. Horror-stricken, Sigrid grabbed for her as together they slid, and Michael with them.

"Help! Someone—save the children!"

She had lost the little girl.

"Herre Gud—Lord God!" All of her heart went out in

her prayer, as sliding swiftly she slipped into the dirty water of the Chicago River.

Dr. van Vlaardingen hung the telephone receiver back on its hook, then lifted it again and called his son. "Bring the car around, *quick!*"

"I'm sorry," he said over his shoulder, to a man patient sitting in the consultation chair beside his desk, and picked up his satchel and took long steps out of his office. Hatless, without a word, he strode past the dozen persons sitting in the waiting room and jumped into the car. "Hurry! Start 'er up!"

"Where to?"

"Downtown."

Nico fed gas, accelerated, and they tore down the street. Must be an awful emergency; he had never seen his father like this.

"It can't be possible!" the doctor blurted. "In a narrow river! Why, it's not a hundred yards wide!"

"Would you mind"—shooting worried looks toward his father, Nico asked—"telling me just what happened?"

"The *Eastland* has capsized in the Chicago River."

"Dad!" The car swerved before it slowed. "That's the boat Sigrid was—"

"Maybe I'd better drive."

The Ford leaped forward. The rattle of its "tin" kept their voices from being heard, one by the other, if, in fact, they spoke.

"If"—the doctor at last raised his voice above the rattle —"things are as bad—as—you'll see whether you want to be a doctor or not."

The son did not answer; he had not heard.

The father covered his face with his big hand. "I can't understand it. Right in the middle of the city. They're calling all nurses and doctors. They said nets are being put in, down the river—to catch the—bodies—"

Beside the sound of the catch of a young man's breath there was only the sound of a rattling Ford.

Again the car swerved before it came to a stop. Aghast, they saw there, in the narrow river, in the center of the city, lying as devastatingly as though it were the last remnant of a disaster on the great limitless ocean, the remains of the flashy excursion boat. Even the smokestack was submerged, and the part of the hull that was exposed already was being gutted with big holes so divers could enter to search the flooded interior.

Men lined every inch of the bridges and the river's banks, casting out lifesavers, flinging out ropes; tugs hastened to do rescue work. All through the day Dr. van Vlaardingen ministered to the injured, the dying, or signaled for conveyances to come for the dead. Twelve hours after he had reached the scene his feet took him, wearily, to Leaping Lena.

A figure came running. "Did you find her? Did you see her?"

"No, Nico."

Terror and dread heavied the feet of the son as he followed the steps of his father to the Second Regiment Armory on Washington Street. "The Red Cross has established a mass mortuary here."

"*Mortuary?* Oh, Dad—not—"

"Yes, Nico." It was a moment before the doctor could go on. "To be open to the public—who may be able—to—help—with the identification of the unknown."

Midnight. The doors opened as they arrived, and two of more than thirty thousand they followed the serpentine paths between the double rows of dead.

Muffled sounds of shuffling feet made a weird sort of music; deep, indrawn breaths, sniffling noses, played in a minor key; piercing sounds, shrieks rang through the big building, tearing asunder the air that never knew sunshine; or low sounds of moaning came as another victim was identified. And the doctor grieved, for here his profession was of no moment at all; these were beyond his skill.

They shuffled along, the searchers, each with his vision before him. And the doctor envisioned them all: "I'll wipe the dishes, Mama," would never come from this little one whose ringlets spread gold on the armory floor. "Buy me a taffy apple, or a balloon, or a train, Papa?" would not again elicit a "Hush, boy," from the one who knelt over him now, knees unfeeling of an armory floor.

The woman, with hands raw and torn, so soon to have brought forth a being in the image and likeness of God, little had she known or guessed that her childbed would be a hard armory floor.

The doctor stopped, stopping the others behind him as a freight train does, so that the rear brings up with a humping. With Michael bound to her body, there lay Sigrid on the armory floor.

11

Slowly the doctor knelt, and except for Nico the others passed by, shuffling, scraping their feet in hopelessness and dejection. The man knelt in grief for his neighbor, for this girl whom he and his son loved; but the part of him that was the physician reached to feel Sigrid's wrist.

"There's a pulse!" He could be sure he had screamed, but no echo came from the rafters of the huge armory. Only Nico heard; and with a wide swimming motion his arms opened a path for his father who carried the forms of their neighbor and Michael.

"I'll get Lena, and drive it home!" Nico shouted. "You take Sigrid and Mike—Dad—here—driver! *Driver!*"

The doctor sat on the floor of Marshall Field's delivery truck holding Sigrid and the baby on his lap while the driver raced to the parsonage. Nico was there when they arrived.

"You, Nico, take care of Sigrid—remove her wet clothing—while I tend to the boy! Pastor, put water on to heat! Run over to—to anywhere—and get all the dry blankets you can.

"Nico! *Take off her clothing,* I said!"

Color mounted from above Nico's collar line. "I—I can't do that—"

Swiveling on his heel, the doctor snapped, "Why can't you?"

His father didn't understand, so what should he say? "Dad, she's a girl."

"What's that got to do with it, when a person's sick?"

What could he say? "I—I—" Oh, any excuse would do! "The fellows would kid the daylights out of me."

"And you expect to be a doctor." The father spoke low

100

and evenly, measuring his words, all the while working to make sure the baby's lungs were clear of water. "You are preparing to enter medical school. Are you planning on practicing on—on studying—only the male body?"

"No. But—but *Sigrid!*"

"Let me tell you, son, a doctor is born, not made. Whether you are twenty or forty, if you are a doctor at heart, it makes no difference." Satisfied that the baby was all right, he opened Sigrid's shirtwaist, removed her skirt. "One does not approach our ministry, Nico, with a question as to what someone else will think of him—boy or man—but with a plea as to how he can serve—a thankfulness for that privilege of being able to minister to the body of one who needs us." His voice faltered, and it was a moment before he finished. "For it is not only the physical body—"

Nico removed Sigrid's shoes.

"It is the house of the soul."

A sob broke from the son.

"Sigrid needs us. How badly, you have no idea. Are you going to turn away, 'Doctor'?"

Turn away from Sigrid? He hadn't meant to turn away. "No, Dad."

"Michael! Michael!" she screamed, and "Don't let go!" "I'll marry you, Jack, only don't drown!" She did not know that Jack had not gone to the picnic, but had been out looking for a better job, intending to surprise her. She saw that blue eyes were close to hers, and drowned herself in the depths of them. They were Jack's eyes. But they changed, to become the doctor's. Then they were Nico's; but they couldn't be his, because she loved those eyes. Now they were Pastor Bedell's. Again they were Nico's. But now they became the eyes of someone she did not know.

Outside, Nico saw the figure that hourly paced there, as if by looking at her window he could bring help to the girl he loved. And the name of the watcher was Jack Yingling.

By Monday almost every little home in Calico Row had a crepe on its door; and there were two on the O'Tooles'. Whole families had drowned. Every block in the subdivision gave, to add to the figure which was to read over eight hundred dead. Each day saw corteges pass the parsonage, but Sigrid did not see them. She rose from her bed only to care for Michael. "Take care of him till we get back!" rang in her mind incessantly, crowding out all other sounds.

It took almost the full time of Hattie Allspaugh and Taina Heinebach, the woman from Finland who lived across the street, to answer the solicitous inquiries about Sigrid and the boy. Even Cholly Peterson, one of the head foremen at the plant, came to ask about them. Taina met him and Mrs. Allspaugh on the front porch. "Yes, I jumped," he said. "There isn't a better swimmer in the city of Chicago than I am, if I do say so myself. Why, I've swum in the North Sea! I thought I'd be over to the opposite bank before you could say 'Jack Robinson.'" His voice reached the shrieking point. "I swam like *hell,* and I just stayed in one place!"

It must have been the suction, Cholly reckoned, that kept dragging on him. His big frame shook, and a wild look came into his eyes before he buried his face in his hands. "I can't stand it!" he cried. "Thinking of those women and children!" His hat came off, then, and he held it over his heart as a long lumber wagon carrying six coffins rolled by. There were not enough hearses in the whole of Chicago to carry the *Eastland* dead to their cemeteries.

Cholly had tried to save some of the children and women, even one with pink underwear on. "And you know what *they* are."

Hattie Allspaugh nodded knowingly.

He had not been able to save a single person. Not one. He had gone down, and been saved, without even knowing it until he woke up in the rescue boat.

"He'll go off his trolley if he keeps on thinking about it," Mrs. Allspaugh whispered to Taina Heinebach.

"Come right down to it," the Finnish woman asked. "What happened? What made the boat turn over?"

"Someone put the water ballast into the wrong hold; that's what they say. Ballast should've been shifted to the other side when all the passengers flooded the port side. Mind, I'm not saying that—that's what 'they say.' Of course I suppose nobody'll ever really know."

Taina had asked the question so many were asking.

Summer and her flowers did their best to lift the pall which hung over Chicago. Though gaudy zinnias flaunted showy reds and oranges and yellows, they might as well have been smoke-colored. Calendulas picked up the gold of the rising and the setting sun, but the days had more the purple sadness of a winter's twilight.

The wake of disaster widened: it meant that, with some, happiness over rescue changed to despair over aftereffect. It meant that all of the doctors must do double duty, for hundreds of men, women, and children had to be inoculated against typhoid fever; the danger of epidemic was great, so many people having been exposed to the contaminated river water.

Despite precautions, it was little Michael whom the typhoid struck.

Days of fever.

Nights of fearful watching.

"Let me stay up with him, Sigrid," begged the pastor, "so you can get some sleep."

"No. Night is his low time. I'd rather watch." She could not trust his care to anyone else, not even to the pastor. It was she whom Molly had charged, "Take care of him—"

She sat on the bed, bathing the baby's hot brow; but when she looked at the thermometer she called for help. "Pastor!"

Asleep on his good ear, he did not hear.

One hundred and four and six tenths! "He's going to die!" Michael's lids were open, but the eyes were rolled back in his head. Only the whites showed.

". . . take care of him . . ."

What had the doctor said, as a last resort? A little brandy, dripped into Michael's open mouth; the washtub, set it beside the bed—fill it half full of water—cold water! Chop off some ice from the piece in the icebox—put an iced cloth on his forehead; rub him—dip him gently into the tub; keep rubbing; add ice to cool the water more; keep rubbing, from head to feet—keep one finger on his pulse—"Oh, God, for *more arms!*" Now lift him carefully —roll him in the blanket—

—he is shivering!

—*his lips are purple!*

—a few more drops of brandy!

She fell to her knees. "Dear God, don't let him die! I

have done all I know to do. Only You can save him now! He is so little, and sweet—don't let him die!"

Seldom was the pastor's doorbell rung so insistently. Sigrid hurried to answer it; glanced at the calling card held out to her by a slim woman, not young but young-looking. "I am Miss Christianson. Miss—? Come in."

"Hartz is the name."

"Miss Hartz, please come in. The pastor will return shortly. Will you have a chair?"

Sitting primly on the edge of the chair, the visitor said, "I've come to see about the O'Toole child."

"How nice of you! I'm so happy to be able to tell you that he's getting well."

"He's been ill?"

"Oh, you didn't know?" Something prompted Sigrid to give a second look at the card.

. . . Child Welfare . . .

"I've come to—" the woman began.

"He nearly died of typhoid. But Dr. Van says he's almost as good as new now!"

"Of course, in the case of illness, we shall no doubt recommend leaving him with you until—"

"Until—?" Sigrid twisted the big ring nervously.

"Then, as soon as possible, you can be relieved of the responsibility of his care."

"Relieved? I don't want to be relieved! He's mine! His mother gave him into my care!"

"And what did you think of doing?"

"Of course I'll adopt him."

"Have you had any—Do you know anything about the adoption process, or—"

"Why, no, but—"

"You said you were 'Miss'?" At Sigrid's nod, "We would not recommend adoption by a single girl."

"You mean—you would take him—from me?"

"He would be nicely placed."

"No. I'll never give him up. No." She felt herself weaving as she walked to the door and opened it. "Miss Hartz—"

She closed the door after the visitor and leaned against it in order to stand. Of course the woman was right. She had no legal claim to Michael, but she would *fight* them—fight to keep him!

All of the maternal instinct, growing through ages past, welled now in Sigrid as she knelt again beside Michael's bed. Praying, she grew calm. "Heavenly Father, don't let them take him from me. Please, if it is right that I should keep him and care for him—*show me the way!*"

12

The years of silence were broken. Now words came from the lips of Jack Yingling, "I love you, Sigrid."

This was not the way she had dreamed of being proposed to, in stark bright daylight, she sitting on one chair in the parlor and her lover sitting in the opposite corner. *It should be in the twilight hour, standing beside broad water, hands clasped, watching the big round ball that lights the day slip slowly into the pocket between the sky and sea—his kiss upon her cheeks should come as silent echo to the sun's kiss on the cheeks of the white clouds, bringing blushes—*

"I'll never care for anyone but you."

—tinting the languid, rippling waves with gold and orange and crimson, until the fiery ball would bow politely and slip out of sight, leaving its golden rays to blend with the purple of the night—

"Will you marry me, Sigrid?"

—or standing in a forest with the moonlight flowing through the lace of oaks—

"I've thought it all out. I know I'm only a dumb Swede, but I'll take such good care of you—"

—or, loving, rising as eagles with pinions lifting their two souls above the rainbow's arc—

"And when we grow older—"

—or if it must be day, then standing in the marsh, at noon, knee-deep in spiderwort, the ephemeral blue-violet flowers brushing their hairy stamens on her lover's clothes and hers—

"We'll have our minds—"

—standing lips to lips until the blue flowers closed, for day had gone—

"We'll have our common interests, reading and—"

—or in a lashing storm, with boughs of tall trees bent like grasses on the meadow—or on a carousel—

"Answer me yes."

—or in a library, the warm colors of book bindings reflecting the warmth of a big log fire—

"Please, Sigrid?"

No, not in a library, for then it would be a van Vlaardingen who was asking her. The room was a kaleidoscopic blur until with effort she quieted the mental fragments of colored glass that had brought varicolored dreams. Dreaming, she had forgotten it was Jack sitting there.

(Oh, Jack, if only you would not brush your hand back over your pompadour so frequently!)

"I've got a fairly good job at last! And I'm going to night school, at Coyne's." And he was losing his Swedish accent.

"Yes, Jack. I'm so proud of you."

"Then will you marry me?"

(Jack! Jack! Why do you have to pick at your fingernails so?)

"I—I think I'm too young, Jack. There are things I want first."

"I'll give them to you!"

"But they are the sort of things I have to get for myself."

"It isn't that there is someone else?" He came to her now and sat beside her. His hands were hot on hers. "Look at me, Sigrid, and tell me there isn't."

Her eyes were closed; against the darkness of the lids was the picture of Mr. Wessly, drawing away from her—as if she were a leper—

"You haven't promised anyone else?"

"Jack, tell me—you aren't *afraid?* You know the 'health risk'—and you aren't afraid—of—me?"

"Oh, Sigrid, Sigrid! No!" Kissing her, he drew her breath to mix with his, to prove his "no." "Now will you marry me?"

Had she always intended saying it? Then why did it frighten her so to hear her lips say "Yes"?

Again she closed her eyes: there was someone else. Michael. If she was married, maybe she could keep Michael.

The pastor found her sitting in the doctor's book-lined room, glassy-eyed; no book was in her hand, none on her lap.

"Sigrid? Are you all right?"

Without expression, "Yes."

She made no move, so he drew the small rocker close to her chair. He noticed that he hunched the rug with the rockers but, although bothered by them, he made no effort to straighten the humps. He leaned toward her, waiting for her to be the first to speak.

"I've had a proposal of marriage."

"And you have refused?" His eyes narrowed until they became little slits.

"No. I have said 'yes.' "

He rocked, with little staccato rockings.

"Aren't you going to ask me—who?" she asked.

"No. If you want to tell me, you will."

"If a person loves you, a person who hasn't had much happiness, someone to whom life, so far, has not been very kind—"

Nervously the pastor propelled the chair.

"—and by marrying him you'd not only make him happy, but—I—I—oh, Pastor—" Again came sight of Mr. Wessly backing away from her. "Who else would have me?"

The little chair snapped upright. "You mean you would consider marrying—without *loving?*"

She looked at him dumbly.

"Ah, Sigrid! That would be blasphemy!"

The rocker rocked, and the clock ticked, until at last he spoke again. "Sometimes we pity, and mistake it for love. Sometimes we think we love when, as you suggest now, we are overcome with a wave of gratefulness, undeserved as it may be, but this, that you say you would do—"

The clock on the bookshelf made the only sound. The minute hand went round and round. She knew her pastor expected her to say something, but she who was so seldom at a loss for words could think of nothing to say. At last he broke the silence. "Love. Mythology explains it well by saying that the gods separated man from woman, and those gods have been trying ever since to effect their reunion into the whole; and that attraction of the two halves, *to each other,* is what we call love."

He reached for her hand, and she gave it to him. She felt, more than saw, that he leaned close. "God makes man and woman one in the sacrament of marriage. But even He cannot effect the perfect whole unless the two halves are properly matched."

The clock ticked on.

"Only through love should a union bring forth seed for the coming days."

Only through love. Did she love Jack? How could she know? "When love comes—how can we be *sure?*"

"You will know, Sigrid. You won't have to ask anybody, not even me!" He smiled, and leaned closer. "In the book your father gave to you, *Les Misérables,* do you remember when Marius writes to Cosette, 'I have met in the street a very poor young man who was in love. His hat was old, his coat worn, his coat was out at the elbows, the water passed through his shoes, and *stars through his soul!'* "

She had never noticed, before, how truly beautiful the pastor's face was.

13

Sigrid laughed as Beda said, "One more baby to take care of, days, won't make no difference to me, 'smany's I've got!"

There was to be a hearing in the courthouse, but not until after the first of the year, to decide the future of the orphaned boy. In the meantime, with Beda caring for Michael while she worked he was hers to mother. She taught him to call her "Sigree," and, to the pastor's delight, to call him "Grampa."

She taught him to walk, and he toddled precariously from chair to chair; taught him to say *"Tack för maten"* at leaving the table after a meal.

The days passed, until with December came the Christmas letter from Sweden. Sigrid went to the shelf and picked up the mechanical bank; because of good neighbors it still jingled; even the doctor would not send a bill. With every coin that had been dropped into the slot the Atlantic Ocean was narrowing. And so she smiled at the sound of the clinking coins.

For the tenth time she read over this letter from Norden, not only in her grandmother's hand, but with postscripts from Big Johann and Aunt Elisabet and her husband and their children. And Young Johann wrote, only a little note in an unsteady hand, and she wondered why, but it wasn't the kind of thing she felt she should ask about; and Herman Nikodemus—how she loved that name!—and Marta, Agda, Patrik and Tuppie, and Maria and David. They were her kinfolk. Her fingers lovingly caressed the figure on the bank, then moved to stroke the satin finish of the bread tray Mor Sigrid had fashioned for her. Apologies in great number had come with the gift: the old fingers were not as willing as once they had been, the birch was not as

110

fine a grain as formerly, she had not been able to bring it to the smoothness she desired; she should have been able to think of something new and different to send to the granddaughter in America. A like tray she had made for each of her own daughters, and for their daughters in turn. But here it was, a homely gift; it should prove useful, for "everyone serves bread."

Its edge was carved with quaint squat letters, *"Vårt Dagliga Bröd"*—Our Daily Bread. This was another touch of her grandmother's hand, a message of love, a blessing.

As on last Christmas and the Christmas before Sigrid was with them in spirit at her father's old home, walking with them into the woodlot, selecting the Yule log, lugging it home, all the while singing; watching the log burn in the hearth as it burned away all past wrongs; she partook of the *lutfisk* at Christmas Eve dinner; went, in line, to dip bread into the large kettle to taste the savoriness of Christmas ham boiled with cabbage.

"But," the angular penmanship said, "with all of the celebrating, with our ceremonials, some older than Christianity itself, we never forget the real meaning of Christmas —Christ's Mass—heralding the birth of our Saviour. Think not, ever, that the opening of the gifts is the climax of Christmas! Oh, no, all of the Yuletide's coming, the preparations, the giving of gifts, lead up to this hour when early on Christmas Day comes the time to go to *Julotta*. Church bells, pealing, call us to solemn worship. All must go, and God sees but does not frown as a peppermint candy silences the small one to whom the service is interminable. In sleighs we ride to the church. Oh, you have never heard the sound of Christmas until you have heard silver sleigh-bells ringing in the cold, crisp Swedish air, making accompaniment to the songs and the greetings, *'God Jul! God Jul!'*

"As is the custom, each member of the family carries a lighted torch. The larger the family, the brighter the glow; the brighter the glow, the happier the family will be in the year to come.

"You can imagine, Sigrid, the splendor of the glow on my large family!"

Although she sat in Calico Row, so great was the power of the written word that with that family Sigrid entered

the church. Julotta began. Majestic was the song to greet
the newborn Day,

> "All Hail to Thee
> O Blessed Morn!"

The organ's swelling in the chancel vault reached Sigrid's
ears through her grandmother's telling—from last Christmas morning—from next—from every Julotta since the
beginning, and every one to come. The full vibration filled
her ears, her heart, her soul. It was a song of love—for
Michael, for the pastor, for life.

And for Jack? She had promised to marry Jack. . . .

Once more she and the pastor trimmed a tree set on the
Geib piano, and Michael sat on the floor with legs spread
wide and watched with open mouth, and reached little
hands out and closed them to secure imaginary bright trim-
ming balls.

Christmas Eve. Not many presents, but—

> bells ringing—heavenly bells—

"It is the doorbell, Sigrid." The pastor laughed as he
brought her thoughts back to earth.

"Hope no one's needing you," she said, and hastened to
open the door.

There stood a woman. A taxicab was at the curb. "Right
place for the lady?" the cabbie called.

Whoever she was, she was welcome here; this was the
parsonage.

The driver went. Sigrid took a step forward. The woman
was old, her face a beautiful lace pattern of wrinkles; a
tricornered scarf had fallen to the back of her head, showing that her straight hair was combed tightly back from
the high, shiny forehead so prominently showing heavy
blood vessels leading upward from the temples. Her hair,
skin, brows, and eyelashes all were about the same color,
tan-gray, as was the thin line of her lips compressed over
toothless gums, the pointed chin, and the strong, heavy
nose with long hairs showing in the nostrils. There was a
heaviness of the eyes; and as if she were too tired to focus
them both, one eye strayed to the right as she looked

ahead. Sigrid noted all of this, yet her thoughts were not on the woman's appearance.

She half-closed her eyes. The woman carried a large, woven knapsack in coarsely mittened hands: it was the immigrant standing here—bringing a flood of remembering of parents to overcome Sigrid, until in some way it brought understanding that this woman had come as a gift from God—on Christmas Eve—

She took the woman in her arms. "You—*you* must be Michael's grandmother!"

The old woman walked stumblingly, with Sigrid's help, into the parlor.

"It's Michael!" she wailed. "Pat's Michael! Thanks be to God I lived to lay my eyes on him!" Gasping, she slid to the floor and crumpled into a heap beside the child.

How had she come? Who had sent for her?

Revived, the granny told. For hours she told: it was her son. Pat, before he died, had arranged for sending money every payday to the bank in Ireland, so that when there was enough to pay for passage his "ould" mother could come and live with Molly and him and Michael. Then there was the insurance money left to her. It had taken long, longer than it should, to get the papers, to sell the little she had in Ireland, so she could come to Michael.

"Say 'Granny,' Michael," Sigrid prompted, before she knelt beside the pastor. With his hand on her head she poured forth her thanks to Him who answers prayers: Michael would not be taken from his own kin!

Seated on the floor beside her grandson, Granny rocked herself back and forth. "It was the neglect of me was to blame. Shure, and weekly I brought the six loaves of bread, warm bread it was, after I heard about Michael's coming. I carried them right over to Father Murphy, and I says, 'Father,' I says, 'give these to the poor, please, Father, so's Saint Anthony will know and keep, good, the little one.'"

Sigrid squeezed the old hand. She loved the way Granny said the boy's name, as if it were spelled Mi'hawl.

"But"—Mrs. O'Toole blew her nose and swiped at her eyes—"'twere the child I asked the good Saint to take care of, not the grown ones; I didn't ask for the parents—

for the busyness of me thinkin' of me grandson, for me own son I did not ask—"

"You did the best you could, Granny."

"If only I had brought bread for them, too." Granny wept openly now. "But"—she looked heavenward—"it was the will of God. The young wun is left, with no father—to—Oh, if 'twere not for the likes of you and the—" She sent a grateful glance toward Pastor Bedell, and the wrinkled hand reached to lay itself on Sigrid's hand. "I know that out of the goodness of their hearts the parish will want to put Michael in an orphans' home—and do not mistake me, it is good there are such—and me, now that I'm here, me in a home for the aged. But e'en though I be here, near Michael, there is no way"—her lips all but failed to make the words—"for us to be together."

Sigrid cleared her throat of the lump that came. "Dear Granny, you are a blessing, straight from heaven! A Christmas blessing! You couldn't know! We didn't know! But if we had known we would have sent for you, if we could, to come to live with us."

"Here?"

Did Granny's question include the one which suddenly entered Sigrid's mind? Would the Lutheran congregation welcome an Irish Catholic into the parsonage?

"When death comes, Granny, you have to think of the ones that are left. My father used to say, 'When death comes, never linger on "The King is dead," but follow at once with, "Long live the King!" ' "

"That would be a part of the ould country that he brought with him."

"Yes. And we all must live. Michael and his granny. And they have to live together." She looked for, and received, a nod from the pastor. "We'll manage somehow. Think of how wonderful it will be for—for a person to come home at night, not having to start from scratch to get a meal, but to a home where, when the door opens, there'll be the smell of stew cooking. Irish stew!"

Swift swipes with her sleeve did not clear the old woman's face of tears.

"We'll work it out, Granny. And now, Pastor, let us say our Christmas prayers."

"Tack för maten," piped Michael.

With still-brimming eyes Granny O'Toole said "thank

you" in her own way, "God bless you, Sigrid, for bringin'
loaves to Saint Anthony."

Now, who was that a-knockin' at the door? Granny
ripped off her kitchen apron and flung it to a chair back.
"Pastor Bedell! Come in, sir. Come on in."

"Sigrid isn't here yet?"

"No, sir. She's a-workin'—wor-r-rk all day—wo-r-rk all
night, or go to school; all the same thing, says I; that's
all she knows, wor-r-rk, bless her heart. I've never seen
the likes of her."

"I am glad you are going to be living together here in
the O'Toole cottage." He accepted the proffered rocker.
"It was right, so right, that the three of you should come
here, to what is now Michael's house. The payments are
not too heavy for Sigrid to manage, and the parsonage,
with only two small bedrooms—it wouldn't have held us
all."

"Still, right as rain, sir, or not, you're a-grievin' because
she left: and she's a-grievin'—should she have left you,
or shouldn't she have? Oh, you sit there tellin' how right
it is, tryin' to make yourself believe it; and her—oh, she
don't say nuthin'—but I'm not blind—and it's all done for
me—"

"We live so close, Granny. I'll be running in—often."

"Little did I ever think that Kathaleen Bridget O'Malley
O'Toole would ever be-a-questionin' a man of God! The
Lord f'rgive me, but why did you tell her that you wanted
her to go?"

"Mrs. Granny Kathaleen Bridget O'Malley O'Toole"—
a boyish grin spread over his face—"because it was the
thing she wanted to do, if it could mean keeping care of
the child."

"That I know." Granny's head nodded affirmatively.
And what *she* wanted to do, and would do, she vowed to
herself, was that she would be running over to do his
housework; only a little house, the parsonage; a man
alone couldn't keep it up; but she, she'd find time to keep
it neat and clean for him.

"And I knew it was only a question of time"—he
stopped, as if it hurt him to think the thing he was saying—"until I would have had to be without her. She has
told you that she expects to be married?"

"Yes, sir, that she has. And she's a-fixin' the attic up into 'a grand room,' as she calls it, for the two of them. Her and Jack."

Pastor Bedell stilled his jowls, forcibly, with his hands. What Granny said further did not penetrate his mind until he heard, "We are of such different faiths, sir. It worries me, the thought of it. Is it fair to be askin' Sigrid to have fish, always, on Fridays, when it's her who's providin'?"

He smiled. "It is good, Granny, for everybody to eat fish at least one day a week. We could all profit by the doing, all of us Protestants. It's brain food, you know."

"Oh, the likes of you!" She pretended to be exasperated with him. She had always known that priests were smart, but you couldn't get ahead of the pastor, either. Nothin' short of astonishin', it was, to hear him tell now that it would be good for Sigrid that Michael was to be brought up in the Catholic Church, that by getting intimate knowledge of two beliefs she would grow.

He turned to leave, but she touched his arm. "But, sir, how can she feel about my clingin' to my own church, goin' in the mornin's, and I a-livin' in what will really be her home?"

He took her hand. "I'll tell you how she feels, Granny. I talked with her, at length, about this difference in religion. These were her words, 'We can step over the threshold of one home into two different churches just as well as from adjoining houses.' "

All through the night the summer breeze had danced the big old elm tree, at the same time tapping the dance tune with gentle raindrops on its leaves. Sigrid had lain sleepless: there was so much to think about; after they were married she would place their bed under the sloping roof next to the east window; she would nail wallboard against the two-by-fours. Too bad Jack wasn't handier with nails and a hammer. And she'd wallpaper the sloping ceiling and the walls.

All through the night her taut body had seemed to hang suspended inches above the mattress; only now, when it was almost time to get up, every muscle was willing to relax and she could give her body heavily to the bed. This was a good mattress. Hair. It fluffed up so nicely when aired in the sunshine. A good bed. Funny, but the ceiling always looked too small to match the floor space that gave room to her brass bed, her mahogany veneered dresser with the neat plain brass escutcheons on the drawer fronts, the little pine commode with a rack on each side holding hand-crocheted lace-edged towels, and the tiger maple chair with cretonne to hide its torn cane seat. Maybe it was the living she had done with these pieces of furniture that made them so lovely to her; but she would say her mother had done well, buying off of Mr. Ginsberg's junk wagon. . . .

No sooner was she dressed, than, "Yankee Doodle Came to Town!" came from the direction of the front door.

"Riding on a pony!"

"Well!" She had to stop short, she laughed so hard. There was Bobby Schmotzer straddling a painted pony head, and astride the broomstick behind him were his mother and father.

"Stuck a feather in his hat"—Bazile shoved a long black willow plume into the band of his straw hat—"and called it macaroni."

She threw open the screen door, grabbed the side seams of Bazile's coat, squatted as if she, too, rode on the pony's back, and with Granny and Michael beating time the four of them pranced up and down on the porch singing "Yankee Doodle Dandy!" until the floor boards creaked.

"You've got them!" she panted.

"Yes, sir! We've got our citizenship papers." The Schmotzers stood three abreast and seriously, with hands at sides, with Bobby's head thrown back watching his parents' lips and filling in a word whenever he thought he could, they repeated the Preamble to the Constitution.

"Bazile," the wife looked at him adoringly. "He knows it all, the whole Constitution of the United States, by heart."

"Do you mean to say you don't?" Sigrid teased.

"No-no." Abashed, Emilie blushed.

"Neither do I."

"And you went to the American schools?" Bazile was dumfounded.

"Congratulations to you both." Sigrid shook their hands. "And Michael and you and I, Bobby, we are citizens without our half trying."

"I hope," the father worried, "that because of that none of you ever forgets to be thankful for what you've got here."

It was the immigrant speaking, her father and the doctor and Jesper Seastrom and many thousands upon thousands more, speaking with Bazile Schmotzer's tongue.

"America has been good to me," he said now, and turning to his wife, "This time, Emilie, you tell."

"Something more? What are your mama and papa keeping from me, Bobby?"

"I dassn't tell."

"It is for Emilie to tell, yes."

"No, Bazile, you."

"You first, my dear Alphonse!" Sigrid laughed and bowed low with a sweep of her open hand. "But whatever it is, let's go inside; it will be easier to talk while holding a glass of lemonade."

They sat around the dining-room table. "The invention," Bazile began, and Sigrid felt her lips curl involuntarily. "It is going to make us rich."

"Oh, not millionaires, Bazile. But rich!"

Sigrid shivered.

"Too much ice in," Bobby warned, reaching to touch her elbow. "You should be like me, like Mama says, no ice in." He drained his glass.

"Tell me about it! How glad I am for you. How glad I am, if someone could have an invention turn out well."

It was some kind of an improvement on an electrical switch that was bringing good fortune to the Schmotzers. Bazile explained it, but she did not quite understand. If only Pa, poor Pa, could have known some of this satisfaction!

"I knew a man in the old country, he made an invention, but it was a man of higher class stole it from him. The gentleman got the glory. Got the money, too. Not so here. Here, in America, the poor man has the chance the same as the rich man. Every man is a gentleman." Abruptly changing the subject, "I see you got the coal stove down for the summer."

"We took it down only yesterday."

"Stoves! You, Sigrid, should not have to do with an old-fashioned stove no more."

"We don't mind, do we, Granny? We call it our *Nürn-*

berg Stove, and we forget that our backs are cold and our fronts too warm, because we see that it is beautiful."

Emilie wiped her eyes. "Tell now, Bazile."

"The men will come, from the Austin Sheet Metal Works, to put you in a furnace."

"Oh, no!" Still she had to smile. Put you in a furnace, said as Mr. Horgan would say it. "No, positively no," she repeated.

"Yes," Bazile insisted. "We have to share all that this country gives us. It gives so much to us."

"No, Bazile and Emilie. We could not take that from you."

"No." Bazile moved to one side of his mouth the large piece of ice that had flowed in with the lemonade, and it clicked against his teeth. "That is right. Not from us, no. It will be a present to you, *from America.*"

America.

America must be prepared, for Europe was at war.

For hours Sigrid's feet had slipped and turned on the rounded cobblestones of Chicago's streets, trying to keep in step with the music of the bands, marching for "Preparedness." Close beside her Taina Heinebach's feet slipped and slid. Taina, too, was marching for Preparedness. So were the hundreds and hundreds of others. Thinking of the length of the parade, it seemed to Sigrid that everybody in Chicago must be here, marching. She gave a reassuring squeeze to Taina's hand at seeing how sad her friend looked. It had been almost impossible to understand why Taina, a married woman with as fine a husband as Louis, should have gone to work at the plant, until she had learned that Louis had been laid off from his job as toolmaker in the shop on the North Side. They didn't want any "damn Germans" around. And she had thought, that day, that the assassination of the heir to the throne of the Austrian Empire could not affect Americans; she had been one to agree with local public opinion that it made no difference to Americans whether the Germans invaded the Balkans and took them for their own, or left southeastern Europe to the Slavs!

She could be glad of one thing, that Bazile had made himself so valuable to his firm that they forgot his nationality and his background.

"Preparedness," Taina shouted over the blaring of the bands. "Doesn't that really mean, when you come right down to it, building for war?"

Sigrid fell out of step, and had to skip and shuffle to get back in. How could she answer Taina, when her woman's mind found it impossible to understand in what way "arming to the teeth" could be the surest way of preserving peace? She turned sharply at hearing Taina say the very words she was thinking. "It doesn't make sense."

"Building for war?" War was young men dying on the battlefields. Young men, like Jack. What was it she was marching for? She stopped still, but the one behind her in formation bumped into her, shoving her forward.

"Louis feels so bad, Sigrid. Would you come over, if I have a party for him?"

"Yes, I'd like to very much. If you make it on a Sunday."

"Even if Louis—is—from German parents?"

"Of course! Why, I know your husband as well as I know, oh, almost as well as I know Pastor Bedell."

"I thought of having it on the Fourth of July, of making it a sort of celebration of a housewarming for our new house, and of our Finnish Midsummer's Day, and Independence Day, all rolled into one." Over the sound of the bass drum and the tuba Sigrid heard Taina's plans, but her mind kept asking, what *was* it she was marching for?

She kept on asking herself as the days followed each other, until came the day of Louis' party. Although it was the Fourth, the welcome must be in the Finnish manner, Taina explained happily; so Sigrid found herself being led to a huge circle surrounded entirely by birch trees, young and slender. Transplanted to form the circle, their lithe trunks were set close together, "To keep the evil spirits out." In due seriousness Taina parted the saplings to allow her entrance, all the while speaking traditional good-luck words to keep those evil spirits from entering at the same time, then quickly letting the saplings go, to snap back and close the opening tight. That ceremony was repeated for each of the guests as they arrived to enjoy this summer celebration, this *"Lehti majan juhla."*

Inside the circle Sigrid saw that a large table was spread. "A *smörgåsbord!*"

Taina laughed. "With us it is *voileipäpöytä*."

"Both," Pastor Bedell enlightened them all, "essentially, 'spread bread.'" He went around carrying a smoking piece of punk and smacking his lips.

As Sigrid watched for Jack to arrive, she saw that coffee brewed on the top of the wood stove set up to one side of the table; one pot boiled over and the coffee magically was transformed into tiny balls of liquid crazily chasing themselves over the surface of the stove, hissing in angry protest against extinction. It reminded her of the war.

Soon the guests were gathered, Granny and Michael, and the pastor, and the doctor and Nico, and the Swedish stair-builder and Beda with their family, and Mr. and Mrs. Allspaugh, and Jack. But somehow the ancient ceremonials took on special significance; these fireworks associated always with America's Independence Day had greater fire today because they matched the fiery eyes of the van Vlaardingens. Combined, the ceremonies joined the past with the present, the old countries with the new, and in the going seemed in some strange way to bind her close to the doctor and his son.

"Midnight is the time for serving the spread in Finland." Taina caught their attention, and memory made her deep voice vibrate. "Midnight, in midsummer, when still the night is day."

But this was America, and so they ate by twilight. Toothless Granny O'Toole liked best the clabbered milk, lumpy and watery. "It's the peasant in me," she boasted. Every one of the guests smacked his lips at sight of the pancakes, both meaty blood pancakes and *blini*, heaped with sour cream, and caviar.

No, the day was not long as it was in the north countries. Night crept in, but no one noticed. Torches, tall flares stuck into the ground, made day of night for the revelers, along with fountains of red stars, white stars, blue stars, and bursts of light flashing from nowhere and on the instant gone. Michael slept in the arms of his loving Granny. The rest spread themselves on the ground and sang, and the stirring birch leaves sang with them the song of Finland, followed by the anthem of Sweden.

The doctor rose.

Sorrow had left its lines on that face of the doctor's, and to Sigrid, as he stood there towering above all with his six-feet-three, or more, of body—in spite of his dignity, the stateliness of him—he seemed like a little boy. She felt a sudden urge to put her arms around him to comfort him.

"Immigrants," he said slowly, "like Taina and Granny and the Yinglings and the pastor and me"—his head was bowed, but only for an instant; then it raised and he stood as at military attention, head high. "Oh, I stand and sing 'The Star-Spangled Banner' feeling as deeply as any one of you who were born here in America—and as sincerely—but, even as I say the words, deep within me I cannot forget the words of 'Wilhelmus van Nassauen'." With voice full and strong he sang the song of Holland.

After the song, silence. Sigrid looked up into the sky. So this was the way immigrants felt; no wonder her father's and mother's eyes had glowed when they sang, "Du Gamla, Du Fria!"

But poor Louis, no glow was in his eyes; he sat there downcast. Why, and with friends gathered in his honor? Yet she could guess. At the completion of each country's song she had seen him open his mouth as if to begin one, then hang his head and close his lips tightly together. She tried to catch Jack's eye; but Nico had read her mind. Already he was uncoiling his long legs, almost as long as his father's now. With his finger raised as a baton he called the "chorus" to join in "O Tannenbaum!—Oh, Hemlock Tree!"

"Thank you!" Louis' eyes were overflowing. *"Danke schoen!"*

"Louis!" There was terror in Taina's voice, and she looked about, as a trapped animal, going to the birch saplings, spreading them, peering out into the night. "Not to speak German, Louis—the song, it was enough—"

"Oh"—Sigrid laughed—"I learned that German song in grammar school!" And in an effort to put Taina at ease again, "What a conglomeration of nationalities we have here, Irish, Finnish, German, Swedish, Dutch—"

Again the doctor rose, and included them all in the wide sweep of his arm. "This—this is what America *is!*"

America. Full hearts gave thanks to God for America.

Full throats gave forth the song natives and immigrants had learned to love,

"Oh, say can you see, by the dawn's early light—"

and eyes were full as they finished,

"Oh, thus be it ever when freeman shall stand
  Between their loved homes and the war's desolation."

War. The Fourth of July, echoing war.

Sigrid pitched do, mi, and sol. The men took the do, and hummed it; the women took the mi and hummed. Nico took the bass. The ones who did not know the words followed the refrain, humming as best they could,

"We are tenting tonight
      On the old camp ground,
  Give us a song to cheer
      Our weary hearts—"

"Weary hearts," Dr. van Vlaardingen interrupted by repeating, and they stopped singing at the pain in his voice. "Not necessarily English hearts, nor German hearts, but human hearts!"

The flares burned low. To misty eyes the cookstove became a giant cannon, the birch trees were a circle of tents in the half-light. Beyond, the foliage of poplar trees fluttered and shone in the torchlight but held mysterious shadows in their depths, as choked voices harmonized,

"We are tired of war
      On the old camp ground—"

Only Nico was able to finish,

"Dying tonight, dying tonight,
  Dying on the old camp ground."

"Oh, God!" His father paced the grass. "What is to become of nations? *Can* America stay out of the war?"

It seemed such a natural thing that in this moment all should want to pray, each in his own way. The dead calm

was broken when, with a sudden gust of wind, in the
western sky such a pyrotechnic display as none had ever
before witnessed tore the sky: ragged, jagged streaks and
sheets of lightning ripped the heavens, then hung as a
burst of glory at the edge of a heavy black cloud; and
Sigrid burst into the song,

> "Mine eyes have seen the glory
>   Of the coming of the Lord—"

but stopped short at hearing the doctor's anguished cry,
"Can even the Lord keep the god of war from striking at
America now?"

14

Chastened and tired, the women cleared the remains of the feast; the men piled chairs on top of the picnic table and spread a tarpaulin over all, against the rain sure to come before morning. Dread, the dread of war, heavied their footsteps as the neighbors went to their homes.

"Can the United States keep out of the war?" That question crowded all else from Sigrid's mind as days went on. Only by voting for a Republican, the doctor assured her. But the posters were so sure: "Vote for Wilson! He kept us out of war! *He'll keep us out of war!*"

The pastor was a Republican, too, but not Hattie Allspaugh, who shouted, "Vote for Wilson, he'll keep us out of war!"

Now, on the night of November 7, 1916, in Chicago, Republicans and Democrats alike, west siders turned their faces toward the east, south siders toward the north, north siders toward the south. All eyes were focused on that spot in the sky, over downtown Chicago, under which the Tribune Building stood. Holding their breaths, all waited for the first sign of the election returns.

No voting populace, the *Tribune* had announced, should be expected to have to wait until extra papers could be set up, printed, and distributed, at such a momentous time in the history of Americans, and so it had planned an ingenious way to broadcast the early returns of the presidential election.

"Pretty fine of them, I'd say," Dr. van Vlaardingen said warmly. "Because this is bound to cut their sales of extra papers."

Sigrid looked up, for it was in the sky the returns would appear. A huge searchlight mounted on the roof of the Tribune Building at Dearborn and Madison streets would signal to the city and surrounding territory the news of

125

the contest. As long as the vote for president was in doubt a clear white beam would be shown, pointing straight toward the zenith. Any apparent swing to the Republican, Hughes, would be marked by a change of the stationary beam from white to green. If President Wilson led, the beam would turn red. When the election of either candidate was assured, the beam of light would be lowered and would circle the horizon. A steady, level sweep would mean that Hughes had won. A zigzag sweep would indicate that the country had re-elected Woodrow Wilson.

In Calico Row eyes waited, not only men's eyes, but the eyes of women, those of children who would report to schoolteachers of the lights they saw to announce the election of a president of the United States, and the eyes of immigrants who, not yet, were entitled to write their preference down. The neighbors were gathered in the streets, waiting. Sigrid looked about, now, at the familiar scene.

Perhaps the community might better have been named Calico Rows, for there were street after street lined with rows of the cottages, all built after the same blueprint but each painted a different color, gray with white trim, white with gray trim, salmon, brown, barn red with trim of startling white, shades of green from light to dark to chartreuse, light yellow, and a yellow that was almost orange. Occasionally the plan had been reversed, so that the front door and the dormer were to the left as one viewed a house, instead of to the right as most were. But that was their only structural difference.

It was in this same spot she had stood so many years ago watching the northern lights. She had been proud of her father that night! When the heavens had burst forth into wild flame, fear had struck at the hearts of suburbanites until her father had silenced the hysterical screaming of those to whom the sight meant the "end of the world." He had outlined the scientific explanation of that electrical display of nature, and told them of his homeland where he had grown to know the aurora borealis, as his mother had taught him to call the northern lights.

Sigrid's fingers played over the necklace of wrinkled berries, and her eyes looked far—far beyond the site of the Tribune Building—a half a world away—as a shaft of light came, piercing the sky.

She felt an arm slip about her waistline and turned brusquely, only to return Jack's embrace and stare at the beam that pointed upward. It was not white, meaning that the vote for president was in doubt. It was *green!*

"I'm going to collect my bets!" Jack shrieked in delight, brushing her cheek with a kiss. "It's going to be Hughes!" And he was lost in the crowd.

Hoarse whispers picked up and repeated what he had said, "That means that Hughes is leading!" But in the main the crowd was silent. She saw that it was disappointment dumbed the Democrats, and that even the Progressives who had turned to Hughes when Teddy Roosevelt decided to support the regular Republican candidate stood without cheering, tense. Was it that they, and even the Republicans, were afraid? Did they, too, hear little voices deep inside of them speaking, "Wilson and *peace* with honor," "Hughes with Roosevelt and war"? She put her hands over her ears. Still she heard, "This is no ordinary presidential election year when at most a change affects our daily lives by having our postmaster kicked out of his job at change of administration; this is a year when the election decides whether we'll be mowing our own back yards or mowing down men on a battlefield."

"It can't be true! We wanted Wilson! He kept us out of war!" a mother screamed. "I've got four boys! I wanted Wilson! He's the only one who'd keep us out of war!"

Sigrid buried her face in her hands, until someone cried, "What's the matter with all you Republicans? Haven't we got the courage of our convictions? 'Republicans and war!' is only the Democrats' way of electioneering!" Then with the rest of the Republicans she cheered as the words suddenly awakened them to the good taste of victory. As they cheered, children danced, and far into the night the steady sweep of the beam circled the horizon, telling that the election of Mr. Hughes was assured. Extra papers came: Mr. Hughes had carried the populous states of the East. By midnight the paper which Sigrid bought told that earlier in the evening Mr. Wilson, himself, had conceded the Republican victory.

Came a shout, "You Democrats may as well pay your election bets *right now!*"

It was a sight she would not soon forget: big, burly Patrick O'Reilly, the policeman, trundling Dr. van Vlaardingen in a wheelbarrow; nor would she forget the sight of Nico laying peanuts on a chalk line on the sidewalk, for the O'Brien family—twelve strong, counting Mr. and Mrs. —to push along with their noses to the corner of the block!

Wednesday's *Tribune* greeted her with the headline, "HUGHES LEADS IN HOT FIGHT." But the day lengthened; returns from the West came straggling in, and with them startling news. The votes for Wilson were piling up. Returns came from California, and the tide was turned. Maybe Mr. Wilson had been re-elected, after all? By Thursday it was certain that he had.

Her candidate had lost. But this was the way she had learned was the American way, the will of the majority was the one to which she would be loyal; she hated a poor loser; let her think it was just as well. Thinking of "Wilson and peace," let her think it might be better this way.

Thursday evening saw the doctor good-naturedly pushing the big policeman around the block in the wheelbarrow while a crowd followed, laughing; saw Jack returning the bet money he had collected; saw Nico skin his nose while using it to push a peanut down the chalk line on the rough cement sidewalk. But some of the fun seemed to be gone from the paying off of election bets. . . .

The winter seemed longer than a winter should be, for only three weeks had passed. It was Thanksgiving Day. Frosted patterns spread over windowpanes, blue shadows lay in contrast to the golden-orange tinge of sunshine on frosty crystaled yards as Sigrid walked with Granny and Michael and the pastor toward the Heinebach's home, answering their invitation to dinner. Icy branches of the trees tinkled faintly, with crystal melodies, like Japanese glass chimes on a summer porch. But in Taina's little house there was no coldness, only warmth. True, it was a little steamy, not only from the cooking, but from the steam bath in which Taina had indulged: no Finnish person would come to a feast without first going to the *sauna;* but it was not a Finnish menu prepared by Taina for this day!

"Have some more turkey? White meat or dark? Eat up! The doctor brought the gobbler, and he wants us to eat!" Louis carved and passed.

"Tack för maten," lisped by a sleepy boy, soon to be

two years old, was the only hint so far of the ancestries of the friends gathered for this truly American day, Thanksgiving. The guests leaned back in their chairs, surfeited; the men slid belt buckles along to the next notch.

Thanksgiving Day. They sat and pieced together its story, as the native-born had learned it in the schools. The story was the same, of 1621 and 1916, Thanksgiving Day, when all the people in the land, with voices raised, recognized God's blessings and gave thanks for His goodness, for bountiful harvests, for friends, and for peace.

Peace!

A day for rejoicing, yes. A day for eating. But a day for prayer. Pastor Bedell spoke, and his voice trembled. "Let us pray, in thanksgiving, silently. And let us pray for peace."

Each, in his own way, bowed to pray, fulfilling the meaning of this day. Each, in his own way, thought of the war, coming closer, like a raging forest fire.

At sight of Hattie Allspaugh's lips opening, Sigrid choked the gasp that came. This was no night to talk about the election. With the lively diversity of political opinion housed in these neighbors, this day might well end in quarreling if Aunt Hattie got started; she was always one to spark an argument. "Please, Granny, before Michael falls asleep in your arms, tell us the tale of Tam."

"Aye, Sigrid. 'Twas on the moors o'Scotland." The Irish woman's voice rolled, and the r's were broad and thick. "And them dew-dampened—oh, the mists, they were so heavy that wet dripped from the air as well as from the tree branches." She loved the telling of stories, and it showed in her telling. "As wet was the air as the gentle river flowing—flowing—then, was it a tinkling cowbell the tipsy Tam O'Shanter heard, that made him stop to listen?"

Only Michael's rapid breathing made accompanying sound, and Sigrid noted that it was not only she who stopped eating after-dinner mints the better to listen to Granny tell of how the witches nearly caught the tipsy Tam! Then, like a shot, Michael leaped from Granny's lap to hers. *"Rida Ranka* me, will you, Sigree?"

She laughed. "What a combination of American and Irish and Swedish you are! You're getting awfully heavy for this, but I guess Granny will be glad for the rest."

As she rode the boy on her foot she saw Granny reach for the thin slip of a holiday paper, scan it, take off her spectacles and stare into space, wipe the glasses on the hem of her apron, put them back on her nose bridge, and read. The spectacles came off again. As if there were no one else in the room, she looked upward toward the ceiling. "It's that glad I am, Pat," she said solemnly, "that you bought a cemetery lot big enough for me, too."

"Why, Granny!" Everyone in the room leaned forward, stopping the crunching of nuts and munching of mints.

"Here it says, well, it says a poor widow woman is going to be buried in the potter's field tomorrow."

"No." A deep silence fell.

"Yes. It says, like this, 'Mrs. Gertrude Shaughnessy, eccentric recluse who lived for over forty years in a shack next to the railroad tracks—'"

Sigrid set Michael down so she could take the paper from Granny. The letters in the filler at the bottom of the page grew and grew before her eyes: "Aged recluse found dead."

"Why," she stammered, "that's Crazy Gerty!"

"Did you know her?" Nico came to stand beside her, to read for himself, but she had dropped the paper to the floor.

"Really, no. But my parents knew her, and I grew up with knowledge of who she was. Mother told me she saved Pa for her once, when he would have gone to the Yukon, except for Crazy Gerty. It seems that in helping the poor soul home one bitter cold night he got sick from overexposure, so he couldn't follow the 'gold rush.'" She looked around, sending a plea to each to understand. "Will you excuse me? I have to go. It says 'tomorrow' she will be buried—so I'll have to go now—"

"You can't go out tonight." Jack jumped up. "It's too cold!"

"Where are you going?" came every other voice but three.

The doctor knew. With an unpredictable maturity of understanding, Nico knew. "Let me drive you. The weather *is* bad. All right, Dad?" Expecting an affirmative answer, he did not look toward his father to see that he, too, had risen and followed Sigrid with hungry eyes.

Granny knew. She followed the two young people to

the door as the doctor resignedly resumed his seat. "The teapot," she whispered. "You know where it is, in the china closet. Take what's in it, too."

"I'll go along, then, Sigrid." Jack went for his coat.

He might have been a stranger, the way she looked at him. "No, Jack," she said sadly, "there is no need for you to come."

Nico kept the engine running as he waited for her. Through her lighted window he could see that she went to the shelf where she kept her mechanical bank. Though he could not see, he knew she slid the bottom open.

There was a rattle of coins as Sigrid shook them out; there was a little clink as she piled coin on coin to count them. Wordless, she rode with Nico to the North Side; they found the old tarpaper-covered shanty alongside the tracks. A lighted lamp sat on the window sill. "Please let me go in alone?"

"I'll wait here."

Inside she met old Mr. Ginsberg, from whose "rags-and-ol'-iron" wagon her mother had bought most of her furniture. He sat, chin cupped in his hands, on the edge of a sagging white iron bed. His watery eyes shone in the poor light when she told him she was Ellen's daughter.

"So vell I remember when you were born, oh, so vell. Such a fine mother as you had! I lost track of her. I did not know that she died." He ran his coat sleeve under his nose. "And here you are, her daughter. I lost track of Mrs. Shaughnessy, too. It is the great remorse I know, now, that I did not find time to keep the poor woman in my thoughts after I moved away to a stylisher neighborhood."

Together, with Nico driving them, they found the morgue and the slab on which Gertrude Shaughnessy was laid out.

"Togedder ve pay."

Sigrid pressed Mr. Ginsberg's hand; yes, together they would see to it that Mrs. Shaughnessy was put to rest in consecrated ground, and a Mass said for her. There would be a respectable funeral for Mrs. Edward Shaughnessy whose given name was not Gerty, but Gertrude.

"Somehow," Sigrid said to Nico as he left her at her front door, "I feel so close, so good and close to my parents tonight, Thanksgiving night."

"God bless you, Sigrid." He pressed her arm. "Good night."

Slowly she walked into the house. Granny's teapot, the one that had been a fourth full of nickels to help pay for a set of false teeth, was empty. So was the Salvation Army lassie bank. The wide sea, which had narrowed as the bank filled, had grown wide again.

Sweden was far away.

Had the re-election of Woodrow Wilson been less because he had "kept the country out of war," than a decision "not to swap horses while crossing the stream"? Was that "stream" war? Republicans and Democrats alike suffered qualms, and Sigrid trembled with the multitude, until on April sixth of the next year the answer came.

"WAR DECLARED!" the headlines blared, in letters inches tall.

"God help us," Granny begged, echoing Sigrid's prayer. Looking at Granny, how she wished that she could draw. There in that face was the fear of war, a woman's solicitude for men who would go to the battlefield, the discouragement of a Christian—the foundation of whose thought is peace—all there, written in the face of Granny O'Toole. And yet, transcending all, there was that aura of hope which only faith can give.

If only she could draw. She needed that picture, to carry with her wherever she went, to remind her that no hate showed in Granny's face. It was hard not to hate. She raised her voice with others',

> "I will not breathe
> Where God's clean air
> Is soiled by a German tongue!"

She repeated, "Don't say *German* silver, people will think you are a Hun! Call it nickel silver now!" There was a certain joy in marching in parades, in helping with Liberty Loan drives, in singing of loyalty. And in damning "the Germans." But could she be loyal to her country only by being disloyal to her friends? How about the Schmotzers? And Louis Heinebach? It seemed that war touched familiar things, and changed them: sauerkraut, served now, came to the table as Liberty Cabbage. Even the funnies: overnight "The Katzenjammer Kids" became "The Shenanigans." And people changed. People threw rotten eggs against the swinging sign at Taina's gate, splashed and splattered the name, "Louis H. Heinebach"!

Louis chose a new name, "Bill," to be known by; but not one that others chose for him. "Hun!" "Slacker!" they called him; and strewed yellow feathers in front of his gate.

Now he was gone, enlisted in the Army. "He loved America," Taina cried. "As much as I—as you, Sigrid!" But "Hun" was the name that had sent the man who had been "Louis" into the infantry, to go across the ocean and fight his blood brothers.

Then, on the twentieth of July, the draft was conducted in Washington. Numbers ranging from 1 to 10,500, written in red ink on small slips of paper, were enclosed in black celluloid capsules and were mixed in a large glass bowl. If there were only some way that the eyes of the nation, not merely the thoughts, could be on the Secretary of War, Mr. Baker, who blindfolded drew out the first capsule! Everyone in the whole country knew that number, now, that he had drawn, Number 258. After the sixteenth hour of drawing more than a million men had been drafted by number, and one of the first of the numbers to be called was Jack's.

Sigrid mourned: the bitterest of all the results of war was that it changed people. Jack, who had been so refined in his speech, said now of Nico, "Lucky bastard, of course he won't have to go; they're going to exempt guys who are studying to be doctors." And, "It would be my foul luck to have been born so I'm 'between the ages of twenty-one and thirty-one.' "

"You should be proud"—halfheartedly she tried to console him—"to be able to fight for the cause of freedom."

"Ha! Proud to have your guts shot out?"

She shuddered. What had gotten into Jack? Still, she did not have to ask herself, for she knew: panic. At thought of the battlefield he was afraid. And who would not be?

Only in small ways could she help the boys who were fighting, and so she no longer pared apples before making salad or a sauce. Mr. Herbert Hoover called on all Allied peoples to conserve food. "But it takes us women, doesn't it, Granny, to see that it makes a prettier salad or a more colorful applesauce if the red skins are left on?" No longer did she peel the rhubarb down, so that from the stalks came thin curls like shavings of pine that had used to come from her father's plane. But she would have no more rhubarb sauce until sugar was less scarce; the thought of it made her jaw glands hurt. Sugar was needed for the boys "Over There." Still, the plants had to be cultivated. Twilight came and blended into evening as she wielded the hoe. It was getting too dark to work; she picked up the trowel and scraped the hoe clean. That feeling, of being watched, came over her, and she turned sharply.

"Jack!" He stood in the glare of the porch light.

"Sigrid." He pulled her to her feet. "You *will* marry me, right away, before I have to go?" In desperation he pleaded.

The way he said, "have to go," cut through her. Conscription was an ugly word. Her father had hated the word! Did it do to all men what it was doing to Jack? Would she be any different if she were a man—conscripted? She pitied Jack.

"Be my wife before I have to go?"

She forgot the pastor's words as Jack crushed her to him, so that her breath was lost, and she sank against him. She felt little, felt as Ellen must have felt with her Carl, secure in the protecting arms of a man who loved her, who would take care of her.

"Yes, Jack, yes. I'll marry you—before you have to go—"

Now she knew she would wear the little golden bridal crown, the *brudkrona*, that beautiful treasure, the crown of solid gold, worn by every daughter of her mother's family through all the generations. With Jack as her groom, it would top a filmy white veil on her head.

Not every family in Sweden was proud possessor of such an heirloom. "Indeed not!" her mother had declared so often, excusably boasting of her grandfather's being a *Rikstagsman*. It was from him had come the Viking ring. Learned man that he was, that grandfather who had been representative to Sweden's National Assembly, had never learned that his "little pet, Elin," had become a servant girl on her arrival in the new country. "Ellen," she had called herself in America. But, Sigrid thought now, the

Swedish version of the name seems to have fitted her best. It fitted her memory best. From now on it would be as "Elin" that she would think of her mother. And Pa. His name seemed more rightly "Karl" than "Carl."

Such courage as Elin must have had, to come alone to a new land while still not much more than a child. Only fifteen years old, and hired out as a maid in a big rooming house in New York City! Less than five feet tall —such fortitude to make the ninety pounds of her do the work of servant girl, office clerk to her dentist employer, and nurse and companion to his consumptive wife!

Such pride, too, as Elin must have had, not allowing even her father to know her whereabouts until she had become what she considered a success. Twenty-two years without so much as mailing a postal card to her own father! How could she have done that to him, she who was always so kind to everyone?

"My mother could never have yearned for the closeness of family the way I have." Sigrid shook her head. Or had she? Could it be that which had been the great lack in Elin's life? To have made her the half-sad, girlishly forlorn creature she had been? She had always been so proud, too, of having a golden crown as family heirloom; so proud of having a daughter who, one day, would wear it at her wedding.

She looked up. A song sparrow lit upon the telephone wire, clasping it sharply, making it dance, bringing consternation to the pairs of his English brethren as the wire trembled in up-and-down motion; and such scolding as went on before some of the couples flew away! But more waited for the wire to steady itself.

Three accented notes came from the songbird's throat, followed by a medley of clear and joyous whistles; again came the accented notes, a reply from the bushes, and Mr. Song Sparrow dived for the tangle, pumping his tail up and down in characteristic motion.

If only her mother could be here to witness her marriage! If only Elin could see her wearing the golden crown!

With the closing of her eyes she could see the mellow gold of it, six-pointed, the points flaring outward and each tip ending with a little golden ball; snub-ended five-pointed stars, tiny gold hearts dangling from their arches, and six oblong-cut aquamarines, the semi-precious stones standing for hope and happiness and love. "The blue of those stones," her mother had said, in singing tones, "remember always that blue is the color of honor, and this is a virgin's crown, a crown denoting purity, to be removed from the bride's head on her wedding night by the man who is her husband."

Only the rich families in Sweden owned such a dear and costly object. Still, many a peasant girl had been able to follow the lovely custom of wearing one because of some person's bequeathing the family *brudkrona* to the parish church where any maiden might borrow the use of it on her wedding day. But woe to the one who boldly posed as chaste, but who in truth had given her flesh, for the stones would then take on a cloudy look, and the promised hope and happiness and love would most certainly be changed to lucklessness, and the bride would fall on evil.

"A fine way to teach a daughter to be good." Sigrid smiled at memory of her mother, who had brought the crown to America without the knowledge of the customs officials. For her own gentle mother in Sweden had baked it inside a big round loaf of brown bread for the willful daughter who would choose to go to America rather than attend school to learn to be a midwife, according to her father's stern command.

The remembered voice of Elin gave way to three accented notes, followed by a medley of clear and joyous whistles. How dearly her little mother had loved Pa, the big brash Karl. Whatever else there may not have been in that marriage, ease, or material success, there had been love. Had her mother been sure of her love *before* she took the marriage vow?

The marriage vow. . . . She and Jack would be married in Messiah Church. The dear old pastor would be the one to read and perform the sacrament; and it would be the next best thing to having her parents there, to see his white tabs shining against the black of his suit, framing his dented chin.

"Why don't you wear gloves, Sigrid?"

Surprised, she looked up, then rocked back on her heels and smiled at her good friend. For once she could look up at him, she who stood so much taller than the pastor. His loose-hanging jowls swayed as he shook his head in looking at her dirt-covered hands.

She spread them. "They aren't beautiful, are they?" Ruefully, then, she looked at their palms, their backs. "But I do like to dig in the earth with my bare hands. I love the feel of the soil. With gloves on, it's different, I seem to lose something."

"As I have always said, you are a real dirt gardener." He smiled broadly. "Not only do you have green thumbs, your fingers all are green, every one of them. It seems you can make anything grow."

Now she smiled, a teasing smile. "Was it not my own pastor who, only last Sunday, read from Corinthians, 'I have planted, Apollos watered; but God gives the increase'?"

The pastor's face lighted up. He wished all of his parishioners listened to his sermon's as intently as Sigrid!

Frog music hung over the nearby swamp, and now, as the wind shifted to the north, it brought a crescendo from a thousand bulbous throats. "Oh, Pastor," her voice sang in unison, "Jack says he will take me to Sweden; he says he wants to take me 'home.'"

"To *live?*"

"Oh, no! On a honeymoon."

One eyebrow lifted, and the pastor turned his face away. "Let me help you." He pushed up his cuffs and pulled away the little wheelbarrow filled with winter's debris and dumped it on top of the compost heap back of the full tall lilac screen near the alley fence. Returning, he laid his hand on Sigrid's head and tilted her face to his. "If, Sigrid, you know you can take this young man to your grandmother in Sweden and say, 'Farmor, *out of all men in America,* this is my choice,' then—then—"

For a fleeting instant she hesitated before answering, "Yes."

"You have my blessings, then, and God's. But please, please, will you wait until he comes back from the war? So many things could—"

"It is too late for that. I have promised Jack to marry him before he has to go. I've promised—"

She would have them all, "Something old, something new, something borrowed, and something blue." Now, after all the years of longing, she would go to Jake's Pawnshop and ask the price of the blue cloth hanging there. She would make her wedding wrap of it. Again there were some coins in the mechanical bank.

The dingy shop looked dingier than ever for the low gaslight in the rear, in front of the safe, was not burning to make a bulbous silhouette of the three gilt balls hung over the front door. The shop was closed: Jake had enlisted, and was gone away to war.

She set her jaw. She would try to see the good in this. With the shop closed, nobody else would be able to buy it either. She would have to wear something else of blue on her wedding day, over the dress she was going to make out of the old white quilt that had been preserved by loving owners from the time of early colonial American settlers until at last it had been discarded—worn thin through all the years, but its texture still showing handstitched woodland ferns and doves on the wing—and she had found it for sale in the new Ye Olde Antiques Shoppe that sold things so much cheaper than Jake's Pawnshop.

She bent over the dining-room table, lengthened to its full size with three extra leaves, and spread the pieces of a Butterick pattern on the quilt; laid the pattern on so as to cut around the stubborn spot of rust which would not come out with lemon juice and salt and sunshine, then held the pieces up against her before the mirror.

She wished that the Schmotzers did not choose to stay so much to themselves these war days; she would have liked to have Emilie help her make her wedding dress.

She was going to be Jack's bride; and when the war was over he would have saved enough money to take her to Sweden on their honeymoon.

Swedish Interlude

"Such a thick letter as this one is, come from Karl's daughter." Mor Sigrid's fingers held the envelope between them, pressing as against a padded quilt to show its springiness. "It shames me when I think of the one-page letters I have sent."

For a long time she stood silent, holding the envelope. Yes, she had written letters to her granddaughter, but poor excuses for letters had they been. She had not even made mention yet of the way every one of the family had rallied to her plea that they drop a bit of money into the earthen jug over there in the corner. Maybe, maybe it was just as well. It would take long to save so much as to be sufficient for a passage ticket from America to Norden.

There had never been much money at Norden. There was so little to bring money in, so little market for the things they had. But they were rich in other ways. Stoutly defending her home place to herself, in her mind she named over her riches: plenty to eat, fish from the sea, grain from the ground, birds and fowl from the sky. There were the strong walls of house and barn, protection from the weather be it hot, cold, or stormy. There was the roof; no rain or snow had ever entered through that thatch. There were the lands, pasture for sheep who in turn gave warm wool clothing; for cows that gave the butter, cheese, and milk; for horses that pulled the plows and wagons. Yes, Norden's folk were rich! But so poor in money, they; so poor in coins.

"Read what the young Sigrid writes," a happy-sounding voice came, from where the wheel chair stood, to break the silence. "Then we may all write a page or two and send even a thicker letter in return."

"Always the one to think of a fine way to do." Big Johann went across the room and patted his namesake on the shoulder.

Mor Sigrid's brows knitted: not yet had she come upon a way to find a work that Johann could do and not rely on hands and fingers.

They drew together, the three of them, and young Patrik came from the fields to join them, to listen to the news from America. Mor Sigrid slid her chair along the floor to make a place for his: Patrik Bror, it was, who had stayed at home to run the farm when all of her other able-bodied children had found their livings, or moved with their spouses, elsewhere. Patrik was born after Karl left home, and Patrik was thirty years old already. It had been long. . . .

With difficulty she drew her eyes from seeing far, so far away as thirty years ago, to bring them to rest on the words of the letter beginning, "My Dearest Farmor and Family." Then she looked, and looked again, before she said excitedly, "Sigrid is to become a wife, it says here!" And, "His name is called Jack in America, but he was born Enoch Yingling—*från Småland!*"

They must interrupt the reading while Patrik fetched the map of the United States. There, at that place where Johann's crochet needle pointed, was where their Sigrid would be wed! "But read on!"

"Aye." The mother's eyes read faster than her tongue. "Aye, but listen to *this!* 'Jack says he will bring me to Sweden on our honeymoon.'" In her excitement she half-rose from her chair.

She settled in the chair again. It was as if God had spoken to her through young Sigrid's words. Her eyes roved to take in sight of the earthen jug. Even by the time of the ending of the war, when travel could be resumed, could the family have saved enough coins for a passage

ticket from America? Aye, this was God's work! If the
young Jack was to bring her to Sweden for the wedding
journey, Sigrid would be coming without the use of the
moneys in the jug. She, herself, would be able to use
them. Mor Sigrid's eyes flew now to rest on the floor beside the wheel chair. The ball of linen thread, restricted
from rolling by being imprisoned inside a little china teapot, scarcely made a sound, its movement was so slight.
Her eyes followed the thread coming from out the teapot's spout. So slowly it came, and traveled to where
gnarled and stiffened fingers fed it to a hook.

Now she knew. In Sigrid's words a message, somehow,
had come. It was for her son, Johann, not for the American granddaughter, the coins in the jug had accumulated.
But how should they be used? How?

Her lips finished reading the letter. Her head hurt from
thinking. Her eyes saw the corner fireplace, surely she
must be seeing it, and the old cradle with the rockers
running lengthwise instead of sidewise, the rugs on the
floor, but it was as if those reminders of daily living were
not there; only did she see Johann's hands. And above
them, a smile.

As if she were feeling her way, she could have been
blind the way she walked, she left the big room and
walked out into the dooryard. The frail aspen tree whispered a message. Her hands clutched at her temples.
What—what did it say?

The trees, the grass, the sky, all reflected that smile of
Johann's. How big could a human being be, to smile in
the face of what Johann saw before him?

As a sleepwalker finds his way, she walked to the
water's edge.

The lovely sky spoke, aye, of Johann; but always the
sea would remind her of Karl. In Johann's place, how he
would be raging! Just as the sea could do, and ofttimes
did. That book she would write of Karl, if she could
write a book, would be of both the sea and him; both, yet
only of one, for in Karl was the story of the sea. Broad,
gentle, knowing, true, and wild. "But one does not lose
his love for the sea because in a storm it lashes angrily
against the shore." Her head bent. "Nor does one love
it less because sometimes it kills the one who loves it
most, throwing the body aside carelessly." So had she

known, even when Karl had gone. Better, she knew it now, after the passing of the years.

She stood now on the outmost rock, stretching her hands toward where the water met the sky. "Ah, Karl! You were my eldest son. The eldest always deemed the wisest in any family, if you were here mayhap you could tell me what to do for Johann."

Waves came, and broke, and rolled over her shoes and wet the hems of her garments. Sea wind blew her clothing against her, showing the shape of her body, whipping her skirts now so that her legs showed to the knees, drying the skirt hems.

How happy Morfar had been to learn she had named Karl for him! To think of the sea, to see it, was to think of Morfar, too. If he were here—then—then he would tell her what to do for Johann! No longer were the hems dry, for the garments she wore swirled in the water as she knelt on the rock.

Softly, at first, the sea spoke. As a child does, raising its voice to attract a mother's attention, the swish and swirl spoke louder; each wave that came, each swell, intensified its tone, mounting on the scale. Her bowed head raised. This was the voice of God! Of the sea, and of Morfar, yes; but this was the answer to her prayers, hearing Morfar—as if yesterday were now—"I hope that at least one of your sons, See'ri, will make his life's work of the sea."

She ran. Wet soles slipping over the rocks, wet garments flapping against her in the wind, she ran to the dwelling. Inside the door she calmed herself and walked in easy manner to her chair. No care now for the dripping salt water to the clean floor; no matter, such as that, for she had the answer.

"This young man, Jack," she heard Patrik say, "so Sigrid says here, is an automobile mechanic. Knowing nothing of that kind of work, still it seems to me I should like to learn to be such a one." He laughed. "If it brings wealth enough for ocean travel."

"Nay," she countered. "If I could choose a life's work, I should not spend my time studying such."

"And what?" her husband asked kindly, trying to keep his gaze from the soaked skirts. "What should my See'ri study?"

She loved to hear his soft, colloquial pronunciation of her name. It had been Morfar's pet name for her; Big Johann had picked it up from him. "Always"—she wore a pensive smile—"and I suppose it was at least partly because of Morfar and his work, I have loved the sea. My work, if I could choose, being I never could be an able-bodied seaman"—deliberately she looked away from the place where the wheel chair was—"would nevertheless have to do with sea life. I would study—" Her voice became sad. "It was Morfar's wish and hope that one of my sons should choose a work that would involve the sea. But such was not to be: that is a cross for me to bear, that Morfar, who was so good and generous to us all, should not have had his wish."

"I," crippled Johann laughed, but looked at her as if to bore through both the soul and body of her, "I volunteer! With Herman Nikodemus the kind of farmer who draws with a pencil, and Patrik a farmer who draws with the plow, there is none other. Name the work—"

She cut him short. "As for me, as I started to say, I would learn—"

Big Johann beckoned to Patrik, unseen by Mor Sigrid, and together they went out into the dooryard.

The mother walked haltingly to the wheel chair. "Do not, oh, please, Johann, do not be light with me; do not belittle the thing I said. For I want this more than anything before in my long life."

"To study, you mean?" How tender his look was.

"Aye. I want to use the money in the earthen jug to buy proper books—"

"For *you* to study from?" His eyes danced.

"To study the laws of the sea. To study the laws connected with navigation and commerce, and—sinkings—and—"

"Splendid!" A gnarled hand rested on her wrinkled one. "I can see, already, my mother standing proud at having passed the examinations, and being admitted to the bar!"

She shot a quick look at him. "But, but you must help me, Johann. Without you, studying with me, helping me, I could never—Oh, will you, Johann? Will you?"

The smile he wore changed, but it was still a smile. *"Min mor,"* he spoke with untold tenderness, "I sit here now and think of the time when you told me it was in answer to my wish 'to sit and crochet all the day long' that I was made to sit so. I think of the time you pointed out the King on the playing card. Oh, no, it would not have been like you to have said, 'Here, copy this, Johann. It will help you to take your mind off of—of—It will help you to while away the lonely hours if you will copy this.'

"No. You found a way to make me think it was a blessing come to me that I must sit; you found a way to make me think that it was I who thought of doing the crocheting. 'Look closely at the cards, Johann,' you said. 'Do you see they are not drawn with lines? I never noticed that before.' And I asked, 'How do you mean, Mama?' And you answered, 'See, the picture is printed on the cards by using tiny little squares of color. See? That line looks curved, but if you look real close you can see it is done with those tiny squares.'

"I looked, and then I saw. Oh, I remember to this day the way you looked at me, searchingly, when you said, 'It is like filet crocheting.'

"Min mor, you looked at me again in that same way just now!" Quickly he continued, not allowing her time to speak. "But I asked you at that time, 'Do you mean I could make a king like this in crocheting?' And what did you say? *'You* could, yes.' "

His eyes were brimming now. "You drew a pattern for me, and I copied the King. That was the beginning."

He reached and took both of her hands in his, as best he could. "I do not say, Mor, that I realized then what you did for me. No. But, in looking back, I see. I know. And I know what you are doing now."

She looked up sharply.

"Aye, you do not fool me. I am a man, now, with a man's insight and understanding, a man's comprehension."

"But I have, Johann!" With all of her age, how naïve she was; how could he help but smile at her finishing, "You know I have always wanted to study."

"I know." His smile was broad even as he looked down at his hands. "I can still hold a pencil, and if the day comes when the fingers will not, I can always tie a pencil to the wrist."

"Johann, *don't!*"

"But it is the head that needs to know the law, not the hands. Let us thank God that my brain and head still—"

"Dear, dear Johann!"

"Aye, Mor. There is more in life than lace."

And the lace had been his life! His mother closed her eyes and bit hard against her tongue.

"The young Sigrid," he went on, "she will do well with this mechanic man for husband, that is sure. And, as he will bring her to Norden, yes, Mor, if it will bring even a moment's happiness to you, I shall take the benefit of what books that in the earthen jug will buy. I shall study the maritime law and do my best with it."

Holding his stumpy hands in one of hers, trembling as with the shaking palsy, she raised her head, calling, "Big Johann! Patrik! Where are you? Come! Come! Ready the boat! I go at once to the mainland—to Göteborg!"

"To Göteborg?" The suddenness of it astounded Patrik so that he stood with his jaw dropped and his mouth hanging open. "What for?"

"To buy textbooks! Lawbooks!" She danced to the corner of the big room and picked up the earthen jug.

15

"Please ask your beloved Jack to plan that your wedding journey to Norden shall be in springtime," Sigrid read from her Farmor's letter. "I cannot tell it as it is; you shall have to experience the tremendous surge of spring as it comes, here in the North country, fantastically, so dramatic, so unbelievably beautiful!"

Not slowly, with the gradual opening of flower buds, did the season come to Sweden, but with a spectacular suddenness, coming almost as if the world were a stage and the scenery was being shifted by rolling on a backdrop of spring even as the winter "set" was being rolled away.

Her beloved Jack. Only four days more, and she would marry him.

She barely knew she entered Messiah Church and bowed her head. "Help me to know I love him! Please, God, let my marriage work out well; help me to be a good wife to Jack. Help me to *know* I love him!"

From the empty church she went to the parsonage. "We are having meat balls for supper," she called in the front door. "Why don't you come over and have some with us?"

"You know I shall be glad to come," the pastor answered happily.

Saturday night.

Before time for him to come, with the meat balls simmering in mushroom gravy over a low gas, and Granny and Michael calling on Mrs. O'Leary, she would work in her garden. It was a war garden now, where tomatoes replaced menarda; carrots would give orange color below the place calendulas had caught the color of the sun before war came; beets, and vines of cucumbers and squash drew nourishment from the earth where old-fashioned flowers had heretofore. Every inch of ground must give food; but she would steal space enough to plant the gladiolus bulbs Nico had brought her. "If you stagger their planting," he said, "you can have blooms all summer, way until frost."

She took some of the bulbs from her lap and laid them on the ground, judging how far apart to plant them, when Jack came through the narrow gangway, between the houses, leading from the street.

"Only four more days." He pulled her to her feet. "And you will be my wife." He did not lack words, now, as he planned for the three days they would have together. "And then, while I'm away, you can decide what to do about the boy—"

"The *boy?* What do you mean, 'about the boy'?" One hand held up her skirt, making it a pocket in which the gladiolus bulbs hung. With the other she pushed him from her.

"It's you I want, Sigrid, not the kid and—"

Her face reddened with indignation before it purpled with anger.

"Why, Sigrid, surely you haven't been thinking that Granny and Michael would be living with *us?*"

His words came like a puff of wind to blow the gleed of Sigrid's anger into a blazing, burning coal of rage; she glared at Jack across the few feet of garden.

"Sigrid, listen to me. I only mean—I can't support them, too!"

"I'll keep on working then."

"Oh, no, you won't! A man's wife working! What do you think I am?"

"I'll never leave Granny and Michael—to—How could you *think* such a thing? Why, I was with Michael when he was born! And his mother asked me to take care of him."

"But, Sigrid—"

"Get out of here!" she screamed. "I never want to see you again! Never!"

There he went! He—who looked for kindness from others—he would have her desert Michael and Granny! Let him *go* out of that gangway—for *good!*

That gangway! It was like the little doors on the astronomical clock at Lund, in Sweden, that Pa so often had described to her, like the wings of a stage, with actors coming in and going out of it, as if on cue. She hurled a gladiolus bulb after Jack and hit him on the back. A display of hot anger such as she had always contemned in her father now overpowered her. Such was her rage that she did not notice that the "actors" changed places, and another had come in answer to his cue, an invitation to supper.

Bewildered, sad, half-unbelieving of his own eyes, Pastor Bedell watched her face, watched the shadow grow into a cloud.

No. No! With all of the good that had been passed down from her forebears into this young woman, was she also to inherit such as this?

The loose-hanging jowls shook as he saw the cloud grow darker and watched as that same rage—which, unchecked, had cut like a knife of Swedish steel the ties which had bound her father to his home, his family, his country, and his God—made Sigrid blind as she pitched another bulb and hit him squarely in the eye.

The next morning's sunlight coming through the small colored pieces of stained glass making up the tracery in the rose window made Sigrid's fingers blue, her hand gold, her wrist crimson. Her arm was banded with green and a light yellow, a yellowish-green, and purple. She could not bear to look at them. Her eyelids squeezed tightly together and teardrops fell from between them.

Nor could she bear to look at Pastor Bedell, for those were the colors of his closed and swollen eye. Telling the story of the Man of Uz, using the full book of Job, telling the whole of the philosophical drama, recounting the series of impassioned dialogues culminating in the speech of the Lord out of the whirlwind, taking the whole congregation into the spacious setting in the Golden Age of the patriarchs, he was addressing his sermon, nevertheless —she knew—to her.

"In essence," he said in his gentle voice, "Job's story is all just a simple tale of piety rewarded after great suffering." The common phrase, they had all heard it and all used it, he was sure, "the patience of Job," was the underlying idea. His one open eye looked, now, straight at her, "Patience, *the overcoming of anger*."

He scanned the congregation. "Job, with anger, scorn,

and despair answers the traditional insistence of his friends that his sufferings are a punishment for sin, until the argument is ended by the Voice of the Lord when He says: 'Where wast thou when *I* laid the foundations of the earth?

" 'Wast thou then born?'

" 'Hast thou entered into the treasures of the snow?' "

Her pastor's head shook from side to side, emphasizing his own incapacity of understanding. "And Job, overwhelmed by divine majesty, admits that the problem of evil is too deep for the human mind to solve.

"Magnificent poetry," the pastor described the many verses continuing the questions which Job heard as though spoken by the voice of God. It was as though God were confronting Job with all of the mysteries and marvels of the universe. "And Job *is* overwhelmed with awe, but at the same time his spirit enters into peace."

Job could not understand his own affliction. "But why should he?" Pastor Bedell asked. "Why should any one of us, when there is so much else that is mysterious?" He paused, as if for physical strength to continue, but did continue, "Thus it is that the drama of Job does not present any smooth answer to the question with which it is concerned. It does not explain why the good suffer."

Now he drew in a deep breath; but his rare humor made him go on. "Do you think I speak of myself, and my suffering with this black eye?" A little ripple of laughter answered him; only a little ripple, for they were in church.

"It is not of body pain I speak. The travail of the body is as nothing compared with agony of the mind."

He knew. He understood her so well.

"But,"—his voice was firm—"the story of Job does deny the glib arguments of persons like Job's comforters who explain prosperity or calamity as being weighed out exactly according to man's goodness or his sins." It had always seemed to him, he said, that this was the Book of the Old Testament which opened the way for the New Testament and its picture of Jesus who suffered not for any sins of His own, but for the sins of others, and through His sufferings helped men in a new way to understand the love of God.

She was missing some parts of the summing up in fitting the whole sermon to herself; but now came the concluding words, "With these words from Job I shall pray for you: *'Cast abroad the rage of thy wrath.'*

"Yes, I shall pray for you. But as the Lord tells Job,

> " 'Then will I also confess unto thee
> That *thine own right hand can save thee.'* "

The sermon was ended. Addressed to the whole congregation, but meant to help her. She could not join in the singing for thinking of the thing she had to do: cast out the rage of her wrath. "The acorn does not fall far from the tree," Hattie Allspaugh had said. But in this, with all due respect to Pa, she had to grow to be unlike him.

Her own right hand. Pastor Bedell meant that only she could change herself; only she could thrust out this inherited weakness of uncontrolled temper.

Oh, Pa, if you could know the courage it takes to leave this pew and follow the line to shake the pastor's hand!

Oh, the loyalty of Pastor Bedell, not to incriminate the one who had injured him, but to stand at the exit shaking hands, answering his parishioners' questions by joking about having "bumped into a door!"

"Isn't that what is usually said?" Laughing, he parried the questions, until she extended her hand.

If he turned from her she would not blame him. If he pointed a finger and said, "She—she is the one who—"

But no. He pressed her hand in friendly warmth.

She could not lift her eyes to meet his. "I'm sorry," she stammered.

The pastor stared after her as she tore her hand from his. He was not quite sure what the next communicant said to him, but he awoke to the fact that he had answered, *"Jaså,"* to one who was not Swedish.

Now, as never before, she needed a father to turn to....

Sigrid twirled the Viking ring, polishing its silvery-satin sheen. Her right thumbnail passed along its face, noting the notches around the oval's edge: shallow notches for land conquests, deep notches for conquests on the seas. One space was smooth. Had it been left for her to notch?

That would take strength.

To think of strength was to think of Dr. van Vlaardingen. She had always likened him to a rugged oak tree. He was the only one she could go to, only asking to feel his strength, taking of it what she needed to face her beloved pastor—to face her friends—and tell them she was not going to be married after all.

A million muted hammers on the leaf drums told her it was raining. Unmindful of the rain, only unpleasantly half-conscious of the slushing of her toes inside of her wet shoes, she passed the little house where Granny and Michael awaited her return and went next door and entered the doctor's library.

He found her there, leaning against the doorjamb.

"Sigrid! You are ill?"

Yes, ill. Sick. Heartsick. Too sick to cry.

"What has happened?"

"I've found out that—Oh, Doctor, I can't marry Jack! I don't know if I ever loved him—I don't know if I did, or not—but I can't marry him!"

"Dear girl. Perhaps you were in love with love, and have stood looking into the brightness of that sun, into the terrible bright beauty that is love." He grasped her elbows and held her at arm's length. "So do we all at some time in our lives."

He did not speak pity, but she saw it in his eyes. "Then, when we have to turn our faces—"

She stiffened.

"We find ourselves bedazzled. Forgive me; we find that we are foolish, irresolute things, deprived of sight from having looked too long into the sun."

His arms relaxed, bringing him closer. "Now you must choose. Will you be blinded, from this time on living in the gloom of—of—injured pride, allowing hate to rise from the once-lovely fire; blinded, uncertainly feeling your way about, until you become accustomed to that darkness?

"Or will you cast this bitterness aside, believing that each experience, glad and sad alike, is the thing that makes us grow? Knowing that God sends laughter, always, to follow tears?" His voice was like a breeze audible in an oak's leaves, soothing, with a little "z" sound to the "s's."

Now tears came; and she gave in to them, sobbing on his breast.

She could not be sure if it was he who spoke, or if it

was the voice inside of herself: "Now is the time to think of all the lovely things you know."

The ceiling changed into the range of sky; storm clouds chased each other until they disappeared beyond the horizon, and by the light of a clear sky she could see some of the lovely things she knew: the sight and sound of wind; a buttercup; the intricate green veins in maple leaves turned gold; a red geranium on a window sill; and, after a storm, when the sun has broken through, a world of dazzling snow, hard-crusted into shallow curly waves, with tracings of orange-gold on their ripply edges; the taste of strawberries; Michael's button nose; the smell of fresh, clean clothes gathered from the lines on washdays; the van Vlaardingens on their knees planting an apple tree *outside the fence* so passers-by could help themselves to fruit.

Her tears, like pelting rain bringing back life to parched and shriveled crops, lent their miracle to wash away the dust of broken pride. Here, in the doctor's sheltering arms, was self-respect.

Saturday. Jack was leaving.

She had had to come. . . .

Hidden by the crowd at the railroad station, she looked for him. He was going to war. Was the certainty of her mind, after her rage at him, the real truth of her feelings?

But Jack must have felt a similar certainty. He had not come back.

There he was.

The train came in, and stopped. "Next stop Rockford!" the conductor yelled, and a hundred khaki-clad boys took up the refrain. "Next stop Rockford!" Then they changed the words and chanted, "Next stop Berlin!"

"You are brave, Jack!" she heard Beda say.

He turned brusquely. "Don't talk bravery to me! I'm not going because I want to go. I'm going because I *have* to go! Just when I was learning to be a good automobile mechanic I have to throw it all up—forget all I've learned —to go *killing!*"

Sigrid's head swam: as a mother would, she felt pity for him, for all of the men who stood between their homes and the desolation of war. From between the heads of the bystanders she saw that his eyes softened, filled with tears, and he looked around. "She didn't come, did she?"

"Jack!" She nudged her way toward him, but he had not heard her.

A soldier with an M.P. band on his sleeve moved toward him also and took a firm grip on Jack's arm, leading him away.

Most of the Swedes she knew, and Swedish-Americans, were almost fanatically patriotic toward America, sympathetic to its cause, eager to help in the "war for Democracy," but now she heard the elder Yingling brother snarl, "Better we should have stayed in the Old Country. Sweden is not at war." Crying then, without shame or apology, the big Swede ran and tore his younger brother from the M.P.'s grasp and clasped Jack to him. "Adieu, Yack," he cried. "Adieu."

Khaki suits jammed the railway cars' interiors. Was that Jack who waved? Sigrid craned her neck, trying to see. Or was it the butcher's son? Or was it someone else? The train lurched forward, but still she saw strong-armed men lean out of open car windows and hold girls up from the platform, against the sides of railway cars, for one last kiss. Frantically, all waved.

The train slid out. It's rear end grew smaller and smaller. Sigrid put her hands over her face when, *"Cannon fodder,"* she heard the Swedish stairbuilder say bitterly.

16

Months of war are longer than months of peace. And the winter months of war were longest of all.

A summer of war, and in Calico Row full brown heads of the cattails bent as large blackbirds sat to rest; deep red showed on their wings as the birds flew from the swaying stalks.

War was a time of watching the news, dreading to look at casualty lists, of longing to help in some way and not knowing how.

Now the days shortened, but not for Sigrid. On Mondays, Wednesdays, and Fridays, after the day's work, serving as hard a taskmaster as Mr. Horgan, her body cried out for rest. But she could not be tired yet—not for at least three more hours—not until she had stood, a teacher, facing her night-school class, facing it with eagerness, giving help, giving encouragement, facing it smiling.

But then on Tuesday and Thursday evenings came the reward! The university classes—a student, learning—learning—learning!

And finally the greatest rewards of all: the doctor's library; home; Michael, Granny, and stew. It was a revelation the way the Swedish pastor grew to like Irish stew! And the times the neighbors gathered in the little house. How much good it did her just to see the pastor sit in the little chair he always chose and close his eyes and lay his hands over his stomach and rock.

They had been talking about the war. Suddenly the rocker stopped, and she was surprised to hear its occupant say, "If only I were younger, I would go."

"To *war?*" Sigrid asked.

"Yes, I would go, to do my bit, to help win the war for democracy! Oh, you cannot know, Sigrid, what that word means. You cannot know what it would mean for an American to have to bow before a kaiser!"

Again it was the immigrant speaking, lauding the way of life she so easily took for granted.

"And," the pastor continued, "although we immigrants came to exploit America, our exploitation can now become a benefit, so that now, in turn, our United States can help the countries from which we came—helping the European countries in their time of need, we can teach them the true meaning of the brotherhood of man. Yes, I would go. Why the whole mass migration to America would have been for nothing, if the Kaiser should win!"

Mrs. Allspaugh, letting her eyes rest first on the doctor and then on Nico, said vehemently, "He's got more guts than *some* of the men around here."

"Oh, Aunt Hattie! That isn't fair!" They all knew of the long hours Dr. van Vlaardingen worked. Besides keeping up his own practice he took care of that of Dr. Swindells, who was now a captain in the Army, to say nothing of all the examinations he made for the draft boards.

"When our country calls me, personally," he said, "I am ready to go. But I cannot, deliberately, step up to join the forces of war. My work and my life are dedicated to healing, to helping bring life into the world, not to killing, not to joining forces bent on hastening lives out of the world." His eyes shot that steely fire. "We hear it all around us, 'Kill the Germans!' 'Kill the Kaiser!' 'Kill!' 'Kill!' Even our gentle women raise their voices, 'If I could get over there, I'd kill that Kaiser!'" The fire of his eyes was almost shut in now by the half-closing of the lids. "What can we expect to accomplish through killing?"

"But we *have* to kill the Kaiser to end the war! To end all wars!"

"Oh, Sigrid, do you think for one minute that the Kaiser's death would bring an end to wars?" He did not wait for an answer. "Do not think that I am afraid to go, or afraid to die. I have had too close an acquaintanceship with death to be afraid. But in this day of hysteria, of hate, of lust to kill, I hope to God that I may keep on an even keel, to serve our country, not with hate, but with love."

She felt goose pimples cover her forearms as the pastor rose and went to the doctor's chair, put his arm on the broad shoulders, and said, "Doctor, you should have been the minister as well."

"I Didn't Raise My Boy to Be a Soldier," Mrs. Allspaugh whistled between her teeth.

Nico's face was flushed. He would not ask, he said, for deferment; when they called him, he would go, but not because he would be any more convinced than at this moment that war was a way to bring peace.

"To think that young men"—the doctor's eyes rested on his son—"should be sent to a battlefield, given ammunition, and told to kill—to *kill!*"

Sigrid felt a faintness sweep over her. To kill—or to *get* killed! And Jack was on the battlefield! Oh, it would have been the least she could have done to have bade him good-by!

September came. The day of the third registration. Men of eighteen to forty-five years went forward to answer the call of the draft, and when Sigrid came from work she saw father and son marching in her back yard.

"For-ward, —rch!" called the doctor.

"Halt! One! Two!" came from Nico.

Yes, the father admitted later, he had thought to keep up his son's spirits with the gayety, but he well understood that Nico had marched along, holding Michael by the hand, thinking to keep *his* spirits up. For the doctor, as well as his son, was included in this third registration.

Far into the night Sigrid sat alone in their library.

Why should they have to go? She could pray that they need not. But she had prayed that everything should work out well between Jack and her! "Why, then," she had asked Pastor Bedell, "why did it all end, even before it began?"

"I only know His ways are good," was how he answered her. "I do not know the 'whys.' "

Tightly young fingers intertwined, in prayer, on Sigrid's lap.

The color she loved, blue, that rare blue of an October sky, came with the first day of the month. But with it came another color. Khaki. She saw, through tear-filled eyes, the doctor's khaki-colored cap, cordovan shoes, and matching stiff, shining leather puttees with straps buckled tight to show the shape of trim, youthful-looking calves; every detail she saw; the neat jacket, five-buttoned, the shoulder straps that had captain's bars pinned to them; and on the stiff-standing collar the caduceus, emblem of the Medical Corps.

Nico, too, was in uniform; that of the S.A.T.C. He was taller than his father now, and that day he had stood, one of a hundred and fifty thousand members of the Student Army Training Corps, and taken the oath of allegiance to the American flag. He and all of those student soldiers were to be allowed to continue their studies in colleges and technical schools, under military discipline, following a curriculum prescribed by the military authorities. At least for a while. But if the War Department was to fulfill its plans to have three million men in France by March of 1919, no one knew when any man in uniform might go.

The doctor and Nico were ready. To go to war.

Granny O'Toole sat counting her beads. Dr. van Vlaardingen rode Michael on his knee. She could not know what went on in the doctor's mind, until at last he said, "We've been trying to get along, since our Norah left us to join the Red Cross, but we're simply going to have to hire another housekeeper."

Granny looked up, as he hoped she would.

"Someone to come in each day for a few hours and dust—"

She could find it in her heart to smile. She knew what he was driving at, and might the Blessed Virgin smile on him for the driving. The pastor's house took so little time of a morning to redd up—the days were long. "Might I do, Doctor, to apply for that job?"

"How much?" he sparred, but his face bore a look of happy relief.

Granny hesitated. Mrs. O'Leary was getting five dollars a week, doing about the same for Mr. Singleterry. Would she be overcharging if she asked for three? Would she, now? Or had she better make it two and a half? Shure, and it would be takin' a little of the burden off of Sigrid, God bless her, if *she* could earn two and a half a week! Or had she, who had never worked for anybody before in her life, for money, better make it two? Er, well, she would take a chance. "Would two and a half a week be too much? For a few hours every day? And I could start your suppers, peel the vegetables, and—"

"Make it f—" He stopped. "Make it ten!" He slapped his hand on his thigh so hard that Michael jumped.

"Ten? You mean ten dollars a *week?* Oh, I wouldn't be worth that to you, Doctor! No ould woman would be worth that much."

"I'll be the judge of that. Ten dollars a week it is, then; and you will start work tomorrow?"

Granny's spectacles slid from her forehead down to her nose where they belonged. "Oh, I'll keep it up good, Doctor. I'll keep it up good." She could not trust herself to say more, nor to stay; wiping her eyes, she went to her room, leaving the doctor to usher himself out with Michael's affectionate assistance.

That night, in her bedroom, Granny could not sleep. Ten dollars a week. She would set aside a dollar of it, each week, for the church; they had carried her for nothing, practically, all of this time. And oh, the thought of it, she could put the rest toward her support and Michael's!

Think of it, for doing a little bit of housework, ten dollars a week! "Pat," she raised her eyes heavenward, "and aren't ye proud of your ould mother?"

And think of Sigrid, who had deprived herself all this long time, so's to keep an ould woman and the boy from being parted. What was there she could do for Sigrid in return? What would be the grandest gift she could make for this valiant young woman? Something of Ireland, it must be, to show her gratitude deep from the Irish heart of herself.

The grandest? "Carrickmacross, that's what!" Net in plenty was there in the old trunk, come after her from the Old Country; and there was the fine cambric, too, to draw the pattern on, and to use in appliqué. "A day must surely come when Sigrid can welcome one who will worship the music of her talk, the joyance of her laugh, and the bigness of the heart of her! Then, come that happy day, then will a handsome weddin' veil be waitin' in readiness!" There would be other nights for sleeping; instead, she sat drawing a pattern of daisies for the border of a veil of lace.

For Sigrid, none but the finest. And the finest was Carrickmacross.

For the doctor? Oh, she would repay the doctor. Such a

clean, clean house as he would be havin'! Such good puddin's, such good cakes!

Now and again Granny's low voice broke the night stillness with, "Ten dollars a week!" It would be the first money she had ever earned.

Such friends, one helping the other; and they weren't all Catholics, either! The wonder of it—the loving-kindness—

"Ten dollars a week!"

A wonderful, wonderful country, America.

"Ten dollars a week!"

17

War was a time of such great longing for peace, the time came when hearts had to believe there was an end to fighting although an armistice had not yet been signed. The neighbors gathered in the streets at rumor of a "cease-fire order." Michael marched up and down on the porch, with Granny following.

"Extree paper!" a newsboy called. Sigrid reached for one. "Wait until the armistice has been *confirmed*," the headlines begged. A man skipped by her and grabbed the paper, tore it into bits, and tossed the bits into the air, screaming, "It's over!"

Suddenly she was in the firm grip of the doctor on one side and Nico on the other, and they flowed with the surging crowd. She stretched her arms through the links the men's arms made and covered her ears to keep out the clang of streetcar gongs, removed her hands only to have the earsplitting explosion from a motorist's cutout automatically bring them back, where they stayed to protect her from hearing the noise of opened mufflers. Still, over the screech of a horn she could hear, "The Kaiser's licked!" A grown man came down the street rolling a big garbage can. "The war's over!" he screamed. A woman, pounding on a skillet with a stewpan, bumped against them. Crazily happy the crowds were. "The boys'll be coming home!"

They stood and watched delirium reign. Half-crazed men shouted; women screeched and, swept into the arms of strangers, danced into the night. Strangers? No, there were no strangers. Joy united the throngs crowding the streets, a common joy, the war was over. Believing made it so, even before the news was confirmed. There was bedlam in the streets. In nightshirts, in nightgowns, with paper hair curlers, in all stages of dress and undress men, women, and children hooted and howled and screamed, "It's over!"

"*Everybody's* dancing for joy!" a woman shrieked.

"Except the cigar-store Indian!" Sigrid shouted, and at her words a score of men pushed at the heavy base and rolled the Indian from his place in front of the corner store, out into the street. The dancers formed a circle and skipped around him, screaming and yelling, "No more wars, *ever!*"

"Would to God they could be right!" the doctor said sadly.

If all of the New Year's Eve celebrations since she was born, Sigrid decided, were rolled into one and added to all of the Fourth-of-July celebrations of her twenty-three years, and all let loose into a few hours, they could not have matched this celebration at rumor of an armistice. "It's over!" rang on the air around the world.

It was only a rumor, but a forerunner of the true word of armistice. At eleven o'clock in the morning, on the eleventh of November, the last gun fired on the battle front.

No one read the news with greater thankfulness than Sigrid.

Now no more lives would have to be sacrificed. Now Nico would be able to stay and keep on with his study of medicine. The doctor, who did not believe in war, would not have to go. Taina's "Bill" would return, or would he be "Louis" again now that the war for democracy was won and men would live together forever as brothers?

And Jack would be coming home. . . .

Nothing repeated can be as spontaneous or as soul lifting as the original; she had guessed it at the time of the re-election of Mr. Wilson, when bets were paid and later paid again; she knew it now as throngs filled the streets for the second time in such a few days.

"The war to end all wars is over!" women repeated as they danced up to the cigar-store Indian and let out war whoops.

To Sigrid's eyes the Indian became Dr. van Vlaardingen, both tall and big, both with faces strong and serious and sad. The doctor's words came back to her, "Do you think for a minute that the winning of this war will end all wars?"

"No more wars, *ever!*" men said again.

Did the wooden lips move to speak? Or did she hear across the hours, "Would to God they could be right, 'no more wars, *ever!*' "

As if she had no will to keep her eyes from it, she gazed on the figurehead in its place at the door of the corner store. Inscutable the Indian stood, his hand shading his eyes, looking ahead.

Slow-falling snow came with November days. It outlined the red-and-yellow, blue-and-green, feathers of the chief's long headdress; it placed a white "ash" on the tips of the handful of cigars he held. It laid a white mitten over the hand shading his eyes.

It was like lifting a board that has been lying too long on the ground, showing the growth beneath it blanched and lifeless and sow bugs darting quickly to find a shadier place, and soon in the sunshine green fills the grass blades and the pale spot regains a look of health. In that same way, lifting the blackness of war from the country, the paleness of worry on its people faded. Anxiety gave way to cheerfulness and hope, especially as more of the boys came home.

Taina's Louis came. His eyes were sunken deep in his head, his shoulders were stooped, and oh, how he coughed! Louis had been gassed. His lungs were practically eaten away by the mustard gas. German gas.

Jack came home. And *how* he came.

"A hell of a welcome," he grumbled. "And some reward, I'll say, to come home to a dry country!" He was not the only one, either; all of the guys, he said, wanted to know why, why prohibition? The war was over, there was no further need to conserve grain, "if that was truly what had been behind the passing of the Eighteenth Amendment."

There was a way out, and Jack found it. Not only did he patronize the bootlegger who, like the sow bugs, crawled into dark places; Jack became one.

"It's all your fault, Sigrid, that he started drinking," said his brother Jonatan.

"*My* fault?"

"Ya, yours. If you hadn't called off your wedding—and left Yack in the lurch—he wouldn't have started—"

It was *war* that changed people.

"He never touched a drop before you—"

"If you would tell him you'll marry him now?" Beda suggested meekly.

"Ya, Sigrid, he wants to know—will you marry him now?"

"He asked you to ask me?"

"Ya—he—he—"

"Jonatan, in American history we learn of a woman who said, 'Why don't you speak for yourself, John?' Let Jack come to me, and speak for himself, and I will answer him."

"Yust remember—this drinking—it's your fault!"

Sadly Sigrid watched Jack's decline. His eyes had that hunted look in them, always outside the law as he was, bootlegging. She avoided him, but she knew from Beda that he resented any interference; whatever help might come to him would have to come, not from friends, but from outsiders. Late last night, Sunday morning actually, she had looked out of her window to see the yellow light from Nico's study lamp still sending a path across the dark; Jack had passed by, and leaned crazily against the lamppost.

At break of dawn she rose. Maybe, in walking, some plan to help him might come to her. As was her custom she headed first toward the pawnshop. In front of it she stood and stared. It was gone! The beautiful blue cloth was gone! The window was dismantled. There was a circle on the glass, cleaned, and in the center was a printed notice. Jake was not coming home, for he was in a government hospital; his wife was going to sell out the business. All owners of pawned properties were requested to present their tickets before thirty days had elapsed. And remaining articles, at the expiration of the thirty-day notice, would be sold at public auction.

She had lost it! The lovely blue—the beauty that had become almost as an altar of hope.

Forlorn, she walked on, past the city limits. The blue sky seemed to be trying to make up to her for the loss of that other blue. It and the many-shaded, moody beauty of the great green prairie soothed her as she walked. How could she feel sorry for herself when she thought of Jonatan and Beda? Loss of an inanimate thing was nothing;

loss by death was sorrow, but loss of such a one as Jack, in the way he was going, was so much worse. And Jack, himself, oh, such loss as he must know with respect for himself gone, seeing his friends turn from him!

Retracing her steps, she came to the parsonage. The pastor already had visitors, Beda and the doctor, bent on the same mission.

"I have tried talking to him from the standpoint of health."

"I know, Doctor." Beda sniffled. "That made you 'an old sourpuss, buttin in,' " she finished artlessly.

Dr. van Vlaardingen sat musing. Then, "This is the natural aftermath of war," he said. "It is not only Jack. He is merely the personification of the hopelessness, the materialism, that has started to sweep over the whole country; of the profiteering and recklessness of living. Maybe he suffers from that letdown feeling, the feeling of disillusionment, for war has not ceased in Europe. Entrance into the League of Nations is not meeting with favor in the Congress. Perhaps he asks, and justifiably, 'What did I fight for? Has it all been for nothing?' The aftermath of war is striking Jack harder than some. We have got to save him from this curse of drink. By helping one, we will be helping to stop this wave of disillusionment."

"But, Doctor"—the pastor bent forward—"how can we appeal to him?"

"What are his weak points? Besides the drinking."

"Well," said Beda. "He likes to be a bigwig."

"What are his strong ones?"

"He can do anything with automobiles." Sigrid's tongue tripped, she talked so rapidly as inspiration came. "He is a wizard at fixing them! The Army didn't waste any time learning of his mechanical bent!"

"And making the most of it," the doctor finished for her. "Both for the Army and for him."

"I wonder." Talking to herself Sigrid left the pastor's parlor and walked out again to the prairie. "I wonder if he would—"

The next morning she entered the private office of one of the superintendents of the plant. She did not see the chair to which he waved her. "From taking dictation I happen to know that you are planning an automobile trip into Canada." She knew the roads were poor. She knew they were anxious about repairs. She knew they needed a chauffeur-mechanic. She sat, then, and told Mr. Rasey the story of Jack. "If he could get away, get a new start. He was a good boy before he went to France. And he knows automobiles."

Mr. Rasey stroked his chin. "Does he mean so much to you?"

"I owe him— He was one of those who went to the battlefield for us— We owe him—"

"There will be absolutely no liquor available, if he should go with us."

"That's what he needs!"

"I'll ask him if he wants to come. We were, as you know, being more or less held up, looking for a good mechanic."

"Could you—sort of—build him up when you ask him? Sort of treat him as an equal—well, almost, anyway?"

"I shall do my best." He shook her hand and ushered her out.

The following evening Jack came to tell her he was going away. "And when I come back—let's start over again, Sigrid?"

"We'll see."

"And say, that's a swell car I'll be driving for Mr. Rasey!"

He was proud. Best of all, he was sober. How long would that last? She could only hope.

"Good luck, Jack. The best of luck!"

She could cry; she had to cry, as when he turned to go she saw that the back of his coat shaped itself over a flask in the hip pocket of his pants.

Saturday. Sigrid heard the auctioneer's unintelligible chant as she pushed her way through the crowd, and it sounded as if he said "Ha—m—I—bid—sev'—mumble, mumble—eigh'—eigh—SOLD—for eighty-five!" An old mandolin went, a wall clock, a diamond ring. "Now, we have here—" The auctioneer reached in back of him.

She drew in her breath. He held up the blue drapery cloth, "her" blue cloth.

"We have here—a Swedish shawl."

Swedish? Maybe that was partly why she loved it so! But a shawl? He must be mistaken. A shawl so big? So wide and long, a shawl?

"So fine," the auctioneer was saying. "See, I can crush this much of it into the palm of my one hand!"

"What's the material?" a woman on the far side of the room asked.

"Knitted. Knitted of fine wool—hand knitted—extremely valu-ble. You'll never see another like it! What'm I bid?"

"Ten dollars!" Sigrid spoke up, clearly, confidently. There must be about ten dollars in the Salvation Army lassie bank.

"Ten dollars!" the auctioneer sneered. "Ten dollars wouldn't pay for the *yarn* for this much of it!" He held it up and with his thumb and forefinger marked off a small part of its length.

"Twenty-five dollars," came from the woman on the far side of the room.

"Twenty-five, I'm bi'—twen'-fi'—twen'-fi'—who'll make it fif'—'m I bid fif'—fif'—fif'?" the auctioneer chanted.

Sigrid felt her body grow more and more tense; she heard someone whisper into her ear, "Don't seem too anxious." But she *was* anxious!

"Thirty-five!" she shouted. The sweat poured from her. She had to have that shawl. She had wanted it for years! She simply had to have it! She would cash in a Liberty Bond! For *that* she could cash in a bond!

"Forty," came a muffled voice from the rear.

"Forty-five," another man's voice said calmly.

"Fifty!" came from the woman across the room.

Sigrid slumped, and leaned against those standing close to her.

"Fif'-five—fif'-fi'—I'm bid—who'll make it sixt'—sixt' —sixt'—?"

She looked around, but could not see the rear of the room. Was this the way auctions were conducted? Nobody was saying anything now; the woman did not speak up again. Craning her neck, Sigrid merely saw one man adjust his glasses, another only waved a hand weakly above others' heads, and yet the auctioneer kept going up, to sixty-five, to seventy, on up, and then she heard, "Going—

GOING—*GONE!"* His gavel came down. "Sold," he barked. Sold, for a hundred dollars!"

A hundred dollars!

The beautiful blue of it—the exquisite blue of it—sold —to somebody else.

18

"Mr. Rasey would like to see you in his office."

Sigrid laid the receiver back on its cradle, but dallied, running her finger over the instrument, tracing the shape of the cradled phone. If Jack had done anything he should not have done, what would that mean to her? She had recommended him. Would she lose her job? Hesitatingly she knocked at Mr. Rasey's office door.

"Come in. It's a fine day, Miss Christianson." He drew up a chair for her. "I think of all seasons perhaps I like fall the best."

"So do I." He was being very considerate, and so she smiled. "But then," she admitted, "when spring comes, I decide I like spring the best!"

"And summer? And winter? I suppose it's the same with them?"

She nodded.

"I thought as much." Changing the subject. "Did you major in psychology?"

"Why, no, sir. Not *yet*."

One eyebrow lifted at the hope in her voice. "I wondered." Then, half to himself, " 'Make him feel like an equal,' you said." Drawing his chair closer, "I suppose you are wondering why I have sent for you?"

"Yes, sir." Her handkerchief was now a tiny damp ball rolled into her palm, and the ball grew tighter and smaller as she listened to Mr. Rasey's telling of his misgivings at approaching her friend, Jack Yingling. Momentarily she relaxed at hearing of Jack's fitting in with the superintendent and his colleagues, of Jack's pride in handling a fine car, of Jack's adding much to the conversation, "having been to France, and all," until—Her knuckles grew white on hearing of the look of silly anticipation on Jack's face as he produced a hip flask; of the look of surly questioning about his standing with his companions when they refused a drink; of his withdrawal as one of them; of his caressing the wheel with an almost loving gesture, as a person does when he pets a child, but in this case a child he anticipates having to leave. "That night he tossed and turned. When he thought I was asleep he got up and walked out into the softly moonlit night. I followed him, keeping in the shadows. I saw him stand, slumped; twice he raised the bottle to his lips, but brought his arm down again. Then, pulling himself up tall, what a pitch he made! The bottle crashed against a tree!

"The days that followed were not easy for him, I know. But, my dear"—Mr. Rasey touched her arm—"you were right: he has so much good in him. As a mechanic he is priceless. As a man—well, if I feel a year from now the way I do now, I am going to back him, set him up in the garage business. I believe it is a coming thing. By the way, I have not told him of your speaking for him. I thought you'd rather I did not. But, oh, how much that boy owes to you!"

It hurt, he clasped her hand so tightly. "The thanks are to you, Mr. Rasey. You are the one who gave him a chance."

"I hope everything works out well between you two." He smiled warmly.

"It has. It has!"

And then she did an unheard-of thing: she took the rest of the day off, so she could bring the good report about Jack to Beda and Jonatan, and tell them that Jack was to stay for a while in Canada on a job for Mr. Rasey.

Later, the neighbors gathered, as they had used to do before the war, in the little cottage. "It looks as if there is going to be an artist in the family," the pastor said of Michael, who sat drawing. "For a boy who won't be five until January—"

All agreed with the doctor, then, that Michael had a fine teacher in Sigrid. "But, say," he added, "what do you think of this new organization, the American Legion?"

"I'm going to join." Louis was quick to reply although since he coughed so much he had not a great deal of breath for talking. "They are all for vocational training for us fellows of the A.E.F." His eyes lit up. "I hear there is talk of them even going to bat for a soldiers' bonus!"

"There'll be many a mortgage paid off on little houses, if that comes true," Mr. Allspaugh filled in as his wife drained her coffee cup and set it down.

Then, for Sigrid, the sky fell. *Was she seeing things?*

Hattie Allspaugh had brought a sack of Bull Durham tobacco from her pocketbook; the fingers of her left hand held a small white paper so that it was depressed, length-wise, in the middle; over the paper she sprinkled tobacco evenly from one end to the other; holding it steady in the left hand, her right brought the little cloth bag to her mouth and with her teeth holding the string she pulled the bag to close it, then laid it on the table. Her fingers jiggled the paper sufficiently to settle the tobacco evenly, then she rolled it. She ran her tongue along the paper's edge, rolled the cigarette around smoothly, and pressed the dampened edge to seal it. One end went into her mouth, and she struck a safety match and lighted the other end. Then she puffed. The smoke rose from her rouged and artificially placed lip bow and traveled into dilated nostrils, leaving a gray path on the little valley and two ridges between her lips and nose, and soon came out of her nostrils.

Sigrid stared. Aunt Hattie smoking? It was not possible! No one who had not known Mrs. Allspaugh as long as she had could fully appreciate this. Why, the very first time she had seen Aunt Hattie was on the train, when Pa had been smoking, and she—a total stranger—had practically called him a swine because he had a cigar in his mouth! Oh, if Pa could be alive to see Hattie Allspaugh sitting here, tilting her head back, blowing smoke toward the ceiling!

Her next words closed Sigrid's gaping mouth, "Oh, don't be so old-fashioned, Sigrid. My goodness, all of the girls are smoking."

Granny choked on her coffee. Girls, indeed! Mrs. Allspaugh was as much on the shady side of sixty as she was! Girls, "with the grandmother faces," Michael aptly de-scribed them. "Girls," she mumbled, way into the night. She would not forget that very soon. *"Girls!"*

Nor would Sigrid. "Hattie Allspaugh, blowing smoke rings!"

Fall was done; winter and spring followed, and summer again lay lush on the prairies. No, no longer prairies, truly, but plots of ground growing smaller as Chicago grew larger. Year by year the big city had stretched her hands farther to the south, the north, the west, and gathered the prairies to her.

One finger pointed toward the east, but—grow eastward? How could it? The lake was there. Grow anyway! Fill in the lake! Grow!

As the city grew, week by week Sweden grew closer to Chicago. Not geographically, perhaps, but to Sigrid as one after another she laid four quarters on the tambourine held by the metal lassie on the bank, and pushed down the lever.

"Look!" Granny came running in. "Sure'n I wish I was a child myself!"

"I, too!" Sigrid agreed, and followed Granny out-of-doors. The doctor's auto sat at the curb; he and Nico watched a team of strawhatted horses plodding down the street pulling the sprinkling wagon. From the perforated brass arcs at its rear came, in thin arched spray, cooling water to wet the asphalt steaming in the hot Saturday afternoon sun. Barefooted, in their underwear, little boys and girls followed, screaming in delight under the shower.

"They have more sense than we grownups," Nico said as he helped her pick up Michael's suit, socks, and shoes from the curb where he had flung them.

"This is one more reason I have hated to see horses go."

"Yes." The doctor came to stand beside her. "With horses will go the sprinkling wagon, as we know it, and the waffle wagon."

The doctor spoke, she sensed, with an overwhelming longing for his childhood. And what was this sensation she experienced? A sudden sadness—a feeling of having aged —of growing old.

She was, of course. Twenty-five years old. The wave of nostalgia swept over her, too, remembering: the German band, a casualty of the war, was gone. Gone, too, was the old Italian organ-grinder—

"Don't let Dad make you feel blue." Nico bent over her. "Something always comes to take the place of things that go." He pointed. Here came the one-man band. "Such an aggregation of talent!"

"But hardly musical, would you say, Nico?"

"Looks as if he needs treatment for St. Vitus's Dance!"

"Right you are, 'Doctor.' "

His smile thanked her. Not much longer now, and he would have earned the cherished title.

"Over There!" was the song Michael requested for his penny; and the one-man band played on. Happy tunes or lively tunes, he played, but his eyes were sad. Peering from beneath heavy, bushy brows, they told as well as words that soon he too, would vanish. Pennies did not feed a man, or clothe him, as high as prices were now. He walked away, and Sigrid knew that for the last time she had seen the too-big derby resting low on bushy eyebrows and bent-down ears. "Keep the Home Fires Burning." The strain came back to them as he turned the corner and was gone.

Gone was the one-man band, the German band, the Italian organ-grinder; gone the horses' drinking troughs with the few catfish in to purify the water. But come the day of full suffrage for women; come the passage of the Nineteenth Amendment to the Constitution. From the month of August 1920 the world would see American women take an increasingly active part in the political life of the nation.

"Wouldn't your father have liked to know," Nico asked, "of women all over the country casting ballots for the President of the United States?"

"Yes. Yes. He often told me about how he had grown up to believe in full suffrage for women because of the teachings of his mother's Morfar. Yes, he believed in women's rights, even as he believed in America."

President Wilson was a sick man, now confined most of the time to his bed; more than partially paralyzed, he was mentally exhausted, intellectually embittered. His League of Nations was as good as dead. The country was tired of the high-minded idealism of the war years and wanted normalcy. "Normalcy" was Harding's keyword, and so Sigrid and Taina joined forces with Pastor Bedell, the doctor, and Nico, with Mr. Allspaugh and Louis, and walked solemnly to the polls, there to cast votes for the Republican who was to win, Warren G. Harding.

But not Hattie Allspaugh! She announced loudly that she had voted for the losers, Cox and Franklin Delano Roosevelt. Pulling a deep draw on her cigarette, holding the smoke for an unbelievably long time before letting it come from her nostrils—to look to Sigrid for all the world like the charging bull on the package of her tobacco—she said, "You mark my words, we ain't heard the last of that young man Roosevelt! With the women voting, and him as handsome as he is, I wouldn't be a bit surprised to see *him* moving into the White House come another election!"

Michael was not interested in presidents beyond the wearing of celluloid campaign buttons. He spent his days playing "doctor." But an ill-trained doctor he was, to be taken so by surprise at coming one day to call on Sassy to find her blanket bed squirming with kittens.

"Granny! Sigree!"

"We'll keep this calico one." Sigrid picked it up and held its fuzzy softness against her cheek. "What shall we name it? I've about run out of names."

" 'Cal' would be good," offered Granny. "It could stand for calico, and for Cal Coolidge, our new vice-president."

"Splendid, Granny! Even though the *kitty* doesn't look as though it had been 'weaned on a pickle'!"

"No." Michael's lips and chin quivered. "I wanted to name it. Why can't it be the name I want?"

"And what"—Sigrid returned the kitten to its mother and drew the boy to her—"what would you like to name it?"

Unhesitatingly his answer came, "My Cousin Tissappee."

Her eye caught Granny's.

"Don't laugh!" came with all of the seriousness of a young man who is old enough to attend kindergarten. "Don't laugh. Every morning we sing the song about My Cousin Tissappee." He tried to pitch the tune, to demonstrate, but each note he uttered sounded exactly like the last one. "I love my song. I want to name my kitty after my song."

"All right, lamb. It shall be My Cousin Tissappee." A silly name for a cat, but if it made Michael happy, that would be its name.

With the passing of a month moody skies, clouds hanging low, heavy with snow, let go, and the air was filled with dancing flakes. White and black, the out-of-doors was a series of etchings in contrast to the cheery dining room as the neighbors ate of the roast goose Sigrid and Granny had prepared. In the parlor white paper snowflakes hung on lace curtains; tinsel icicles dripped from the chandelier; attics, belying their hidden gaiety with festoons of gray cobwebs, had loaned big red shining balls, and blue-and-gold and tinsel garlands, and angels, with which to trim the Christmas tree. At its topmost tip was Elin's star, cut from cardboard and covered with tinfoil, uneven in its points, not so shiny as once it had been, but oh, the happy memories it brought to Sigrid!

Perhaps she should have planned to have the gift giving now, on Christmas Eve, as Elin would have done, but for Michael they would do the American way, so he would be celebrating as were the children he knew. Having the dinner on Christmas Eve was a concession to the doctor, who expected Mrs. Holgerson's baby to come on Christmas Day. Only the Yinglings had not come.

Jack had come back, she knew. She had invited them all, but they had not come.

With his usual *"Tack för maten,"* Michael slid from his chair, danced around the table shaking hands with each of them, shouting "Merry Christmas!" Never once did he forget to add, "We're going to get our presents tomorrow morning, don't forget! Presents! And—next summer—I'm going to the sirr'cus!" To make absolutely sure, "Ain't I, Sigree?"

"Yes, Michael, dear. You are going to the circus." She turned to the others. "Can you imagine the circus putting up posters so far ahead?" Then, "How does a person go about eliminating 'ain't'?"

"There ain't no way," Nico teased her, smiling broadly.

Sigrid broke the ensuing silence by humming the pitch to begin "Silent Night." All voices joined; low, high, and medium, they harmonized. "Christ, the Savior is born." Church bells chimed.

" 'Music from on High,' we always said, at home, when I was a child, when we heard the church bells ring." The doctor closed his eyes, hearing their sound all the way from boyhood. "We of the Low Countries have beautiful bells; not only chimes, but, ah, our carillons!"

They let him go on, for they could see how earnestly he wanted to explain their making. "Oh, if I could describe to you the heavenly music of the carillon—cascading softly from the sky—"

Sigrid sat drinking in the sound of him. How much she had learned from this man. She listened now with half-open lips as he went on to tell of the artistry necessary for the making of every single bell, of the great bell casters of Amsterdam whose carillons found homes in France, in Germany, in Sweden. "And yes, the carillon is one of the many lovely bits of European culture which have become integrated with America."

After he told of the tuning of the bells, how each bell has five tones, and they must be tuned at correct intervals so as to form a perfect chord, and that after a bell is in tune with itself it must be in tune with all the other bells so that the carillon as a whole is perfect, Sigrid sat wondering: was it only she who likened the beautiful bells to these friends, "Made in His Image," so tuned as to be in tune with all the others?

The candles on the tree flickered, casting the only light into the room. Their glow brought remembering—the story of Dickens' *Christmas Carol;* Andersen's *Little Match Girl;* her mother sitting listening, with Tony on her lap, as Pa read to them, until the candles snuffed out their lights. The street lamp shed a weird, faint luminosity to replace the candles' gleams.

Christmas. It was at Christmas that nostalgia for childhood and longing for loved ones no longer here came strongest.

The clock struck. "One, two . . . ten, eleven, twelve."

"It came upon a midnight clear,
    That glorious song of old—"

Heads raised abruptly. A pair of eyes in every head opened wide, to question. What was this spell that could bring heavenly music to their earthly ears?

"Peace on earth,
    Good will toward men—"

The creaking sound that comes with cold shoes meeting an icy, snowy stair came nearer and grew louder. The singing was right outside the door! Sigrid threw the door open, as the pastor brought up the rear.

"From heav'n's all gracious King!"

Jack, his brother, and Beda and the children, stood on the top step and finished the song. Soft-falling, large flakes of snow lit on their shoulders, on their caps.

> "The world in solemn stillness lay
> To hear the angels sing."

Solemn stillness, yes, it lay upon them all; upon Sigrid to whom came full realization of the meaning of this visit: it was Jack's way of asking her forgiveness and renewing his suit; it was the brother's way of thanking her for whatever her part had been in restoring Jack to his real self that she read from his eyes and handclasp.

"Merry, Merry Christmas!"

Of course they must all have coffee, and finish the mince pie. But it was getting late, and if they were to be awake at the time Michael would be prancing out of bed in the morning, they had better seek their homes and beds.

Mistletoe?

Yes, Hattie Allspaugh had brought a sprig of it and, "unbeknownst" to Sigrid, hung it above the doorway to the hall.

Sigrid stood with Granny, both of them hostesses, shaking hands.

"Merry Christmas!"

"And a Happy New Year!"

The doctor glanced up and saw the mistletoe. His face flushed; he looked inquiringly at his son and, self-consciously, shook Sigrid's hand.

"Gosh, what's mistletoe *for!*" Nico grabbed her and placed a kiss full on her lips, leaving her breathless, tingling.

Now came Jack, with "Merry, Merry Christmas, Sigrid!"

"Merry Christmas to you!" Instinctively, after the fervor of Nico's kiss, she stepped back.

Jack looked up at the white berries and smooth green leaves, and his handclasp tightened as he moved to draw her close; but Michael came running, jumped toward her, and tackled her around the knees with so much force that she staggered away from Jack.

"I *am* going to the sirr'cus next summer, ain't I, Sigree?"

They couldn't help but laugh.

"Providential," Mrs. Allspaugh blurted, and threw a dark look at Jack.

Sigrid knew it was because Aunt Hattie had said he "wasn't worth the powder to blow him to hell," and would never quite forgive him for proving her wrong in her appraisal of him.

19

As American as "The Star-Spangled Banner," the Fourth
of July, or Washington's Birthday, or goldenrod, was this
day toward which Michael looked with such ecstatic eagerness, circus day. He stood, in shivering delight, waving
good-by to Sigrid as she left for work on the Friday morning before *the day*.

"Tomorrow! Don't forget tomorrow! G'-by, Sigree—you
know tomorrow is the sirr'cus!"

"I won't forget."

"What a bunny hug the boy gives you!" Granny's big
smile faded. "But do you notice that Michael, least of all,
now misses the ones who should have been everything in
the world to him?"

Yes, Sigrid had noticed. He clung to Granny as he would
to a mother, and waved good-by to her each morning for
all the world as if she were a father!

"Wait a minute!" Nico came running. "I'll ride in with
you. Got something to tell you!"

Running, half backward, so she could wave until she
reached the corner, Sigrid turned it and together she and
Nico dashed for the streetcar.

"My, but Calico Row seems dead. Where is everybody?"
he asked.

"Everybody, except us, has gone on that excursion to
Starved Rock. I wouldn't have minded going myself, but
of course tomorrow—"

"Yes, I know." Jostled and bumped, they clung to the
ceiling straps and Nico, almost like a second Michael,
poured out his excitement in the anticipation of the morrow. Naturally it was to be a different kind of day for him,
but what a day! One of the big days of his school life, for
he was to listen to the reading of a paper dealing with the
work on insulin, which, if it worked out according to Dr.

Banting's expectations, would bring added years to diabetics' lives.

"I just can't tell you, Sigrid, how much it means to me to have the opportunity to get this firsthand knowledge on the pancreas."

Yes, tomorrow was to be a big day.

So it had seemed in the morning. But now it was evening, and Sigrid's heart was fallen as low as her shoe soles. How could she go home and tell Michael that she had to work tomorrow afternoon? How could she? She couldn't. Her heels dragged. She lagged along, missing the streetcar. It was not that she minded working overtime on a Saturday, but why couldn't it have been any other Saturday? If only Granny felt able to go all the way in to Chicago. If only Beda or Taina had not already gone to Starved Rock, and taken the Schmotzers with them—any one of them would have been glad to take Michael to the circus. Maybe if she walked all of the way home she might get up courage enough to tell him.

But he had lived for going to the circus. For months!

"Granny," she telephoned from a drugstore, "I'll be late. You had better put Michael to bed."

"Oh, for pity's sakes, he's already in—in preparation for circus day."

"Good-by, Granny."

When she reached home Granny was serving lemonade to the van Vlaardingens on the front porch. "Here, sit down, m'dear. Where've you been?"

"I walked home." If there was a song in her voice now it was a threnody. In the almost dark the three shot glances at one another.

"Is—is there somethin' wrong?" Granny leaned toward her, urging a tinkling glass into her hand.

"I have to work tomorrow afternoon. There is to be a conference of all the heads of the company. And I have to cover it." Before she finished, they had grasped the significance of her announcement. "So I can't take Michael to the circus."

Impulsively Nico cut her off. "You can't *do* that to him, Sigrid."

"What can I do? I can't afford to lose my job."

Nico sat on the top step, his long legs stretched from him, reaching halfway down the flight of steps. Now he drew the legs up and clasped his arms around them. His chin rested on his knees. "Once," he began slowly, seriously, "I read a short story. I can't remember where, but it must have been in a magazine. I have never been able to forget it."

He sat, looking ahead. "It was about a little child, a girl; her mother had promised to take her to a carnival or something. At any rate, the whole story was a glimpse into the child's mind, the way it stored up visions of seeing, of being a part of, this entertainment which had been promised her. The building up, the anticipation was so great that the child lived only for that coming day."

"Just as Michael has." Sigrid's voice was low.

"Yes, just as Michael has." Nico seemed older than his own father as he sighed. "The day came; the child dressed herself in her Sunday-best dress, and danced into her mother's room, ready! The mother was dressing, too.

" 'Why are you all dolled up?' she asked the little girl.

" 'Because this is the day we're going—'

" 'Oh, no. You can't go with me to my card club. You go and change your dress again, and run out and play.'

"The child's world crumbled." Nico turned to look at Sigrid, and by the light of the far street lamp she saw that his eyes were glistening with moisture. "The title of the story," he finished, "was 'Only a promise to a Child.' "

"But, Nico, what can I do?"

"You've got to take him."

The doctor came and sat beside her. "You attach too much importance to this, Sigrid. Every child has to learn how to meet disappointment."

She drew away. "You—you don't understand."

All through the night she lay awake, trying to make a decision. Her work came first; it was their livelihood. Michael came first. "You can't do that to him, Sigrid!" "No—no—Nico—I know! But, my job—"

What should she do?

And in the doctor's house they were not sleeping.

"It was as much you, as anything," the father scolded. "If you had not come up with that sentimental story—"

"All right, Dad. Try to make me feel like a sissy. I don't care. It's so long since you were a child, you can't remember—"

"But it is one chance in a million; you cannot absent yourself from the reading of that paper."

"Dad, that kid has got to be taken to the circus. Since Sigrid can't take him, I'm going to."

"If your education is that unimportant to you, on the very eve of your graduation—"

"Dad! Why do you have to *be* this way? The paper is bound to be printed."

"Are you sure—it—is the boy you are concerned about?" The doctor narrowed his eyes. Did Nico guess of his love for Sigrid and resent the thought of its coming between them? Was Nico taking this way of turning Sigrid against him—making her feel he did not *understand?* Was that why Nico had made reference to his age—to make the thought of love ridiculous for one so old as he? Did Nico guess?

"What do you mean, Dad?" If his father answered him Nico did not hear. What did his dad mean? Did his dad think for a minute that he was doing this to play hooky from school? My God, he couldn't think that!

Father and son listened to hear each other toss and turn the night away, until at dawn Nico, hearing the doctor's deep, even breathing, rose, dressed, and slipped quietly from the house.

"Sigrid." He flattened his nose against her kitchen screen door. "If you'll put on another egg, and feed a guy breakfast, I'll take Mike to the circus."

"Oh, Nico! No!" She stopped at hearing his happy-hearted laugh.

He might have been only six, too, as he skipped with Michael and caught the spirit of circus day. He went along with the boy by the hand, singing, "I'm going to the circus," in the same tones and with the same inflections as Michael had been using, heading toward the grounds.

Such ecstasy, such anticipation! Michael could scarcely breathe.

Came the sounds! Wheels rumbling; hoofs clattering; the oomp-pah-pah of the big brass band; the circus parade; and then came the sight of it! With Michael perched on his shoulder, Nico fell into step with the music. Spectators were packed so tight, looking down, to Michael they seemed like a solid pavement, but as the band ahead struck up a new tune, he slid from his perch and in the small space he could find to stand he danced up and down. He could not contain himself to speak. Standing on one foot, trying to hop—changing to the other foot—clinging with both hands to Nico's arm, he stammered and screamed, "My song! It's my song! That's 'My Cousin Tissappee'!"

A big smile of comprehension spread over Nico's face. And wait until Sigrid heard! As the band played the spectators, large and small, added the words; but the words they sang to the tune of Michael's song were, "My Country, 'Tis of Thee!"

It was almost more than a person could absorb, this sight of the parade; but then came the circus itself. How could a pair of eyes follow five rings at a time?

Michael's did.

Greater than Thanksgiving Day, greater than his birthday, or Easter, or Halloween, greater even than Christmas —circus day! So much to see. So much to cheer. So much to remember. "Peanuts! Popcorn! Cracker Jack!" Fall asleep? Not Michael. As brothers, he and Nico talked over each clown's antics; they held their sides for laughing at the way the clown had picked Michael right out of his seat and ridden around the circus with him on the handlebars of his bike.

"Weren't you afraid?" Granny exclaimed.

"No! It was the sirr'cus! You don't be afraid at the sirr'cus!"

All over again it must be told to Sigrid, and repeated again when the doctor came to share the supper Granny had prepared. As they ate, Sigrid kept her attention on Michael. He was happy. This beautiful day he would have, to be his, always; he was old enough to be able to recall this day through all the years of his lifetime. And he had it because of Nico. Nico had given up the great opportunity to listen, firsthand, to the paper on insulin. Sitting there, munching hard-boiled eggs and boiled ham and hardtack, he gave not the slightest indication of his disappointment.

He needed no formal "thank you" from the boy, but how could she tell him how she felt? She took his hand. "Nico, *tack så mycket.*"

At his father's look, she was not sure why, she dropped his hand.

"Var så god!" Laughing. "I had a swell time, myself," Nico assured her.

Far into the night Sigrid sat at her bedroom window and looked at the yellow light streaming from Nico's study lamp, looked into the darkness, thinking. The doctor's son had grown into a man, a good man, like his father—his higher education was not changing him, as it did some; he was still the same fine boy who had come to join the neighbors of Calico Row, the boy who was a man now, a man whose eyes had been filled with tears as he recalled "a promise to a child."

20

The purring lawn mower of a Sunday early riser woke Sigrid. And no sooner had she reached the kitchen than the two next-door neighbors were at the door.

"Have you seen the morning paper?" Nico was excited. "There's something here could be terrific!" His father followed close, as a child does who doesn't want to miss anything.

She reached for the paper.

"No." Nico put it behind his back. "You've got to promise to do one thing before we show it to you. Doesn't she, Del?"

"Tease." She laughed. "So you two are in league against me?"

"He is serious, Sigrid."

"Will you have a cup of coffee, you two big kids?"

"No, thank you." Nico, his spirits fallen, moved to go.

She had hurt his feelings. And after his kindness of yesterday. "I'm sorry. I promise. Whatever it is, I promise."

His enthusiasm returned. "Swell!" He marched her into the dining room, opened the newspaper, and laid it on the table. "Look!"

There was a full-page announcement, and in tall black letters at the top of the page, "$1,500 IN CASH PRIZES!" Under that were listed: "$500, First Prize," "$250, Second Prize," and on down, with prizes for Honorable Mention. It was the last reminder of a writing contest, first announced in the spring by the Biggs publishing house, for the best story of Chicago, its beginning and the beginnings of things "that have made it great."

They read through the fine print: "Use your imagination, so that your book will appeal to young adults as well as grown-up readers."

"I didn't see the original announcement, did you Sigrid?"

She looked up. "But, Nico, I can't write!"

"I didn't say you could!" His excitement was undiminished, and it proved to be contagious.

"Oh, you are going to try for it?"

"Sigrid"—Nico's eyes shone—"I can't write worth a darn. But don't you see? Your father wrote, and Dad and I think your father could *write*. You have some papers he wrote about Chicago. Come, get that shoe box out! Let's read those papers and see if his story qualifies under these rules."

She went for the shoe box, and lifted the corner of each paper until she came to the folded sheets on which was written, *"Chicago."*

Father and son drew up chairs, and Nico's hands reached toward her in helping motion. She waved his hands away. "Calm down," she said nervously. "I never won anything in my whole life, except the Wide-Awake Club button from the *Daily News*."

"Well, that's sterling silver," he reminded her. "And, anyway, this wouldn't be you. It would be your dad."

Her dad. Quickly she unfolded the sheets. There was his note: "If we could understand the voice that sings and whistles, or howls and moans, according to its mood, might we not hear from it the history of Chicago?"

She read, then, the allegorical story her father had put on paper, on closely spaced lines covering both sides of the long sheets:

Chicago

Men call Chicago "The Windy City."

I am the wind.

The sky—and I—have watched the Indian come and go; have watched the white man come, and the city grow.

I, alone, have touched the pink blush of cherry trees in each and every spring.

I, alone, have swayed the grasses since the first; only I have kissed the cheek of every maiden, red, white, and black, and yellow; and I have found all fair.

On, on, from the vantage point of the ever-present wind, to Sigrid and her listeners the glaciers of the Ice Age retreated; the reign of man began, near a wide basin filled with blue water; an infant came to the prairie, the first child born in the Windy City, and its skin was red.

The big blue water, "Lake Chicago," it was called now.

She-cau-go, playful waters.

Che-ca-go, strong smell—for garlic grew along the riverbanks.

Gitchi-ka-go—a thing great or strong.

All of these, Chicago. Before the time of the white man Chicago had her name.

Called by the wind the white man came: low, the wail of a newborn babe—white-skinned—mingled with the cries of Kickapoo and Potawatami infants. Tenderly, now, the wind blew, a gentle silk taffeta swishing through the poplar trees—a lullaby.

Beginnings.

The building of Fort Dearborn, the first doctor, the first Protestant sermon, the stockyards, the first public building, the Drainage Canal, the wind witnessed the coming of them all. . . .

More cattle! More wheat. More lumber! More iron, more steel! More men! More, more of everything, Chicago needed, to grow; and Chicago got what she needed, and grew at a tremendous pace with block after block rowed with pretty wooden houses, "frame" houses, one, two, and even three stories high. But the Chicago *Tribune* saw them as "miles of firetraps, pleasing to the eye, looking substantial, but all sham and shingles."

In September of 1871 the *Tribune* issued a solemn warning.

In October—*the fire.*

The voice of the wind spoke on, as Sigrid read:

I can be kind. I can be cruel. Men who listen to my story may call it madness that I should call my part in the Chicago fire a kindness. But, "Burn! Burn!" I cried, fanning the flames from the west side eastward. Kindling wood, that bunch of shanties was, and so I blew a gale. It was like setting fire to a box of matches!

Burning, the flames had all the beauty of a lovely song.

I could not have stopped it if I would, for I am not the Force behind myself.

Not if I could would I have stopped it, for I could see into the future, a new city, bigger, stronger, for having her poor beginning wiped off the face of the prairie. Those rows of wooden stores and homes and barns—they were no fit beginning for the city that should rise here in the heart of America.

And so I blew the flames hotter—hotter—

Now men can be glad, for when the ruins at last were cleared away, there began the rebuilding, the beginning of Chicago as men know it now, where my breath meets walls of skyscrapers in the Loop and storehouses of culture on the lake front, blows smoke from tall industrial stacks all over the city, directs the rain to wash the cheery windows of a half-a-million homes—and yet—in her abundant forests tall oaks, by growing close together, defy my breath so that their seeds may fall and little oaks grow in the shelter of parent trees—and in the springtime, violets bloom.

21

" 'And in the springtime, violets bloom—' "

Sigrid's moist eyes looked first into the doctor's, then were held by Nico's. "Those words tell you more about my father than any I could put together."

The three sat with chins cupped in their hands propped up by elbows resting on the table. Softly she spoke again, "He was so big, so brash, so clumsy in a way, so stubborn, so headstrong; and yet he was so tender, so gentle."

"Please finish reading." The doctor glanced at his watch.

"To think that so short a time ago," she went on, for she had not heard him, "a ferry, that was a canoe, paddled to a little wooden hotel at the 'Y' in the river where we can stand now on the bridge; and beyond, when night falls, we see huge buildings with their many lighted windows become black giants rising against a near-black sky—giants, throwing their diamond-studded shadows into the dark river, the white jewels sparkling in the constant rippling of the water—"

They all sat silent, until impulsively she dropped her arms and raised her head. "I *love* Chicago! When I stand there—"

Flushing, she bent her head to read again, through the voice of the wind telling of new beginnings, a new Chicago. They lost sight of the fact that she was reading: this *was* Chicago!

She finished the story of great beginnings; but as she ended the written words, so great was her father's faith in the city that he left them with the feeling that this ending was only a beginning—for Chicago—a greater Chicago.

"It will have to be typewritten." Nico gathered the sheets. "Can you do it during your noon hours, do you suppose?"

"Yes, I suppose so. But you see it is only natural that I should like to read the things my father wrote, because reading them brings him and my mother back to me. But to send it out—I couldn't bear to have anyone ridicule him—his language is simple, and what about the grammar? I am not sure of—"

"Sigrid, it would be a terrible mistake to demand the same stereotyped sentence structure from every writer. Your father had a way of putting his words together, a style of writing all his own. Refreshing in its simplicity, it—at least to me—is more appealing than if it had absolute rhetorical accuracy. And maybe it does? How can we know what it is worth if you do not submit it? Type it up, Sigrid, and we'll send it in. Remember, you promised." He grinned boyishly as he pushed his chair back, and the sound gave emphasis to the finality in his voice.

To a watcher in the kitchen the chair's scraping sound was a signal. "They're through!" And Michael dragged Granny in by the hand.

"F'r gracious' sakes alive! Do you fiddle-faddlers know what time it is? Not a bite of breakfast have you had, and here it is almost dinnertime! What in the wor-r-rld?"

Sigrid had not know how hungry she was until Granny's frying bacon told her through her nostrils. But the doctor ran, with, "I've calls to make! Good-*by!*"

"A-wastin' the whole blessed Sunday," Granny scolded. "And Michael and me a-havin' to slip out, quiet-like, on tippy-toes, so's not to disturb the three of you, readin', and clishmaclaverin', and us havin' to eat out in the back yard to keep from disturbin' you, and to keep us from starvin'!"

"Oh, Granny." Nico danced around with her in his arms. "Say a little prayer."

"Nico!" Now it was Sigrid who scolded. "Don't you dare mention this to anyone, not even to Granny! There's no use building any hopes, not even our own."

"Whatever it is"—Granny winked at Nico to make him understand that she could guess—"I'll not be inquisitive." She folded her hands. "I'll make a novena."

The cicada's shrilling announced the coming of frost. There would be only six weeks more of summer; and only a little more than two months in which to typewrite, in stolen moments much too few, the pages of a book, "—on one side of the paper only, each page titled and numbered, double-spaced neatly—" Sigrid stared at the calendar, "—manuscripts must arrive on or before October 1, 1921."

Every morning, a half-hour earlier than usual, she boarded the streetcar and was at hand when the watchman opened the gates to the plant, to spend the precious minutes at the typewriter. And each Sunday morning she listened to Pastor Bedell, preaching from Messiah's altar. Despite his cheery greetings, despite his efforts to be gay, she sensed his loneliness. It was hard for a man to grow old alone. And he was growing old. There was that filmy veil over the pupils of his eyes, so easily seen as she removed his spectacles to wash them. Did he never shine the glasses between times? He and Hattie Allspaugh must be nearly of an age, yet the pastor appeared to be so much older now than Aunt Hattie. They were meeting the years so differently. As long ago as when she was only ten or twelve years old, her "Aunt Hattie" had had white hair, and had seemed to be an "old woman." Pastor Bedell's thin fringe also had been white, but where his was still white, now Aunt Hattie's was a reddish black; her face was well cosmeticked, and she had youthful ways; this no one could deny, watching her smoke cigarettes!

The pastor clung so to her hand as she said good-by. Strange, for so many years she had been turning to him for encouragement, now it seemed almost as though he turned to her. And then, although she had admonished Nico and his father that they might not "tell a single soul," she told Pastor Bedell of working each morning on the plant's typewriter to get her father's story ready to send to the publisher's contest.

"My prayers shall join yours, Sigrid." They shook hands, and in the pressure of the pastor's hand was none of the feebleness of age.

Now summer was almost spent. Tall phlox blossoms, the van Vlaardingens' and hers, their stems interlaced through the fence slats, stood at evening perfuming the air; stood in the dusk, sequined with fireflies.

Fall came, and Labor Day. The holiday was not so important as the day after, for Michael went to the first grade. Granny dressed him ready to go, and hung the asafetida on a string around his neck to keep contagious diseases away, and put two white handkerchiefs in his pocket, "one for show and one for blow."

The early mornings, the weeks, sped to the tune of an Underwood typewriter. Again the van Vlaardingens sat at the dining-room table in the little house and Sigrid concluded the reading from a pile of yellowed foolscap sheets.

"Not a typographical error!" Nico laid the sheets face upward in the box in which they had come from the stationer's shop. On top he laid the transmittal sheet: "Written by Karl Mattias Petersson, deceased. Submitted by his daughter, Sigrid E. C. Christianson." Her address appeared below. "But don't you think there should be some sort of dedication?"

Without hesitation Sigrid wrote in the center of a sheet and handed it to him. *"Till min mor*—To my mother. I am sure that is what he would have written there."

"We're just in time, aren't we?" Nico and his father answered in one breath the dour look on the expressman's face as they glanced at the timepiece on the wall. One minute until nine.

"It is really very important," Sigrid apologized, "or we wouldn't bother you right at closing time. You see, it's the last day."

Mr. Wolfson gave her a receipt. "Huh, you're not the only one's tryin' fer this," he sneered. "I've had six parcels go to this contest already."

Nico ignored his tone. "Will it go out tonight?"

"On the 'lev'n-'lev'n."

"Thank you." Sigrid led the way into the night.

"It's simply *got* to get there in time!" Nico insisted.

Poor Nico, believing that Pa's book might have a chance. She sent a knowing look to the doctor. And yet—if it could win! "I think I'd like to walk home."

"G'by, Dad." Nico tossed his father the car keys. "I'll walk with Sigrid. "Or—he turned—"is there anything you have for me to do? Would you rather I'd go back with you—in the car?"

"Go ahead, son. The walk will do you good."

The tall height of the doctor shrunk, as, shoulders slumped, he stood watching them go down the street.

But Sigrid hardly noticed Nico's presence. Tall, thin spirals of smoke from leaf piles rose, to be lost in the darkness of the sky; that smell of autumn hovered in the air; boys, late in finding their homes, made scuffling sounds by dragging their feet through dry leaves that had been swept into street curbings. A sere leaf drifted awhile before it fell—another—and another; the gentlest of breezes brushed her face and passed to her companion, a benediction, she fancied, from the one who had set the story on paper.

"What have you planned to do with the money, if it wins?" Nico broke the silence and leaned down to look full into her face. Would she use it as his dad and he wished she would?

"The money?" She paused. "Oh, yes, the money. I had not especially thought about the money."

The light of the far street lamp showed her face to him: no painted Madonna that he had ever seen had had a lovelier face than Sigrid's was at this moment.

"I have been thinking—oh, what if she—his mother—could see the words her son had written—between the covers of a book?" Her eyes looked far; her hands spread wide; her head moved slightly from side to side. "In her own hands—to hold—his book—"

"Do you suppose, Pastor, there are many such neighborhood groups as ours who keep on meeting year after year?"

"No, I do not suppose there are, Doctor, especially when one considers the infinitely different temperaments, interests, and occupations represented here."

"We all know what it is that has kept us together; we never should have meant what we do to each other if it had not been for Sigrid. It is she who—"

"I'm *ravenish!*" Hattie Allspaugh's voice drowned out all others. She pounded the stub of one cigarette into the center of an ash tray before lighting another, and the pastor watched the smoke as she inhaled, exhaled. Mrs. Allspaugh was one of the women who, with a collective frenzy in imitating one of the masculine vices, visualized themselves as having reached their goal, "equality with men." How little they comprehended the true worth of their sex, never inferior, never superior, simply the other half of the perfect whole.

"Come, Michael," Sigrid prompted, and smiled as little chubby fingers swished a paintbrush in a tumbler of water, turning its pinkish yellow to a muddy brown, then wiped the hairs on an old white stocking and cleaned mixing squares in the three-color paintbox.

"Come when you're told, do as you're bid; shut the door softly and you'll never be chid," Michael repeated mischievously, and set the tools of his love labor aside.

"Last time I heard that, your mother was teaching it to you, Sigrid." Mrs. Allspaugh brushed the back of her hand over her eyes.

All eyes followed Sigrid, setting platters of food on the table and spacing chairs around.

"Nights are getting awfully cold." Hattie turned the conversation. "I'm glad I got all my blankets *laundreed*. Ain't you, Taina?"

"Not too cold," Jack broke in, "to have another band concert tomorrow night."

"As late in the year as this? I thought there never were any after Labor Day."

"Never have," said Beda. "This, though, is to be a farewell concert. I heard at the store that it was going to be the last one—for keeps."

"You mean the last for good and all?" Nico stopped still, holding a hot dish full of savory Swedish meat balls and mushrooms.

"Yes," said Jack. "For good and all. They say the attendance has dwindled so, on account of moving-picture shows and automobiles."

"You can be glad for those! The automobiles, I mean." Nico set the dish on the table and blew on his fingers.

"You *said* it! We all ought to go, though, on the last night."

All could not, but to Sigrid there was a poignancy about the memories of the band concerts in Town Hall Park; if she went she could live over those glorious evenings when, as little more than a child, she had walked hand in hand between her mother and father, skirting the edges of the crowd, walking rather than sitting because while in motion the mosquitoes "did not bite so bad."

"Will you go with me?" Jack leaned close.

"Yes, thanks. I'd like to go."

Granny heard, and bit her lip. As she sat, late that evening, in her bedroom taking tiny point stitches on the daisy-petaled border of a wedding veil, furrows dug deep into her high brow and her lips were pursed. It might have

been a heavy rug she worked on, so hard she jabbed the
needle in. Now she muttered under her breath, "Her a-goin'
with Jack—when—" And the lace work went into the
wrapping of the old cotton sheet; resignedly she laid it
in her bottom bureau drawer.

It was not so much Jack as it was nostalgia, Sigrid would
have told Granny, that lured her out to this Saturday-
night band concert. Nostalgia, and October, for October to
her was a gaudy siren, her cheeks touched with the rosy
glow of maple, oak, and sumac; lips the color of bitter-
sweet berries. Sniffing the pungent smell of leaf smoke,
Sigrid walked alongside Jack, unmindful of him. Into her
mind flashed pictures of remembered Octobers; now she
could add another with its beauty, add her new buoyancy
at her pride in Michael's drawings, for he did not only
copy, his brush could paint the very images that grew in
his imagination.

The strains of "K-k-k-aty" came from the Park. Jack
hurried their steps. As they neared, from under the red-
roofed octagonal bandstand came, "When You Wore a
Tulip," and they sang in harmony, "And I wore a red,
red rose." The leader raised his baton, his white-gloved
hands waved, or shush-ed, as wind instruments of all
shapes and sizes blared. The alternate high spears and low
spears on the fancy, lacy iron railing at the edge of the
red shingles shivered; a piece of white-painted "ginger-
bread" trembled and fell at her feet from its place between
fancy, turned uprights. The bandstand was going to pieces.

She was glad she had come; a sort of sad-gladness it
was, for this was farewell to one more landmark, one more
identification with her childhood.

"Put On Your Old Gray Bonnet." The band played
them all, all of the favorites, to "The Star-Spangled Banner." Then what an ovation greeted the now-bowing
bandsmen!

Listeners drifted slowly from the Park, by families, in
couples. Reluctantly they folded blankets they had brought
to wrap around their legs in the fall chill, and put the
bandstand, the music, the summer, behind them. Children's
voices warned, "Run, sheep, run!" Desperately they played,
as if their whole pleasure of childhood had to be crowded
into this one evening, perhaps the last night before snow
came. And Sigrid strolled with Jack. Softly, now, strains

of an encore reached them, "Should Auld Acquaintance Be Forgot?"

She sighed. It was a parting with summer, a parting with an old small-town tradition in this, one of the many "small towns," now rightly called suburbs, which made up Chicago.

"Say, I'm doing swell," Jack said. "In my garage business."

"I am glad for you."

"I'm going to branch out, set up another one. Have you noticed how many autos there are on the streets now?"

"Yes." She had noticed. And how few horses there were, too.

"It's bound to be the coming business." Impulsively, "Why do you keep on going to night school? What good is a degree ever going to do you if you become a housewife?"

He didn't understand. Why should she take the trouble to answer him? He would never understand.

"Together, in my business, we could— Oh, Sigrid, can you ever forgive my—youthful mistakes? Can you forgive, and forget?"

"I forgot them long ago."

"Sigrid, I love you. I have always loved you." He stood in front of her, to stop her. "Will you marry me now?"

She stepped back so she could look at him; he was fine-looking, really handsome. His success showed on him, in his way of carrying his head, in his clothes.

It might be asking too much of life to know a love with perfect understanding, a love in which there was not room for question, in which she could respond wholly and without reservation to the man who claimed her. It might be better to take what came her way and make the best of it than to yearn for perfection. But she would not forget the pastor's advice, and she knew she must live a life of spinsterhood rather than accept the doubtful advantages of a marriage in which understanding, in which love such as Pastor Bedell had described would not have a place. It would not be fair to Jack, either, to accept him, knowing that she, her inner self, would have been lost to him even before the wedding day. Jack had chosen her; but not of Jack could she say unreservedly to her Farmor, "Of all men in America, this is my choice."

"No, Jack, I cannot marry you."

"But you said you have forgotten?"

"Yes, and I have. I am fond of you, Jack. Terribly fond. I hope I never lose you as a friend, but—"

"You mean you won't marry me ever?"

"I can't."

"Why?"

"Because I don't love you, Jack." Pastor Bedell had said that "only through love should seed be brought forth." There was a time when she had tried, yes, she had tried to love Jack.

He grabbed her arms roughly. "I know why! There's someone else! It's the doctor, isn't it? You won't have me, because there's someone else—"

"Yes, there's someone else. There's Michael."

"For God's sake, Sigrid, don't rub that in! I've always been sorry about that!" Sobbing, he buried his face in the curve of her neck. "If you could only *know* how sorry! But when a man's pushed against the wall—by lack of money—"

She drew away. "You'll find someone, Jack. Any girl will feel proud to have you propose to her."

In silence they walked toward home.

October, beautiful in the light of the street lamps. November soon would come. To herald its approach, to force the lifted head to nod to coming winter, soft-tinted, never-fading weeds drew Sigrid's gaze downward.

Winter would come. Winter—in her thoughts an old man sitting by the hearth. But melancholy need not come with winter: pleasant, too, was the sitting close around a fire, the sight of orange berries overflowing a satiny copper bowl in a friendly room.

To herself, Sigrid murmured, "Autumn goes, and winter comes. But in the winter we are nearer to spring than we are in October."

For spring would come—a young girl dancing.

Then summer—the woman fruitful, beneficent.

And fall again.

For such was the rhythm of the seasons—the reassuring rhythm of the seasons—the beating of the pulse of God.

22

Diamond dust on every branch and twig and dormant bud; Granny called it hoarfrost.

Dazzling sunlight on white earth and fence and slanting roof; Michael called it winter.

To Sigrid it was fairyland.

"Look, Michael." Breathless at the beauty of the out-of-doors, she gasped. "Look—at the rainbow colors—the frosty little spears!"

If only she could draw. But Michael could! Taking his hand, she walked with him into the wonder of winter. "Look, Michael, look!"

Damp, heavy snow fell. She formed a snowball, patting it with mittened hands, and dropped it, urging, "Roll it!"

"It grows bigger and bigger!" Excited, Michael, who had forgotten other winters, rolled; and Sigrid helped him, picking up the blanket of snow in a circular path around the yard, until the ball was as big around as a snow man's body should be, and green grass showed on the ground where they had rolled the ball. With coals for buttons, a corncob pipe of Louis', and an old felt hat of the doctor's, Mr. Snow Man stood ready for winter.

The deep of winter came, and frost on the windowpane. "Look, Michael!" Ferns, not forest green, but white, grew before the eyes of the astonished boy, and she marveled with him at the labyrinth of fronds, overlaid one upon the other, the long, graceful sweep of one drawing the boy's finger to trace its path across the foreground, sweeping, curving. All of the magnificence of a fern dell was here on the windowpane, an enchanted fern dell, which in filtering the sun's rays showed sparkling, jeweled spores.

Snow came, falling to place crazy top hats on the cattail stems. Snow stayed, piled on the pointed carrot nose of the snow man, making white "smoke" above the hole of his pipe.

Snow settled, forming little white turbans to sit jauntily on the topknots of stark Queen Anne's lace whose umbels were drawn tightly upward. Ladies with white turbans they were to Sigrid and Michael. Ladies, too, were the goldenrod; their sweeping dried flower panicles were willow plumes; and now the plumes were heavy with snow. Nodding, the goldenrod stood, their wandlike stems swaying, stopped, as ladies on their way to church, their pods round "muffs" held sedately before them.

Holding hands, Sigrid and Michael walked and ran and played in the head-clearing, lung-clearing cold air of winter. "Look, Michael!" She pointed out the blue snow, shadow shapes of lampposts, trees, and cottages; she called his attention to the rosy-hued snow when at sunset red clouds cast their glow over everything, but still a bit of October blue had been forgotten in the sky. "Look!"

She could not draw, but she could show Michael the beauties of the season, of every season. Through his eyes and heart and gifted hands he would put them on paper for her.

There was beauty for Michael to see, but there was pain also for the boy. Through his mouth, now, into the kitchen came shrieks and yells, for this was agony he knew, the thought of having a first tooth pulled. "There, now, don't fuss. Just hold still." Sigrid slipped a length of string around the loose tooth and tied a knot. The other end of the string already was tied to the doorknob.

"When are you going to pull it?" he whimpered. "Will you give me jiggers?"

"Oh, we'll wait until Granny comes in. She's coming right now! Hear her? As soon as she comes in—then—"

The doorknob turned and Granny came blustering in. "My glory be, but it's cold out!" The string sprang from its tautness and fell to the floor.

"Ow-w-w! Now you'll have to tie it on all over again," Michael moaned. But then, "Oh, Granny! Sigree! Here's my tooth—on the floor!" Amazed, he looked first at the tooth, then incredulously at his elders.

"See? It didn't hurt a bit."

"Wrap it up, darlin'," Granny advised. "Put it under

your bed pillow, and in the mornin' I'll bet you find a penny there."

The lucky penny came to Michael and he laid it on the table and put white paper over it, first on one side and then on the other, and drew lines across it with a soft pencil so that it showed the Indian head on the front and the pattern on the back; then cut the circles out and pasted them together. "It's a lucky penny for you, Sigree." He made certain she deposited it in the side pocket of her purse, then said seriously, "It *will* bring you good luck, you just see!"

She wished for the faith of a child, when on the next day she came home from work to find a letter from "The Biggs Publishing Company." She turned the envelope over and over, and held it close to the lamp globe: it was a letter, not a cold printed rejection.

Not a rejection slip! What if it should say—? That what she had sent in had won? Fantastic. Such things happened to other people, not to a person's self. Had she ever, in her whole life, known anyone who had won anything big? No, those were only the people one read about in the newspapers. Her lips formed the words as they would most likely be written within the envelope: "We were interested in the story, 'Chicago,' but—" or, "We thank you for—but—" Oh, yes, she knew without looking what the letter was going to say. How eloquent a few words, rightly placed together, could be. How decisive!

"The front doorbell!" She looked to Granny. "Now, who do you suppose would be out on a stormy night like this?"

Michael turned on the porch light. "It's Unc' Nico and Dr. Van!"

"Please let them in." Sigrid's tenseness left her. They would be here to soften the disappointment by sharing it.

"We're already in." They shook snow from overcoats and hung them in the hall. Overshoes came off. Nico sat himself in the rocker. "I see by the paper that the winners of that contest are to be notified today."

The doctor settled himself on the sofa. "So we thought we'd come over and wait for your telegram to come."

Why should she know disappointment? She had been certain all the while of the thing the letter would say. She was not disappointed; she had not expected Pa's work to win. It had not occurred to her, but of course it would have been a telegram that would come if Pa had won; naturally it would not have been only a letter. Holding it up, she forced a smile. "I have already heard." She shrugged her shoulders, at the same time lifting both hands, then dropping them, expressively, to show that she knew the whole thing had been hopeless—hopeless—

She sat on the carpet between the two visitors, slid her finger under the envelope's flap, and tore it open. Slowly she picked the ragged raw edges clean and handed the scraps to Michael to put into the wastebasket. More slowly she removed the letter, and unfolded it. It began as she had known it would, "We thank you for submitting—"

How she got to her feet she never would be able to guess. How she was swept first into Nico's arms and then into the center of the room, dancing, whirling around and around with Nico's hand in one of hers and the doctor's in the other, and Granny and Michael rounding out the circle, never would she know.

"Listen! 'We take great pleasure in informing you—' "

"First prize!" They'd have to call the pastor right away, to tell him!

"I have to make a sick call," the doctor volunteered. "I'll stop by and tell him."

Breathless at what this would mean to Mor Sigrid of Norden, Sigrid fell into a chair while Nico did the explaining to Granny. Pa's story would become a book!

"Glory be!" Granny clasped her head.

"Jumpin' gee whillikins!" said Michael.

When breath returned to Sigrid she spoke her plans: "The book will go to my father's mother. And I can buy Pastor Bedell a radio, complete, with a big battery, and a charger, and I can—"

As she listed all of the things that she could do, the look in Nico's eyes was not a fiery one, but a look of blue steely tenderness. So often he had noticed that Sigrid was, as she was now, without thought of self. But he knew her better than she knew herself; she had given away her secret longing as they studied the Swedish language.

He waited until Granny took Michael to bed. Then, "Did you realize, Sigrid, that the letter said the five hundred dollars would be considered as an advance against royalties, that if sales should go above a certain figure—if the book 'takes'—you will be paid additional royalties?"

"If it takes!" She laughed. "You speak of it as if it were a vaccination!"

They read the letter over again, to be sure. "So"—he hesitated—"for this money you should—"

"Should what?" She had already said what she planned to do.

He stopped walking up and down, stood before her and held her elbows in his two hands. "We'll get a radio for Pastor Bedell. Dad and I'll see to that. I should have thought of it before—"

She winced at the pressure of his hands.

"The opportunity will always be here, to go to school, to set aside money to send Michael to the Art Institute, to do all of the things you say you want to do, but your grandmother won't always be there."

As he dropped his arms she went to the rocking chair, her eyes filled with tears; tears dropped to her waist front.

"Please, Sigrid, use this money to go to Sweden."

Of course she could not go. She would not dare broach the idea of an extension of her two weeks' summer vacation; she could not afford to lose her job. But she could dream of visiting her grandmother. Of course she could not *go;* she could not very well leave Granny and Michael. And yet—to go!

Some peace of mind came with her impulsive writing of a letter to the publishing house. Oh, in this she knew no indecision. If they had no definite plans for the dust jacket, might she suggest that they print on it a picture of Chicago's old Water Tower, the house of the standpipe of Chicago's first water works? It should be in color, with sunshine lighting its crenellated turrets, the majestic structure standing as a castle against a blue, blue sky. Complete with battlements it should stand, its long, narrow windows showing light and shadow, its heavy stones describing the strength of the tower, the only major building to survive the Great Fire of 1871. Its few green trees should add their color and their low height against it.

Pioneer of Chicago's early days—

Memorial to the Great Fire—

Symbol of the spirit of the city—

Chicago's old Water Tower.

A part of the heart of every Chicagoan, it would travel
to Sweden.

Of course *she* could not go, but that part of her would
go with the book to her Farmor in the Old Country. . . .

One of Granny's hands slid into a boy's sock, and a
heel hole spread over the clenched fist. The other hand
held a darning needle, first flat against the sock then weaving up and down. The needle hand stopped its work now
and again to rub across the darn to feel if it was smooth.

Those hands, so capable, so long in use, wrinkled, old,
how much longer could they be useful on this earth? As
she looked, Sigrid saw other hands, older, two years older
than these before her. What were they doing now in
Sweden?

She looked down at her own; they were big, but they
had long, slender fingers; they were shapely, but they knew
calluses on the mounds. The coal and snow she had
shoveled were bound to leave a mark; and the tips of her
fingers were snub-ended from pounding against typewriter
keys.

Granny's lay in her lap, still for a moment. Old hands,
conditioned by life, their shape changed by work and
time.

Sigrid started. She had to see her own grandmother's
hands before it was too late. It was almost as if her father
spoke, reminding her of his wish that she should see his
old home and know his mother. Her eyes closed. Why had
he left *this* story, when she knew he had destroyed many
another of his writings? Why had the contest been one
into which his story had fitted so precisely? Why had it
won?

It was as if she were meant to go. Her father had provided the way. Truly this means had stemmed from the
Old Country; it should be used to know her kinfolk. And
if she went, she herself could lay the book that would
mean so much to Mor Sigrid into those hands—the ones
which had held the books from which her son, Karl, had
learned to read—the hands which had taught him to write!

"I am going to go!" The words burst from her.

"I am glad." Granny looked closely at her darning
stitches. How could she and Michael do without Sigrid's

presence? How long would she be gone? Granny dared not ask, for fear Sigrid might change her mind.

Sigrid moved to the writing desk.

"I am glad," Granny repeated, "that you have decided to go."

Sigrid picked up the pen. Was it actually she who had decided? It seemed not so much by her own compulsion that the decision had been reached; it seemed more that it was the Hand of God, working out the pattern of her life to answer the prayers of the mother of a son.

"Kära Farmor," she wrote. "Do not ask me how, or where I got the money. Do not ask me anything. Only know that when the summer comes I, too, shall be coming." Before she dropped the letter into the green letterbox on the corner she pressed it to her lips.

Never had the hands of the clock passed each other so quickly, and yet so slowly, as in the months that followed. The twilight sky blued evening snow for the last time. March winds came to send kites soaring into fast-moving clouds. Chicago's grounds and buildings, splattered with dirty suds of snow, waited for the spring to send a cleansing rinse of rain water. Day after day Michael, sent from home "spankin' clean," sprawled on his stomach, oblivious to all around him, intent on the game before him, the visor of his cap over one ear, his eyes squinted, nose wrinkled, tongue out of one side of his mouth but caught tightly between what front teeth were left, his thumb held trigger taut. Then, with a slight muscle movement, after marbles clicked, dusty, and with dirty hands and handkerchiefs, he found his way to school.

Robins came; sparrows dust-bathed under the porch, making the gray ground move in fluttering ripples; a brown bird lay prone, stretching first one wing and then the other to fan them in the sunshine.

"All you have to do, my dear, is to wash your face in the early-morning dew on May Day." Granny gently pushed Sigrid out of the door. "But all the whilst you have to be a-wishin'."

"Such an old maid as I, being so—"

"It always worked in Ireland. I don't see any good reason why it shouldn't work in this country." Granny knew the ritual: if rightly followed it would bring, during the year, knowledge of her heart's love to a maiden.

Sigrid smiled, a half-sad, wistful smile, her face wet with the morning dew.

That was a day to remember, the day the postman delivered the book. A day to circle on the calendar; a day to count almost as the beginning of time; but no day to shout and celebrate; rather, one to spend in solemn thankfulness.

"In sure and certain hope of the Resurrection unto eternal life," Pastor Bedell had said at Pa's funeral. The words resounded in her ears; this was a resurrection, for her father would live on, immortal through his book, as long as a book could last.

Her lips moved slightly; now they opened slightly, and her tongue moistened them; opened wide to help her wide-open eyes see all on the illustrated end papers inside the binding of deep Lake Michigan blue. Somehow the artist had caught the feeling of the wind, swaying long grasses; and as Sigrid looked, soft clouds seemed actually to be traveling across those two front end pages.

Looking at the back ones, she could feel the force of that wind being stopped against the stone and marble of Chicago's skyline.

Lightly her forefinger traced the outline of the City Seal depressed into the front center of the binding, the "Y" of the Chicago River, and the motto, "I WILL." And the dust jacket was as she had visualized it, as she hoped it might be. The tower stood "alive."

Under the spell of the marvel of her father's book she completed her term's evening classwork. Now she had a better feeling of the Swedish language, could understand the endings of names other than "son," which always had been clear enough: "strand," for shore; "lund," for a grove or clump of trees; "ros," for rose; "kvist," for twig—but mostly spelled "quist"; "holm," for islet; "gren," for tree branch; "dahl," for valley; "blom," for flower; "blad," for leaf; and "berg," for mountain. Poetic names, when a person knew how they had been derived, were "Dahlgren," or "Lundquist." She could see how the Swedes in Middle Western America solecized their native tongue; often, seemingly speaking Swedish, men lapsed into speaking of the "roof-et" of a house, or they added an "a" to words where an "a" did not belong.

She bought her ticket on the Swedish-American Line, from New York to Göteborg: Second cabin on the *Drottningholm,* $330 round trip. Not so grand as cabin class, not so sumptuous as first class, but it was a ticket to Sweden, to the home of Mor Sigrid.

There was no need for new clothes to make the trip; what she had was plain but good; and nobody there had seen them, so they would be new to them. And her shoes. What did it matter that the soles were thin—they hardly touched the ground now that she fairly flew wherever she went!

Her friends were happy for her. But Mr. Horgan: "A month? Do you have to be gone a whole month? What am I going to do?"

"It will be only a month," she reassured him. "You'll get along fine without me."

Every day was a step over a threshold, every day different; but now a day had come to mark a turning point for her. For one whole month she was not to be a working girl clinging to a streetcar strap, not being jostled by rough, smelly men. The neighbors had come with her, and they all piled into the railroad coach. "No Pullman?" the doctor asked, disturbed. "I didn't realize—do you mean you have no berth accommodations?"

"I don't see how you're ever going to get along, not knowing the *langridge* any better'n you do." Aunt Hattie, too, was distressed.

"Now, these parcels are for you. But don't you dare open any of them until you are on your way!" Nico admonished her.

"I won't." Her voice cracked.

"ALL ABOARD!"

"Good-by!"

"Good-by! Be a good boy, Michael!"

" I will."

I WILL. The motto of Chicago, her home. Her throat filled; it was as if her heart jumped into it. Now she could well ask herself, why, why had she decided to go?

One after the other they kissed her. "Hurry back!" Nico said.

And the doctor, "I'll count the days till you come back."

And the pastor, "God bless you, and send you back safe —to us."

"A-L-L A-B-O-A-R-D!"

The little sea of faces looking up to her blurred, as objects in the mists of early morning, then slowly slid away.

Haltingly she returned to her seat. The green mohair-covered seat was piled high with parcels; each had a note attached, but her eyes could not see to read; they only saw that little sea of friendly faces, and as she sat there, those faces all merged into a Dutch composite—two into one—and out of it shone steely blue eyes.

Swiftly she sped into the night. The lights that sprang from nowhere were those eyes, then in a wink they were gone.

She sat up, braced against the pillows, with her window shade rolled up. Often the steam engine's whistle, a lonesome voice with heartbreak as its core, wailed two long and two short blasts through the night. Sometimes an echo came—two long and two short—and the heartbreak sound was stronger. She was leaving home and friends behind.

It was as if there should be no time taken for sleeping, traveling as she was. She wished she could make the acquaintance of the towns they passed through, and walk on the streets of the cities when the train stopped. A town was only a clump of lights approached, blurred, and left behind; a city, the dark brick walls of a railroad station broken by a barred window inside of which a night light burned weakly over a littered desk, a sign, "American Railway Express," a four-wheeled cart piled high with mailbags being pushed or pulled along the platform by a bent old man. As those neared, she pulled down the window shade and peered through a crack left at the bottom. No different looking than Elmhurst or Geneva or Oak Park were the little she saw of Gary, Columbus, or Wheeling.

Now she saw mountains, great points of land, pushing against the clouds, and she pressed her nose against the car window the better to see land that was not prairie. She stared in wonder at unfamiliar towns as they sped by.

New York City was different. Was it only because she had left the train and become one of the populace, or was it because it was daytime and she could see the character of the city? Nothing about the city seemed strange or new. It was almost as though she had been here previously;

but of course it was through her mother's telling that she knew New York.

Here was the brownstone front in which Elin had lived; there was the English basement, the first floor, the second floor, the third. There, that window, high above the entrance door, would be the one in the little hall bedroom her mother had known as her first home in the new country. The Philadelphia rubbernecker, rusted, with clouded and cracked mirrors, still protruded from the sill of the second-story window. Would it be possible that Dr. Osgood or one of his family still lived here?

"No," the maid responded to her ring. A Miss Flynn ran a boardinghouse here now. The section was known as Greenwich Village, and was inhabited mostly by artists.

Sigrid lingered on the steps. Her tiny mother had walked these steps, had *scrubbed* them. She ran her fingertips over the handrail lovingly. Oh, if only she could have her mother back for just one day—one day, in which to crowd all of the things she should have done for her and never did; one day in which to say all of the kind things she always meant to say but never said.

"Min lilla mor," she whispered. "You seem so close to me here, closer even than in Chicago where we were together."

It seemed to her as though Elin took her hand and led her to the dock, walked with her up the gangplank, went with her to her cabin and returned to the deck to bid "Au revoir" to America. Countless boats wove a complex wake pattern over the water, and it was as though Elin's eyes led Sigrid's eyes over the pattern to gaze at the Statue of Liberty; as though her voice told of one day, long since, climbing up into the arm which held that torch, into that huge hand, all growing smaller and smaller as the *Drottningholm* now moved toward the open sea.

23

Mothered by an inland prairie, christened by clear blue water, Sigrid, child of Middle Western America, stood leaning over the rail of the *Drottningholm*, looking down at the green and churning salt water of the Atlantic, watching its intricate shifting patterns.

Begrudging the time spent in fostering shipboard friendships, reluctant to spare the necessary time for eating, all she asked was to stay with sailors' stance on deck, feeling the spray and wind against her face, watching the teasing, pulling, slippery waters, seeing the huge waves dash their white-lace-edged jade against the prow. Now, here, she could find it difficult to recognize the well-known fact of birth from a flesh-and-blood mother and father, so much a child of the sea she seemed. Now the Viking spirit rose to outdo all other heritage. Let poets moan of sorrowing seas, or empty seas: she loved each salty drop.

The doctor had come over these rolling waters, even as Elin had come, and the big blustering Karl. He, even as they, had walked ship's boards over this very deep. Only a ship's chartered course it was that they had followed, the immigrants, but to the hearts and souls of those many it had been the broad pathway to the Land of Promise. But, oh, if the waters below could speak to tell of the heartaches they had left behind, and *carried with them!*

Thinking of heartaches was to think of Pa. "The story of the immigrant to Chicago, Scandinavian or any other nationality, around the turn of the century," the head of the Swedish Mission had said to her one day, "could never be fully told without taking into account his intemperance." Was it the transplanting that had made Pa weaker than he might have been if his roots had remained undisturbed? And those others? What about them? No one would ever know. But such as they had made a home for

such as she. Perhaps Pa had floundered, never able to know
the assurance which would have come with the habits of
generations in his own country; but he had given her firm
ground on which to grow. He had given her America.

Suddenly the deep draught of adventure turned her
stomach and she was overcome with homesickness. Grop-
ing, she left the deck. Where was her cabin? Where the
gifts to bridge the long way to home and friends? She
rushed to find them, and did not see the marks her tears
made on the tissue-paper wrappings.

One by one she undid the parcels, unwrapped the gifts,
and closed her eyes to see the giver and set herself in the
mood to "hear" their voices as she read each message on
the cards attached. One little parcel bore a much too large
card marked with printed letters, "Something you like,
from Michael"; and in it was a box of Cracker Jack. Who
could be so composed as not to bury her head in her arms
and sob for home, for friends?

As a child she always had "kept the biggest until the
last," and now one parcel remained unopened. "Something you like," had been copied from Michael's card,
"from the van Vlaardingens." Which one of them had
printed it? It was surgeon fingers which had wrapped the
parcel, with the corners of the blue tissue paper folded
carefully, precisely.

Lingering over the wrapping, she removed the ribbon,
coiled it around her fingers, laid it on top of the folded
tissue. Slowly, savoring each second of anticipation and
suspense, she slid the box cover off.

This was one of those moments in life when fingers,
hands, arms cannot obey the order from the mind to feel,
to lift, to hold a gift aloft; when knees bend, when eyes
can only close, and fingers only intertwine.

Here, come as a gift from the high bidder at the auction,
was the blue shawl.

Sigrid of Norden stood on her boat landing, Sigrid the
mother, Sigrid the grandmother. The wind blew her clothing, to show the shape of her tall, spare body, fluttering
her skirts behind.

Of all of her children, and her grandchildren, only one
was not of Norden. Of all, only one had not rested as an infant in her arms. This one, how would she be? This grand-

daughter, who was an American, who was one of them through her letters, yes, but in the flesh of her, *how would she be?* When she saw how they lived on this rocky island with its seck ground, what would she say?

What if the young Sigrid should be disappointed in Norden, and display that disappointment before the others to make them sad? What if the young Sigrid should be disappointed in her? After all, she was only a peasant woman. What if this American girl should be ashamed of her? She looked at her hands, then quickly hid them in her skirt folds.

What if this Sigrid, kin though she was, should feel upon seeing them that the ones here were not good enough for her?

Whatever she was, however she was, she was Karl's daughter. Mor Sigrid turned from the sea. Moving with the rhythmic grace that was so much a part of her, she strode toward the dwelling. There all was in readiness. As in anticipation of Yuletide every inch of the buildings, indoors and out, house and barn, was newly scrubbed. The animals, too, were fresh from soap and water, clean smelling.

But such buzzing as there was in the big room as she entered! Lissie came to greet her, hugged her tightly, and panted, "Oh, Mor, isn't it wonderful?"

"Aye, Lissie, aye." Mor Sigrid's throat was choked with —with what she could not say, except that the well of happiness inside her was full beyond the point of overflowing. Her hands clasped and unclasped, clutched at her breasts as if the greatness of her joy brought pain too great to bear. Here were her children—all—all come for the meeting with Karl's daughter. And yet she was afraid. What would the young woman from America think of them?

"Remember, now, we are to say 'Welcome'!"

So it had been agreed upon: they would make the newcomer feel at home, all chiming in to say the word their hearts felt; but in English it must be spoken, this first word.

"Go, Lennart, go." She almost shoved Lissie's husband from the room. "So shall we wait, and the minutes shall be as hours until you return with Karl's daughter."

"Have the coffeepot ready!" Lennart called back, and rested on one oar so he could wave; and his boat headed toward the mainland. From thence he would go on to Göteborg.

So slow, this trip seemed. At last he stood at Göteborg Harbor, with the west wind blowing into his face, and that was good. "One need not be a sea captain to know that the wind from the Atlantic blows warmth to Sweden," he said, joining a watcher on the dock: Lars Ahlsén, the rich man's son, scion of the family who owned the fleet of ships he called his sea home.

"Nay, not like the east winds from the Russian-Asiatic continent, cold." Lars forced a shiver, then broke into a hearty laugh. "What brings you here, Captain Lennart? I thought you were taking land leave while your ship was in dry dock."

"I have come to meet a passenger on the *Drottning-holm*."

They stood together, looking toward the sea they loved. Suddenly, impulsively, "Beautiful," Lars said, scribing an arc to take in the scene before them with the wide sweep of his arm: ferries skimming across to Hising Island; fishing boats, low in the water, leading the way for countless gulls.

"Lars sees beauty in all except women. How is that, sir? So fine a young man as you should—"

"My heart is given to the sea, I guess." Again came the hearty laugh.

Unspoiled by money, by social position, Lars. Lennart laid his arm across the younger man's shoulders. He could wish one of his sisters was of age for Lars; he loved the boy.

"There she comes!"

There came the *Drottningholm*.

The American Sigrid clutched the rail. It was as if she and the boat stood still as closer, closer came the land of her forebears. The sea, its loud and mighty turbulence spent, now crawled in slow and gentle motion toward the shore. These were the waters where the Skagerrak and Kattegat joined.

Buildings making up the skyline of Göteborg grew; trawlers lined up in the fish harbor took on shape, and shapes were repeated, rippling, upside down. Those characteristic points of the city's profile, Skansen Lion and Skansen Crown, enlarged in size for Sigrid, just as so many years ago they had diminished in the sight of her father as he had bade farewell. No, not farewell; she was sure he had not used, even to himself, that most final of words for he had truly planned on returning "someday." "When he got rich," he always said, "then would he return to Sweden," carrying this to his mother, that to his sisters. Oh, he would go home laden with gifts. "When he got rich," he would go home.

"Home." Always that wistful, longing quality to the word.

True, he had spoken, had written, of America as his home; but there was a tinge of reserve, a hesitancy, as when a half-grown child learns to call a new stepmother "Mother."

What would he say if he could see her now, steaming straight ahead toward his mother to lay the richest gift of all into her hands?

The two forts, Skansen Lion and Skansen Crown, grew bigger. Since the seventeenth century thus had they enlarged before the eyes of those nearing Swedenland, and now Sigrid's eyes drank in their outlines. Reflections from the old canals, fishing boats, nets drying in the sun, church steeples reaching toward the high blue sky, all this had filled her parents' sight. This, before her, was what they had chosen to leave, yet had never entirely left behind—their homeland; home of her ancestors whose blood coursed through her veins.

Born to the new land's prairie, nurtured by its inland waters, Sigrid stood profoundly touched by sight of rugged shore lapped by a now-tamed sea. Distant hills rose and fell with the rise and fall of the *Drottingholm's* deck. Bottle-green water churned and swirled about the slowing hull.

The ship hardly scraped against the pilings.

Sigrid, mothered by a new land, stretched out her hand to make acquaintance with the old. Lennart grasped the hand, and through his smile, with a little Swedish lilt, came, "Welcome home!"

Lars, the sea- and sun-tanned son of Swedish noblemen,

had followed, and now he grasped her other hand and
echoed Lennart's welcome.

The big room always seemed big enough till now.

Even rich, it had seemed, with fuchsias growing in pots
set in the deep window sills, with the little white curtains
made more than a half-century ago of the cloth her schoolteacher on the mainland, the Widow Kvalvog, had brought
her from Norway. Mor Sigrid bit her lip. Before Peter had
come into her life she had counted those threads and made
the Hardanger pattern; Peter, father of all her children. It
was long since she had given him thought; the happy years
with Big Johann as husband had all but wiped out the sor-
did memories of Peter's lust.

A pair of the curtains still hung at each window. So
many times had she had to replace the crocheted rings,
worn out by sliding over the poles; so many times the curtains had been laundered, and still there they hung beautiful in age. To her! But what would they be to the American
Sigrid? Merely "old curtains"?

"Let her hurry and come, so I may know." Her hands
clasped so tightly that the knuckles grew white. Again she
clutched at her bosom to ease the pain. Her head tipped
sidewise as she strained her ears to hear the sound of oars
over the happy chattering of her gathered family.

The sound of oars—such heartbreak as that sound had
brought to her on that day when Karl left home.

"Dear God, let his daughter be kind." Her eyes rested
for an instant on each one in the room. "Whatever the
American thinks of us here, let her be kind."

Aye, this was indeed so small a room in which to stage
a welcome for the granddaughter from America. Best she
go to the boat landing to greet the young woman from the
rich land across the sea—out in the open, where she could
breathe.

She started toward the door.

The sound of oars!

Were her feet glued to the floor, that she could not move?
Before her eyes the room moved, but she stood waiting,
until there in the doorway stood Karl's daughter.

"Välkommen!" From sixteen tongues the Swedish welcome came. With all of the coaching, with all of the reminding, after all of the determination to remember to

speak the word "Welcome," none, not even Mor Sigrid, remembered.

With all of Sigrid's resolutions to show that she fit in by saying, *"Tack!"* the words that came with overwhelming emotion were, "Thank you, thank you all!"

Mor Sigrid came forward. Outstretched hands clasped outstretched hands, and the two Sigrids stood looking deep into each other's eyes. "You are Karl's daughter." Evenly, Sigrid of Norden spoke. Here was, indeed, the answer to her prayers, for in this lovely young woman Karl had returned. She *was* Karl, his frame, his forehead, the color of his hair, the color of his eyes, the protruding eyetooth. Perhaps a firmer, stronger chin than Karl's—perhaps—but oh, she would have known, had she met her anywhere on earth, that this was Karl's child!

They stood, hands clasped, looking at each other, drinking in this new good taste of kinship.

Sigrid closed her hands tighter over the older ones. This was her grandmother. Taller than she—and she was tall—straight; there was no gray noticeable in the blond hair braided high over the most kindly face she had ever seen. Her father's mother resembled him, the same large frame, the same high forehead, the same blue eyes. A softer face, more marked with mercy, love, and humility; a little squarer, firmer chin—maybe—than her father's; but had she met this Swedish Sigrid anywhere, anywhere, she would have known her as her grandmother.

She looked long and steadily into the eyes of Mor Sigrid of Norden. "Home," Lennart had said. "Welcome home." Home was in Chicago, in America; yet, somehow, here, with her grandmother's hand in hers, she knew that she belonged. And oh, it was a good feeling!

Tears welled in four blue eyes, tears of gladness. Then Sigrid spoke, *"Farmor, älskade Farmor!"*

"Karl's dotter!" Their arms went about each other and they stood, love flowing from heart to heart.

"Praise God," the grandmother said. "Once more I see the power of prayer." How could she have wondered how the young American woman would be? How could she have doubted that young Sigrid would be—be Sigrid? This was Karl's daughter, her own granddaughter, her own blood. She was one of them. And she was home.

"I have been selfish." Her face colored, and Sigrid mar-

veled at the skin, like that of a young woman, not gray
and wrinkled in seamy patterns as Granny O'Toole's was.

"Here we have Lars," Mor Sigrid curtsied. "It is good
of you to come to grace our lowly home. You will stay, of
course, for a few days? A fine surprise to see you! And to
what are we indebted for this visit?"

Lars drew her up from her curtsy and placed his arm
about her. "Mor Sigrid, it is good of you to make me welcome. *Tack!* And as for my coming—nothing could have
kept me from coming." He looked, unabashed, toward Sigrid.

She blushed. Suddenly something brought back the memory of Granny's ritual on May Day, brought recollection
of the feel of morning dew on her face as she had stood
wishing, reminded her of Granny's promise that the year
would be sure to bring knowledge of her heart's true love.

Now came a thrill such as she had never before experienced at seeing Lars stoop to kiss her grandmother's work-
worn hand. And then Mor Sigrid said, "We have so many
to meet our new Sigrid. Now, here is—"

Young Sigrid touched her arm. "Please, may I ask one
favor?"

"Aye, aye, indeed."

"Please, first after you, may I know Lissie?"

"Lissie?" The mother's breast heaved, her chin quivered.
"You know Elisabet as Lissie? Your father told you about
Lissie?"

As Elisabet stepped forward the poise that marked Mor
Sigrid was gone. She was as a child. Eagerly, naïvely, she
stammered, "Karl told her about your being Lissie to us!"
Oh, there had been times when she had questioned, when
Karl did not write, when he did not come home; times
when she had doubted her son, had worried for fear he
might have been careless in some of his ways, that he
might have forgotten his home, but no!

Sigrid could not keep her eyes from her aunt Lissie's
face, the face that Pa had said, in a kindly way, was ugly.
He had told of an awful birthmark on the left cheek, one
from which long, bristly hairs protruded and hung as from
a bear's hide. Pa had not known, but the bearskin mark
was gone. There was a scar, but years had mellowed it,
and Lissie's face was beautiful. So was her hair, worn low
in a large figure eight, covering the back of her neck.

Big Johann filled his eyes with the sight of the three of
them, Mor Sigrid, Lissie, and Sigrid, as mutely they stood.
Always he had said, and it was brought home to him now,
that some are closer to God than others. Dear Morfar was
one, his See'ri is one, Lissie is one; and now, seeing Karl's
daughter, there was about her, to him, that same indefin-
able quality of goodness. Merely to have them in the room
invested the place with the dignity of love. Even as Lissie
was, Sigrid was a likeness to his See'ri. No greater tribute
could he pay.

He shook hands now with young Sigrid, and she could
tell from the warmth of the handclasp that she had passed
inspection.

Lennart she knew from having come with him from
Göteborg; knew of his deep love for Lissie, his deep appreciation for her acceptance of his son, Tuppie. Elisabet
and Lennart's son, Karl-Johann, bowed next to her. Four
or five years older than she, he had finished at Uppsala
University and was now an architect. And there was Justina, Lissie's change-of-life baby, only ten years old.

In the sequence of their ages her Farmor's children were
presented: Maria, and her sculptor husband, redheaded
David; Young Johann, who excused himself, smiling, because he did not rise. It was with an effort that Sigrid
looked away from him, he was so crippled; but none of
the others seemed to notice his great handicap, or cater to
him because of it. He had no wife, nor yet did Herman
Nikodemus. "Full of the 'Old Nick,'" Pa had used to
describe the boy who was now a man. But still the mischief was in his eye.

Oh, there were plenty of stories they could tell about
Herman Nikodemus! Now Mor Sigrid did show indulgence
to crippled Johann to the point of breaking the chain of
introductions so he could tell of the time, as a stripling,
Herman had tricked his schoolteacher—nearsighted the
man was—given to thrashing his charges on the nearest
provocation. Well, perhaps not so "mere" in the case of
Herman; but, sure of a thrashing when called to the front
of the room, the boy had filled the seat of his pants with
ripe lingonberries.

The teacher struck. Herman Nikodemus howled. The
lingonberries burst their skins and red juice flowed down
the boy's legs to the floor.

"My God! My God! Blood!" the nearsighted teacher had cried, and run screaming from the schoolhouse, holding his head and begging forgiveness from above.

Herman himself finished the telling, "Well, never again did he thrash a child in his schoolroom!"

His mother sighed, but the sigh belied the laughter she held inside; no, Herman Nikodemus was never meant to be a man of the Church, as she had hoped when he lay in his cradle. Born on the birthday of Jesus, yes, but the devil must have thought that was enough: full of the old man with the pointed tail was Herman.

Aye, her children's lives were like books, each a story in itself. Who could have dreamed on that Christmas Day, which was the first page of the book of Herman, that ensuing pages would disclose his life's work as that of drawing funny pictures for the newspapers? Was there a child in Sweden now who had not followed the capers of the thirteen children of one imaginary farm family? Or *was* the family entirely from Herman's imagination?

Oskar Rudolf, and the two others, ah, too soon the books of those little ones had ended. Tenderly she had laid them away. But the book of Karl; not even after learning of his death had she laid that book aside, for deep in her heart she had know she would see its sequel. She had begun to read that sequel now, and its title was *The American Sigrid.*

Such happy books were those of Lissie, and Johann, and Maria, and Marta. Marta Linnea was next to be presented to the newcome family member. Marta, svelte, comely, richly groomed; so right was the mind's eye picture of Marta standing on a concert stage bringing forth music from her precious old violin.

"Someone has to make up for all of the race suicide in this family!" Agda laughed as she and her husband, Tuppie, came forward with their brood.

Tuppie must bear resemblance to his dead mother, Sigrid decided; he was small of build, dark-haired, and his eyes were much like those of Granny or Michael, with an Irish twinkle in them. He limped slightly, dragging his right foot. Agda and Tuppie, partners in a fine tailoring business, were the proud parents of Hjördis and Nordis, Helga and Tora, four girls ranging from twenty years to two.

Sigrid shook her head; she might have been a queen, the

way they welcomed her. Women and girls curtsied before her, and the men bowed lowly to "Sigrid, the daughter of Karl"—except Johann, who sat in the wheel chair, and his welcome shone from deep blue eyes.

Patrik Bror was last. Her father had never mentioned Patrik.

"It is almost thirty-five years ago Karl left," her grandmother said on presenting him. "My youngest is a living reminder, for Patrik was born in the August after Karl left home."

In the silence that followed the very air semed to reflect the heaviness of hearts. Then Sigrid's nostrils widened: the air was imbued with the redolence of coffee!

"He is no gentleman, nor lady, who drinks it not!" Herman Nikodemus set a tray on her lap. "Aye, that's the virtue of the coffee drink—it will prevent drowsiness—it much quickens the spirit and makes the heart lightsome. Partake of this homely brew, child of the berry which grows upon little trees only in the deserts of Arabia!"

She could not drink for laughing.

"Drink! Drink!" he urged, playing the fool. "It is to be taken as hot as possibly can be endured; the which will never fetch the skin from off the mouth or raise any blisters by reason of that heat. It is a simple, innocent thing, composed into a drink by being dried in an oven, and ground to an almost powder, and boiled up with spring water. Drink! *Skål!*"

Laughing, they all raised their cups. "Skål!"

Now Sigrid must sit on the little three-legged stool in the honor corner, and before they told more about themselves Mor Sigrid must hear about Karl, his work, everything. And about Elin.

Sigrid told first about her mother, the little Elin her father had loved; come from Halland in Sweden, so tiny, so frail in body, but so strong in character, so rich in faith. She brought out the little tintypes and unhooked the brass clasps on their worn coffee-brown leatherette folding frames. "Taken on their wedding day."

It was a miracle that any likeness remained on the tintypes, so eagerly sight of them was devoured.

It was a sight for those eyes of Karl's mother, to see him sitting in a carved chair, even with his clothes much too tight-fitting, and a funny small-brimmed derby on his head.

And on looking at the other, her head swayed; and she said, glancing toward Lars, "The long, thin neck of the aristocrat—so well Karl married—"

As Sigrid talked on, again it was as though Elin brushed her cheek to bid her tell only the good of Karl. It was not that it would matter to this family; there was one trait of theirs which stood out, already, on this short acquaintance, proclaiming their everlasting consciousness of the fact that they were members of a family group. She knew it would not matter to one of them, how widely scattered they might become, how high on the ladder of success one might climb, how deep in failure another might descend, they would still be that family group, still loyal to each other.

No, she knew it would not matter what she told. Still, she would heed the little voice and tell only the good. Elin had had such pride!

His family knew of his magnificent and heroic deed as he had died, and so she told of the many little ways in which Elin had showed her love for Karl, the many ways in which Elin had been a good mother; but as she told, and looked at her grandmother, it seemed more as though she and Elin had been contemporaries, *syskon*, siblings, and that Farmor Sigrid was mother to them all—Pa, Elin, Tony, and her.

Mor Sigrid. Together those two words spelled "Mother" in its biggest sense.

"Mor Sigrid"—having the sound of poetry.

There was Tony to tell of, the little brother who lay beside Karl in Rose Hill. And Elin: never had the soil of the new land nurtured her transplanted roots to make them hold, and so when her father had sent her a ticket, she had gone home.

"I was wishing that maybe I could go to where my mother is buried, and see her grave."

Mor Sigrid cast a glance toward Maria and David. At their nod, "You shall go. We wish not to spare you for a single day; but the way shall be found for you to visit your mother's resting place in Halland province."

"Tack! Tack!" Sigrid remembered to use her Swedish now. But she must tell all—all—and so came the picture of the night the northern lights showed above Chicago, of the skiing her father had done at Rockville; and it was

only kindness that kept her from telling of the expedition's disastrous ending, his coming home with a broken hip.

"Karl went on ski, in America?" His mother's eyes shone. "It was I who taught him to ski, and he had not forgotten!" She was excited, and her words came tumbling out. "Let me tell you! One time when he was only a boy, Karl excelled in competition—and won a—*wait!*" She rose and went to the chest room. "Come, Sigrid, and see."

In the chest room, on poles stretched across the room near the ceiling, hung rounds of *knäckebröd,* known in America as hardtack, an off-center hole in each. "Those on the far pole are yours, baked when I learned of your birth; there they are, waiting for you when you shall marry—" She cut herself short and drew an arm around Sigrid. "I am sorry."

"No matter now, Farmor." Sigrid smiled warmly. But the touching part of seeing the wedding bread was that ever since her birth she had been a part of the life here. She, who had mourned the lack of family, had been a part of the family at Norden all the time.

Big Johann had followed them. "Draw back your hand, See'ri; I shall lift this heavy lid." As the chest lid closed, and they walked back into the big room, her grandmother laid a pair of diminutive silver skis on her opened hand. "Aye, Big Johann was there and saw it all. And no more proud are you than we all were on that day Karl brought them home; than he was himself! I was going to send them to him. I had sent one of his belongings by Georg, but I never learned if it reached him or no; and Georg went to California, and—" Mor Sigrid's look begged Big Johann to tell her Georg Ahlgren was still among the living only, like Karl, slow to write. Sadly he shook his head, and she spoke on, "When I never had answers from Karl, to my letters, I saved the skis for you." A smile came. "But never did I dare to hope that I could lay them in your hand."

Sigrid's voice trembled as she told of her childhood and her father's gifts to her, gifts made by his own hands: the peach-pit lavaliere; the little violin fashioned from a wooden cigar box; the theater made of a shoe box; of the surprise gift, when it was not her birthday or Christmas or anything, the book of Victor Hugo, and how he had read it to her—

Mor Sigrid sent a quick look, a look of deep satisfaction, to Lissie before her eyes dropped their lids. But even lids pressed tight could not contain the drops that had to fall. Karl had not forgotten!

Well she remembered the birth time of her son, how she had prayed that she might have marked Karl with the love of good reading, and writing, too. Had he ever written after leaving home? Again she moved quickly, this time to the fireplace. "The King's men, in all of their inspections, never found this bit of laxity, this neglect of proper repair." Two loose bricks in the fireplace wall gave to her fingers, and reaching into the gap she brought out its contents. Lovingly she stroked the two books, *Les Misérables* and *Andersen's Fairy Tales,* before replacing them. The rolls and little stacks of paper she handed to Sigrid.

"Before Karl came I called this 'My Niche for Literature,' and after he was old enough to show interest in reading and in putting his thoughts on paper, I changed it to 'Our Niche for Literature.'" An indulgent smile lit up her face. "Not literature, of course, are these: only little stories, written by the boy Karl."

But Sigrid laid them aside. Now was the time to tell. "Uncle Lennart," her breath came rapidly, "will you please bring me my suitcase?"

"I'll get it." The visitor, Lars, fetched it and laid it at her feet. "Only today," he said, in all seriousness, "I said to Lennart that the sea was beauty enough for me. Little did I guess what treasure the *Drottningholm* was bringing."

As she might to an impulsive child, she gave him an indulgent smile. Then, while opening the lid of her suitcase, reaching inside for a tissue-paper wrapped parcel, she began with her grandmother, and her eyes followed to each one of the kinfolk, then rested again on Mor Sigrid. "Have you not wondered how it was that I was rich enough to cross the Atlantic?"

"All Americans are rich," blurted Justina.

"No. All Americans are not rich, no more than all Swedes have finished at Uppsala." She smiled toward Karl-Johann. "Year after year I saved, in a little bank, dropping a penny, a dime, or a quarter toward passage, but I should never have been able to save enough. Then, when I had about given up hope, when"—again she looked around the circle, and her voice lowered—"when I began to feel resentment against my father for—for cheating me of knowledge and nearness of my own family, he provided the way." Now came the story of her life after her parents' going, the telling of Michael and Granny, of the van Vlaardingens, of how they had been the ones to encourage her to send her father's work to the publisher's contest.

Mor Sigrid's mouth was open wide. She gaped, for as Sigrid was speaking she had unwrapped the oblong parcel. Finishing, she walked across the room to where her grandmother rose to meet her. The American Sigrid curtsied in a simple gesture of respect. "Here is your gift, dear Farmor; through this came the way, the way your Karl provided."

The book shook in trembling hands. No longer could she stand; pressing it against her breast, to try to crush the pain of joy that pierced her heart, Mor Sigrid slumped slowly into her chair. *"Chicago,"* she read. "By Karl Mattias Petersson."

She held it out from her, at arm's length, then drew it close under her spectacles; brought the book away and drew it back, reading the letters as with the movement of her arms they grew larger, smaller, larger, smaller: "Karl Mattias Petersson."

These were words he had penned, her Karl, the little boy who had written stories about the trolls in the woodlot and the fish in the sea, and about Hjärta, his horse—words Karl had written had been placed in print! These were *his* words, here, between the covers of a book!

A book! A seed planted for eternity!

"Oh, dear God," she breathed. "That any one human being should receive so much on earth as this!"

The past came before her. She saw the book of Victor Hugo, the book of Hans Christian Andersen; and now, in her hands, she held the book of Karl's writing.

Her dreams had come true!

Her heart would sing as long as it could beat.

24

Into the corner of honor in the big room the book must be placed close to Sigrid's chair. "Here, Johann, set the little table here."

Mor Sigrid placed the book upright on the table, spreading the covers so it could stand; and the picture of Chicago's water tower showed grandly in the homely dwelling in Sweden, and the name Karl Mattias Petersson showed from the corner of honor, that corner where distinguished visitors ever were seated, or the eldest of the group, or the one whose birthday it was, or whose Name Day. At Yuletide there stood the tree. There had dear Morfar lain in his casket; there had the golden cradle stood. Of all of this she told the American Sigrid.

"You will find the story of Norden's part in the restoration of the cradle to its rightful owner, the King, in those papers there. Together with the legend of its burial by the pirates, Karl set it down."

Expectancy hung heavy in the air. The littlest ones, though silent as it behooved them to be, expressed with their faces the demand to hear the saga once again. And Mor Sigrid was not one to disappoint them. Sounds of heavy breathing filled the room as she finished, "Ah, so proud was Morfar to prove the family honor by cleansing Norden's souls and hands of pirate greed, for before the introduction of Christianity and the baptism of the Vikings it had been considered honorable to kill and rob." She looked toward the corner of the big room. "There it stood, as a member of the family. After the emissaries from the King came to take the cradle to him, the corner stood bare. Would anything, I asked, ever be as beautiful or seem so much at home there as that golden treasure?"

She stepped back and looked hard and long, her head

swaying. "Aye, aye, as beautiful, Karl's book; and ever so much more at home."

There let it stay, in the corner of honor.

Sigrid stood the tintypes, one to either side of it, spreading the leatherette frames so that the gold scrolls shone around the gray ferrotypes.

Mor Sigrid wiped her eyes. "Tomorrow, perhaps, when you have rested, you will read Karl's book to us? But now you are tired. Let us seek our beds. Tomorrow, early, we will begin another day, another glorious day with Karl's daughter." Warmly she kissed the daughter of her son.

"Good night!" from everyone. "Sleep well!" "God bless you!"

Sigrid lay in the Gustavian bed, which had stood like a chair in the daytime; even the exquisite feel of fresh, cold-mangled homespun linen sheets did not bring sleep. If she pinched herself from now until morning she would hardly believe that she was here.

Through the half-closed door opening to the big room she watched the burning embers in the grate. Beyond she saw the curtains of the bunk bed move. Mor Sigrid parted them and swung her legs over the side, pulled her white linen night shift down to cover her feet, and sat looking.

Soon her husband arose, to sit beside her; his linen shift came only to the knees. They sat, his arm about her, gazing toward the corner of honor. There was a whisper, a loving look, and Big Johann went from the bunk bed, tiptoeing past the bench on which Young Johann slept.

Sufficient firelight came from the coals in the grate to cast a huge shadow up the wall, on up over the ceiling. Soon the husband returned, and Karl's book passed from his hand to Mor Sigrid's. A greater fire shone from her eyes than from the burning coals; and she held the book tight against her bosom while Big Johann drew the curtains across the opening of their bed.

> *"Rida, rida ranka,*
> *Hästen heter Blanka!"*

Little Tora laughed as Sigrid rode her on her foot, up and down.

"Not 'Rida ranka'?" the grandmother exclaimed. "It cannot be that in America there was room for that?"

"Oh, yes." Now Sigrid laughed. "Not only my father taught it to me, but my mother taught me the Halland version, too!"

Mor Sigrid gasped; how could she believe that the little verses, varying but little in the various provinces, handed down from generation to generation in Sweden, should have found their way to America and become a part of the life there? "America. I remember Morfar saying how he would have liked to visit America. So should I like to go." Dreamily, "For a part of me is there." Leading the child, Tora, from the room, "I confess to you, Sigrid, at the call of the chanticleer I found some chore, away from the dwelling, for each one of the family to do, so that I might have these few moments alone with you. They are setting the breakfast board out in the open, under the sky; it is so beautiful out-of-doors, and, after breakfast, you will read us what Karl wrote?" Quickly, "It is not that we do not understand the written English words, but understanding comes so much fuller on hearing them spoken. Slowly you will read it? A foreign tongue seems spoken so rapidly to those who are not good students of the language. Then, tomorrow, you shall go to Halland. I know you must go. David will carry you there over the mainland for he has an automobile, one of those frightful horseless carriages which gets its power in some mysterious way from the petrol he pours into its tank. I do not want to hurry you away, but you must be back at Norden for Midsummer's Day! Take all the time you wish there, but hurry, hurry back!"

At those last two words Sigrid closed her eyes, not reckoning the seconds as they passed and she stood silent. The wind came from the sea, but with closed eyes she stood envisioning the shore line of a Middle Western American metropolis, and it seemed that the warm winds blew landward from the wide blue lake.

No, it was not the neighbors in Calico Row she heard, it was the sound of voices of aunts and uncles and cousins and Lars. "Good morning!" "Did our Sigrid sleep well?"

Our Sigrid. Her heart beat hard; again she felt how good it was to belong. And now she must meet Fru Alvardsson, the good neighbor, the nurse trained in midwifery who had attended Mor Sigrid so faithfully and often. In looking at her Sigrid felt that she did not really see the long, pointed nose with a large wart on the end of it, or the wart on the eyelid which rested comfortably enough when the eye was closed but which pushed the lid into little creases to make room for its bold self when the eye was open wide, or the three warts set in front of her right ear, looking like the three-balled sign in front of the shop that had been Jake's.

The coarse white hair, parted severely in the center and drawn back tightly, forming a hard knot at the base of her neck, only framed the generous, kind soul whose light shone from small, dark eyes. Tiny, frail, dried, shrunken, was Erika Alvardsson; would a gust of wind, if it came, blow her away? Sigrid looked at her hands, and experienced a strong impulse to curtsy, or to kneel. Instead, she shook one of the hands and murmured her pleasure at this meeting.

"*Varsågod!* Please come to breakfast!"

"You make better coffee than we do at home," she admitted.

"Cleared with a fish skin; that is what gives it such a fine flavor!" Herman Nikodemus grimaced.

Softly in the breeze the leaves of the aspen tree sang to them as they made a celebration, a banquet, of their breakfast. Such a different kind of breakfast this was from the snatching of a piece of toast and gulping a cup of coffee, almost while on the run to catch a streetcar. There was no rushing in Sweden; even in Göteborg she had noticed that everyone moved about leisurely, politely. Not once, in the big city harbor, had she seen anyone shove or push. Rather, always on the air was a soft-spoken, "Thank you."

They sat sipping coffee, and Sigrid could not remember how many times her cup had been filled. Geese called from the barnyard; the grunt of a hog sounded, and the moo of a cow. It was a scene of contentment. Peaceful.

The morning meal over, they arranged themselves in a semicircle, and Sigrid went into the big room for her father's book. On the way she stopped to look closely at the Hardanger-patterned curtains, finger them, and gaze admiringly at them. Her grandmother saw, and caught her breath in a deep sigh of gratification.

"Come. Sit here." Big Johann set the chair for Karl's daughter so all could see her face and hear her as she read.

First she passed the book around so they all could look again at the picture on the cover, and so that Fru Alvardsson might see. It was a long, long time it took for the two old friends, Mor Sigrid and her midwife, to decipher those three familiar words, *"Till Min Mor."*

Then, *"Chicago,"* Sigrid read. "By Karl Mattias Petersson." Chills crawled up her spine at sight of the rapt faces before her.

Two-year-old Tora did not interrupt, for children were well taught that they were to be seen and not heard; nor the twelve-year-old Helga, nor ten-year-old Justina. But Mor Sigrid interrupted. "It reads just like him."

Again, "The wind. He always spoke of the wind as if it were a friend."

And again, "Aye, always was he interested in glaciers, 'the timeless, majestic, blue-white glaciers', once he described them."

Or, "It was while studying with Karl that I learned of how thousands of years ago, when the ice sheets melted, the land began to rise and how this part of Sweden still rises a little fraction of an inch every year, even now." Her lips closed then, with, "Oh, excuse me." She glanced around, embarrassed. "Forgive me."

Smiling, Sigrid read on, slowly, clearly.

"Aye," again the mother interrupted. "He loved the noble leaf trees; he loved the pines—"

Her head nodded, "Aye—aye—aye."

"Aye." As an amen she spoke the word.

The folk of Norden, in Bohuslän, in Sweden, listened to the story of Chicago, in Illinois, in America, a story told by the wind through the pen of their kinsman; they heard the rustle of tall grasses on the prairie, they saw the blue of chicory blossoms.

"Karl," Mor Sigrid whispered. "Always he loved the color blue."

Grain ripening, even as here, they saw. Rivers whispering, lake roaring, they heard. Even as here waters continuously chattered, or roared, or whispered softly in sibilants. As Sigrid read, " 'And in the springtime, violets bloom,' " the air was heavy with emotion. No eye was dry. Chicago no longer was only a dot on the face of a paper map. It was a beating, pulsing city—warm—with an almost human heart.

When she had finished, Sigrid sat looking at the end papers. How should she break this spell the reading of the book had cast over the listeners?

Though she may not have known of the great philosopher, she knew the meaning of his words: "Where there is Love there is music, and where there is music there is Eternity." In the short time she had been in this home she had seen how the family accented a story hour or other gathering with a song, as they had in the home of her childhood, as she often did in her own home; and so she sang, her voice full but quivering,

"By the rivers gently flowing,
        Illinois, Illinois,
    O'er thy prairies verdant growing,
        Illinois, Illinois . . .

"Upon the inland sea
        Stands thy great commercial tree,
    Turning all the world to thee,
        Illinois."

She passed the book to her grandmother.

"If never I know heaven above," Mor Sigrid responded, "then these days, this day, shall suffice; for if ever a mother knew heaven on earth, it is I."

Now, when she least wished it, came a rush of remembering to Sigrid, and she found she did not recall only the good; came knowledge of her father's drunkenness, his terrible, uncontrollabe temper. But let her bow before this evidence of faith—his mother, standing tall, but with her soul kneeling to the memory of a worthy son—*in her heart worthy*, and so his worth was real.

"Now I am glad Karl went," she was saying. "Even as he did, for only in America could this have happened so."

"I shall translate it," crippled Johann said excitedly, and raised a knotted hand. "Into the Swedish language, so all of our friends may read it!"

"I should like to help you, if you wish," Karl-Johann offered, and smiled broadly at his uncle's nod.

With the book clasped tightly to her breast, Mor Sigrid walked into the dwelling. She had to be alone with her son.

Big Johann followed, but only with his eyes. Proud, proud, was he; as proud as if he, and not Peter Kristiansson, had fathered Mor Sigrid's Karl.

25

It hurt for Sigrid to think of breaking away, even for as short a time as it would take to make the trip to Halland province, from this home so radiant with love, so beautifully furnished with objects made exquisite by loving hands. It was easy to see that, though having fewer of material possessions than the Americans she knew, those things were chosen with greater care than if at their acquiring the knowledge had not been at hand that whatever they chose would remain in the home for a lifetime. For many lifetimes. Here were no gaudy knickknacks, chosen to satisfy a fleeting impulse, to cheapen the richness of the home, a richness grown more rich with age.

She wished the neighbors at home could see this room: the fuchsia plant on the east window sill had grown much too robust for the recess. Shoot after shoot trailed upward and sideward and downward, hung looped over the curtain rod at the top, and were tacked here and there to the wall at each side to make a vivid-colored living frame for the window and a patterned wall covering way around it. If the pastor were here, he would be able to tell from whom her love of flowers had come!

"The big room," they called this. Not the parlor, nor the sitting room, nor the dining room, but "the big room." In this room the living was done; a homely, lovely room, with big spread board, bunk beds, handmade rugs, carved pieces sitting on deep sills and making every effort to distract attention from the flowers. Forcibly it came to her that it was no accident that some of the greatest woodcraftsmen are known to be Swedish. Through such folk as these at Norden the ancient peasant culture of Sweden still survived; those who had carved, those who had painted on furniture and walls, had written in their work testimony of a fine talent for beautiful form in decoration. But more, they had given evidence of the high esteem in which the home was held.

"Summer is dearly bought, for the winters are long," Maria had said; and Sigrid could understand how the long winters, with their dark, cold evenings, in forcing all members of a family to spend their time within the home, had fostered the inborn desire to have beauty a part of their regular daily-living necessities in the household. She turned an old drinking vessel over in her hands. Carved out of a piece of birch, the outside at one time had been painted black and the long neck gray, but the crest still showed its gay red. "Since before the time of earthen bowls, or glass, or metal—"

What a rare experience, this, seeing firsthand how this family lived in an atmosphere rich in tradition, faithfully preserving the customs and handicrafts of their forefathers. And hers!

Beauty in every inch of house and furnishings, and everything represented family members' ingenuity in using the meager materials at hand to meet everyday needs beautifully. Her grandmother had braided the rugs on the floor when a bride, before the son Karl was dreamed of, and he would now be fifty-four years old if he were alive. Oh, if only he could have lived, to have returned with her to this house where he was born, to see it with the more appreciative eyes of manhood!

In that carved bunk bed in the corner all of Mor Sigrid's children had come, excepting her first-born son, and he had come in the deep snow while she was shoveling a tunnel to the barn. No wonder Pa had loved the snow; it was his heritage.

On the damper pull Sigrid saw the petit-point portrait of Morfar; he stood, a foot forward, walking toward her with his arms outstretched. Her arms raised in return gesture. Morfar had been no stranger to her before, but now he truly came alive; again she could hear his stories through her father's telling, stories of the trees of Bohuslän standing strong against the wind. Long and hard, then, she looked at Mor Sigrid's hands. Those hands had wrought a picture in yarns which could carry the likeness of a godly man through all the years. Impulsively she clasped the hands in hers. "Oh, Farmor, how glad I am that I could come!"

"You glad? Then think of what a song my heart sings!"

Tapestries hung from ceiling and on walls, some made by her grandmother and some by other Sigrids long since gone. "It is not the fashion any more to have tapestries hung so; the hanging is but a relic of the time when housewives sought to cover bare walls and low ceiling rafters, but"—there was no apology in her tone—"I like it so."

"I like it, too," Sigrid answered. "And I have already decided that if the time ever comes when I can build a home, exactly as I'd like to have it, I am going to copy it after this one—with the corner fireplace—"

"You have not, as yet, seen Lissie's home. It sits beyond," a quick nod denoted the direction. "Matching the timbers, the window framework, the roof, matching all of this old, old home."

Both turned at hearing, "Nor is it the only duplicate." Karl-Johann had entered the room. "Agda and Tuppie's home, too, matches this homestead inch for inch."

Sigrid started pacing off the floor.

"There is no need to measure in such style." The young architect laughed. "I have the plans, all drawn to scale."

"May I see them, please?" Sigrid's interest was high.

"Not only may you see them"—Karl-Johann laughed aloud—"you may have a set. A half-a-dozen sets, if you wish! I have enough of the blueprints to wallpaper the barn!"

"It was Karl-Johann's first practical work," Mor Sigrid said kindly. "And a good job he did, too."

"But I wasted much good blueprint paper."

"Perhaps not so." She came to his defense. "When the American granddaughter wishes to own a set of plans, who knows how many more—of Norden's—"

"There will be sufficient for all." He came from the chest room, laughing and rolling up a set of blueprints which he presented to his cousin with a low bow.

"Are you ready?" David entered and went directly to his mother-in-law and placed his arm about her waist. "We have decided, all of us, that Mor Sigrid is to come with us to Halland province, and Big Johann too."

"But there is much to do, still, to be ready for *Midsommardagen!*"

"Have you not trained your daughters well enough?" Lissie winked at her sisters. "That they can cook and bake to prepare for one Midsummer's Day without their mother?"

"Aye." The mother turned to gaze thoughtfully at the little tintypes. "And a good deal I would give to visit the resting place of Karl's Elin."

"Hurry, then, so we may start."

"No. Do not hurry." Lars came and stood before Sigrid. "Please do not hurry away—ever—leaving me behind—"

Before she could respond her grandmother came to her. "You will need a shawl. There is always a breeze. Here." She reached to drape a knitted shawl of lichen shades over the young shoulders. "This one is becoming."

"Thank you, Farmor. But no, excuse me, I have a shawl. I—I have the most beautiful shawl in all the world."

Sigrid went to the spare sleeping room, opened her grip, and under her breath said, "Dear friends!" If they could have seen her joy at the opening of the parcel! If they could see her now, and know how much she loved the shawl!

Halfway through the doorway into the big room, with the shawl draped over her upturned hands, she came to a stop. What was the matter? The lively chattering had stopped abruptly. And the way they looked at her!

"What? W-what?"

Mor Sigrid swayed, to be steadied and held upright by her husband. She, Big Johann, crippled Johann, Lissie, Maria, David, Marta, Herman Nikodemus, they all stood or sat open-mouthed, as if they saw an apparition from the grave.

Sigrid could not keep her lips from trembling, or her chin. What had she done? "What is the matter?"

"You cannot know." Big Johann was the first to compose himself. "No, you can never know what this means to See'ri of Norden."

"Georg found him!" Mor Sigrid was weeping now; the tears ran down her cheeks, dripped from her nose; but she was not aware of them. Tears of gladness do not scald. "Georg found him. See, Johann, I knew America was large. I told you so. I knew the outer world was large. But Georg found Karl, and gave him his shawl!" Her clenched fists pressed against her chest. "Morfar told me, 'Faith is all you need,' he said. Aye. Faith. I knew—I *knew* the shawl would reach Karl. I knew." Then to Sigrid, "Had he it—a long time?"

"No, only—" Sigrid closed her mouth that had been hanging wide open. Piecing the words together, as with a puzzle, she comprehended: this shawl, the exquisite blue shawl, had been knitted for Karl by his mother. And it had found its way to her; not only had it found its way, but it had become the symbol of hope to her.

No. It could not be! In real life? No, such a thing could not happen. The walls of the room swam around her. Then her heart spoke: it was not coincidence, this. No. This was God's way, moving each one of them in studied manner, with each move planned, executed, in His way, to make the lives of a family intertwine.

And so it was, too, with Sigrid of Norden, that the room swam. From joy it swam, from seeing heaven right before her eyes. Karl had received his shawl, but it was more than a piece of knitted yarn, it was his forgiveness from home, his knowledge that its every stitch spoke of his mother's love. If he had had it sooner, she knew he would have written home again.

Well did she remember the time the inspiration for its making had come to her. She had been sitting in the early morning sewing christening mitts for newborn Karl when she saw the frost pattern on the windowpane. She had decided in that moment that this she would knit into a shawl for her son, of the finest wool that she could card. And she had; she had used the pattern sent by the winter; she had given her best workmanship, her finest stitchery to the working of the pattern on the shawl.

Her message of love had gone with the shawl to Karl, in America; and now it had returned, a message of love from her son.

Doubtless Karl had described its making to Sigrid, but the young Norden children did not know, and so, "See, see the pattern in the center?" She lifted the shawl from Sigrid's hands and spread it wide. "The long fern fronds, the icy plumes, the frosted fingers, can you see?"

Yes, they could see the pattern which had thrilled each one so many times as winter came to decorate the window-panes. And they could see the border of snowflakes, no two alike; some simple, some complex, delicately their all-over pattern was traced against a background of simple stockinette stitch.

"Your father—did he show you the name—the way I named the work?" Mor Sigrid eagerly brought her face close.

"N-no," young Sigrid stammered. She stood resolving never to release the secret of the way the shawl had come to her, no matter how proud she would have been to tell it was a gift from the dear friends who had made it possible for her to keep ownership to the home Elin had loved and worked so hard for; never, from anyone, should she allow this happy mother to know that in truth the shawl had not come to Karl's hands, that its blue had hung dusty and begrimed in a dirty pawnshop.

"But of course he would not have paid such particular attention. He was a man, and for a man—if a shawl is warm—"

Big Johann could smile.

"Aye." She fingered it. "Here it is. See?"

The casual glance, not even the more observing look, would tell that the six spears of one snowflake had been varied from the perfect form. But now the artist's fingers of Mor Sigrid spread one corner of the shawl over the back of her hand. On close inspection they could see an S, an I, a G, an R, an I, and a D, forming the points of a star so different from the rest; and yet, resting in the corner of the shawl, its dissimilarity would go unnoticed except to those who knew.

"The King never owned so fine a shawl," Big Johann said; and there were those in the room who remembered that they were the same words he had uttered on that Christmas Eve when the shawl had been the mother's gift to Karl.

"I made it of blue," Mor Sigrid reminisced, "little knowing that would be the color he liked best as he grew older." For the benefit of the American, she continued, "The love of blue is deep in all Swedish hearts. Though we can make our dyes of red and yellow, and all other colors that we need, from our roots and barks and berries, there is no indigo in Sweden. And so some say that it is only natural that, in our lack of it, it becomes more precious. Be that as it may, Karl's love of blue was more pronounced than with most. But that, at his infancy, I could not know.

"I made the shawl of blue because his eyes were blue. Blue is the symbol of heaven, from which the Christ Child came; and I have always liked to think it was a shawl of blue that Joseph draped over the head of Mary as they began their long journey to Bethlehem, that it was her blue shawl which reflected its color into the eyes of her babe when He first opened them, making them blue; and God, the Father, deeming the appearance of the color a singular auspice, thereupon decided it should be the color of all newborn babies' eyes." As if in defense of her surmise she looked about. "Many a baby's eyes have I seen at birth, and everyone's were blue.

"So it was of blue I chose to make the shawl, blue—the color of Karl's eyes—the color of truth, and of honor."

The big room was wrapped in silence as she finished.

Blue.

To Sigrid came the sight of the sparkling steel-blue eyes of the van Vlaardingens, the blue of Michael's eyes.

To Lars Ahlsén the color of the wool was faded beside the eyes of the girl whose shawl it was.

Big Johann could not keep his gaze from the tableau before him, Sigrid of Norden, Elisabet, and Karl's daughter, sitting with the shawl across their laps.

The blue shawl—years, it had been in the making—as fine as a spider's web—fair as the color of flax flowers.

Ah, the beautiful blue of it, repeated again in the eyes of the three women who held it!

The blue of truth, yes. The blue of honor. But, too, the blue of faith. The ineffable blue of the sky.

26

If Mor Sigrid was to go, then, Lars insisted, it was best they change their minds and go by boat to Halland. His boat. For was it not lying in readiness only a few miles up the coast? Sigrid's delight was unbounded, and her grandmother beamed on her. "Yes, we of Bohuslän's coast, we are a sailor stock."

Then it was Lars, not David, with Lissie's husband as mate, who would be the one to steer them south.

"With the seamen Big Johann and Captain Lennart manning the boat, to say nothing of Mor Sigrid's seacraft, this will be a sailing to remember." Lars helped Sigrid aboard.

She waved to the family, crowding the boat landing, as swiftly and smoothly the vessel under her cut the water. Thrilling to the tossing and bounding—with breeze filling their canvas and salt spray swishing over the boat and breaking into little bubbles—they sailed down the waterways of the Vikings, along the ragged fringed shore, now near, now farther away, past fishing boats high of bow and broad of beam. A stork, tardy in its spring migration from Egypt, flew northward above them. There, strong fishermen were laying nets, methodically preparing to extract their living from the sea; there, birds basked lazily in the sun on flat slabs of rock.

The southwesterly breeze made a funny cock's comb of Lars's hair but on Sigrid, sailing over these waters so rich with memories of ancient times, this kingdom of Bohuslän's skerries exercised a curious spell. Enchanted, she watched the changing colors in the clear water as clouds passed overhead graying the granite below.

"Has then," Mor Sigrid absently queried, "the saga of Beowulf also reached America?" Her hand took in the shore line with a wave of widest sweep. "Here, in these waters, so men tell the tale, lived the evil mother of the

237

evil-devouring monster, Grendel. Look deep below, Sigrid, into the clear waters. See the caverns of granite? See the intricate channels? There the mountain streams, coming from underground, pour through rocky caverns into the sea. By night fire glows on this water. Ah, how Karl loved to lie floating, trying to catch the phosphorescent wavelets!

"When the wind stirs up the waves, they churn so that the air above grows thick, and thicker, until the very heavens weep; and 'twas here Beowulf came with the mighty sword, Hrunting, its biting edge hardened with blood.

"But Sigrid knows the tale."

Not aloud could she liken the story of Beowulf and this mere to herself. Not with her lips could she speak to tell that just so had this water seemed to her, as to the Geats, when they had sat sick of heart, wishing without hope that they might cast their eyes once more upon their lord. For thus had she stood, even as they, looking out over the sea after the sound of oars had carried Karl away.

In the saga a marvelous working took place: Beowulf swam upward through the cleansed flood, and as he swam to the shore the water of the mere grew still.

As in the saga, for her, too, a marvelous working had taken place. Stilled were these waters now; no longer would she stand, wondering, straining her eyes to look out upon the sea. For Karl had returned to her in Sigrid.

"My heart is light." She placed an arm around her granddaughter's waist and drew her close. "For you—came —home."

Home. Sigrid was stirred at the sound of the word. And yet—?

"There, to the landward, that island shore is Marstrand," Lars explained. "There many of the residents of Göteborg come to spend a day of outing, or a weekend holiday. There came King Oskar, when he lived, to spend his summer holidays."

"Sigrid of Norden, here," Big Johann interrupted, as proud as a man could be, "had audience with our beloved King Oskar."

His wife nodded slowly. So much of happiness surrounded memory of her visit to Stockholm after she had carved the set of chessmen. Yet that visit had forerun the saddest sound that ears could hear, the sound of oars pull-

ing from the shore as Karl left home. But now, now she
could forget that sadness. Smiling, she called attention to
Karlsten Fortress, and young Sigrid saw quaint cottages
rising one above the other on the rising granite, leading
the eye upward to the thirteenth-century castle.

"Let us anchor, so Sigrid may see the shore line from
the tower."

Big Johann saluted Lars crisply and set the prow landward.

Lars walked her up the rising rocky island; they climbed
up the steps of the old gray tower and stood leaning
against the parapet, looking down and beyond. The salt
water raced in, broke against the rocks, receded slowly in
frothy indifference, raced in again, and broke. The rhythm
of the movement fascinated Sigrid, almost hypnotized her.
Or was it the invigorating air, so free of smoke, so clear
and clean and sharp, that made her tipsy with joy at sight
of the scene below?

Had her father ever seen this sight, the little sister
islands lying in sun-sparkled waters, the jagged shores, the
fishing boats, the whole archipelago of the western Swedish
coast, the Pater Noster Skerries clustered on the horizon?
Had he seen this beauty, to which he had been born, and
been able to tear himself away to live in a little basement
flat on a dirty street in the city of Chicago?

Below was the promenade. Yonder the fishermen's nets
were spread in picturesque array to dry in the sun; there
cliff walks called; boats rolled at anchor or lay tied to
home-built docks, or darted over the blue water leaving
spreading wakes behind. Below was beauty, such poignant
beauty as to make the bosom ache at sight of it. And Pa
had turned his back on this!

She felt Lars's arm lay itself lightly on her waist and
turned to look into his eyes. "You feel the beauty of it,
too," he whispered, then took her hand. "The ring—you
wear it well—and, do you know, it was the home of the
Vikings—those waters below—"

"From which those warriors set out in their long ships,"
she wanted him to know she knew, "with the single square
sail and twenty pairs of oars, or more—"

He interrupted, "To capture hamlets in Ireland, to take
most of the Scottish Isles as their own—"

She placed her fingers over his lips; this was hers to

say: "From which they set out for the shores of North America!"

"Home of the Vikings!" he said again proudly.

Her head shook slowly. "No words are fine enough to describe its beauty."

"And you, Sigrid, you are of Viking blood." He breathed it softly into her ear, as if it were a secret, but all the while he caressed the Viking ring. "Should not this compelling beauty, then, be your chosen home? Sigrid, it is soon, I know—to ask you for your hand. But I love you. From the moment I saw you, coming from the *Drottningholm,* I knew the sea must, from that instant on, be satisfied with second place within my heart."

"But my home is in America!"

"You will have your home here—our ancestral homestead sits in just such a spot as this, overlooking the Kingdom of Bohuslän's Skerries. Stay, Sigrid, stay, and marry me? Learn to call this beauty 'home'?"

Mor Sigrid had pleaded: "Stay, for this is your home, as it is ours." "Welcome home!" Lennart had said.

And yet this was not home.

What did the word really mean?

"Sigrid, the Viking, stay—for this is your rightful home—"

"Oh, Lars, if I had been born to this, or raised to it, how easy it would be to call this by that magic name. But, even though I should stay, could this ever be home to me? Would you, Lars, want to tear yourself from *this,* to go, for instance, to my country?"

"Twice a year, oftener if you wish, you could go home on one of the ships of the Line—to the country where you were born."

"It is not merely the spot of biological birth, Lars. Home is the place of first awakening to life, the place of the learning of one's loyalties." It was long before she spoke again. "Do you know, I have never heard an immigrant, no matter how long in the new country, no matter how long naturalized to citizenship, speak of his old country without saying, 'At home we did thus and so,' or 'At home it was this way.' Even people removed from one state to another speak of Pennsylvania or New Jersey or Maine as 'back home.'"

He held her close, but she leaned from him to look

below. There was beauty here, ah, yes. Forbidding, stern, perhaps, yet, paradoxically, serene.

"Home is something more than a shore line, more than an ancestral home, or a hill, or a sea or a view—something more—"

"Is it that you cannot care for me at all?"

"At home, my pastor— Lars, you would love him as I do! —he said that when I cared enough to marry someone, I would *know* I loved him. You ask me, and I do not know—"

"That will come! Oh, I will give you everything! When I heard you tell of how you have had to work—to skimp —I could not stand it! You will never want for anything again!"

"Dear Lars, your home, your—anything you have— would never make a bit of difference to me. If I loved you I would not care if you hadn't an öre to your name."

"*Sigrid,* then say that you will stay? I will teach you to love me!"

Almost as if she spoke to herself, she asked, "Could I ever choose to be like my mother, who came to a new country and left her heart behind? And my father, too, deny it as he would."

"I do not love you less, Sigrid, for your knowing the loyalty you know." He drew her to him, holding her close with one arm while with the other hand he brushed her hair back from her forehead. "I see that you must return to your homeland. Go, Sigrid, go—satisfy yourself that you could come back to Bohuslän—and me—and be happy here."

Chicago—?

The skerries of Bohuslän—?

Home was where love dwelt; and certainly love dwelt here. Never had she felt so welcome, so at home without being at home. Let her always be thankful to God that He had let her know her grandmother's love. And Lars. It seemed as if she had known him always.

He bent to kiss her, but she turned to look over the parapet.

Though caught under the spell of the grandeur of the sight below, knowing that never would she be able to free herself from the enchantment of the skerries of Bohuslän, suddenly she felt an awful homesickness for

Michael, for Granny, for the pastor, for the doctor, for Nico. She drew the blue shawl closer around her.

"Come, Lars. Come." Big Johann appeared. "Night falls, on time, always."

Sigrid freed herself from Lars's hold and threw her arms wide, then drew them slowly to clasp them across her breast. She must hold sight of this forever close, her father's homeland. . . .

More rugged coast line, more little islands showing only as flyspecks on the map, more little white-trimmed red cottages, *torps,* sitting snug against the rocks. Big Johann said he thought he would be safe in saying that from the shelter of every one of those rooftrees at least one child had gone to America.

They sailed southward, each with his own thoughts, with foam streaking along the scuppers, dipping and heaving, talking, and singing some. As if posing for pictures for a storybook swans cut the darkening blue sky with white, a stork stood on one leg atop a chimney on the shore. Frequently now the cottages were half-timbered, with white-washed walls and thatched roofs; the growth around them was more lush. Now the river Ätran emptied her waters into the Kattegat. They had reached Falkenberg.

"Welcome." The sister to Sigrid's mother spoke. "I see you wear the ring." It was Eleonora who had sent the family heirloom; Eleonora, twenty years older than Elin. There was Sture Sven Eklund, the husband, already known to those of Norden for having come one day to tell them of their son and how he had worked on the farm in Småland, and of the time Karl had shaken the hand of his king. The warm, good feeling spread again over Sigrid. These, too, were kinfolk, welcoming her "home."

"So this is little Elin's daughter," over and over Eleonora said.

Sigrid wished she were of smaller size, somehow it seemed almost blasphemy that she should be so tall, and be the child of "little Elin."

They went to the churchyard. "Come, Lennart and Lars," said Johann. "Show me," and aside, "Let them go first, alone. As much as the thought of Elin means to us, she is more theirs than ours."

"We can learn much from you," the younger man

answered. "In the matter of thoughtfulness and consideration."

The others walked the curving lane past the deep-recessed door with the cross above; and there, with birch trees leaning tenderly, protectively, over the resting place, was where Elin was buried beside her mother and father. A little stone told, "Elin Benedikta Sibylla Nilsson Kristiansson, born 29 July, 1875. Died—"

Sigrid could not see for the flood in her eyes, but she did not need to see; she remembered the summer of nineteen hundred and twelve. It was ten years since Elin had left America and gone home.

"Karl's Elin," her grandmother was saying; and kneeling together they pressed the soil around the roots of a seedling golden rain tree, brought with them from Norden, so that a part of Karl should be here with Elin. "So shall you have seed, for a golden rain tree, to take with you to America."

As Sigrid knelt so many, many scenes returned: the time her mother had told her to put her penny inside of her woolen mitten so she should not lose it. But, she had thought, mothers couldn't know everything: she knew how to carry a penny without losing it, even with mittens on, she knew. But she had lost the penny. And there was the time Elin had said, "Never judge another person; there is always the seed which falls on stony ground. It isn't the seed's fault, alone, if after trying and trying to grow it gets discouraged." She had meant Pa. And there was the time her mother had come and stood beside her at the open attic window—and she, thrilling to the roar of thunder and flashes of lightning—and with the rain pelting their faces, thought Elin was enjoying it the same as she, when she felt the little mother shiver, and heard her say, "Pa has not come home."

"Oh, my poor little mother," she cried. *"Min mor, min lilla mor!"*

They let her cry, until at last she felt the peace of the churchyard fill her. Quietly she listened: was it the wind singing in the heart-shaped birch leaves, or was it the spirit of Elin bade her not sorrow?

"Be glad, Sigrid, for I am glad," it seemed the voice was saying. "Glad that you have lived with a clean heart, and true; glad that you placed a kiss, that day, on the

full and friendly lips that their Maker had forgotten to
make strong, that day Pa gave his life; glad, oh, so glad
you came to Sweden to know your own."

"Oh, Farmor"—Sigrid whispered low so only her grandmother could hear—"I cannot explain, but sometimes it
is as though I feel my mother near, as if she touched my
face with her fingers, but it is only the breeze. As if she
spoke, and I hear what she is saying—but all is silence.
As if—if I tried hard enough—I try, and try; oh, how I
try—but then I have lost what I almost held, and I am
exhausted from the trying. I cannot explain—"

Mor Sigrid answered low. "You do not have to explain,
not to me." And she thought of the many times she had
seemed to feel Morfar's presence near, as though he were
speaking to her, encouraging her. "Thus it is, dear Sigrid,
that a good spirit lives on and on, in memory, in the
hearts and minds of loved ones left behind."

With Sture Sven and Eleonora they walked the cobble-
stoned streets of Falkenberg; they rode in a surrey to see
the surrounding countryside. Grain fields crowded close
to a churchyard's walls, to the inside of them, telling as
well as words of the farmer's insistence that the soil should
be as much for the living as for the dead. Silhouettes of
drying hurdles for the grain stood bare and prophetic
against the lowering sun; here and there Sigrid could see
a trousered figure climb one, as he might a mast on a ship,
making repairs against the harvest day.

Thus had it been when her mother was young and spent
her days here. Life went on. No matter who was laid to
rest, life went on. To her this moment would stand out,
apart, to remember as the one which suddenly brought
realization that she—she, herself—would one day go, and
life would go on as usual.

The sun would set. But she would not see it. Then,
"Look at it now," a drumming inside of her screamed.
"Look at it now!"

She looked, and as she looked the Kattegat that Elin
had loved became a sea of gold. Its beauty was more than
she could bear. "Take me to see my mother's home," she
begged.

They went to the little house at the crossroads, a place
of rare poetic setting, where Time had indeed stood still,
a place it would be easy to call "home." The little house

was covered with vines so that of the framework only the casements showed, and the whole walls were undulating waves of green.

Twittering birds made accompaniment to the haunting song the leaves sang.

Together the two Sigrids stood listening, hand in hand, as to them the vines repeated the same story they had heard the birch trees sing, "Be glad, for I am glad—

"Be glad."

27

In the grace of a dipping sea gull, in churning patterns woven by deep salt water, in the changing color of sea and sky, in the short night-black of water, Sigrid could see the face of her aunt Eleonora at their parting.

"Farewell," they had said, both knowing that it was farewell.

But the kinswoman could not go empty-handed from Halland. Eleonora had thought it fitting that the daughter should own the little carpet Elin had treasured. Seeing the kind of home her mother had left, Sigrid could understand Elin's longing for what America never had provided her. She was not one of those for whom it had "not been so good," at least materially, in the Old Country. She should never have been an emigrant: it was right that she could go back where she belonged.

Now Sigrid showed the carpet to the family at Norden, a thick, fluffy black-and-white one, unlike any she had ever seen, a dear little carpet woven with a woof of hare's hair. She ran her fingers through the softness of it. And the golden clock, by whose face Elin had learned to tell time, also had filled her hands upon leaving Falkenberg.

"You are happy at thought of carrying a Swedish clock to America," crippled Johann said. "And we, here, are so proud to own a clock from America! So goes it." He was looking at the little mantel clock. "It was given me in part payment for a case—"

Here every tongue interrupted, and joined to tell Sigrid about Big Johann's namesake. "To be famous for making fine lace—that was not enough!" "No! To have his handiwork blessed for the altars of cathedrals, not enough for Johann!" "No—he would not rest until he had studied—and studied—and studied—and passed examinations!"

Sigrid followed the look he sent to his mother before

246

he reached with knotted stumps of hands to wipe his tears away. For the rest of her life she would try to describe, to herself, that look.

"And now he stands well to being one of the topmost maritime lawyers in Sweden!" "In the whole of Europe!" "No, in the whole wide world!" Justina finished, looking adoringly at her uncle.

He spread the hand stumps out wide, shrunken palms upward. "You see, Sigrid, what a family does? Makes a person feel so—so—worth-while." Now his face shone. "But I have done only what my mother expected me to do, filled my life with something besides pity for myself. But, as I say, that is a man's family for you, always seeing the thing he does greater than it is.

"In truth, the great thing that has been done has been done by my mother." It was seconds before he trusted himself to go on. "By Lissie, by Big Johann—by all." He included all in the circling of his arm. "Big things they have done for me. And little things. Oh, I could tell you about my pet sea gull, Lucifer; a pet means everything to a growing boy, and *min mor* and Lissie, and, yes, the rest, made it possible for me to have my pet. For over thirty-five years they cleaned up after him." Johann's eyes grew soft. "Lucifer. At last he had to go. One day he cawed to leave the house. We saw him lie down out on the rocks near the water, and we could tell that life had left him.

"It was my wish, of course, to bury him in the corner of the dooryard, and so Mor started from my side to bring him to me.

"It had been well enough for him to bide his time, crippled as his wing was, here on the land; but for the first time in all those years he had tried to get away. His action almost told us that for one not fit to battle the sea the land was well; but in death, no. And it was as if his family understood his wish that a sea gull should have no such ignominious burial—in a dooryard—but in death they would see to it that the sea claimed its own. For his brothers came.

"As Mor stopped, they dipped and gently two gulls picked Lucifer up with their bills and flew with him out over the water."

So silent the room was, the only sound the ticking of the

clocks. Johann picked up the handwork he had laid
down. This his stumps could do: his arms and hands
kept working, to fascinate Sigrid. On his lap he held a
thick board into which had been drilled two rows of holes,
graduated in size from an inch in diameter to a thread
size. He had started with a foot-long strip of pewter and
pushed it through the largest hole, then through the smaller
and smaller ones. As the diameter grew less, the soft alloy
of tin and copper lengthened. At the last it would be a
thin metallic thread; and Johann told how it would be
used by Agda to complete an altar cloth his hands had
once begun, to hang rich metallic lockets and chains on
five wise virgins—crocheted virgins—

"But come, my granddaughter, there is much to see and
do in these few days."

Woodbines clinging to the stone fences swished in the
summer breeze as the two Sigrids stood to look over the
home place, the house looking down upon the barn, the
orchard beyond. Stone fences everywhere. And green
grass was in the yards and in the sheep lot. The woodlot
carried the eye farther, on to the birch swamp, to the peat
bog, as far as their eyes could see stretched the land of
the island farm, Norden.

"No more mine than yours," Mor Sigrid said. "Rightly,
it should at this moment be your home."

"No."

"Yes. For you are Karl's daughter, and Karl was the
eldest son. As it stood for generations the eldest son inherited the farmstead on the death of the father, if there
was a son."

"But think of all the others!"

"That was the law. And if no male issue, to the first-
born daughter. Had Karl stayed, Norden would have been
his and so, in turn, yours. But"—she looked querulously
toward her granddaughter as if, from her face, she might
read an unspoken plan or hope—"it is of course a poor
peasant home. Compared to that of Lars Ahlsén it is poor
indeed. He is—did you know?—of the nobility. Lands,
and lakes, and woods, all kinds of wealth are his, beside
the shipping line his family owns.

"Yes, there would be a husband who could grant a
young girl's every wish.

"I miss him now that he went home, and so, I presume, do you?

"I have seen the Ahlsén homestead. There it sits, like a castle—and it *is* a castle—overlooking the skerries—"

Young Sigrid's face told nothing.

"That was the law," Mor Sigrid repeated. "Had Karl stayed, Norden would have been his and so, in turn, yours. But now the law is changed. After the world war so many things changed. But this is, and always will be, as much your home as ours."

Again that warm, good feeling spread over Sigrid; and the two women went on further inspection. The inside of the barn was as clean as the house, even to the white-ruffled linen curtains at the windows out of which the cows looked at the rolling landscape. The cows were like children in the family; there was not the slightest quivering down the flank, nor the faintest suggestion of apprehension in the eye of a single animal as she and her grandmother walked along the gutter. Birgitta, Greta, Kirsten, Birthe, Marjatta—and as always there must be a Lisa—answered as their names were called. They showed the results of being brushed several times a day; and their tail switches had been combed to silky smoothness before having their ends caught up on the ceiling hooks. Hoofs and horns were waxed and polished so they gleamed. Ecstasy showed in the rolling big brown eyes of Lisa as Mor Sigrid scratched her behind the ear.

"You take such good care of your cows—"

"And why should we not, Sigrid? Think of how much they give us: milk, cream, butter, cheese, fertilizer for our fields, calves for veal, beef, hides for our leather shoes—even the heat from their bodies kept a 'bedroom' warm for your father—for up that ladder, in the barn loft, was where he slept when he was a boy."

She helped lift the neck boards and release the tails; but instead of hurrying out after their milking the cows loitered so each in turn might rub against its mistress.

As her grandmother talked on, to tell of Norden's beauty in other seasons, Sigrid could see the frozen grandeur of winter melting drop by drop, drops gleaming in the sunlight as they fell from house or barn roof; could feel precocious spring come suddenly, whispering to the flowers to pierce the snow and show their cup or star-shaped faces.

Charging the air with a peculiar magic, summer drew its
own description for her, but even in the intensity of the
sunlight, as she listened to Mor Sigrid describe opaline
mists rising over the meadow, she could experience a
strange longing for dim grayness of winter, a half-sad yearning for a darkened room lighted only sparsely with candles
so as to leave the greater portion of the room in mysterious
gloom.

As if she read her heart, her grandmother said, "It is
that Viking melancholy we know. It is that which I had
hoped might make Karl's writings great."

They passed a covered well with a big iron wheel and
an old wooden bucket, and one with a bucket hanging
from the end of a long, slender pole levered in a crotched
post before they returned to the dwelling.

"The morrow being Sunday," Big Johann greeted them,
"how would our Sigrid like to attend church services on
the mainland, going in the old manner in the church boat?"

"The islanders have planned that for the churchgoing
all will dress in their provincial peasant dress to make it a
special event for Sigrid, the American. We have seen how
you love the old," Lissie purred, "and so, while you
journeyed to Halland, at Mor's suggestion I delved into the
chests and found the oldest dress of all."

Now, freshly laundered, the costume was being fitted
to Sigrid. She slipped her arms into a hand-woven white
linen blouse. Tiny smocking stitches gathered the full
sleeves into the body at drop-shoulder height and also into
the narrow tight cuffs edged in linen lace. The cuffs closed
with small round fancy silver buttons, as did the neck
which was framed by a fine net collar embroidered with
flowers in a running stitch of silky thread. Over the blouse
Lissie slipped a full skirt of dark blue wool, in basket
weave, with a hemline of black velvet which appeared
again as the lining in the tight red bodice whose short full
peplum at the back was tacked up to show its lining. The
bodice was red, but its color was subdued by years, and
close inspection showed that it was woven in a damask
pattern of roses and rose leaves. Lissie laced it up the front,
through pewter lacing rings, *maljor*, shaped like hearts,
with long black lacings on whose ends were heavy-
patterned needles to facilitate the lacing; and then she
tied a bow at the waistline. An apron—no, two aprons—

no, three!—were part of the costume: a work apron of thin leather, one of finest wool woven in multicolored stripes, and one—to wear to church—of white linen with fine blue cross-stitch design at the hemline. Whichever one was worn, or if all three, the streamers would be tied in a neat bow below the upturned peplum of the bodice.

Stockings, striped round and round, were next. And then the shoes. They fitted her well, quaint shoes, short in the toe, decorated with rose designs above wooden soles cut with shaped heels far under the hollow of the foot. Now Lissie tied a woven headcloth, folded tricornerwise, under her chin, then kissed her roundly on the mouth. Dancing into the big room Sigrid felt more than ever at home.

"So shall you go to services," Mor Sigrid smiled, "in the local dress of your kinfolk of Norden. In your own dress."

It was hers, to own, to link her with Norden and its past—to show the neighbors at home! Too overcome to speak, neatly she curtsied her thanks.

To crown the gift giving of this day her grandmother laid a porcelain plate into her hand, and Sigrid caught her breath sharply. It was as much the reminder that she had been present in their thoughts and hearts since the beginning of her life as it was the translucent beauty of this glazed bit of kaolin clay that made this, indeed, a crown to top the gift giving.

"Bing and Grøndahl of Denmark have made many *'Jule Aften'* plates since," Mor Sigrid said. "One for every year. But this was their first, 1895, marked for the year of your birth. You were six months old when Johann," she glanced fondly at her husband, "bought this plate for you, and brought it here to me."

It had a name, *Behind the Frozen Window;* and there, in the apogee of the potters' art, were long fern fronds, icy plumes, frosted fingers—sent to the artist by the Frost King, even as he had sent the same pattern to Mor Sigrid for the blue shawl.

On Sunday morning, all clad in traditional dress, they waited on the landing for the church boat. Elaborately embroidered shifts, worn by the men, kept Sigrid's eyes busy. Magnificent designs in bold color.

But no, not color on all of the men. Fru Alvardsson's

son, Erik, served as oarsman on this day, and he, dressed all in black, with long frock coat and stovepipe hat, stood straight and tall and solemn in the boat's stern, manning the long oar. Without a sound, except the water's lapping, he steered the long church boat against Norden's pier. Green birch bows lined the boat's sides and dipped their leaves into the water, or bent to greet their rippling reflections.

Already some of the islanders had settled in their seats, but Norden's family filled the boat. Children dragged their fingers over the sides; the grownups sat with holy mien as the sunshine made brighter their costumes' bright colors. Much too short for Sigrid was the trip across the water to the mainland. Up the winding lane, walking in double and triple file, soon they came in sight of the church. Its tall spire led their eyes heavenward; from the spire's square-louvred base came a welcome song from scores of bird throats.

"Always, here," said Mor Sigrid, "I like to stop, and stand and bow the head and give thanks that we may come to this beautiful place."

It was a different scene that memory returned to each one as all stood with heads bowed; but to Sigrid the moment was filled with heart pain. To want to go and leave all this, and yet not want to go!

The church doors stood open. Through these doors her people, from the first building of this old, old church, had been carried as infants to the baptismal font, had walked in solemn privilege to confirmation, to communion, had entered happily as bride or groom, had been carried out. In Pa and her had come the breaking of the chain. But it was not broken, really, for now her eyes, too, gazed on the doors which had in turn opened for each generation before her, doors of heavy oaken planks so covered with designs of iron mounts that the sight of oak was almost completely lost. Through the doorway she, with the family of Norden, entered. Tall tapers burned in silver candlesticks and wall sconces, and she could not take her eyes from the beautiful stained-glass window showing Christ, the Shepherd. Below, small white letters set in a bright red background told,

"In Memory of my Beloved Sigrid,
Karl Ivarsson of Norden."

Norden, the home of so many Sigrids; how could she think of leaving it?

"The Lord bless thee and keep thee." The minister spoke the benediction.

If he could have read the hearts of two of his congregation he should have heard the Sigrids say in unison, though unbeknown to each other, "So much have I been blessed; let me say ever, and forever, not pleading, 'Bless Thou me,' but 'Bless I Thee Lord.'"

Sigrid walked from the church; it was a blessing, too, to be able to see the resting places of her forebears. With the movement of the sun the tall spire counted the tombs in the churchyard. This was Time's sundial—gravestones, low and sunken, were the hours; the steeple was the gnomon, long, tapering, shadowy.

Unconsciously aware of old roots striking deep into the past, of old customs still surviving in one whose ancestors for so long had followed them, she raised the garlands of thick-grown vines and dropped a coin into the poor box at the gate.

Norden! Its people, its island, its church on the mainland! Rightly her home. God seemed very close as she dropped her hand over the side of the church boat and let her fingers slip through the water, and watched the little wake they made widen, widen, just as her world had widened.

At the same time, from Mor Sigrid went a special thanks to God. This would be the first Midsummer's Eve for all these many years that she would have a full family to celebrate the ripening of the year.

Midsummer's Eve.

The exquisite freshness of the day saw them go to the fields and meadows, with woven baskets over their arms, to pluck flowers; to the birch swamp and the beech grove to cut boughs with which to deck the Maypole. Singing, they carried Nature's bounty home; and Sigrid vowed that next year, every year, she would do this lovely thing in America—gather leafy branches and wildflowers to deck a Maypole, even if the pole would only be the clothes post in the back yard. Michael would love this joyous way of celebrating midsummer.

They bound boughs around the pole so it became as a tall leafy tree trunk; they wove blue and yellow flowers into long streamers; and as it lay full length upon the ground every one of them, big and little, knelt to dress the pole and fasten the streamers to the top. Not as in some villages, nor in some provinces, would they dress only flowery yardarms, or wreaths to hang upon them, or a large heart to crown the pole. "No." Mor Sigrid's voice shook. "Always at Norden there must be a streamer for each of the young people." Not one for her, nor for Big Johann, of course; and someone must play, so not one for Lennart, as fine as Lennart played music on his accordion.

Amid sighs of pleasure and screams of excitement, rejoicing in the magic of the year's "high noon," they pulled at the ropes and raised the pole. "Oh!"

"Ah!"

Midsummer's Eve.

The day on which the sun puts off seeking its bed, never caring if it sleeps.

The day on which night comes; but when it comes, it is not night at all, but a fairy twilight, unreal, ethereal.

Mor Sigrid's eyes followed as, in their old-time dress, the sons and daughters of Norden selected their streamers, blue cornflowers marking the sons', and for the daughters' yellow marigolds and cowslips and sun-colored flowers from the garden.

Music came from the accordion.

Lissie started the dance, going clockwise, and Herman Nikodemus going counterclockwise. Young Johann, too, must take part in the dancing, and take his part in weaving the pattern of a family; and it was here Big Johann took his part, piloting his namesake's wheel chair. In and out they danced, singing, laughing. Sometimes Lennart drew the music out slower, so they could stop and bow low or curtsy to the ones who happened to be beside them in their contrariwise stepping. No bumping against one another, not even with the wheel chair!

Mor Sigrid stood watching. There was a lump in her throat, a big lump. Karl's streamer no longer hung limp against the leafy pole. The ribbon that would have been full blue for her eldest son was woven half of blue and half of yellow flowers. Held tight in Sigrid's hand, she danced with it, in and out, in and out, with all of the other children and grandchildren weaving the intricate pattern of yellow and blue at the top of the pole.

No streamer dangled now, unclaimed. In Sigrid, Karl had come home.

The pattern crawled down, down, making the streamers shorter, lowering the canopy over the heads of the dancers. And Mor Sigrid stood watching the pattern grow, watching the perfect pattern grow.

Big Johann caught a glimpse of her, and he knew that for her this day was not only the apex of a year.

It was the apex of her life.

Midsummer Day—*Midsommardagen*—

Laughing and singing still, waving to the weathercock that Mor Sigrid had carved many years ago to place on the greased tip of the Maypole, they came from church services; for this was Saint John's Day, too, the good saint having claimed the festival day of the heathen Balder as his own. Carrying their baskets for a picnic in the woods, where they could sit soft on the carpet of leaves and pine needles, the young people waved to the mistress of Norden as she stood, unseeing of them, looking up, gazing at the blossomed streamers as they imprisoned birch leaves on the Maypole, forming the pattern of a family at the top.

She stood with Karl's book held to her breast, in stillness, as the dew descended bringing the scent of lilies of the valley, as the sky became a velvety blue when day and night clasped hands—no, not day; not yet night; but Midsummer's Day—the day for which long winter had prepared the earth by giving it its rest. The day for which brief spring had played her prelude. The day of bloom and ripening of grain—golden grain—golden wheat—golden flowers—golden hours—

Yes, Mor Sigrid stood looking. But now she knelt, still looking upward. The pattern at the top of the Maypole was unbroken!

Ah, this was knowing the ripening of the golden fruitfulness of life, sharing in the golden glory of fulfillment!

"If the day of life could last into the year as the day of Midsummer lasts into the twenty-four hours around the clock, there would be no need to cross the line to heaven," Mor Sigrid said to herself.

Sigrid, too, sat meditating in the big room, and did not speak. If a month could stretch beyond one page of the calendar, then she would not have to think about returning to her work at the plant. How should she remind them here? Her grandmother took it for granted she would stay, seemed to have forgotten that she must go. And for herself, how could one heart hold two such great emotions, sadness at thought of going from this place and those so dear, and happiness at thought of going home?

"So, now, we go to our rest. Until the morning, all!" Her body was tired; Mor Sigrid rose unsteadily and went to the honor corner, picked up Karl's book and held it close. Hands, she commanded, press the book hard against the pain—hard—harder—against this joyous pain—

She started toward her bed, and Big Johann did likewise; but she stopped to place a kiss on Sigrid's gold-colored hair. "God bless you, for being true to your parents! He will bless you for keeping His commandment to honor them! Aye, He will bless you for all of your days."

She stopped also at the wheel chair. "Dear Johann—dear Johann—" She choked, and the words came haltingly, *"Until the morning—"*

Big Johann steadied her as she swayed, and led her to the bunk bed. The day had been long and full, and she was weary.

"The oars!" she cried. "I hear the oars!"

Heads raised, and Sigrid's raised with the rest, ears straining to hear, but there came no oars' sound to them.

"No Fool's Mate, Morfar!" Mor Sigrid spoke it clearly, leaving no doubt as to what it was she said.

Now, as the family came closing in to question, Big Johann saw the smile he loved spread over the face of his See'ri. It did not wane, as in life, but laid a mask on the dear face. . . .

At long last Lissie came and lifted his head from the silent form.

"She is gone. Mor Sigrid, my See'ri is gone." He sat holding her hands, picking up one finger, stroking it, stroking another, stroking each hand, kissing it, holding them both until Lissie took one and folded it over Karl's book and pressed down the lids on her mother's clear blue eyes.

"Thank God," she said, "the sound of oars had changed its tune in time from sorrow of those bygone years to gladness at your coming, Sigrid."

"Aye." Big Johann scarce could form the words as he

bent over his beloved. "It was more joy than your dear heart could hold. Ah, *my See'ri*—you stated it well at Sigrid's coming: 'A sound to erase forever the bitter one.' " He kissed her lips. "Aye—aye—" he murmured. "We shall seek to know—as you would have us know—if the end be well, then all is well."

Sigrid would stay. The plant, the job were far away. Sigrid would stay and help prepare her Farmor for the grave.

Clinging, as she had, to the old, they tried to discern what the wishes of their Mor would be; and so in her shroud, next to her heart, they laid the little triangular woolen diapers she had knitted for the twins never to know life except in her bosom, the little garments to tie together the spirit of the mother and the spirits of the babies who had lived—but had not lived—to tie them together into eternity. A small clipping of hair from every one of her children they laid beside her, and she had borne thirteen.

Heart treasures they knew were dear to her they laid there. Into her palm they placed the öre to pay for her last journey. Clasped by both of her hands, over her heart, they placed the book, *Chicago,* and inside of its cover Sigrid's first letter that she had wanted always to have as "part of her."

Thus it was that Sigrid of Norden was carried out of the church where she and Big Johann had been made as one, into the churchyard, carried shoulder high, following in the shade of the steeple as the bell chimed the seventy-four years of her age.

Lars Ahlsén, not of the family but dear to the family, returned to lend his willing arm to the sorrowing American.

Over the green grass the islanders and the family walked, excepting one who rode in a wheel chair, to escort the loved one and to lay her head to the westward in the quiet of the churchyard, near to her little ones, near to Morfar.

Big Johann stood as in a trance, hiding the wish that the bell might be tolling an additional seventy-two for him.

The pastor stood conning his book, but he made no word sounds. He tried, and could not; the strongest pillar of his church had laid down her work. A swallow spoke for him, and as the casket lowered slowly the sun momentarily hid behind a summer cloud and rains from the heavens came downward.

"Do not weep, skies!" Young Johann's voice came clear and strong, "Nay, do not weep, any, for she lives still!"

Laboriously he lifted his crippled arms high. "Even in these hands of mine *she lives!*"

28

The fierce, discordant, beautiful music of sea gulls drowned out the humming music of industry in Göteborg's harbor. The graceful birds grew fewer in number until at last one lone gull wheeled above, then dipped into the brine before turning back toward home.

Sigrid drew the blue shawl tighter over her shoulders. "Look, look, look long and hard against that shore that never shall your eyes see more," the rhythm of the water seemed to say.

Surely now her heart would break.

"No, thank you," she replied to meal call, and clutched the rail. The waters grew a darker blue, a darker green.

Now the sky was filled with stars. So close, the stars; so big, each one sending a moon's worth of light to make the black water's froth into the white outline of a ship. And the wake rippled aft, bent on returning to the shore of Sweden, even as her thoughts. "Think of us at Norden, as you care for it and watch it grow," Mor Sigrid had said as she pressed the seed of a golden rain tree into her hand.

Her breath came heavily, and her knuckles whitened against the rail. As if she would need a reminder to think of them!

Many gifts rested below, but the stories from the Niche for Literature could not be entrusted to the hold. Quickly she left the rail to open her grip and be assured that the sheets of paper were safe.

Sleep would not come, and so she read the stories her father had placed on these papers, stories of trolls in the forests, birds in the air, fish in the sea, stories of children and flowers, and Christmas and Easter, and about the golden cradle; and the stories about Hjärta.

Dreaming, she saw Pa smile; and then it was not Pa at all, but her mother, the little Elin of the vine-covered house; soon the door opened and streams of children came from the doorway, each little one carrying a book.

A band of sunshine the size of a porthole woke her. Would the dream tell truth, that Mor Sigrid's hope would see realization and these stories make books for little children to read? Would there be other books bearing the name Karl Mattias Petersson?

Soon she could know; and now she was anxious to be done with traveling.

Hurry, ship! Hurry! Hurry!

How strongly now she felt the pull of the prairie—its scorching heat, or windblown snows—smooth, level land where no hills or mountains raised the sight, no stately firs, no salt-sea spray. But it was home!

Ahead, the restless waters of New York Harbor waited to play a tune of "Welcome!" The instruments they plucked were scarred wooden piles. Liberty awaited her, and would speak to her, as the big statue had to so many, many others,

> "For you I lift my torch,
> For you my coronet
> Is rayed with stars . . ."

Yes, Sweden was beautiful, the pull of family ties was strong. Lars—oh, she *liked* Lars—he would wait, he said, to hear that she was coming back to Sweden and to him; but now, nearing America, Pa's words came strumming in her ears: "Would an Abraham Lincoln have been able to become king, head of government, in any foreign country? No! But he could become president of the United States! Only in America could a path lead from a little log cabin to the White House of government. What country but America could have produced a Henry Ford? What country has?" The churning waters on the shore ahead would sing, "Land of Opportunity," while the large, full lips of Liberty echoed the Song of the Immigrant.

The very air repeated her father's words. "Every country can say, 'Next to our own country, in America there are more of our nationals than anywhere else.' " America —upon whom the whole world was depending for guidance. America—the only country related to all countries by blood, thereby necessarily being the one to take the leadership in joining all countries of the world in friendly bond.

"And America is my home!" Speaking aloud, Sigrid heard in her own voice that same quality the word "home" had had coming from Mor Sigrid's lips on her speaking of Sweden, as the word had had come flowing from the lips of Elin.

Once more it was as if Elin took her by the hand, to lead her. Her mother's love was as a benediction, more so in these moments than it had ever been before. For now it was as though Elin opened a door so her daughter could see. Seeing, it was to Sigrid as if this was the first lighting of the world—not by sunrise, but by the fiery light from steely blue eyes, for suddenly she knew whom it was she loved!

Rising and dipping with the ship, she stood near to the prow; together she and the ship hesitated at the top of a wave, trembling, then crashed into a water valley, only to rise again to the crest of an oncoming wave. Reaching, she could almost touch the clouds, they hung so low.

Again night fell. She strained her eyes to search the low sky; no moon, no stars, were there. There should be stars above to tell of this, which now she knew!

Where were the stars?

Her pastor's words, gleaned from the book she loved, *Les Misérables,* gave her the answer; remembering, "I have met in the street a very poor young man who was in love. His hat was old, his coat worn," she felt a wave rush over the deck, felt the water pass through her thin-soled shoes.

And the *stars passed through her soul.*

29

The roaring waves knew and spoke his name, "Nico van Vlaardingen."

Going over her friendship with Nico it was like seeing a green bud that gave no hint of the flower it hid until, suddenly unfolding, it gave sight of a full, glorious, beautiful blossom. Everything with Nico had been fun, always; they had been able to do anything, build anything, together; but she had never given a thought to *love!*

It had been her meeting with Lars, and Lars's proposal of marriage, that had forced her heart to make her mind aware of its true feeling. She would write to Lars, telling him that once again her pastor was right: when true love comes, one knows no doubt.

Nico. Although the card said the blue shawl had come from "the van Vlaardingens" it must have been Nico who had bid for it at the auction; only he and the pastor had known of her yearning for it. She had never spoken of it to the doctor. Thinking back, it was soon after the auction that Nico had stopped working midnight hours at Bradley's Drugstore. It must have been to buy the shawl for her that he had worked to get that extra money.

If he had been tantalizingly mysterious about "saving for something," she might have guessed, as often as they had pressed their noses against the pawnshop window to look at it; but he had never let on. . . .

New York City, the fast-passing landscape across the country, were behind her. "Chicago!" the conductor called.

There they were! "The whole *kit and kaboodle* of them," Mrs. Allspaugh screamed, had come to welcome her home, except Granny, who had stayed behind to have the meal on the table as soon as they arrived.

Michael took a running jump and threw his full seven

and a half years of growth into her arms, almost throwing her. *"Sigree!"*

Hugs for each, from each; ah, it was good to be back home. Best of all, though he was now *Dr.* van Vlaardingen, Nico had not changed. But what had she expected? It was only in her own heart that he had changed. He was as he had been before she went away, so full of ready laughter. And the look that came from his eyes when he saw the blue shawl over her shoulders! He reached to embrace her, but in all eagerness his father came between them, saying, "That's a mighty pretty blue shawl you brought back with you. Becoming. And is this all of your baggage?"

"No." She looked up at him sheepishly. "I have added a lot."

He took the claim check. "Parmelee Transfer will deliver it." Smiling, "No matter how much it is."

They piled into the streetcar. Michael sat with her and pointed out the river, the bridge. Outside of the grimy window was Chicago. Home. Dirty, with men and women rushing, rushing, but it was home. So different from Sweden, yet the same bright sun shone over both, and—a smile flitted over her face at noticing an Old-World custom—a housewife had hung her bedding out to air. Caught by the lowered sash of a window on the second floor of a brick flat building, the blanket fluttered in the lazy wind, the pillows fluffed big in the warm sun, just as the ones had done hung on stretched lines in Bohulsän and Halland.

"Glory be to God!" Granny O'Toole hugged Sigrid, sniffled, and kissed her. "Thank God you've come back; that lonesome we've been without you."

"Granny!" Hattie Allspaugh scolded.

As Swedes would have done, Granny had cleaned the whole house against her return. Nico had beaten the rugs, and then Granny had swept them, good; she had cleaned the china closet, washed all of the windows; she had scalloped strips of newspapers, and cut openwork designs in the scallops, to make new shelf paper for the pantry. "But you'll have to be excusin' the kitchen curtains, just a-hangin' so—"

"Uh-huh." Michael strutted. "I took the tie backs to church school."

"What in the world for?"

"For ruffles, Sigree." He posed in military fashion. "I'm gonna be the British general in our play."

Now they had ham for supper. "The left leg ham," Granny expounded, so it would be tender; not the right leg, that a pig always uses for scratchin' itself all the time so's "it'd get that tough." And custard baked in all of the cups that were chipped or had broken handles.

"Now tell us about Sweden."

"It would take forever." Yet she began telling.

"Did they have electric lights, and everything, as we do?"

"Yes. And they wanted to show me all of the modernity in Göteborg. Oh, they seem to be so very proud that their country is modern and up to date, but—I didn't want to see that—I did not want the sight of apartment buildings or cooperative stores to bring disillusionment, to burst the bubble of the romantic past to which my parents belonged. And my grandmother, in a way, at Norden, it was as if she had helped Time stand still, awaiting my visit, so that I could see it as my father knew it."

At speaking of her grandmother she left the room, to gain composure, not to dampen this welcome home with sadness; and as she passed Nico the look on his face reminded her in some way of Big Johann.

When she returned, he said, "We know you. Most likely you never even noticed if they had electricity in Sweden!"

"You know me all right. I was entranced, simply entranced, at sight of the old."

"Did they speak English? Or did you speak Swedish?"

"It was a mixture." She laughed at remembering. "Strangely, though, I think I spoke more Swedish, once I got started, than they did English."

"And you didn't have any trouble making yourself understood?" Aunt Hattie's jaw dropped.

"They are so polite over there that if you can say, *'Tack'*—thank you—you've learned a big portion of the language!"

"*Jaså.*" Pastor Bedell nodded.

And then she told of Lars, told all.

"A fine family," Pastor Bedell said when she was through. "Almost as well known as the King. Well known and respected. Highly respected."

"Are you going to go back?" Nico leaned forward.

"My heart says no."

"Parmelee!" The call interrupted her, and the drayman carried in an old dower chest. Out of it came the snow shovel, *Far;* and she passed it around for everyone to see. "It seems as though they name everything. Even their tablecloths!"

"Such as?" Aunt Hattie wanted to know.

"The very best one was named *Drottning*—Queen; and there was *Qvinna*—woman; and one was *Teofil,* for no good reason that I could learn."

More solemnly she passed around a small figurine, molded by the famed sculptors, Maria and David Henning, known far and wide for their great work, *"The Mother,"* in whose hands they had told the story of fertile days. The model for the statue and the model for this little piece were the same. Even on this small figure the hands told a story of work, of little play, of strength, of gentleness, of fingers oft entwined in prayer. *"Mor Sigrid,"* it was named.

In the room in Calico Row there was a long interval of silence.

Now from out of the chest came a gift for Pastor Bedell: an old Swedish Bible bearing a notation from the pastor of the church he had attended in childhood. Sigrid wiped his glasses so he could see better to read. In the little time she had been away he had grown so much older. The lines of his skull showed clearly under transparent skin—the hollows for eyes—the jawbone—

Gaspings of delight veered her thoughts as the neighbors caught sight of the little silver skis, the golden clock from Elin's home and the carpet made from hare's hair, and the provincial dress.

"I came back as laden as a peasant immigrant. With wooden trunk and all!"

"You certainly came home richer than you went," said the pastor quietly.

"Yes." Her voice reflected the fullness of her heart. "Yes, richer. All of my life I shall be a better woman for having come to know my grandmother."

This was the time to tell them the story of the blue shawl, as much a story as anything she had ever read in books. She showed them the name in the corner, making one snowflake so different from the rest. At his quick intake of breath she turned sharply toward Nico. With their

look came that flash of absolute understanding which sometimes comes, so fleetingly, between a man and a woman,
and she knew that with the blue shawl he had given her
his love.

Again silence fell, until from the pastor came, "Wondrous are God's ways for His people. Wondrous are His
ways."

"A mantilla of four-leafed clovers, that shawl," said
Granny, her eyes a-twinkle, for with her new bifocals she
could see deeper into hearts than some.

The blue beauty stilled their senses.

Sigrid's heart beat wildly. Yes, it was beautiful; but had
they noticed the blue glint coming from under Nico's wide-
open eyelids? She had to turn away, not to reveal to all the
feeling that she knew was written on her face, and so she
walked to the window and looked out. A sudden flash of
lightning showed shining backs of the leaves of a silver-
leafed poplar against dark storm-blue of the lowering sky
—like changeable taffeta—

Like silver flames!

Like Nico's eyes!

She would be back before he knew it. Sigrid cuddled
Michael and reassured him.

"Don't go away again."

"I have to go to work. But I'll be home before dark."

"This same day?" Michael waved good-by, but against
his better judgment let her go from his embrace. She had
stayed away so long the last time.

It was good to be back! She greeted the friendly streetcar conductor, fellow streetcar travelers, the watchman at
the gate, and tripped toward the building that housed Mr.
Horgan's office and hers.

"Good morning!" she almost sang to the girl who sat in
her chair.

"Did you wish to see someone?" Haughtily, the head
turned.

"I'm Miss Christianson. I've come back."

"Come back? Did you leave something here?"

"Why—why—this is my desk. This is my job."

"Who're you kidding?" As a cat stretches itself to a
standing position the young woman rose and walked to the
files.

"Is Mr. Horgan in?" Sigrid started toward his office door.

"No. He isn't here any more. But I can tell you this, that I'm hired permanently for this job. That much I know for sure. I'm sorry, but—"

Sigrid walked from the office, from the building. They had given her job to somebody else, doubtless because she had overstayed her vacation time. One foot set itself in front of the other aimlessly. Then she stopped short. Where was that first impulse which she would have known, in the past, to become enraged, to stamp her foot and cry, "It isn't fair!" And perhaps add, "That's a big firm, for you, promising you that you could come back and, well, what more could you expect?"

Perhaps the faintest urge to it was there; but it was melted so far into the background, it could be happening to someone else. She had changed. She was able to control what, in herself, had been the uncontrollable—a display of rage.

She walked down the street, through the well-kept grounds. It was surprising to see even one weed, but near the fence was a lone milkweed standing tall, a wild morning-glory wound round and round its stem, but the end of it, reaching out into the air and finding no support for the frail tendrils, blew in the breeze. Fascinated by the animated totem pole, she stopped. Robins, sparrows, and a lark followed each other in quick succession to stop before their shrine, bowing their heads, thanking for the summer. Yes. Not only picking up fallen morning-glory seeds, but bending their heads in thankfulness.

A rush of heartfelt thankfulness to God spread over her. She had so much, so much. Only the memories of this past month were worth all the jobs in the world. She would find another job. The important thing was that she had reached Sweden in time.

And she was glad beyond measure that she had not allowed her temper its sway when she learned there was a better position awaiting her. Mr. Horgan had been promoted: he was a general superintendent now, and when he learned of her return he sent for her. "Of course I want you to continue as my secretary."

"I do appreciate you considering me."

"Considering! Why, I wouldn't *have* anyone else!" He

slammed his fist on the desk, making his pens and pencils jump.

She thanked him. "But in the past few days I have decided to—" He made it hard for her, glowering as he was, but she told him of submitting her father's papers and that out of his stories, taken from the old home's Niche for Literature, would come books for little children. "Their sale will provide sufficient money to pay for my studying on campus at the University of Chicago. I couldn't earn a degree without that."

"Enough money so you won't have to work?"

"I'll keep on teaching evening classes at the business college; I'll need to do that."

At last she was a member of that mystical body, learning by going to school. The seasons' passing brought her closer to her coveted degree and closer in her joyous friendship with Nico—Dr. Nico van Vlaardingen, Jr. It was he who renewed her courage with sympathetic understanding when the way seemed hard; he who helped her shovel her snow, and put up her storm windows; he who wrenched stubborn screens loose; he who studied with her in the book-lined room and read aloud when her eyes grew tired. Closer in friendship, yes. But though love flowed from his fiery eyes like some astounding bit of news from others' lips, he never spoke of love.

Not so the pastor. "Have you never found a man whom you could love?"

She poked her needle up from below, through the white percale stretched on the quilting frame, and stuck it down. The American quilt, for which inspiration had come as she first held in her hands the coverlet her Farmor had woven, was almost completed. Stilling her needle, she answered, "Yes."

"May an old man venture a guess?"

"You—know?"

"I guess. And he has never spoken of love to you?"

"No."

"Maybe he never will."

She looked up sharply. "Why?"

"I do not know. But if in all this time he has not, there must be some reason. Perhaps he is one of those who marries once, and only once."

"What!"

"You—Sigrid—you must know the doctor loves you?"

She let her needle fall, and grasped the arm of the chair for support. "No. I—did—not—know."

Did Nico know? Was that why his lips did not put into words the declaration of love that his eyes poured forth? Dear God! It was the *doctor* who loved her!

So did she love him. She would love to call him "Dad." Was Pastor Bedell right? Then why had not the doctor spoken? Could it be that he also saw that Nico loved her?

How did she know Nico loved her? How? There were some things she simply knew. Although it was not summer, and the trees were bare of leaves, still the broad, rugged lacework wrote "oak" in black on the fog-gray sky page. She did not need the leaves to know it was an oak. She knew. And, even without foliage, graceful, drooping fringe wrote "willow" in chartreuse. Nor did she need the leaves to know, as she saw the tracery against the blood-red streak on the horizon, that that was a Lombardy poplar that raised its arms to hide the legendary pot of gold. No! No more did she need Nico's words to know he loved her.

Why, then, did he not speak?

With what the immigrant had brought, America had provided the way. "The Promise of America." Sigrid held the physical manifestation of it in her hand, and walked back to her seat on the platform. This was the parchment that would tell the world she held a degree in the Science of Education. Now she could teach children history in the schools, and she would do as Pa did, try to make it real to them.

Michael's house was paid for; Granny and he could rent their little house and come with her to wherever she was assigned a school. Walking from this platform she was entering a new world.

"Congratulations!"

"Sigrid." Bazile Schmotzer squeezed her hand. "So shall my day come, and not too far away, to wear the cap and gown."

"Yes, Bazile. You were not too old, after all, were you?"

The neighbors drove home, and it was at the pastor's

door Sigrid lingered longest. "My parents would be glad if they could know."

"Isn't it as easy for you to believe they do know as that they don't?"

She hugged him. "Then they know."

At the curb the doctor was saying, "I'll walk on home. It's a beautiful day." He had suddenly grown shorter, and his son towered above him. Was there a break in the father's voice, or did she only imagine it? "Why don't you take her for a ride, son?"

She rode with Nico in the cool of the late afternoon, until at last he drew up alongside the road and escorted her from the car.

"Look." He pointed. "Does this remind you of any place?"

"Nico! It's for all the world—like—"

"I tried. I looked all over until I thought I had found a plot of ground that had the same 'lay' as you said Norden had—the same rolling hills."

Peals of gladsome laughter rang. "Oaks!" she sang.

Shadows of oaks patterned the ground they walked on; below was water, not salt of the sea, but the fresh-flowing water of the Fox River.

He could hardly keep up with her—she ran from one tree to another, touching, looking up, until, suddenly, she stopped. "Is this land for sale?"

"No. It is not for sale." There was a quivering in his voice as in his emotion he reverted to his father's homeland pronunciation, which had been lost for years, "With a little imagination a home here could be as a houz by the zee."

"A little red house—with white trim—"

"Built from the blueprints you brought with you from Sweden."

"With the big room—the big, friendly room—and its corner fireplace, and a *library*—!"

"Let's build it ourselves, with our own hands?"

"Oh, Nico, do you suppose we *can?*"

"Of course we can! We served our apprenticeship building that garage."

"And it's still standing square."

Was this a culmination of a courtship, with no silent

pressing of bodies, but with joyous laughter ringing as they planned for the future? Yes, for with Nico laughter and fun were parcel and part. Had always been.

"Oh, Sigrid, I could not tell you before that I loved you."

"Why?" If he hesitated it would show that he knew what she and the pastor knew.

There was no pause. "It would not have been fair to you, until you had achieved your great ambition." He laughed lightheartedly. "Now we will have a qualified teacher for our children!"

She was in his arms. "We'll call it Norden," she heard him say.

"And I'll acquire a dad," she whispered. "We're going to have to be awfully good to *our* dad, Nico."

"You bet!"

A kiss placed on the Viking ring made it her engagement ring.

"And we will transplant your golden rain tree here."

And there must be a little birch tree, too, to let its leaves ripple in the song, "Be glad."

The moon, a delicate silver sliver, rose to hang low in the sky. An aura of mist circled the silver crescent before she closed her eyes at touch of Nico's kiss, and her heart recalled the pastor's words, "I do not know the 'whys,' I only know His ways are good."

Cattails in the swamp ripened, became fuzzy with seeds; large blackbirds alighted on them, jabbed their bills into the hearts of them; sat; swayed; then flew, showing the spots of brilliant red on wings. Michael won first prize in the Grade School Art Exhibit. Bobby Schmotzer was graduated from high school, valedictorian of his class. And the foundation for a little red house was set in the midst of ten acres of rolling land.

The oaks turned golden, copper-colored; acorns let go their grip upon the stems and fell to earth, or rested momentarily in squirrels' mouths as the furry-tailed animals harvested the trees' bounty. Frog music over the swamp was stilled, the musicians burrowed deep in the mud. Dried brown leaves fell from the elm trees. Nighthawks, migrating southward, put on their annual exhibition of aerial acrobatics. And the walls rose on the foundation for a little red house.

In the crabapple thicket far to the south end of the plot the leaves now carpeted the ground, and crabapples hung from bare branches like red baubles on a Christmas tree. Dull red colored the oak leaves, racing to match the color of a house.

Poplars paling across the river accented the deepening gold of the birch trees in the house yard and the gold of the tall ginkgo planted by some loving hand long years before. A hickory, flinging naked arms against the blue heavens, waved to them as Sigrid and Nico walked back from the knoll to appraise their building work.

Christmas came and with it, sent by Lissie, Mor Sigrid's carved wooden smoothing board with its handle the shape of a horse. And the roof topped the walls of a little red house. The roof, not made of thatch as on the Swedish dwelling, but of shingles made on the grounds from fallen trees by Nico and Louis and Bazile, and even Sigrid herself helping to swing the froe. The ringing sound of a swinging, cutting, splitting blade echoed through the trees. There was music in the building of a house.

Winter was cold. The cattail stems bent over, broke, and lay in the marsh, frozen. Thaw came and they lay in the marsh, slimy. But soon other stems rose to take the place of last year's, rose full of sap, ready to bring forth other silken tops to give resting stands for red-winged blackbirds. Columbine seeds, from Norden, changed to roots and stems and leaves on a lilac-shaded plot in Rose Hill.

And at the new Norden, on the slope of one small hill, dozens of scilla bulbs sent forth their blue; daffodils bloomed on the next hill, and tulips from Holland; and, as Pa's hammer had sounded,

> "Rat-tat tat-tat'-tat,
> Rat-tat tat-tat'-tat,
> Rat-tat tat-tat'-tat—"

came music, the music of the building of a house. . . .

Midsummer's Day came, and the house was completed, grown after the blueprints and specifications of the cousin who had finished at Uppsala in Sweden. Sigrid and her

betrothed looked on as the neighbors from Calico Row
danced around the Maypole in its house yard.

"The day of the Fourth of July will soon be here."

"Yes, Nico. Our wedding day."

"Granny and me's going to live with Dr. Van!" Michael
met the guests.

"Everything works out. Everything! Just like a jigsaw
puzzle," his grandmother added. "And the Schmotzers are
going to live in our little house."

"Yes," said Bazile. "It is as I have always said: you try
to do a little something for somebody, and it comes right
back to you! Sigrid did not think we should put her in a
furnace. But who did we put it in for? For ourselfs! We
think of trying to keep her warm. And who do we keep
warm? Ourselfs!"

Granny took off her spectacles, to see better at a dis-
tance. The birch tree, trailing its bridal veil of diamonds
and dew, was yielding to the sun, letting it lift the spider-
woven lace to leave sight for the Carrickmacross her loving hands had sewn. Now those hands carried the proper
gift to the new home, salt. A little sprinkled on the threshold, and no evil thing could ever enter, a little in the
drinking water of the well to insure long life, good health,
and protection to the dwellers.

Below, the Fox River wound its way southward, sunlight
shattering its ripples into a million little reflecting mirrors.
Wild grapevines, already giving promise of purple jelly,
claimed the wooden fence as a trellis; young woodbines
had started their climb on a low stone fence surrounding
the house yard.

The house looked down upon a barn—no, here it was a
garage—made of large bricks to the eaves, its gable repeating the maroon red of the house timbers; windows and
doors were arched at the tops, and smaller, narrow bricks
were laid in pattern vertically to form the arches. The large
doors to what should be a haymow in the gable swung
with four wrought-iron hinges, and they spelled, instead of
the names and date on the original barn, "Norden, Illinois,
America," and the year, "1926," in the crude forging of the
iron.

What was it Sigrid had done here?

She had brought a part of the Old Country to America.

Granny wiped her eyes. Sweden was not so different from Ireland.

Not only had Sigrid fulfilled her personal desire to transplant a replica of her father's home to her own country, here she had built a shrine to her Old Country ancestry, had made it possible for her native-born American friends to know how her forefathers had lived in another land; had brought a history lesson to the youth who came and saw.

There were birds singing; a brown thrush darted through the air, a robin came close, singing. Wedding music.

Moss roses, blooming as if they could never fade, laid a living "Persian" carpet on the slope in the full sun. Pachysandra covered thinly the shaped slope; violets' leaves grew large under the oak trees; forget-me-nots bloomed over the tulip bed, lately in bloom; in the house yard tall hollyhocks bloomed against the dwelling's red, fronted by stately delphinium, clear blue, except for one dark blue with ruffly purple petals close to the stamens. One tall digitalis stalk leaned toward the sun, its spotted lavender bells luring a cautious hummingbird.

The guests were assembled in the out-of-doors; Mr. Horgan was there with his family, and Mr. Rasey; there were too many friends for the small house to accommodate, even in the big room. All eyes followed the walk. Between and around the stepping-stones low sweet alyssum smiled, not caring if a toe or heel flattened the blossoms for an instant, so long as the way was beautiful.

The strains of "Ave Maria" came.

They came from behind a screen of shrubs where a phonograph needle, by going round and round on a disc, brought strains from Marta's violin. In this way Sigrid's family came to her wedding, in this beautiful way.

The song was ended, but the melody lingered until from the disc both Marta's violin and Lennart's accordion burst forth with Söderman's wedding march—*"Ett Bondbröllop"* —A Farm Wedding—and Sigrid came down the walk.

Inside the long white dress she wore was a now well-known and much sought-after label, *"Emilie—Modiste."* In place of a bouquet she carried the blue shawl, folded small, and cascading to border the borrowed prayer book carried by Tainas at their weddings since forgotten time. Holding the priceless sweeping veil of Carrickmacross lace

was the old *brudkrona* from her mother's family, the treasure of Elin's lifetime, the golden bridal crown—the virgin's crown—six golden points, six oblong-shaped aquamarines, clear, standing for hope, happiness, and love,
catching rays of sunlight; six golden hearts, quivering, as
Sigrid walked to the altar and Nico came to meet her.

The young birch tree was the altar and before it, under
the high blue-vaulted chancel, Pastor Bedell stood with
open book. Two little yellow butterflies circled around
each other in flight, rested for a brief second on his shoulder; then, playing butterfly tag again, flew close to the
sweet-smelling nasturtiums tumbling over a pile of stones
against the hill.

The music ceased.

"Dearly beloved, we are gathered together here in the
sight of God—"

A golden ray of sunshine came through the clerestory of
the lofty nave's green walls and joined the gold of the
shining crown. My Cousin Tissappee brushed between the
groom's legs, stepping in a serpentine path to leave orange
and black and white cat hairs on both legs of a new dark
suit.

A squirrel jumped from one tree to another, the better
to see, but his was the only sound beside the pastor's voice
and the ones of those to be joined in holy wedlock. "Wilt
thou have this woman to thy wedded wife?"

"I will."

"Wilt thou have this man to thy wedded husband?"

"I will."

"I give thee my troth."

To many of the assembled guests came reminder of the
sweet experience of a wedding day as Pastor Bedell asked
blessing on the Viking ring, which would bind Sigrid and
Nico van Vlaardingen "unto their lives' end."

Sigrid raised her lips to her husband's; their eyelids did
not close; instead, they looked deep into the blue of each
other's eyes. She sensed the waiting of the silent guests,
but she looked deep, deep into her husband's soul. The
maiden's hesitancy of sharing her body had, somehow, disappeared at hearing God's word spoken to make her Nico's
wife. She would rejoice in sharing his days, his work, his
dad, his nights, his bed, his life.

Tonight her husband would remove the crown—the golden crown of little Elin.

Such a smörgåsbord as only the King of Sweden must, up to this time, have seen was laid in the house yard. And there was also corned beef and cabbage, "fitten for any Irishman"; there was German sauerbraten, there were fried chickens which had been rolled in slivered almonds; and there were Finnish nuptial cookies, baked by Taina, called *avioliittopikkuleipiä*, paired and clinging to each other by means of sweet sticky jam. And there was Vlaardingen cheese, from Holland.

There was the *knäckebröd*, baked by Mor Sigrid in June of 1895, that had hung all these years by its off-center holes on the ceiling pole in the chest room at the Old Norden; now the bride broke it into bits and passed it to the guests. With solemn ceremony Sigrid passed the bits on the birch tray with "Our Daily Bread" carved as a border around its edge.

Suddenly the gay conversation stopped, for from behind the shrubbery came voices, and the phonograph gave a message from Big Johann, from Marta and Maria, from David and Lennart, from Lissie, from Young Johann and Herman Nikodemus and Agda and Tuppie—from all—a "hello" to Michael; it was Cousin Michael they called him; to the doctor; to Dr. Nico a "welcome into the family"; to Sigrid, love—a world of good wishes to all from all at Norden in Sweden. Sigrid let her face drop into her hands; it was as if they were here—as if her whole family were here for her wedding—even, in some way, Mor Sigrid, and Elin, and Karl.

"Magic, that's what it is!" Michael announced, "Just plain, unadulterated magic."

Now the doctor, with Old-World courtliness, placed a bright orange-colored piece of glassware into Sigrid's hand. "To my beloved daughter, from Holland." It was an orange of glass, with stem and all, a souvenir in commemoration of the birth of Juliana in 1909. "Juliana," he said, with deep affection, "of the House of Orange; heiress apparent to the throne of the Netherlands."

Sigrid held it up against the sunlight. "I'll use it as a little vase, to hold fresh-cut California poppies." She kissed him on the cheek. "Thanks, *Dad!*"

The slumping shoulders straightened; he was tall again, straight-shouldered, as he had always been.

"The Old Country and the New, blending their beauties in vase and flowers," the pastor whispered aside to Granny O'Toole.

Sigrid was compelled to stand while every stitch on the bridal veil was examined and "oh'd" and "ah'd" over by each guest. The fine machine net was edged all along its yards and yards of length, its long train, its cowl, with a border of daisies, each little petal appliquéd of fine cambric, outlined with a heavy thread over which Granny had taken thousands and thousands of tiny stitches. All over the field she had worked little circles, tiny o's.

"Only the finest was good enough for Sigrid." The Irishwoman was near to bursting with pride. "And the finest was Carrickmacross."

There were many gifts to exclaim over, but none more touching than the gift from the two Johanns. "Love spoons," to be used by the bridal couple, tied together by carved wooden links, all—the whole of it—cut from a single piece of wood, in the symbol of unity. Instead of a flower design, each link bore the initials of one of Norden's family; and in the bowls of the spoons were "Sigrid" and "Nico"; tied together by the magic chain—never to be parted—

The summer evening lingered, even as the guests. Long shadows—long twilight—fireflies rising like vapor from the warm earth.

Michael and the Yingling boys might have been little Balinese boys, putting fireflies in their blouses to light dark mountain passes, the way they ran to catch the little flying bugs with their "electric signs going on and off."

How could birds sleep, with the singing of the wedding guests rising through the trees? They did not sleep, but joined instead in the singing.

Pastor Bedell sat rocking, and thinking. As his thoughts raced, the scallops that were his chin and jowls quivered. His work as a pastor, to comfort the afflicted and afflict the comfortable, soon would be over. But today he had done the thing he had lived on to do, joined Sigrid to a worthy man, joined them in love.

He had watched her grow from a little child, even as so often she and he had stood in wonder at a flower bud's

opening, shyly, petal by petal, until at last its fragrant
chalice lay waiting its mating. The flowering loveliness of
Sigrid was as a picture of the miracle of life, and she was
now about to fulfill her principal purpose, God's purpose;
for she, the flower holding the heritage of countless ages
past, carried in her heart and body the miracle of still another seed, another life.

And best of all, he had lived to see a girl, now grown
to womanhood, weed the garden of her inheritance and
pull from it the thistle that, in her father, overtook the
garden, ruining it.

There had been times—yes, she had cut shoots from the
plant, only that they should grow again—but, at last, the
thistle and its root were gone. She had proved that man
need be slave neither to his inheritance, and refuting her
father's lifelong excuse, nor the frustrations of his early
environment, but can transcend them both.

He could go any time now, happily, to where his Kristin
waited.

A burst of cannon broke the solemn trend of his
thoughts, and the community display of fireworks came to
send a glow of white over the treetops. All jumped at the
sound of an explosion; then, high in the sky, there was a
burst of red glory, followed by another salvo and a glory
of white, followed by another and a burst of blue. Stars
appeared as if by the magic Michael had declared, silver
stars, and fell into the treetops, into the river, bringing to
night the mirrored ripples of sunlit day.

Red stars, white stars, and blue stars burst from some
unseen pocket in the sky and drifted, cascading, glittering,
shimmering, falling, only to be followed in quick succession by others, celebrating the Fourth of July. Celebrating
Sigrid's wedding day.

Stars falling above book ends that were little irons with
"Geneva" molded into their handles; above a Swedish
snow shovel named "Far"; above an early-American hay
rake, handmade of wood, bound round with wire to rein-
force the prongs; over a little Geib piano—

Falling on native oaks, on newly planted birch, on a
Swedish golden rain tree from which each fall long
racemes of golden seeds would hang, like golden rain, falling on a clump of *ginst* from Halland province; on a little

shamrock plant, nestled in leaf moss; falling on tulip bulbs from the Low Countries.

Stars lighting the way home for guests whose ancestry could be traced to the many countries over the globe—lighting the eventide for a bride in whose veins coursed the blood of Swedish Vikings and a groom whose forebears had called Holland "home."

Stars of the Fourth of July—lighting the way for all—For this was America.

The many-colored draperies of Independence Day flickering against the velvety blue-black sky lighted the way of two whose love had mounted through the years until this night, together, they touched a meteor!

30

"April snö
Är så godt
Som fåragö."

The little rhyme, which for generations had told her kinfolk that April snow was as good as sheep manure for the crops, rang through Sigrid's brain.

It was true that snow in April and fertility were synonymous. Not only Swedish peasants had a rhyme for it; there was the Norwegian proverb, and the German, and the Danish. American farmers attested to the truth of it and spoke of the free ammonia, nitrates, and albuminoids deposited in the ground by the action of the snow.

April. A lovely-sounding word, in either language, rolling off the tongue smoothly, with the cadence of music, evoking images of spring.

A gay word, April. And now it was snowing. Chionodoxa laid its bright blue carpet over the white of it on the slopes.

"A woman who sees snow fall in this spring month will bear a child within the year," were her Farmor's words.

"I would like"—she turned to her husband, and smiled up at him—"to name her Sigrid, for my grandmother."

"Her?" A happy smile spread over Nico's face.

"Yes, 'her'; and Elin, for my mother; and Juliana, for yours."

They were silent, until he said again, "Her?"

"Yes, Nico, I seem to know."

His study of obstetrics warned him not to plan on the child's being a girl, but the loving husband knew his intuition told him truly. "Sigrid she shall be named, for the great mother of Norden; Elin, for the one who gave you to me; Juliana, remembering the mother I never knew—

280

but that will make Dad happy!—and for Juliana, Princess of The Netherlands, who one day will be their queen."

"Sigrid Elin Juliana van Vlaardingen," they chanted together.

"A famous name, Vlaardingen." Nico laughed, and she saw the fiery glint of his eyes shine brightly. "Not only do we have a cheese named after us, but a city in Holland."

They would carve the name on the little name stick come with the hanging cradle from Sweden, made of woven birch bark, to be hung from a hook in the ceiling near the table, or near the bed, but near the mother in any case; inside was a little soft mattress of goose down, a coverlet woven in a pattern of ducks and birds. Everything was in readiness to receive the child, complete except for the carving of the name. The columbine and heather flowers daintily placed at the top would leave plenty of room, even for so long a name as their Sigrid would have, and the date of her birth.

"April snö."

Walking in the snow, big fluffy flakes fell on Sigrid's eyelashes. The sun, claiming its name day, showed for an instant and the world became a rainbow-tinted place.

Snow—sunlighted flakes—falling—softly, but it was no longer winter. It was April.

She felt her husband's handclasp tighten as they stopped before the golden rain tree, and she looked hard at where the clean leaves soon would open, their three leaflets spreading like fingers of a tiny hand, a little tree telling of the one who had left the earth and yet had not; for the Swedish Sigrid would live on in the golden racemes that would come to crown this little tree, in the many hearts and souls she had mothered for her own land, in her son's daughter and her issue in America.

Sigrid of Norden, in Bohuslän, she had been. Her industry, her strength, the artistry from her brain and fingers, her charity, her love, her faith—all would live on, in Sweden—

And in America.

She had lived, enriching her own land, enriching the new land; for she and her kind were mother to America.

THE BIG BESTSELLERS
ARE AVON BOOKS